'Tom Cox's books are hedgerows. All about the journey and not the destination. They delicately link one stunning viewpoint to another whilst providing nourishment for the heart and soul, a safe haven for a host of endangered fantasies, musings and stories'

Alice Lowe

'*Villager* is delightfully convoluted, otherworldly and captivating, immersing the reader in the contours and personality of the landscape and those who inhabit it'

Mark Diacono

'A synthesis of folklore, nature and the curious psychedelia in ordinary experience that points to the truths in which we find meaning. Tom Cox is a master of effortless, fluid storytelling and *Villager* is alive with both gnawing edge and Cox's signature flavour of clipped, pragmatic humour which is perfectly juxtaposed with the unbounded imagination of *Villager*'s world ... It's tender and dark and strangely comforting. I loved it'

Laura Kennedy, *Irish Times* columnist

'This is ideal summer holiday reading – to be relished piecemeal or devoured in one fell swoop, as I did'

Fergus Collins, *BBC Countryfile*

'The true appeal of the story is its interweaving of themes and narratives: local personalities, the impact of pylons, the interconnection between past and present, and the relationship between people and the land that, literally, has a voice in the narrative. *Villager* is one of the must-read novels of 2022'

Matthew d'Ancona, *Tortoise Media*

'I gallumphed through the pages of *Villager* as though it was on fire ... Funny, thought-provoking and astoundingly clever ... What will I be able to read after *Villager*? I'll just read it again, I guess. And again. Just cancel all other books'

Adele Nozedar, author of *The Hedgerow Handbook*

'A relatable and compelling read ... anyone would love it'

Dorian Cope

'An extraordinary book ... [Tom Cox] is policing that interesting boundary between what is folklore, what is actual history, and what is natural history'

John Mitchinson, *Backlisted* podcast

'Tom's newest book, his debut novel *Villager*, takes the reader on his strangest and most gloriously idiosyncratic trip yet, on an excursion through interconnected tales that draw the reader off the map and deeply into the story of Underhill'

Writing Magazine

Tom Cox was born in Nottinghamshire. He is the author of the *Sunday Times* bestselling *The Good, The Bad and The Furry* and the William Hill Sports Book longlisted *Bring Me the Head of Sergio Garcia*. *21st-Century Yokel* was longlisted for the Wainwright Prize, and the titular story of *Help the Witch* won a Shirley Jackson Award.

BY THE SAME AUTHOR

Fiction
Help the Witch

Non-fiction
Notebook
Ring the Hill
21st-Century Yokel
Nice Jumper
Bring Me the Head of Sergio Garcia
Under the Paw
Talk to the Tail
The Good, The Bad and The Furry
Close Encounters of the Furred Kind

TOM COX
VILLAGER

unbound

First published in 2022
This paperback edition first published in 2023

Unbound
Level 1, Devonshire House, One Mayfair Place, London W1J 8AJ
www.unbound.com

Text design by PDQ Digital Media Solutions Ltd.

A CIP record for this book is available from the British Library

ISBN 978-1-80018-237-0 (paperback)
ISBN 978-1-80018-134-2 (hardback)
ISBN 978-1-80018-135-9 (ebook)

Printed in Great Britain by Clays Ltd, Elcograf S.p.A

1 3 5 7 9 8 6 4 2

For Ralph, my most psychedelic cat (2001–21)

'The Queen o' Faeries she caught me, in yon green hill to dwell'
'Tam Lin', eighteenth-century ballad

CONTENTS

ME (NOW)

It's a heavy day, and it hangs all over me. I'm deep in it. I'm so far in it, I'm technically invisible, unless you're extremely near to me, and very few people are. I doubt that will change today, but tomorrow could be different. Days like this – the ones that stay heavy from beginning to end – are rare here. Yesterday, for example, started heavy, but became very light and boldly colourful, then was just a tiny bit heavy for the final part, in spurts and streaks. During the light, boldly colourful middle part everything radiated cleanliness, was so thoroughly fresh and laundered that you wondered where all the bad stuff it had washed away had disappeared to, what vast drain or waste tank the world could possibly possess that could have so efficiently put it out of sight and smelling distance. Small creatures woke up in the freshness, and were hungry, in a ferocious way. 'Hangry' I believe it is called nowadays by the young folk. A man walked through a dark corridor cut diagonally across a field of high late summer barley and got seriously messed up by horseflies, to such an extent that he increased his speed to a trot and then a run through the last third of the corridor, waving his arms like a crazy person who believes he is being attacked from both flanks by ghosts, until he reached a shady, thistle-dotted copse, which he decided, incorrectly, might offer some respite. The small mercy for him in all this was his confident belief that he had remained unobserved. The belief was misguided. I saw him and, I have to admit, I did have a good old cackle.

There's a painting which I very much admire. I think it's obvious that it's of, or very much inspired by, the village, but I doubt the person who now has it on their wall knows that, unless they have ever visited here, which I happen to know for a fact that they haven't. I doubt they even know the name of the artist, which was a faint scrawl in the bottom right-hand corner of the painting in the first place and became fainter when the second of the painting's four owners carelessly left it directly opposite a large south-facing picture window in a bungalow overlooking the Derbyshire spa town of Matlock Bath. The painter's name was Joyce Nicholas, and she lived here in Underhill between 1958, when she arrived in Devon from the north of England as a widow and retired teacher, and 1969, when her daughter Eva installed her in a retirement complex close to the stretch of coast known, jokingly by some and more seriously by others, as the English Riviera. She completed the painting in 1960 and, although she did sell one or two other similar expressionist works at that point via small local galleries and a short-lived bookshop owned by a friend, Joyce – always very hard on herself – decided it was not a success, and put it away in the loft. It did not leave her family until 1983 when, after his wife had fled from him and their legal union in a state of antimaterialist haste, Eva's daughter Jane's ex-husband Gerry gave it to the owner of a junk shop in Whitby, Yorkshire, free of charge. Gerry had hoped to receive a small sum for the painting but was hit with an uncharacteristic attack of guilt when, in examining a rug that Gerry was also hoping to rid himself of, the junk shop proprietor's hand came into contact with some still quite damp excrement that had come out of the arse of Gerry's bulldog The Fonz that morning, but which Gerry, in haste not dissimilar to Jane's upon leaving him, had not spotted. The proprietor stared off into the middle distance of a deep back room full of broken clocks, grumbled inaudible quarter words and exhaled spouts of air from both corners of his mouth, and stated he wasn't much interested in the painting. 'The bottom has dropped right out of the market for this stuff,' he said. 'I've got a ton of it in my garage at home and can't shift it for love nor money.' He was, however, playing it cool, having quickly marked the painting out as something a little out of the ordinary and Gerry as an easily manipulated man whose main goal was to exit the building as quickly as possible. The proprietor had been the first to see any merit in Joyce's landscape since a lodger who was living with Joyce, eight years after its creation. It now hangs above the stairway in a house in Edinburgh owned by two retired surgeons. Visitors remark on it more often than anything else in the house, apart from their cat, Villeneuve, who is white, fluffy and comically large.

I should probably pause to point out here, for those wondering, that I don't know everything. I have big gaps, moments of doubt and humility, just like everyone else, just like Joyce. But I do know a hell of a lot.

I love Joyce's use of colours in the painting. I suspect when she was mixing her palette she was thinking of a light day, or perhaps the light part of a day that had earlier been heavy, but certainly not an all-heavy day like today. The gradation of burnt umber to asparagus in the top left corner, then a suggestion of something darker, where the moor begins and stretches on for the next twenty miles or so. There's a hint of something black and jagged here, some shapes that remind me of rusty barbed wire. And beyond, above this kaleidoscopic hillscape that could just as easily be California as Britain's West Country, a swirling heaven or hell, a definite 'beyond place'. Below that, I think I can make out the familiar valley, the way it funnels down into the village and the lane that becomes the steep high street. There's no obvious sea or river in the painting but there is a suggestion that both are close. Houses? Joyce doesn't paint anything as literal as houses, but there are shapes that we could decide are buildings where people live. There's some interesting yellow and white blotching to the right, below that, which makes me believe Joyce was a big fan of the lichen you get on the rocks and older buildings – and even some of the newer ones – around here. The colours of the lichen are answered by the colour of the sun, in the top right-hand corner, or is it the moon... or is it some combination of both, some other unknown ethereal body representative of both day and night. Above this is what seems to me the most literal part of the painting of all: a patchwork quilt of what are surely farmers' fields. What makes it less literal is the fact the patchwork is *above* the sunmoon, and I wonder if this is Joyce's comment on the topsy-turvy nature of the region, the habit the hills have of disorientating you, the knack weather has here of frequently being below you, as well as, or even instead of, above you, or if Joyce was just feeling a bit like tearing down the walls and breaking the rules that day. I like this side to Joyce a lot, the hidden side that only the brushes and canvas saw, beneath the scrupulous account books, the perfectly plumped cushions, the always-mown-on-time grass. Joyce was a person with more layers than her family and neighbours realised, I think, and much wilder, toothier nightmares. In the middle top of the canvas, if you look into that greeny-black, celestial moorscape, you'll see what you might interpret as a wide, beatific, somewhat hirsute face. This is the part of the painting that possibly interests me the most.

I never did get any of the several art critic jobs I applied for.

Where does the moor start? That's a highly debatable question. Where does the true north start? Where do moths end and butterflies begin? Where is the border between 'sometimes fancies members of the opposite sex but doesn't actually want to touch their sexual organs' and 'is definitely gay'? Who decides what's soulful funk and what's funky soul? There's always some hard-bitten unimpressable bastard who'll tell you, when you're on the moor, that you're not on the proper moor, no matter how far into the moor you are. But let's not piss about. This – whether or not it's 'technically' on the moor, as the map defines it – is a moorland village. You know, very firmly, when you're in it, that you're not in London, or Kettering, or Ipswich. You're in Underhill. As you pass from the high ground down that funnel, so exquisitely depicted by Joyce, the air of the uplands remains in your nostrils, the trees have beards, the lanes have ferny green sideburns, and your hair is made of rain. *It's the bloody moor*, you pedantic bastards. I should know. I've been here long enough.

For many years, the first sign of life you'd see when you came down that funnel in Joyce's painting was an old blacksmith's cottage, but that fell into disrepair several decades ago, the more interesting parts of its structure gradually appropriated by passing opportunists in or around the building trade. The road bends sharply just at this point, with no warning, and once every couple of years you'll see a mangled, abandoned bike, formerly owned by someone who got carried away with the gradient and didn't quite judge the turn. The blacksmith's cottage was replaced during the 1970s by the Molesting Station. Despite society's disapproving eyes and the nature of its purpose being far less fashionable than it was during its outset, the Molesting Station isn't shy about telling you what it is. It even announces it publicly. 'MOLESTING STATION' it says in big letters, on the front of the building. OK, I'm not giving you all the facts here. It's actually a garage, owned by Phil Spring, who took it over when his father Brian Spring retired in 2013, and it in fact has 'MOT TESTING STATION' written outside. But as you approach from the north, the split trunk of a beech tree on the side of the road

5

obscures the first 'T' and the roof of the second one, so it appears to say 'MOLESTING STATION'. I'm surprised more people don't comment on it. Whatever the case, the garage does good business, at competitive prices, and has a reputation for honesty. After Phil realised he overcharged Paul Pike recently for replacement brake pads and discs, when in fact his apprentice Alun had only replaced the discs, not the pads, he called Paul immediately and did a bank transfer for the difference plus a gesture of goodwill, which he suggested at ten pounds. 'Call it twelve?' said Paul. 'OK', said Phil. I don't have a car for reasons that will in time become clear, but if I did I would definitely take it here, instead of one of those supergarages, where you not only pay for your repairs but for the flatscreen TV in the foyer and the machine next to it that pisses out bad coffee you drink purely because you're there and not sure what else to do with your hands, and the pointless little matching blazers of the employees milling all around you doing you're not sure what. Beyond the Molesting Station is what is, for now, the village's most northerly residential frontier: twenty-five hugely unimaginative terraces built in the 1990s, once going under the preposterous collective title of Otter's Holt, a name now blessedly forgotten, apart from, evidently, by me. I dislike these houses but I like all but two of the families who currently live in them, which softens the architectural anguish a little.

It's definitely not one of the most fashionable villages in the region, and it's not quite the least. One of the results of this 'middle of the table-ish' standing is that we have an Indian restaurant, House of Spice, and it is a good Indian restaurant. I have observed that the better-known villages and small towns nearby, where house prices are highest, either don't have Indian restaurants, or have Indian restaurants that make surprisingly substandard food. I don't personally take my meals in the village, so this is just hearsay, but it's widely recognised that House of Spice's onion bhajis – judged, at least, by the standards of other onion bhajis made in rural England – are in a class of their own when it comes to taste, shape and accompanying chutney. For a long time, House of Spice was also celebrated for the closing line of its menu, which thanked diners for their costume – a spelling error, rather than a genuine expression of gratitude to those visiting on Halloween or another occasion inviting fancy dress. It took a whole twenty-five months before the printing of a replacement menu, which merely thanked people for their custom, and the length of that gap can no doubt be attributed to the fondness that had grown for the menu in the locality and the resulting reluctance of anybody to point out its imperfections. The story about another misprint on the House of Spice's menu, offering a '15 per cent discocunt on orders over £20' is, however, apocryphal.

The moor has moods, and because the village is so close to it, it is subject to them. When the sky above the moor is storm-tossed and wretched, you'll hear more gossip and backbiting across the tables in the two cafés, especially the Green Warlock, where Jason and Celia, who are bored in their marriage, go on Fridays. When everything is heavy and damp, like today, you'll notice that people don't say thanks as much in the Co-op. Two almost-friends, who'd normally stop and chat on the street, will keep their eyes down and pretend they didn't see each other. It's something purely elemental, not personal, but it spreads. I don't feel great today, and my not-greatness influences those around me. I made a buddleia visibly ill at ease this morning. The tile warehouse, I think, looks particularly lugubrious and in need of a hug, but who is going to give it one? Colin on Weathervane Avenue just poured a pan of boiling water over some ants on his patio then instantly felt terrible about it, although he tried to transfer his anger with himself in his emotionally unavailable way, instructing his wife Mel, when she arrived home from the supermarket, to not spend quite so recklessly on fruit. There's a bad atmosphere in the dentist's waiting room. But if we are honest it's never had a great reputation as a dentist. It's doubtful anybody would go there at all, if they knew that on the exact spot where Jill on reception currently sits, in September 1723, a farmer and his two sons murdered a man from Minehead following a drunken quarrel that got out of hand. An orchard was planted in the same place a century later, but didn't take. It's the other side of town where most of the apples grow: partially russeted Nancekuke, Pengelly, King Byerd. Old, old apples. Apples of the insurrectionary underground. Apples which would upset the apples in your local supermarket with their foul mouths and lack of foundation and mascara. Many of their sweet culinary gifts will be wasted next week in the annual Apple Rolling Festival on Fore Street: a 'revived' festival thought by many local historians to date back to as early as the 1600s (it doesn't).

But it is not all folklore and bygone insular sword death. We have a post office! Jim Swardesley, the postmaster, is forty-five. He has his moods, like all of us. The dome of his head is entirely bald, but he says it's been that way since he was twenty-two. His theory is that it was the result of a rugby squad induction ritual in his university days, where he was required to shave his entire scalp with an old, rusty razor and no shaving foam, from which his follicles never recovered. Now a resident of the village for over a decade, Jim's arrival, with his young family, was part of the first wave of incomers to Underhill from more urban areas in the centre of the country: an influx that never fully took off as some expected and dreaded it would, and still happens in fits and starts, usually as a result of people finding that more fashionable villages nearby have become too expensive. Jim is now entrenched enough in local life to be slightly resistant to outsiders himself, if only for their repeated failure to queue for grocery products at the appropriate counter, despite his many handwritten signs encouraging them to. Two doors down from the post office is the granite cottage where Joyce painted her painting. The rusty wagon wheel that her predecessor dragged down the hill off the moor and into the garden is still there. Her deep red front door isn't, replaced long ago by some now off-white UPVC. It is good that she can't see this. There is a profusion of gravel that would be alien to her. The sports utility vehicle perched upon it would seem to her too big for any practical purpose, incongruous beside the building it belongs to.

Information comes back to me in isolated flurries, like cherry blossom on a strong breeze in spring, and then it's gone if I don't reach out and grab quickly, and grab well. You can never grab much. There's only so much you can know at one time, even if you're me; only so much room to store it. There's so much *to* know. It will never end, I suspect, even when it does. So much in all these lives, so many stories, even in this small place. And I try to keep abreast of the universe beyond it too, if I can. I'm broad and cosmopolitan, despite what many assume.

But I am remembering a little now, from the day she began to paint the painting. I was not feeling fully at my best that day. Some men and their dogs had raced across part of me and ripped an innocent animal into many pieces and the pieces were stuck to me. The rain would not come and wash the pieces off for a while. It was a few years into the era when I first felt new chemicals soaking into me, changing everything. Yet over there was a meadow: corncockle, poppies, yellow rattle. I'd rarely seen so many butterflies in my life. I was confused. I felt I could go either way, emotionally. One of my wicked episodes could easily have happened. They have to happen, sometimes. It's part of the balance. But in this instance I chose purity; namely, the quest to witness some of it. While I searched for the purity, a stallion and a mare began to mate on my back and I told them to piss off but then apologised, admitted that it was unfair of me, and assured them they were not the ultimate cause of my irritation.

She was in her kitchen, rescuing a moth from a spider's web. (It died two minutes later but it's the thought that counts.) Jazz was playing. That was not a surprise. The type of jazz, though, was. Definitely not grandma jazz, this. Not even 1950s hip grandma jazz. Modal. Louche. A little threatening. The back window was open, which, from where her easel was placed, gave her a good view of the tor and the rocks piled on top of it like a little crude stepstool to nowhere. The breeze was gently blowing in, flapping the net curtains, and a very old grey cat – a satchel of sharp bones, with some fur stuck to them in some places – snoozed on the table, next to a punnet of five strawberries that were on the turn. Joyce flailed a wrist, as if loosening up in preparation for an impressive bit of spin bowling, and in one final move, to achieve a state of ultimate looseness before she began, she lifted her blouse over her head and threw it flamboyantly to the floor. I got a bit shy then (I do!) before watching her go into her artistic trance. I'd never seen anybody paint my portrait before and I was very flattered. She had a glass of wine afterwards, and I can't remember the last time I've wanted to join anyone in that particular activity so much. You'd have to go right back to... Actually, I'm not even going to tell you. Blissful scene to watch, though, even if you couldn't be a part of it yourself. Oh, Joyce. How could you go from a day as carefree and wild as this to the retirement scene in Torquaydos, in less than a decade?

It was the following day when she had her misgivings and put the painting in the loft, with a little chunter to herself. She was being self-punishing, but perhaps she was only following the most sensible course of action. Ideally, we'd all put any art we created away for a while before we properly evaluated it. Two weeks? Probably not long enough. Let's call it two years. OK, ten. That will do it. Scratch that. Just to be sure, let's come back and discover our true worth as creators from the afterlife. 'Hi, I'm dead now. What? Yes, fully. I even have the papers to confirm it. Can you finally tell me my true star rating, out of ten?' Joyce, I think, were she able to pop south over the border between the dead and the living, then north over the other one, between England and Scotland, would be pleased at what she saw on the wall of Dr Micklewhite and Dr Micklewhite. But – and I'm not denigrating Joyce's talent for one second here – are enigma and the passing of the years to be given some credit for that? Is it maybe just possible that time itself has changed Joyce's painting? As if some spiritual lichen of its own has grown on and around it, deepening and enriching its texture? And, if so, what good does that do Joyce, now? What we need to do is get her trending online. Death: it's when we decide if everyone is good or bad, right, decide which of the two boxes to put them in, as well as the wooden one they're already in? Let's get her a Wikipedia page, get the conversation going. 'So sorry to hear Joyce Nicholas is no longer with us. I only met her once, for no more than nine seconds, but she was not stuck up at all, and even said hello to my dog.' 'I have always been a huge fan of Joyce, even when nobody was talking about her, and it was super uncool to like her.' 'Graham, can you remind me how much we paid for that picture above the spare bed?' '£300, I think. It was quite a long time ago.' 'Well, I've just found out from this newspaper article that it's worth £55,000 and by someone called Joyce Nicholas. She died in Devon in 1973.' Oh, Joyce, if only you'd have known your artistic worth, been raised in a different generation, and put yourself out there. You could be an influencer now. But you wouldn't have wanted that, you say? Why on earth not? Oh, because the very process itself was the important part of the matter for you? The feeling of being lost inside it, guided by invisible hands. The trance. The freedom. But what about the 'likes', what about the dopamine rush? How *old-fashioned* you are, Joyce. Don't you realise that even the dead have an Instagram account these days? Don't do yourself a disservice. Play the game. Everyone must.

I'm sorry; I've done something I said I wouldn't and permitted myself to get flustered. It's been one of those days. I think I spotted a couple of drones earlier, circling above the boulders. I have a pain in one of my toes and there's a very unwell, publicity-shy and sensitive ash tree I'm on intimate terms with and this morning someone plastered photos of it all over social media accompanied by the hashtag '#sadtree'. I think the toe pain comes from the fact that a pile of old compost bags and a hubcap are caught on a rock just past where the river emerges on the other side of town, almost but not quite, under the Victorian railway viaduct. It's bearable, not so painful, not even comparable to the time they found a dead owl down there, tangled up in a sky lantern. I should sleep. The forecast is better for tomorrow. I can see the bats powering over from their roosts. I heard that nineteen buzzards and a kestrel are flying up from Cornwall at dawn. But I will say this final thing, concerning the previous subject: Joyce isn't the only one. There are a lot of lofts and drawers and cupboards out there. Most of them have stacks of utterly worthless shit in them. But just a few of those lofts and cupboards and drawers contain a piece of art that's special and true and came from an honest, inspired place, didn't get shouted about at the time, and it's probably only going to get more special and true the longer it's left there. We're all getting older, and that has its pluses as well as its minuses. Over beyond the back wall of Joyce's old garden, the river isn't quite as diamond clear as it once was, and its dauntless song doesn't always quite succeed in drowning out the dual carriageway, but the lichen and moss on the rocks have become richer in texture. Quality lichen and moss isn't something you just cheat or shortcut or hack or hashtag your way to.

Here, in my big green hands, I hold some time. Consider it my gift to you. You will probably never receive a finer one.

I'm going to go now. A heavily pregnant ewe just did a very thick and powerful piss on my chin. But I'm OK. To be perfectly honest, I barely even felt it.

GROUND UNDER REPAIR
(1990)

The summer Mark and I found the man in the woods, Mark was sixteen and I was a year younger. We'd been playing a lot of golf that year and nobody much admired us for it. After our rounds and long practice sessions were complete, we'd walk home along the lane that led back to the village, carrying our clubs, and the inhabitants of passing vehicles would beep their horns and shout profanities at us. Considering it was a quiet lane where you'd only see about twenty cars per hour, it occurred with startlingly regularity. One time someone hurled a half-full Fanta can from a passenger window and it hit me in the eye and drenched the front of my polo shirt. When my mum saw the bruise, she refused to believe I had not been fighting. After that, Mark and I started taking a different route, over the corner of the tor and down through the woods by the river. Some of the paths weren't public but Mark worked out a shortcut and was fairly confident we wouldn't get into trouble.

The golf course had two personalities, and no smooth segue between them was in evidence. It threw visitors off balance, left them hot and gorse-scratched and irritated. Many who had begun the day in a positive frame of mind declined to visit the clubhouse for a drink afterwards, instead hurling their clubs into their car boot, not even bothering to change out of their spiked shoes, blowing out of the car park in a plume of exhaust smoke and a loud scrape of metal against speed bump, like people who'd stolen their own cars. For the first nine holes, everything was very polite and neatly mown, a sculpted suppression of nature that, were you blindfolded and dropped into it, would have been hard to distinguish from the one that characterises a thousand other golf courses. But after the ninth green players followed a steep tunnelled path through a small city of gorse and skyscraper ferns and emerged into a primal, unwashed otherplace that they had to trust, going by what the map on the back of the scorecard told them, was the tenth tee. Quarter-sheared, mad-eyed sheep and horned cattle roamed the fairways and tees indiscriminately. Jangly-nerved salesmen and insurance brokers backed off their putts as large dark winged shapes wheeled overhead, mocking them with shrieking beaked laughter. Balls struck sweetly from tees ricocheted off assorted hidden rocks into tussocky bogs, never to be seen again. These balls soared unpredictably owing to the dung caking their surface and sudden corridors of diabolical wind coming down off the moor. It was not uncommon to see visitors holding up play by attempting to herd sheep, cattle and ponies out of their playing line. Regulars were more nonchalant and casually floated their drives over the animals' heads, but even they were not exempt from pastoral strife. Believed to be assured of victory in the 1989 club championship as he strutted the mounds of the final fairway, Tom Bracewell threw away his advantage when a heifer sat on his ball and refused to move. A crowd soon gathered around the cow, the competitors who had been awaiting the result of the event in the clubhouse bar gradually filtering out to watch, until over a hundred of us stood staring at the animal. Christine Chagford, who before taking her job behind the bar at the club had spent a lot of time in close proximity to cattle, finally managed to sweet talk the cow into giving way and letting the group behind play through, but not before she'd planted a kiss on its forehead and posed for a photo which would later be framed and hung on the wall of the Men's Bar. Rattled, Bracewell racked up a triple bogey seven, putting him in a sudden death playoff with Christine's cousin Tony, which Bracewell subsequently lost. A year later, the general consensus was that he had still not recovered: a pallid, stooped figure, seen, if seen at all, staring forlornly at competition result boards and handicap tables in the back room of the clubhouse or down on the practice ground at sundown, scratching his chin and assessing the balls spread diversely in front of him, some or other mail order teaching contraption abandoned on the ground behind him.

Mark explained to me that he was on a mission, and that mission was to shag Christine before his seventeenth birthday. 'I'm working up to it and slowly getting her interested until one day she just won't be able to stop thinking about me,' he said. 'Is she not a bit old for you?' I asked. 'She's sort of thirty or something, right?' Mark waved the question away. 'Twenty-six. I'm tired of the girls our age. I don't want an immature idiot who writes the name of her favourite band on her pencil case then crosses it out next week when she changes her mind. I want a woman who knows who she is.' I was often dehydrated by the time Mark and I had completed eighteen holes, especially in what had been a very hot summer, and would have liked to have gone directly from the final green into the Men's Bar to order a pint of Coke with ice, but Mark always insisted that we followed protocol and visited the locker room to wash our hands and change into our soft shoes beforehand. I soon became aware that Mark, who was otherwise rarely guided by protocol, was driven by an ulterior motive on these occasions, which was to make sure his hair was adequately gelled before he saw Christine. 'How do I look?' he would ask me, after liberally applying the gel from one of the circular plastic tubs of it he worked his way through each week. 'Really good', I would reply, more admiring Mark's hair as a whole than specifically its gelled state. So far, if the gel was having an impact on Christine, she was keeping her cards very close to her chest. To date, the only sentence she'd said to Mark, besides 'Thanks', 'What can I get you?', 'Pint or half' and 'With ice or without' had been 'Ooh, big shot!' – this being in response to the time Mark paid for two pints of Coke with a fifty-pound note, which he'd got purposely from the bank that weekend, after exchanging it for his birthday money and a month's wages from his paper round.

Mark's other goal for his seventeenth birthday was to learn to drive and, when he had done so, very quickly purchase a car and drive it to school where, by which point, he would be attending the sixth form. The comic genius of this plan, we recognised, was that everyone knew that the small council house where Mark lived with his granddad was only seventy yards from the school car park. It was, in fact, the closest house of all to the school.

School was in town, six miles away, and I went there too, but Mark spent a lot of time at our place, in the village, and when he didn't stay over in my mum and dad's spare room, his granddad was always on hand to collect him with uncanny punctuality and obedience. Mark's granddad's name was Leonard, but Mark never called him that, or 'Granddad'; what he called him was 'Old Boy'. 'Hey look! Here's Old Boy!' Mark would say, looking out of our living-room window and spotting Leonard waiting in his Datsun Cherry. Old Boy very rarely knocked on the door when he collected Mark, never seemed anything less than 100 per cent available, never stopped grinning, and always wore a brown tweed cap, which – along with the outmoded and modest nature of his transport – prompted me to think of him less as a grandfather and more as a particularly humble chauffeur. 'It's OK. I'll get Old Boy to take us', Mark would say, if Mark and I had a plan for a trip where public transport was inconvenient, which, in Devon, on the brink of the nineties, was nearly all trips. When Mark and I went to Paignton, to play the slot machines, or to Exeter, to watch Iron Maiden in concert, Old Boy waited in the car, happily passing the time listening to the radio or reading a tattered paperback by Patrick O'Brian or CS Forester or another nautically inclined writer. 'How's tricks, Paulie, my boy?' Old Boy would sometimes ask me. 'Great!' I would answer. 'You just wait, you boys. It's all going to happen for you,' Old Boy would say. But apart from that, he largely just drove and grinned, with what struck me as the most relaxed of old faces. The Datsun was a car in which I never felt ill at ease, whose interior always smelt verdant and warm and earthy, like a greenhouse.

To my knowledge, Old Boy himself had no particular passion for golf, but it was well known that the clubs Mark used had come directly from Old Boy's loft: an assorted collection of irons and woods dating from the 1960s, the 1950s and, in the case of one tiny, hickory-shafted nine iron Mark was particularly fond of, 1912. My clubs were considered out of date by many, being second-hand and all at least four years old, but when I played alongside Mark they made me feel decadent and spoilt. 'You want to bin those sticks and get yourself some golf equipment, son,' Mike, the car salesman Mark played against in the 1988 club matchplay semi-final, had sneeringly told Mark, prior to Mark casually dispatching him by the handsome total of seven and six, less than two hours later. New juniors at the club came and went, invariably carrying hi-tech weapons that glinted in the moorland sun. It didn't bother Mark a bit. A lanky bespectacled boy called Roger Glaister arrived, carrying a gold-shafted driver, hopping casually over the fence from a big house on the lane which his parents had recently purchased, a cigarette hanging from the corner of his mouth. He spat a lot, in a very idiosyncratic way where the spit forked out into the air through his front teeth. Soon, several other kids at the club were spitting this way too, but not Mark. In their one and only match against each other, the score was quite close for the first nine holes, Glaister taunting Mark all the way with under-the-breath remarks about charity shop clothes, but on the final nine – always his favourite – Mark turned up the heat. By the sixteenth tee, that gold shaft had become two smaller crooked gold shafts, languishing in a wooden dustbin 500 yards distant, Glaister's £50 Pringle shirt was damp from where his saliva had rebelled on him in a gust of wind, and his ankles were caked in cow dung. Mark beat him by eleven shots in the end. 'I enjoyed that,' he told Glaister, shaking his hand and taking a grudgingly proffered £20 note. 'We must do it again some time.'

We had both improved considerably in the two years we'd been playing together, coaxing one another on, but for Mark the process was different: calm, creative, unfussy. A bad round never seemed to bother him. For me, it was increasingly a case of three steps forward, two steps back, sometimes with one extra step back just after that. I'd noticed golf had been much easier when I knew far less about how to play it. At this point, when I had become much more than just somebody who hit a ball and tried to get it into a little hole in as few strokes as possible, my mind became fascinated with the margins for error, with the allure of the countless potential negative outcomes, as opposed to the one simple potential positive outcome. I watched the pros at Augusta and Lytham and St Andrews and Troon on my mum and dad's black-and-white TV, and, while there were a few inflamed exceptions – usually men from Spain or South America – the solidly successful ones often came across as robots in jumpers, pastel droids who might potentially sell you some insurance between shots. They did not appear to have exciting brains or, on the few occasions they did, they seemed to have the discipline to make those brains unexciting for the five or so hours they were on the course. They say golf is a game of the mind but that does not mean you actually require one to play it well. It could even be argued that possessing one is a distinct disadvantage. But Mark struck me as more akin to those rare pros who had a bit of swagger to them, who had plenty of intelligence but were able to somehow reduce it, control it, when they were over the ball. It had been me who'd first brought him up to the club, after I took a bag of balls down to the playing field in Underhill and found him already down there, with that prehistoric nine iron of his. I'd barely known him back then, only recognised him as a distant figure from breaktimes and the bus queue, but we'd instantly bonded, and I'd already been in awe of what he could do with just that one Edwardian club: fading it, drawing it, driving it low, more than 150 yards, into a strong breeze, then seconds later using it with great finesse for the featheriest of lobshots. I still had the authority at that point, though: it was me who told him how to grip the club properly, me who recommended his first pair of spiked shoes. I'd overcomplicated it for him, brought him into the universe of handicaps and etiquette and left-hand gloves and deconstructive video lessons and cruel bounces and lip outs and sucker-pin positions, when he could have just stayed happily thwacking balls all day, down behind the village. But, unlike me, he responded to the psychological torments of the game like a Buddha, appeared to sleepwalk through it all, even, shrugging, easy, that looseness in his swing that made him able to power his drives so effortlessly far being a greater looseness; a looseness of face, of eyes, of character, of mind.

That was what made Mark different to everyone else at the golf course: he just never appeared all that *bothered*. When I consider what would have been happening to him hormonally at this point in his life, this now strikes me as more remarkable still. Golf, so our schoolfriends told us, was a limp old man's game, a bollockless sport devoid of fireworks or passion, but every week we saw it transform men three times our age hailing from supposedly respectable echelons of society into swearing, club-hurling cavemen, grey hooligans spinning in enraged circles halfway up a hill. You'd no more try to strike up a conversation with these directors of sales and funerals, these commodity traders, these spiritually beige number-crunchers while they were on a bad run of putting than you'd try to stroke a hyena who hadn't eaten for a fortnight. One week, we bit into our sleeves to stifle our laughter as a retired headmaster greeted a triple bogey seven by taking off one of his shoes, marching several yards into the undergrowth and hurling the shoe into the roaring current of the river. The next, we bit harder still on the fabric as we witnessed an esteemed Plymouth solicitor lose the last of the twelve balls he'd started the day with, turn to a crowd of nearby sheep, and shout, 'MOTHERFUCK EVERY SINGLE ONE OF YOU.' We learned to play alongside those who made their living in outdoor professions if we could: the thatchers, the lumberyard proprietors, the deputy garden centre managers. They were a little less flappable. Still, like the others, many of them questioned why we spent so much time at the club, which was not in fact appreciably more time than the time any of them spent at the club. 'Don't you boys have homes to go to?' the grey hooligans in their pleated slacks would ask, in what, for me, was an early lesson in the fact that, when somebody attacks you out of the blue for something you're doing that isn't hurting anyone else, they're more than likely talking about a wrongness in their own lives. 'Yes, sir, you are correct: it is strange, us spending our free time playing a sport, in our mid-teens. What must our wives think? Don't we have livings to earn, mortgages to pay, kids to feed?' It was as if we were briefly on some upside-down planet, where adults, not children, were expected to misbehave, and indulged for it. Being together on this planet united Mark and me, fortified the walls of our City of Two. And that's really what we were. Other kids were often around, kids from more affluent families than ours, but they never stayed long, never challenged for competitions. In May, there was a proposal – thankfully quashed, in a rare moment of sanity – at a committee meeting to reduce the number of days junior members were permitted to play at the club. The proposal was talked about as if there were juniors everywhere, vast armies of them, running up the fairways every evening, farting on blackbirds and kicking over bins. But it was mostly just me and Mark. Then, after I broke my arm the following month, it was Mark, all alone, fending for himself amongst the grey yobs.

Up to this point, I'd not knowingly heard any genuinely offensive remarks directed towards Mark at the club. But, now he was winning more tournaments and shooting up in height, he was becoming more widely noticed, and I know his appearance would have been perceived as an extra threat by many of these men who nudged one another and muttered under their breath when they saw him take the prizes at their tournaments, this lanky mixed-race child from who knew where, with his untucked school shirt and hand-me-down equipment and that hair springing higher and higher above his head, towering above their combovers. Mark was good at saving the little money he earned from his paper round, and could no doubt have bought the standard kind of polo shirt most golfers wore, or even got his granddad or his mum to buy him one for his birthday or Christmas, but it would simply have never occurred to him as being important. Mark virtually never spoke to me about his parents. It had been close to a decade since he'd last lived with them. I knew from him only that his dad now resided in France. My parents, meanwhile, had told me that Mark's mum was currently 'living in Weston-super-Mare and having some difficulties'.

How did I break my arm? I think the official cause could be cited as 'having shit for brains'. My cousins were down from Walsall for the weekend, we'd taken a dozen cans of cheap lager up to the rocks on top of Underhill tor, and I was showing off. I took a run up and attempted to vault the gap between the two tallest rocks, the top ones on the bit that looks like stairs, and didn't quite make it. Truth is, I was lucky not to hurt myself a lot more severely, as it's pretty high there, and in the crevices between the clitter the granite sticks out like broken crowns in an old mouth. Even with my arm in its cast, I continued to follow Mark up to the practice ground once every few evenings. That's how pleasurable it was to watch him hit balls. That's what we *loved*: hitting balls. Not the shoes or the handicap system or the cut glass or the silverware or the single leather gloves or the wood panelling or the tee pegs or the gold shafts or the handshakes or the reserved parking spaces or the Eric Finch Foursome Matchplay Bowl or the Garden Room or the Men's Bar or the sixty-degree Tom Watson beryllium copper sand irons or the patriarchal badinage but the pure nirvana of metal cleanly strikingly rubber at high speed with minimum effort. I'd played tennis, and football, and squash, and badminton, and table tennis, but nothing quite compared, contact-wise. When you got it right, you felt like hitting golf balls – and here I mean hitting golf balls as a separate entity to the game of golf – was another preordained human need, like eating or breathing, something that was always meant to be here and always would be here. That was why Mark and I were here, at least four days out of seven, every week. That sensation, like sap rising up our arms, blossoming in our necks and shoulders, flowering in our brains like a million of the most vivid poppies all at once. I chased it in the way that later, in the mess of adult life, I'd chase the memory of my most transcendental orgasms. The elusive nature of the pure strike made it all the more appealing. It didn't actually happen that often, for me. But with Mark, it occurred in long, sustained bursts. He hit a sweet zone of rhythmical calm. He was a great player on the course, but on the practice ground, without the distractions of competition, he was an ethereal one, an alchemist, a Zen wizard. I could have watched him forever.

One night in late June, after he'd hit balls until we no longer could see where they landed, we took our usual route home over the jutting, unimpressed elbow of the tor. The last purple streaks of the sun toasted the hilltops and owls made lewd suggestions to one another down in the woods by the river. Mark, however, had not been the last man swinging. That honour went to the Irish Doctors, whose trolleys could be seen very slowly approaching the seventeenth tee in the mauve half-light. At the club, nicknames stuck like dog hair to merino wool. A wiry, anxious weekend player called Phil who'd once missed a crucial putt when he was distracted by the call of a skein of Canada geese overhead was thereafter known to all as 'Quack'. Carl Marchwell, who was infamous for telling all of his playing companions in great detail about his week and lacked the skill of self-editing, hadn't been called 'Carl' by anybody at the club for years; he was always 'Jackanory'. Ian Welcombe, who liked to bet big money on foursome matches but had never, to anybody's knowledge, actually won, was 'The Bank'. Jill, Ian's wife – one of the few female members of the club who actually seemed to enjoy the game – was not 'Jill' but 'Mrs Bank'. Recently I'd overheard people talking about somebody called 'Jam Jar' but I was yet to find out who that was. The Irish Doctors, however, were just the Irish Doctors. No nickname, collective or otherwise, could have been more definitive or catchy than their quintessential Irish Doctorness. There were six of them in all, although legend was that there had at one point been eight. Generally, playing in groups of more than four was severely frowned upon, but special, unspoken dispensation was given to the Irish Doctors, who always operated as a gang. This – and the fact that each of them was in his ninth decade – meant their pace of play was very slow and they spent a large amount of their round standing aside and letting other groups through. Mark and I liked the Irish Doctors, who were the jovial antithesis of the grey hooligans a generation or two beneath them, and we'd have both been happy to play alongside them, were it not for the fact that, not being Irish doctors ourselves, that would have been an affront to the natural rhythm of the earth, and would have made their progress even more excruciating. As was usually the case, today they would not hole their final putts before the light had totally vanished.

We passed through clouds of midges as we came down the back side of the tor and along the sunken track leading down to the river, watery rubble under our feet, the metal in Mark's bag pounding out a clanking beat several yards ahead of me. We always carried our bags on our shoulders, never resorted to a trolley and, as with many child golfers, the spinal damage it caused would be evident in my posture later in life. I heard a distant cry of 'Cracking shot, Seamus!' and a faint, delayed thud of a ball being propelled a modest distance forward by frail hands, then I rounded a sharp bend and all was silent, beside the chorus of the water. I found Mark sitting on the old packhorse bridge, rolling a cigarette, and joined him.

'Look at that,' said Mark, pointing to the liquid beneath our dangling feet, rushing clear over the black rocks and coppery pebbles. 'It's magic, that is. That's what it is. Think of all of what's up on the moor every day: all the dead sheep bones, all the pony shit, and peat, all our pollution, being sucked up into the clouds then rained down back into the streams. But it still comes down here every day, looking like that. You know what I do, the first thing I do, every time I've been away from Devon? I rush straight to the tap and fill a glass. It always tastes so good.'

'My dad said the water in London is full of women's pills and cocaine,' I said. 'So every time you have a drink out of the tap there, you're doing drugs and stopping yourself getting knocked up.'

'You know it's all bullshit, this? All wrong. Well, not this. Definitely not this. But that.' He gestured back up the sunken track, in the vague direction of the course.

'All what?'

'Just because there are cows and sheep and ponies there, just because they didn't get rid of some of the rocks. It doesn't mean it's real. If grass had a choice, it wouldn't do what it's doing up there. It was never meant to be like that.'

'But if it was never meant to be like that, maybe this footbridge wasn't meant to be like this, either?'

I had made a den close to here one time when I was little, a few hundred yards closer to the village, using an old mattress and a few other mouldy abandoned household bits and bobs I'd found. When I told my mum, she told me to avoid abandoned freezers because children climb into them then can't get the door open again and die.

'I dunno. There's natural and there's natural. You know the shit they pour onto that golf course. You know how many insects it kills? I'm just saying. I've been thinking about it a lot recently.'

'I've got to have a piss.'

I was always careful where I had a wee when I was outdoors. It was one of those ways in which golf made me an adolescent with a little more decorum than most. An older playing partner had told me it was very important to choose a surreptitious spot, in case any lady members were nearby, and my habit of doing that carried over into any pissing that I did in the fresh air, even beyond golfing parameters. I mention this because, had I not been so careful about picking my spot, I might not have pissed on the stranger's hand at all. I'd been pissing for several seconds before I heard him – or, as it seemed, the brambles and bracken in front of me – groan and as I did I leapt sideways, spraying urine on my left trouser leg and shoe in the process. 'Mark! Fucking hell!' I shouted, which in retrospect shows me just how much I looked up to my friend, viewed him as, in some way, my protector.

He rushed over and, careful not to touch the foliage that was still wet with my spray, parted the leaves and fronds to reveal a long male body, supine in the mulch below them. The body's eyes were closed and, when Mark asked the face on the end of the body if it was OK, it grunted, as if in dreamy reassurance. In a way the face seemed a bit like the faces of lads just a few years older than us but the paperiness of its complexion and the colour of the stubble on it made me perplexed about how old its owner was. A camera, quite an old one, hung around the man's neck by a strap. He did not look what I would have called healthy and seemed unable to open his eyes yet there was a sense that the reason he was not able to open them was that he was in a very delicious sort of sleep that he was reluctant to emerge from. Mark asked him some questions, including 'What is your name?', 'Where are you from?' and 'How did you end up here?', and when the stranger only answered with more oddly tranquil grunts and did not move, it was agreed that I would head into Underhill to get help. My arm, being still only half-healed, impeded my progress and it took me close to half an hour to reach the village.

My intention was to go home and call for an ambulance but part of me wondered if that would be time-wasting, as the man didn't actually seem hurt in any way, and on my way past the Co-op I bumped into Steve Clayton, who'd narrowly beat me in the club matchplay last year and used to be in the army. Steve

obviously noticed that I looked flustered and asked me what
was wrong and I told him about the man and he said he'd come
back down the path with me. Steve was strong and I decided
that with the help of Mark and both of Mark's working arms he
could probably carry the man back to the village if it came to
that. What had been confusing to me when I'd first met Steve
was that, despite him being very muscly, Steve couldn't hit his
golf ball very far at all, and the strongest part of his game was
his putting. But since then I'd found out that obvious physical
strength counted for nothing in golf. It was all about rhythm and
timing and you often got blokes who looked like Tarzan or He-
Man who barely hit the ball anywhere and people like Mark who
only weighed nine and a half stone but could lamp it into the next
county. Steve's massive arms were a moot point anyway, though,
because when we arrived back at the spot where I'd done my wee
neither Mark nor the stranger were anywhere to be seen. Now I
was embarrassed and felt like Steve probably thought I was lying
again, because last winter he'd asked me what kind of putter
I'd used and it was a Wilson but I'd said it was a Spalding but
only because I'd forgotten and when we played together he saw
the putter and said, 'I thought you had a Spalding?' He was OK
about being dragged out there, though; he just looked at me a bit
queryingly, and said he had to get back to the shop and get some
steaks for his missus to cook that night, and that it was dark and
I should get home soon but that I should call him if anything else
happened or I couldn't find Mark and he would call his mate John
who worked for the police. I didn't walk back down the path with
him because I felt like it might be weird and we might run out of
things to talk about. Instead I went and stood by the packhorse
bridge for a while, listening to the water and thinking about what
Mark had said about it. I could hear a cuckoo up in the woods
round the back of the tor, the first one of the year. My mum had

said there had been loads when she was a kid. I walked back a different way, past a ruined barn above where my gran said they used to hold the old fayres, which always gave me the creeps, like something bad had happened there.

Something about the way Mark was, how thoroughly OK he always seemed to be, made me sure he'd be OK now, and I didn't feel like there was anything very scary or threatening about the man on the ground, but I was still a trolley of nerves for the couple of hours after I arrived home, doing my best to hide that from my mum and dad while also trying Mark's home number every ten minutes and getting no answer (Old Boy was clearly also out). Finally, just as I could hear the theme tune from the *News at Ten* coming from the telly downstairs, he picked up.

'What happened? Where did you go?' I asked, without even saying hello.

'Nothing. Well, some stuff. But nothing bad. He was OK. He got up after we left. We went back to his house. Well, it's not a house. It's a tent. In the woods. He's from California. We smoked some stuff he had. He plays guitar. He's cool. He has a bad head, he says, and it makes him sleep in weird places. But he's OK. It's OK. He coughed a lot, though. I was about to call you.'

'Steve Clayton might have told the police.'

'Steve Clayton? Why Steve Clayton? Doesn't matter. Don't tell me. It's fine. If they come round I'll just tell them it's OK, and he went on his way. I'm not telling them where his tent is, though, as I don't think it's supposed to be there. He's such a fucking sound bloke. He wants all the rivers to be clear and nobody to be able to own land.'

That was the summer Mark left school, which was one of the reasons that our friendship drifted a little after that. He chose to not come back for the sixth form and instead attend a further education college a few miles closer to the coast, which meant that much talked-up ambition of his to drive Old Boy's car all of seventy yards to attend classes was never realised. By September my arm had recovered sufficiently to begin golfing again and I called Mark a couple of times to see if he fancied a round but he was always busy. I got the impression he was making new friends at the college, people far more exciting than me, probably, who knew more about interesting leftfield music and films. I played some of my best golf that autumn and early winter but it all felt a little hollow with nobody to enjoy it with. 'You could be a pro, lad, if you put the work in,' some of the kinder adult members would tell me at the end of our rounds. But I was wise enough to know that there is a very big difference between being one of the best players at a provincial club in Devon and actually being able to make a career from the game. Also, I was beginning to get distracted by a new nagging feeling in my loins. That November on the Geography field trip to Bodmin, Martha Leigh Price, sitting in the coach seat behind me on the way back, leaned over and draped her arms over me and nothing was ever the same again. The following April I forgot to watch the US Masters tournament for the first time in three years. I started listening to The Smiths and, having seen Morrissey do it on an old TV clip, took to walking around with gladioli in the back pocket of my jeans, which failed to cause any of the stir I'd hoped it would with anyone, save for my mum, who – always obsessed with all matters olfactory – told me that Morrissey 'looked like a smelly person' and that at my age with my whole life in front of me I should be listening to music that felt less sorry for itself.

There was also quite a lot of bad feeling at the golf course around this time. In September, somebody had snuck onto the course at night and spray-painted the word 'WANKSHAFT' in huge letters over the fifteenth green. A month later, Fizz, the head greenkeeper, arrived at dawn to mow the first fairway and found the words 'GIVE IT BACK TO THE SHEEP BELLENDS' written in a decorous arc around the devilish pot bunkers situated in the customary landing area for tee shots. By the time a further two pieces of graffiti – 'WOKE UP WITH WOOD' on the third tee and 'GOLPHERS SUCK SAGGY BALLS' on the bank fronting the eleventh green – the story had made the early pages of both the *Western Morning News* and the *Plymouth Herald*, although no leads had been found pertaining to a suspect. It was one of two environmentally themed news stories featuring the area around the village at that time, the other covering around 300 battery hens from Cavendish's farm up near Wychcombe that had been set free on the high moor. The fact that I found the graffiti amusing highlighted the way that golf and I were slowly growing apart. The effort I'd put in to perfecting my chip shots the previous spring, this spring I rechannelled into trying to persuade Martha Leigh Price to kiss me. I had no luck; she'd never really been as effusive with her affection as that day coming back from Bodmin, and in May she confessed to me that nothing could happen between us until she'd found out if a guitarist called Ben Bishop in the sixth form had properly sorted out his feelings for her. This, however, didn't stop me regularly writing letters to her, brimful of innocent passion and hopes for our future, or using all the pocket money I had saved to get the bus to Exeter and buy perfume for her birthday, or walking down along the path through the woods to the river with her at least once a week. Passing the spot where Mark and I had found the American with Martha, I'd wonder about Mark, and the American, and where they both were now. Every so often on these walks Martha and I would also spot a stray chicken or two, enjoying their newfound freedom, in a confused-looking way.

'Do you always make sure you smell nice before you meet Martha?' my mum asked, one day when she found me moping about the house.

'Of course,' I replied.

'Well, it's her loss, then.'

Nowadays, periods of three or four years often feel like commonplace slips in time, as if you've decided to go onto the next song but put your finger too heavily on the button and actually skip three tracks ahead, although only realise a fair bit later that you have. 'Bloody hell! It's 2021, and 2017 isn't actually last year any more. How did that happen? Oh well. It's nothing new, just part of being a person over the age of thirty-two. This is just life now. Better get on with it.' How different to the final days of adolescence, when a three- or four-year period is like a whole country separating two other, bigger countries, one of which you're no longer interested in and the other seeming limitless in the promises its vast landscape contains. When I bumped into Mark in the garden of the Stonemason's Arms in the summer of 1993, it felt like the late twentieth-century peacetime equivalent of reuniting with a soldier who'd been part of a long war and irrevocably changed and emboldened by his experiences in it. He recognised me before I recognised him and I think the reason for that was not because he didn't look like him but because, for the half an hour that we'd been sitting two tables away from one another, I'd caught a hint of him in my eyeline and shied away from looking directly at him for fear of being dazzled by all that he was. He'd reached his full six foot two in height by this point, his hair was bigger than ever and his cheekbones had sharpened, his eyes deepened. He wore a silk scarf, a chunky belted cardigan and these dark green velvet trousers I can't even get close to doing justice to with words, which looked like they were glued to his legs in the softest, most complimentary way. It wasn't a look you'd have found in any fashion magazines in any era, but boy did it work on him. I was much more bashful in admitting my own appreciation of male beauty back then, it being only a couple of years past a time

33

when most of my mates would have called me a poof or gayboy for making even the slightest suggestion that a bloke looked good, but, even so, I was stunned, and a yearning opened up in me. The off ramp from puberty had evidently been a very different adventure for Mark than it had for me. Why hadn't *I* got to spend it at a magic transformative castle of technicolour dreams too? It seemed a little unfair. Nonetheless, I think I succeeded in disguising my awe and envy and I pulled up a chair at the table where he and his friends were sitting so the pair of us could have a good catch-up. He was two years into university now, where he was studying Environmental Science, but was having reservations about going back for his final year. He talked about how he'd come to realise the drawbacks of institutionalised learning. I nodded, doing what I hoped was a decent job of pretending I knew what he was talking about. I was surprised to discover he was living closer to me than before, up at Runnaford Hollow, a small hippie and traveller community, down near Wychcombe on the back side of the tor. He said some of the guys up there were having a singaround later, as they did every Friday night, and that I should come up and join in. As we talked, I glanced back at the table where my friends were still sitting and couldn't help but be jarred by how different they were to Mark's crowd. I'd never thought of my pals – grunge and metal lads, mostly, misshapes and mild outcasts – as boring but by contrast the people Mark surrounded himself with looked like they had slipped through a rip in the space-time continuum. They were all tassels and belts and bangles and soft fabric and stroked shoulders and androgynous kisses. To my mind, they had nothing to do with 1993 and probably not a lot to do with the past or future, either. 'You remember Chris, don't you?' he said, gesturing towards a girl in a floral dress and floppy felt hat two seats to my left, and beneath the paisley I saw the face of Christine Chagford, Mark's old fantasy now turned reality. I asked her if she was still tending bar up at the club, and she merely laughed and offered a hand – the one not holding a roll-up cigarette – that looked like it had never pulled a pint, a hand that seemed French in all the best ways. By the time we all left for the Hollow, the ground was spinning beneath me and I don't think it was solely because of the three pints of Guinness I'd downed. I told my friends that I might catch up with them later, but most of them appeared not to notice, since, for a £20 reward, one of them was being challenged to drink some vomit he had found in a pint glass on the wall behind him. I'm ashamed to admit it, but I can't even remember his name now.

A bonfire was going strong in a clearing in the woods when we arrived at Runnaford Hollow and a crowd of at least twenty people were gathered around a girl sitting on a knoll of tree roots with a guitar and dreadlocks who was singing a song I knew I should know but didn't. A couple of wiry bearded dogs tussled over a stick as their wiry bearded owners looked on. Looking at the living conditions – caravans, tents, an electricity generator but no running water – it was remarkable to me that Mark looked as shiny as he did, but he later admitted to me that he was only bedding down here three nights a week and having deep luxurious baths back at home on the remaining evenings. He fetched us a couple of mulled ciders and we sat on stools carved from tree stumps, a few feet from the fire.

'So, you and Christine... it actually happened!' I said.

'Sort of,' he replied. 'It's cool. We hang out but she doesn't want to be locked into anything. The way I think you'd put it is she's not a one-man woman, and I respect that. She's taught me a lot. All these people have. They're my brothers and sisters, really. The ones I never had.'

'They seem very cool.' I looked across at a broad, bearded man with a strikingly low and dense hairline, who carried a shepherd's crook. 'I think I recognise that guy from the Green

35

Warlock café.' What I did not add was 'where I saw him getting ejected by the owner for trying to haggle over the price of a cup of tea and a doughnut.'

'Rory? Rory is exceptionally hip. A high priest of Extreme Dudeness, in multifarious ways. And of course you probably remember the American...' He pointed to a tall lean man in a flannel shirt, older than most of the people here, who, as if summoned by Mark's words, picked up a guitar and sauntered over to the knoll in the centre of the clearing, high-fiving the girl with the dreadlocks as he took her place on the organic stage. He hadn't changed much in three years, the main differences being that he was now vertical and had eyes that weren't closed. Much like on that day we found him in the woods, I felt like I was looking at a confusing hybrid of age and innocence. His hair was long and curtainlike, like mine and that of many of the other men who were here, but lightly streaked with grey. Looking at his face was like looking at a portrait of an eager teenager in which the paint had been smudged by a fat, rogue thumb.

'Isn't he fucking amazing?' Mark said, as the American began to play. It would not be truthful to say that I agreed. The music was confusing to me, spaghetti-like and intricate and not very angsty or anglicised, not very part of my small English life, the one whose cultural parameters I then kept far tighter than I arrogantly believed I did. Three of the four songs were instrumentals, which was frustrating to me because I was a stickler for lyrics in those days, and the one that did have words – his final number of the night – was far too blunt and folksy for my taste, a bit... old, more the kind of thing my uncle listened to. Yet I will also say this: an echo of that music has stayed in my head ever since, an echo that has blossomed and grown coloured petals, and I have countless times wished I could go back and hear it again in the flesh. I have experienced a similar phenomenon in other ways since, where I have realised with hindsight that the case was not that a piece of art was not good enough for me but that I was not yet good enough for the piece of art, but I don't think I have ever experienced it to quite this extent.

'This is pretty special because he doesn't get up and play much,' said Mark. 'He's a bit shy about it. He's a genius, though. He has his own method of tuning. Nobody has a clue how he does it.'

More people were arriving at the Hollow now. People of many ages, at least two genders, and many miraculous clothes. Sartorially, the crowd suggested a far more diverse and perplexing definition of 'alternative' than the one I'd become familiar with on nights out with my friends, which mostly resulted in everyone dressing in the same jeans and band t-shirts and Doc Marten boots. Smocks abounded; tunics and dungarees and felt hats and cut-off jeans and tweed and trenchcoats and waistcoats and flares and drainpipes. I noticed one girl in a long white blouse stood a little back from everything, watching, in the woods, as if nervous to join in, but by midnight most people were dancing and hugging, flutes and banjos and lutes and guitars were appearing everywhere and the wavy treeline encircling us began to feel more like a crinkle-crankle wall separating us from the world as it had been described to us by every cautious and boring person we had ever met. I did not see the girl in the long white blouse again, which was a shame as she had immediately interested me and I liked the way her hair reminded me of a holly wreath, and I had begun to worry about why she was alone. Christine – who I'd not realised was musical – played some songs, too, and they were good, in a folky, whispery way. The clear sky above me, with all its stars, was yet another element of the evening I did not appreciate enough, although I certainly did not *not* appreciate it, and I fell asleep under it, a reluctant virgin, two months off my nineteenth birthday, in the arms of a woman thirteen years my senior. I suppose to some there might have seemed something poetic about it if this had been the big one, the night I ended up losing it, but in retrospect to me there is a far greater poetry to the fact that it was not. Fran, she said her name was. A baker by profession, down from the other side of the moor. 'This is a weird request, but can I run my hands through your hair? I do so miss the feel of a young man's hair.' Yes, you can, Fran. In fact, please carry on. I am really ready for sleep now and this is helping me ease towards it. But oh, Fran. What would you think if you tried to do the same now, with the spotted stubble that remains there? Would you be surprised if you knew you'd triggered a lifetime of need for head rubs? Where are you now? And were you offended when your hand landed on my belt buckle and I moved it gently away? Did it make you feel like an interloper from full adulthood, a terrible raider of the young? And will you believe me if I said I did not intend to make you feel that way; I just felt it wasn't the right place, or the right time, despite all the bigger rightness of the occasion in so many other ways, plus the mulled cider was stronger than I'd realised and did not mix well with Guinness?

It wasn't yet fully light when I woke up to the sensation of Mark tugging at my sleeve. Christine was beside him, looking like anything but a former golf club employee who'd had less than three hours' sleep on a shared single bed in a caravan. 'Dude,' he said. He was talking like an American now, as well as hanging out with them. 'We're going on a dawn mission. You wanna come with?' Too bleary-eyed to know what I was being asked, but having nothing but an ordinary empty unemployed 1990s day ahead of me, I pulled myself off the ground and followed them through the trees, leaving Fran asleep clutching the ghost of my hair. The car that waited for us on the lane – a light blue Austin Maestro – was unfamiliar but the driver was not. 'How's tricks, Paulie, my boy?' Old Boy asked, placing a book about eighteenth-century Cornish shipwrecks back in the glove compartment as Christine and I got in the back seat. I told him, with total authenticity, that I was feeling pretty great, and the four of us started off for the coast. It was a journey of no more than three quarters of an hour and by the time Old Boy parked up again, beside a gate gap in the hook of a lane overlooking a pitted, zigzagging headland, part of which was home to a moderately venerated and exclusive links golf course, I was still in the dark as to the purpose of the adventure.

'We use environmentally friendly paint,' said Mark, heaving a tub out of the boot of the car. 'It's made from milk proteins, balsam and citrus. The metal can will be recycled. So this is a protest that doesn't hurt the earth. And even if we did use normal paint we'd not be doing a fraction of the damage that they're doing with their pesticides and poisons that they put on the turf every day. It won't take long. It's only about twelve minutes to the seventh green if we go over this field and we'll have the job done in no time. It's private land to get there, though, so keep an eye over your shoulder, because the farmers around here can be massive bastards. What's your favourite bit of swearing at the moment?'

'Pardon?'

'What's your favourite bit of swearing, right now? A word or phrase. Anything you like.'

The sky over the water was a friendly dark green and seemed like it was holding everything in a freeze frame for us, all apart from many dozen swifts who spun around us as we walked as if capitalising on this bonus pause before the uglier part of the day legally began.

'Big badger's arse!' I blurted out, before engaging my brain, and instantly felt disappointed in myself, knowing I could have done so much better.

'Perfect. Then that shall be today's message. You get one word. How about the arse? Chris and I will share the other two.

This is your big debut. It's like a dream come true. So won't you smile for the camera? I know you're going to love it.'

He sang the last bit, like it was already a song, and I grinned, pretending I knew it. I hoped there wouldn't actually be a camera.

*

It rained later that morning: light flicky rain out of a sunny sky, which we felt glad to sit in as it teased away the last of our hangovers. Old Boy, who didn't have a hangover, also appeared reasonably content to sit in it, just as he always appeared reasonably content about everything. Christine, under her floppy hat, still looked serene and impeccable, mysteriously free of environmental emulsion splashback. The four of us ate mostly in silence, perched on a wall above the shingle, staring out towards an arched rock that my dad had once told me was arched because a very strong whale had swum straight through the middle of it. I thought how beautiful the sun was as it glinted through the arch, and how magical the world we took for granted could be, the world already there that we placed all our paraphernalia and meaningless chaos on top of, and inextricably tied in with this realisation was the realisation for the first time since waking up that I was probably still wasted from last night.

'So it was you all along?' I asked Mark.

'Well, yeah. Me. Some friends. Christine, sometimes. But mostly me.'

'But why? I mean, I thought it was pretty funny. But why?'

'You really have to ask? You know what they called me up there, the way they spoke about me. I'd had enough.'

'No. Well, sort of. Yes. No. What? Who?'

'"Jam Jar". The members at the club. You didn't know that?'

'I didn't realise that was you. I always wondered who they were talking about and why they said that.'

'It's a reference to golliwogs, like you get on the Robertson's jam jars. The black-faced dolls. You know the ones. No, they didn't come straight out and call me "golliwog" or "wog" but you know what it means, you know what they're getting at: it's a degrading term for a non-white person. A belittling. A put-down. Thatcher said it, so why wouldn't they? And you know what? I actually accepted it for a while, just decided that shrugging it off was part of getting by, getting by around here, where there are so few black faces, just like my mate Rob who was the only black kid in his town and started calling himself "Chalky" just so he could get in there quickly before anyone else started doing the same thing. It could have been worse. And it was only a few of them. It was mostly just ignorance and repetition. But then I started thinking a bit more deeply about it, a bit more about what I was endorsing with my silence and acceptance.' I was struck by just how differently he now spoke, just how much more than me he was, just how much, again, his time at that magic castle had changed him.

'I'm sorry. I fucking wish I'd known. I don't go up there any more, if it's any consolation. Haven't in a long time.'

'Bunch of wankers,' interjected Christine, wanking off an invisible cock (small) with her hand.

'It wasn't all of them. Not even most. Some decent people play golf. We both know that. It happens everywhere, not just on golf courses. But it just so occurred that when I was having this revelation I was also having a revelation about golf itself, what it is, what it does to the environment. The amount of weedkiller that gets poured onto that course every month. The insects it kills. The waste it is of natural habitat for any number of creatures. All because some well-off people want to hit a ball around. A lot of them don't seem to even enjoy it. Do you know how many golf courses there are just in England? Over two thousand. Do you know how many acres of wasted wild space that is?'

'I see what you mean.'

'Have you read *Silent Spring* by Rachel Carson? Read it. Drop anything you are reading now and read it instead. It's your duty as a human being. She was dying of cancer when she wrote it but she cared so much about the planet she still went ahead and did it. She saw the future, and the destruction industrial farming was doing, the mindless greed of big businesses, and that was in 1962, and now it's more than thirty years later and people are STILL not seeing the future. We are breaking the fine threads that bind life to life and the results are going to be pissing catastrophic.' He was really gaining steam now and I was struggling to keep up, struggling to reshape him from what I had known him as; it wasn't all that long ago that our primary topic of conversation was the escape shots Seve Ballesteros played when he was stuck behind a tree. 'It all started getting bad in the Second World War. People experimented with new chemicals to make weapons and then we started using the same chemicals to blast tiny creatures to hell, just so we could grow even more wheat, expand the monoculture, make the countryside look even more uniform and dull. Look at the names they call these things. They make sure they're long and hard to remember, because if they are people are less likely to address what they actually are and the terrible harm they do. Golf. Agribusiness. It's all a part of the same giant disease. Waste and indulgence and humans acting like greedy, suppressive gods. What do you do with your plastic when you're done with it?'

'I put it in the bin in my kitchen.'

'Of course you do. That's what everyone does. But where do you think it's all going? Do you think it just vanishes? I'll tell you where it's going. Out there.' He pointed towards the waves, and the stone arch, and I pictured that apocryphal whale my dad had told me about, blasting through the stone then gobbling the container that had formerly held the takeaway sandwich I'd bought from the Newton Abbot branch of Boots on Monday. 'What are you doing a week on Sunday?'

'Nothing, I think.'

'Good. Fancy coming to the Quantocks? We're going to mess up one of the hunts up there. Stags, but probably foxes too. It'll be different to today. More risky. People get hurt sometimes. But there'll be more of us. The American will be there. Rory, too. I know some very excellent people. You'll be fine.'

'Er... OK.'

Unexpectedly, the light spaced-out drizzle had redoubled then retripled and become something more disparaging. In attempting to digest Mark's rant, I'd been slow at eating my chips, and now a deferred queasiness was rising in me, and I opted to leave the remainder of them for the gulls to pick at. Undaunted by the weather, a caterpillar of tourist-owned cars was moving down the hill towards the beach café car park. I realised we had lost Christine and Old Boy but neither were far away, Christine throwing a stick for a dog she had met on the beach, and Old Boy beatifically examining the half-sunken slimy hull of an old boat beneath the causeway. Mark turned for the car and whistled and both of them appeared swiftly beside us.

The fact that this was the last time I saw Mark in person is something that I quickly became disappointed about and is a fact that has become a little sadder and starker every year since. That Saturday afternoon I phoned him at home. He was out but I asked Old Boy to pass on my apologies: I had forgotten that I was supposed to go to my aunt and uncle's for Sunday lunch, I explained, and wouldn't be able to make it to the Quantocks. This was a lie, pure cowardice on my part. I loathed hunting as sport but in the end I could not picture myself in a crowd, trying to disrupt it. The prospect scared me. And I think if I was nineteen again, I'd make the same decision, but I do sometimes drift off into a little reverie about what difference it might have made if I'd acted more boldly and adventurously that weekend, and what other path it might have sent my life down. I got the impression it was a one-chance situation, from Mark's point of view, and sure enough I wasn't asked again to accompany him – wasn't asked to write profanities on a golf course, to help save wild animals being put through unnecessary suffering, or even to attend a party in some woodland with people who were a bit more exciting than the people I usually met. Did I call Mark again after that and invite him out to the pub? Maybe I did. Maybe I didn't. I couldn't say for sure. Let's say I did, for argument's sake. But, if I did, he was busy.

I did see Mark one further time but that was on a TV screen in 1996 during evening news coverage of the controversy over the Newbury bypass in Berkshire, when protesters camped out in the wild and, in an ultimately doomed attempt to prevent the destruction of 10,000 trees on the proposed route, chained themselves to trunks and branches ('I wouldn't like to be in the middle of that lot with a fully working nose,' said my mum, who was watching with me). Several celebrities marched to stop the road being built, including the children's television couple Maggie and Oliver Fox. During interviews with the Foxes and some of the other celebrities and protest organisers, I spotted what was unquestionably the left two thirds of Mark in the background, his aura and shine unmistakable, in clothes that he probably hadn't taken off for three weeks. Of course, in the years since then, I've attempted to look him up online, but been able to find very little of substance. Mark seems to have become one of those rare people who have ducked the gaze of the search engine, his soul too tricky and deep to be googleable. His name comes up on a stag beetle survey I found printed by Natural England in 2004 and a list of organisers for an early Climate Change march in Oregon in 2009, and I heard a rumour that – after Old Boy died, fifteen years ago – Mark had fallen in love and moved to the US west coast, but other than that I know nothing. Did he forge a new identity? Change his name? It's possible. Something in my gut makes me sure he is still alive.

Me? This isn't the place to go too deeply into my story. I was still toying with the idea of university back in 1993, but it never happened, and I've done a lot of different jobs you could probably think of since then, and a lot you couldn't. I no longer play golf: partly because I have long since lost the motivation, but partly because doing so would feel like a vote for a lot of what I am against politically. I painted houses. I delivered cakes. I half-completed a driving instructor training course. I acted as a dogsbody for a wealthy fleecer of the oppressed. I wanted to be a writer, and then a musician, and then an artist, but never really gave any of them a proper go. At a party on Millennium Eve I got talking to a girl called Rebecca who'd lived two roads from me for most of my childhood without either of us ever realising, and a year later we were married. We've had our hard times, like most couples I know, and even broke up for two whole years, when I was having a minor crisis about various small ways in which I'd decided I had spurned my life. In 2016 I was involved in quite a significant car crash, which I feel ecstatically lucky to have walked away from with a largely functioning body, and that year I sold the taxi I had been driving, Rebecca quit her job as deputy head of a coastal school with an insalubrious reputation and we opened a zero waste shop in the closest village to us, which we are never sure is going to survive for another year then does, just about, and hopefully will continue to do so. One Sunday every month we arrange a town litter pick, which has now got so popular that some of the regular attendees have started hosting their own subsidiary midweek litter pick. Life is... slightly fulfilling, fast, slow, small, comfortable, numb, scary. Rebecca and

I are very similar in many ways and very not-similar in others. Rebecca likes whenever possible to see every event or incident in the present, purely as an isolated event or incident, whereas I cannot separate anything from the past and the queue of other incidents that influence it. We have learned ways to surmount this ideological disagreement, but it has taken time. We still live within a twenty-minute car ride of Underhill and when I see the tor as I drive by, I always think of Mark and wonder how he is doing. I think of how brilliant he was at striking the ball, where he could have taken that talent and the way he looked it straight in the face and rejected it. And I think of me, a person who has never been brilliant at anything, just a person who is sort of OK at a lot of things. And then I wonder if Mark going with that brilliance I witnessed in him, letting it play out to its natural conclusion, would have truly made him happy, and find myself wondering if being brilliant at something is perhaps a little overrated, as a way to live.

Memory is a sly magpie, a seasoned frequenter of thrift fairs and jumble sales, gradually sweeping the worthless tat aside to reveal the hidden treasure behind it. Like a magpie, it needs to be greeted and acknowledged once in a while, and like a magpie, if you try to get really close to it, it usually won't let you. My own has undoubtedly done some rearranging during its downtime and I find that, amongst the nights of my youth that now seem important, it's pushed that one with Mark up at the Hollow, by the campfire, to the fore, and, within the night itself, it's probably shone a light on parts of proceedings that didn't seem significant at the time and snuffed out others that did. I come back to the music a lot, the smell of the woodsmoke and the hot fermented apples. I come back to Fran's hands in my hair. I come back to Mark, who will never know what an etched part of me he remains, and I come back to the girl in the long white blouse, standing back from everyone in the pocket of the woods that holds her, the intentness of her gaze towards the American as he played. It seemed like such a small part of the night at the time, but I have never forgotten her face or her holly-wreath hair, and I wonder if one of the reasons I come back to it was something that Michael, my chiropractor, said to me during my treatment after my car crash.

Michael – a man who always looks haunted himself, as if his skin is trying to retreat from any room he is in and hide further behind his bones – and I were talking about a very picturesque walk on the west side of the moor, where you follow a path along an old broken pipe from the clay mine. He said one time he was walking up there with an old schoolfriend, and he saw two ghosts, although it was all quite mundane and not at all what he'd grown up to expect seeing ghosts to be, as an experience. It was twenty minutes or so before sundown, he said, and the ghosts wore headtorches and were in the clothes of miners from a century earlier and had walked straight past his friend and him into the very thick and spidery copse further up the hill, without saying hello. Nothing else happened but he and his friend had both been very sure they had experienced something just out of the normal pattern of things, something not quite correct. About this they were in total agreement. I wonder increasingly if that was the way with my sighting of the girl in the blouse alone in the trees, whose face, when it has appeared in my dreams, has made me want to burst into song and has, in some way I can't fully express, left me waking up steamrollered by a great and melancholic sense that my life has not peeled back the layers and found the magic that it should. It is probably all nonsense, of course. She was perhaps just a lonely girl, a quiet girl, a girl who had fallen out with someone, a girl who wanted some time alone, a girl who felt better on the perimeter of everything, a girl who just happened to have been wandering the woods and stumbled on a gathering that interested her. But sometimes when I am seeing that night in my mind's eye, I feel like I am seeing it as her, as a separate bystander, but one with a greater knowledge about what is really going on, in time's larger context: one who sees these people, some of whom are in the midst of the most thrilling twenty-four hours of their life, and sees their folly in not for a moment suspecting that it is the most thrilling twenty-four hours of their life, not seeing that this isn't the beginning of many, many other equally thrilling twenty-four-hour periods, for many years to come.

As her, the girl with the holly-wreath hair, I stand back in the dark part of the place and I listen to the music blossom and expand and I smell the fragrant burning rings of the trees. And then in my floaty blouse I float up and look down on the lights in the clearing, with another ultra perspective, the perspective of the person directing the film. And I see how everything is informed by everything, because there is no way it cannot be. And then I wake up, and choose not to trouble my wife with any of it.

DRIFTWOOD (1968)

He came out of the canyon with his guitar at dawn, queried by the distant howl of coyotes. He was wearing a stranger's shirt and had not been to sleep. The first truck he flagged down stopped and after one more ride, in a hoarse 1959 Buick LeSabre driven by a silent man who smelled of cigarettes and reminded him of his aunt in a way he couldn't quite pinpoint, he reached the airport. Everyone there looked almost but not quite as tired as him. The dehydrated fur all over his brain amplified a paranoia in him, made each of his small actions feel observed. On the plane a stewardess brought him a nest of dry chicken with some lettuce so papery and devoid of moisture it seemed like fake lettuce, lettuce made solely for photo shoots of lettuce. She asked him if he was travelling on some sort of business and a cough-laugh escaped his throat. What on earth kind of business looked like this? He'd told himself he had done enough of going where everyone said you should go, and wanted to try the alternative approach of going just somewhere, roll the dice across a map, but it was a little more pre-meditated than that. 'I'm going back where I come from,' he told her.

As the coach moved sluggishly through the last outposts of the city, it rained, just like it did in the songs. Rain-grey town, known for its sound. None of the flamboyant outfits he'd heard about were in evidence. All of his fellow passengers were wearing clothes mimicking the colour of the sky. As the rain cleared, he saw toy cars, made to measure for the toy road system around them, and the toy driveways of the toy houses beyond that where the toy cars secured their prescribed eight hours' sleep every night.

After a couple of hours, the bus passed over a ridge and the terrain became less populated, a light green moonscape. Big shaved-looking mounds that were more like dunes than hills. A place that looked like it hadn't quite yet decided on its long-term plans. It segued gently into light forest, little stone houses, something more polite, something that was finally like the England he'd been picturing when he set out, the England he remembered, although he didn't truly remember anything. He'd been four years old. Each of the only three people who connected him to this part of the world was at least 5,000 miles away. Yet many miles further on when the bus finally stopped and he got out, he realised a part of him had still been expecting a caretaker or guide to meet him at the station. A second, lost sister perhaps. A cousin. He discovered a new oneliness in the walk that followed, felt it in the centre of his ribcage.

Nearly all the streets in the city were steep, but they divided into two types: the grey ones that looked like they'd just been born from nothingness and the pastel ones that looked proud in a tired, touching way, like senior citizens still wearing their graduation gowns. He took a room on the top floor of a lanky old house that peered over the edge of a hill. He had his own sink in the corner of the room which he pissed into on lazier days because the bathroom was shared and the pipes clanged every time anyone turned on the hot tap, which hurt his head on the mornings after he'd drunk too much, which was quite a few of them. The previous occupant of the room had begun to paint a mural of a squashed face in two shades of orange on the wall next to a tall window where, until the beech trees across the road came into leaf, you could see a one-inch-high triangle of cobalt sea. He figured the docks were the obvious place to find work and it didn't take him long to do so. On Saturdays, he busked, usually down by the coach station. It wasn't much of a music city, but it was easy to score some weed down by the water at night, an area of much dereliction, both architectural and human. Near a warehouse with a tree growing out of it three women a few years his senior who were high or drunk or both stopped him and asked if he wanted to go to a club with them.

'You'll like it,' one said. 'There's music playing.'

'What kind of music?' he asked.

'Jazz, duuddde,' she said, in a mock version of his accent.

He followed them four streets further into the injured concrete core of the city while they whispered conspiratorially and cackled about people and places he didn't know, lagging back out of concern they might smell the odour of oysters that always now clung to his clothes, then finally allowing himself to blur back into the night for good. They did not appear to notice and as it faded their hard laughter mixed with the cries of gulls until he did not know which was one and which was the other. The next day he bought a small pot of liquorice-red house paint and finished the mural. The sea smells were a constant social concern, even though he did little socialising. Oyster, mussel, cockle, crab. He was convinced they never went away, even after he washed. On the roadsides, in the wet dust and weeds, yellow flowers with darker yellow centres were appearing. Down on the containers, they never called him Richard or Richie, only 'Pencil' or 'Flower'. ''Ere, Flower, you sure you can 'andle this?' 'Don't give it to Pencil. It might 'urt 'is soft 'ands. Lovely 'ands, 'e got, like my missus. You seen 'em?' At night, he dreamt he was on his back, with sealife cascading down on him out of a metal chute. If not that, he dreamt of Alison, the girl from Albany he'd met the previous summer, who, upon taking the least amount of drink, would immediately want to jab and prod everyone around her with no little violence, or jump on their backs. In the space of just one weekend, Alison, who at barely five foot was a whole sixteen inches shorter than him, had jumped on the back of Jim Morrison and the rhythm section of The Turtles. During the dreams, he was always crouched in a corner, watching helplessly as the jumping took place, knowing intervention was futile. In the apotheosis of the dreams, he crouched in the corner of a shipping container, his hands over his eyes, as haddock fell on his head and Alison leapt on the back of a giant dolphin who smiled nervously in the manner of someone who will pretend to have fun on the vague promise of sex. A fragile awareness was growing in him that his songwriting was coming on apace. In a temporarily clean new plaza in the main shopping district, he tried out two new numbers and took home the smallest amount of money in his guitar case to date.

When other, more rampant vegetation had swallowed the yellow flowers on the verges, he set out for the docks at the usual time, carrying all his possessions, but turned right, not his customary left, and soon reached the train station. One of the country's diminishing branch lines took him to a village by the coast, where he and nobody else disembarked. At a post office, he bought bread, scissors, knobbly fruit and – with only an intrigued suspicion of what it might be – Marmite. It wasn't just that the tunnelled lanes he walked along, with their floral specklings of pink and blue, merely seemed a simple, elemental contrast to the city he'd spent the last four months in; they appeared to have no topographical relationship to the small metropolis at all, to belong in a whole different country. He helped two men push a rust-caked pickup out of a ditch. Afterwards, they ran him a mile or two further down the road to their place and gave him a cold lager. They asked where he was going and, when he answered as honestly and specifically as he could, their only advice was to avoid Somerset because the people there weren't right. The garden was full of retired machinery, fading gently into the earth. The younger of the two men pointed at two wooden structures on the hill above them that he'd taken for some kind of hutches. 'Bees,' the younger man said, rolling his eyes, but did not elaborate. The sun broke through the clouds after he left, drying him out for the third time that day. At a payphone, he inserted a coin and dialled a number beginning with an international prefix, but when a woody male voice answered he hung up. Further on, in a steep valley where everything hid strategically from the wind he appropriated three cucumbers from a garden and planted a kiss on the nose of a sceptical bullock.

As a result of trial and error, he found a zigzagging path down a landslip which spat him out onto a deserted cove by way of a rusty ladder which bridged the final gap between undercliff and shingle. Huts of varying types were dotted here and there on the cliffside, with flags and tall, tropical-looking plants outside. For the next thirteen days he slept on the beach, although he had concluded, at one point, that he would probably expire before seeing his first morning there, having come out of his initial salty self-baptism with purple digits and teeth that didn't so much chatter as argue with themselves, then failed in his attempts to light a fire without the aid of matches. He had learned the cove's first stark lesson, which was that it was not Malibu or Venice Beach. But by the third day he had grown acclimatised to the water, and, aided by driftwood and the fruits of a nine-mile hike to and from the village store, lit fires, and worked on verses of a song that he felt like he'd reached up and plucked out of the bright waxing gibbous moon above him. It had totally slipped his mind that it was his birthday. He was twenty-two years old.

The sea on his nude skin made him feel virile, and he wished he had a companion to swim with, but also slightly didn't. The cliffs were red, redder than they looked further down the coast, and the sea tasted red too when he accidentally swallowed some of it. The cove was one that sucked in more flotsam than most. One morning he awoke to discover a small metal alarm clock twenty yards in front of his toes, on the tideline. The sea had a sense of humour but you'd probably be mistaken for taking that to mean it suffered fools gladly. Having finished both of the paperbacks in his rucksack, he began to collect driftwood, not having to use any huge amount of imagination to see faces in the knots and bends in it. He wedged it together to make animals, some real, some mythical. He forged further down the shore, looking for even more. One evening he ran back to his base camp with so much of it that he had to carry the biggest piece in his mouth. He realised he was grinning. 'I am a dog,' he thought.

'And what,' he wrote in his diary that evening, as a response to some points he'd put to himself a few days earlier, 'is the benefit when you do get there? Is there a perfect midpoint between feeling the cold indifference of the world and losing freedom and judgement through commercial success and the people surrounding you who will no longer tell you the truth about what you are doing? (Not that I speak as someone facing a choice between the two at this exact juncture in my life.) Everything went so hazy today I lost sight of where the water ended and the sky began. In the quiet, a gull skimmed the water – or was it sky – and the tiny distance between its beak and the surface never wavered, as if measured by some highly evolved internal calculator. You could believe for a moment that this was all there was in the world: this watersky vapour, stretching for eternity, and this bird. Exquisite. I would like to bottle it somehow. I think this, in the end, is the great challenge, once you can write the tunes (which, really, anybody can, with time and effort): the bottling of something else. Something that's not even yours but that's not another person's either. Something on loan from the earth.'

Closer to the weekend, people arrived and unlocked the doors of a couple of the huts on the cliffside. An old man, his face entirely ringed with coarse white hair, came down from one of the huts and swam naked, striding into the sea with all the confidence of someone reclaiming a swimming pool he had dug out with his own gnarled hands. Afterwards, the old man caught and cooked mackerel, the smell drifting down tantalisingly to where he sat scraping the last flecks of disillusioning Marmite from the jar. Later, he heard hammering from the old man's hut, metallic and dauntless. While he listened to the old man hammer, he hacked into his hair with the scissors and threw the clumps into the tide, wondering when and how and where they would biodegrade.

The sea of his new home beach had innumerable moods. Rusty anger. Muscular calm. Pungent clarity. Weedy broth. Blue fog. Stubborn debris trickster. When did one sea clock off from its shift and the other sea come in and take its place? You never witnessed that moment because that was not permitted because if you did that would unlock everything: the big secret to it all. He knew the sea was irascible, not to be trusted but, as its resident, he inevitably began to get his feet further under the table, as residents do. One day, doing front crawl seventy yards out, he realised that his intended movement, back towards shore, was going the opposite of to plan and, worse, that he was on an inexorable downward trajectory. It was all very befuddling, because nothing around him looked particularly vigorous or wretched, and, in his disorientation, he only got the chance to cry out twice before he was completely submerged, garbled protests in a futile language spoken by only one man. His next close-to-conscious realisation was that he was in Heaven and God was looking down on him. Because Heaven would always customise itself aptly to the manner in which you'd died, Heaven in this instance was made of shingle and raucous white birds, but God had a beard, as God always had, no matter what the cause of your death was.

'I thought you were a goner there, kiddo,' said God, who he now realised was not God at all, but the old man from the hut.

*

'You were in a riptide. The thing to do in a riptide is to swim parallel to the shore. You swam towards the shore, which is the worst thing you can do.'

They sat on old canvas chairs on the old man's creaking, salty veranda and ate mackerel and potatoes, which the man salted liberally, in accordance with their environment. 'How's your head now?' the old man asked.

'Sore,' he replied. He had hit the back of it on some rocks close to where he'd gone under, but in the end the impact had also saved his life since it was the sight of him bumping against the rocks that had alerted the old man to his plight, and allowed the old man to swim out quickly, and drag him clear, around the corner of the current, and back to shore.

'I used to do it for the county. Swim. I was pretty good, could have been better, if I'd put the effort in. I had the chance to go to the Olympics. Belgium. I was too busy falling in love. I rarely have cause to swim like that any more, but I've watched six people die in my life and I didn't much relish adding to that total.'

He slept on the floor of the old man's hut that night, on top of a blanket. The head of a nail, knocked slightly loose from a floorboard, poked into the back of his knee, but he still managed to locate sleep with little trouble. He was a person who lost consciousness quickly: on train seats, on beds, on floors, in deep, chilly water. In the morning, he felt the lump on the back of his skull. It was located on a part of his skull he'd never liked, but had had little regular cause to think about, until now. In the light, he took in more of the cabin. On the shelf on the bed he saw a gardening trowel, a thick wool blanket and a bottle of aftershave. Above the Calor gas stove hung two framed photographs: one of a black poodle, and one of a smiling, elfin lady in a thick herringbone coat. The old man came in with a towel around his neck. 'She's dead now,' said the old man, waving a hand towards the photographs. 'And so is she.'

They swam later that morning, and in the afternoon he slept and played guitar while the old man vanished up the landslip to he did not know where. He stretched out on the skin of the water and listened to the shingle moving beneath him. In the evening by the fire he spoke a little about home but mostly the old man talked about his life and he listened.

'I lost Eileen, she's the one in the photo, when I was sixty-one. I was entirely unprepared for it. I always took for granted that we'd have a bit longer than that. Look out there. Seal. See it? I was not always a good man in my youth. I had my... errant moments. But I, we, got past it. People will give up more easily now. But we didn't. We were OK. In the first year that I was alone, I kept coming back to an image, from years before. It was of Eileen, the first day I ever came here. Naked, in the water. Don't misunderstand me. I'm not talking about something erotic, although she was a beautiful woman. It wasn't that which kept bringing me back to it. It was her face, the freedom and happiness in it. It wasn't like her, to do that, permit herself to become naked in a place where she might be observed by strangers. I knew her to be a very cautious woman. She looked so different that day: like every muscle in her face had relaxed. That is a beautiful thing, to see a woman you love go naked into the sea for the first time. If you see it, don't go on in the blithe assumption you might see it again. Anyhow, not long after that, I came down with the dog and built the cabin. I was totally certain I needed to do it, for her. The dog and I brought the wood around on the boat. It took seventeen months, in total. I'm here half the year, if I can be. My name is Robert Belltower. You play guitar very well. Her ashes are up there. Have you thought of trying to secure a recording contract?'

'I had one. It wasn't for me.'

'Well, if it's not for you, don't do it,' said Robert Belltower. 'But make certain you're certain first.'

Above the path on the undercliff, huge, never-tamed buddleia nurtured vast dynasties of bees and bee mimics. The sweet smell of the buddleia dominated the evenings, along with the very nearly as sweet smell of Robert Belltower. Upon retiring on the fifth night, Robert Belltower announced he would be gone for a short while, possibly to Lyme Regis, or the old smugglers' village of Beer, he was not yet certain. Robert Belltower said he was welcome to use the cabin, so long as he didn't burn it down, and left the key to the padlock under the third rock behind the flag. The song he wrote the following day, which he gave the working title 'Sad Photograph of a Dog', felt like an attempt of sorts to finish a conversation. He deemed it an inferior song and, after further appraisal, decided he was certain he was certain.

Storms were spinning in from the west. They vanquished his fires, stirred and steepened the shingle, drenched his diary, conditioned the furze of his hair. He imagined giant clenched fists pulling the black clouds in on a rope with big concerted tugs and little pauses in between. In the strange aggressive sunblast that followed, he became aware of how long it was since he had been touched by anybody except Robert Belltower. He poured cold water on that thought and reconstituted it as the simpler desire to play a song for a gathering of twenty or more people and hear them clap and possibly whoop. He left the four of the driftwood animals that had not blown away outside the hut, so they defined a path of sorts to the front door. The undercliff seemed steeper, twistier than before, as he made his way up it, but he was aware of something more coiled and taut in his calves as they propelled him up the still-damp path, shimmying to one side every dozen or so steps to make way for jaywalking oil beetles. He stopped and peeled one of Robert Belltower's overripe bananas under a yew tree in a churchyard, ate it in three decisive bites. He threw the peel towards a gathering of wild rabbits then set out up a steep unmetalled road and through a latched gate weighted by an old rock. Cows looked up from their all-day meals, discussed the topic amongst themselves then made their way slowly, and then more quickly, towards him. The hillside shook under their hooves and he froze with his tanned arms spread wide, like some fibreglass cattle messiah, and the cows stopped in their tracks, looking up into his face, fascinated and confused, until, one by one, they returned to the more vital business of breakfast. His reverie was broken by a small, worrying question in his mind: Which rock had Robert Belltower said, and how far was it behind the flag?

He waved down the train at another small station, where there were no other passengers, and took it to a different city this time, less greyly rearranged by war, barely a city at all. He walked up a cobbled street to a cathedral and set up directly beneath a carving of a six-mouthed, six-nosed, five-eyed crowned head. All the office workers, even those of his age group, who bit into thin white sandwiches on the green in front of him had much shorter hair than him, even in his newly pollarded state. A woman holding a polythene bag overflowing with clothes stared sadly at him, then, after almost an hour, moved on, limping. Later, he realised a short man with a guitar was also staring at him, not as sadly, but intently, unwaveringly.

'You're in my spot, longshanks,' barked the man, before he had quite finished the song.

'Your spot?'

'Yes. This is where I go. Has been for a long time. Everyone knows.'

'I didn't realise they were reserved.'

'Well, this one is. Scram. Get lost.'

'Well, what if I'm not so down with that, man? There's a lot of space here. Enough for everyone.'

With that, the man transformed himself into a close approximation of a rhinoceros, bending and charging at his midriff with great speed, knocking all the wind from him. He fell back into the cathedral wall, the sore part of his head smacking against cold uneven stone. As he did, the rhinocerman kicked wildly at his guitar case, scattering coins onto grass and cobbles. He scrambled for his affairs and the lunchtime crowd on the green moved in, but nobody intervened or helped. As he flailed for coins and notes, he noticed the face of his watch, which his grandfather had given him, was cracked and the hands had stopped moving. All of the city's noise had become a single muffled high note and he waded in his stooped shock to the other shore of the cathedral green, dragging his possessions with him in a slapdash collection of arms.

He walked for a number of hours that he could not quantify. After leaving behind the last of the nervous almost-villages that the city had coughed out and passing over several successively higher wooded rims, he descended, stopped at a clapper bridge, drank from a small river and slumped in a cradle of moss beneath a tree and rested his eyes. The water level was low, revealing a quasi-wall that could have been built by a person, long long ago, but could equally have been built by nature and time; it was hard to tell. When he awoke again it was dark. When he awoke the next time, the sun was rising, illuminating rougher, higher land ahead of him: the three-buttocked crest of a hill. His head remained sore but his vision had cleared. A sign matted with thick gaudy lichen told him that he was one and one quarter miles from Owl's Gate, whatever that was. It was, factually speaking, very recently in his life that pretty much all of his goals featured people in some way, but now none did, and to him it was as if that had been the state of affairs for a long time. His goal now was to reach the middle, highest buttock of the three on that hill. Nothing was more important to him and nothing ever had been and nothing ever would be.

It took him longer than he thought. With its tough stalks and hard, half-raised root balls, the grass made him sway and stagger, like a drunk returning home from a regretful episode. Lambs scattered at his approach and clamped onto their mothers' teats for solace, as if in the belief that if they closed their eyes and sucked long enough when they opened their eyes the Bad Man would no longer be there to frighten them. When he reached the top, the sun had turned around to get a better look at him. To the south, he could not see the sea but he could see the light blue space where more land would have been if the sea hadn't been there. Everything was wild and bare and voluptuous in the other direction: buttocks upon buttocks, shadowed by buttocks, for as far as the eye could see. Yet down in the valleys everything was a darker green and there were more hiding places than you'd have ever imagined. A person could become this place, he suspected. On a sunken path with a leaf roof he passed remnant chunks of buildings that were barely distinguishable from the immeasurably older stones around them. An increasing dampness. Root and shale walls coated in bearded slime. As he crossed stepping stones in a brook, he was thinking about a summer day three years earlier when a photographer had taken him and the rest of the band deep into the canyon, down a dirt track, to a house that was falling down, and they'd goofed about, climbing on old refrigerators and sofas, then pulling themselves high into a magnolia tree in the backyard, all three of them, all looking down deep into the lens as if it was a future they wanted to undress and ravish, with Frank in the centre, and that had been the shot that was used. He'd ripped his military tunic jacket on the way down. Frank had been the one who noticed and told him.

The sunken path led him to a tiny lane, and another wooden sign told him to walk left, but the gate was padlocked and decorated with barbed wire. He climbed over it anyway, figuring there must have been some mistake, and he was soon in a meadow, high and sweet from months of reinventing itself. You couldn't stand still. It didn't work. Ask meadows. Below him in the valley he could see a village. He dipped below a neat line of beech, with foxgloves growing at their roots. An unseen horse coughed behind a hedge and two longer, thinner meadows later he saw buildings, barns, a house. He was regretting not drinking from the stream and was about to approach the house and ask for water when he saw a hole in its wall, which, because of the relative intactness of the rest of the building, conjured up the image of a small wrecking ball and an administrative error. He clambered through the hole, coughing away stone dust, and was momentarily dazzled by the darkness of the room. Dusty overalls were draped over a chair. A doorway led to a kitchen, with a sink containing dirty dishes and flies. On the counter was a half-full bottom of rum. He took a swig of the rum, which was warmer and thicker than rum he'd tasted before but not wholly unpleasant. He washed it down with a long blast of water from the tap and could not recall a time when water had tasted so good, so much like a drink that had been brewed and planned and fermented, rather than just like water. He found a small wooden door leading to an area of old stone sheds, which formed part of a high mossy wall that enclosed a rear garden on all sides. A huge wooden padlock hung on another door and an extra plank had been nailed across it. Up the stone staircase, the rooms were more bare, with no beds, but he found a bath and soap, and downstairs there were two large sofas. He found a ripped armchair and, discovering the back door to be locked, carried the armchair out through the hole and into the back garden. The grass was high and the air had a weight to it, as if for now it was holding everything in place.

'Ida Richards,' he wrote in his diary. 'She was my first. Her thirst grew in direct correlation with my uncertainty. I had wanted it so much, talked it up with my buddies, but when it came to it, I stalled, procrastinated. I hit upon new hobbies that would keep us out of her room. Eventually, she had to cajole, if not beg. She walked me through it, soft and kind. Afterwards, I was sore. Nobody had warned me about that. They'd told me that only happened to girls. Nobody was sweeter than Ida. We'd walk through the neighbourhood and she'd stop to kiss stranger's dogs softly on the forehead. Sometimes, while I read, she would sit on the bed, staring at me, playing with her nails, examining invisible objects in the wool of her sweater. She deserved better. I imagine that one day I will realise, on some even deeper level, that, by chance, at sixteen I met a rare kind of angel, but how can you know that at sixteen? When I finally ended it she didn't seem shocked. Her far greater disappointment always appeared to be that I never wrote a song for her, or about her. "But, Richie, why nnnnnot?" she would ask, sulking, shoving me, pouting in a joke-real way. "I thought I was special." I never told her the real reason, which was that I feared it would be a let-down. Not because of the lack of love or feeling, but because it could not be enough. The feeling is still the same. That nothing is enough. It is there every time I put down my guitar. Will it ever be gone?'

Two mornings later, dizzy with hunger, he hiked to the bottom of the valley, reaching a row of stone cottages with neat gardens with sunflowers and hollyhocks and runner beans and windows decorated with elegant watchful cats. Clouds followed him down, gave him their brief appraisal then moved out to sea. He crossed the river and reached a main road. Around the bend, three cars were at a standstill on the tarmac. Another car passed them in the opposite direction, very cautiously, taking a diversion up a muddy bank. A large black-and-white heifer sat on the white line in the centre of the road. Beside the cow stood a fretting, long-haired girl in a baggy sweater flecked with hay. 'She won't move,' said the girl. 'She's been here for over an hour now. She's from where I live, the farm. Over the ridge. I would get my dad to come and get her but I don't want to leave her.'

'How far away is the farm?' he asked.

'Less than a mile, really not far at all. I just need to get my dad, and she'll move.'

'I'll wait with her.'

'Are you sure? I don't know. Is that best?'

'It's fine.'

He crouched beside the cow, and put a hand gently on the animal's back, and began to talk softly into her ear. As the girl hurried away from them, a couple more cars appeared and stopped, and the people inside them got out to look and laugh at the cow, and he whispered to the cow about the people from the cars and who they probably were, and told the cow his full name and a little about what had brought him here, and told the cow a little bit about the world, and some of the ups and downs it might contain for the cow in the future, but in a reassuring, philosophical way, not in a hard, cynical way which might potentially have upset the cow and made it even more reluctant to face that future. By the time the girl had started back down the hill with her father and a rope, he and the cow had made it almost all the way up the lane to the farm.

'Well I'll be a dog's pudding,' said the girl's dad.

That night he ate with the girl and her family. They asked him where he was from and he told them California, first a part with lots of trees and fields and rivers, a little like here, but not as green, because he didn't think he'd ever seen anything as green as here; then the city, and then a part that was somewhere in between. They appeared to be greatly amused and delighted by his existence alone, the unlikeliness and potted story of him, and asked him what had brought him here specifically, rather than another part of the UK, and he said he'd always been told to go west, if in doubt, and he'd once briefly lived here, because of his father's job, a very long time ago, but he couldn't remember it at all, and this apparently caused them to be even more amused and delighted. They began, soon, to talk about somebody called Dick, who lived down by the river, sold logs and had formerly kept pet ferrets, and had once been found asleep in the back of a stranger's Land Rover, but only after the stranger had driven it many miles, and the girl's father began to tell some ruder stories about Dick, but the girl's mother told him to stop, as it wasn't polite, and there were children present. After dinner, the girl's little sister wrote an illustrated story in blue crayon on a sheet of paper and said it was for him. 'People had faces but it was a long time ago before there were cars or toast,' the girl's sister had written. 'A woman and a man and a bear built a house at the top of a tree but the tree fell down so they built another house in a better tree. One day another bear arrived as well. The tree still didn't fall down. It only fell down when the sun drowned in the sea and all trees stopped growing.' The girl's mother said she'd heard there was an attic room in the village to rent in Burrow Cottage and her father cut in and said he thought that had gone now and her mother said she wasn't actually sure if that was true, Grenville, but would try to find out for him tomorrow, and he could stay here tonight. Books were piled high and uneven on the window ledge of the room where he was to sleep. Their subjects were various but largely centred around hens and war but not both at the same time. As the girl, whose name was Maddie, made up his bed, he stole a look at her and thought about how her skin was different to skin he'd known before, something earthier, something sun but rain too. He remembered mirrors for the first time in a while and, finding one in the bathroom, saw something similar beginning in himself. He had altered, assimilated, was becoming the place. Tomorrow, he would look different again. He was not a photograph.

The village was called Underhill and Burrow Cottage was on a street that dug its nails into the edge of a steep slope that rose towards the north. Behind that was a far bigger hill, topped with rocks, underneath a sky that kept changing, over and over again, during his walk to the cottage, as if someone behind the sky kept closing and unclosing a heavy drape. He told the old lady who lived in the cottage that he would take her attic room for a month but wasn't sure beyond that and she said that was fine. He'd been lucky: a locum doctor had wanted the room but changed his mind at the last minute, although she admitted she'd been relieved, as he seemed to be what she called a miserable so-and-so. 'A very funereal, slightly cadaverous man. I wouldn't have liked to have him examine me at all. I'd have felt like he was measuring me up for my coffin. You're not a miserable so-and-so, are you?' the old lady asked.

'I have my bright days,' he said.

He had to stoop to avoid hitting his head on the beams but there was a single brass bed that he could stretch out to very nearly his full length on and a wicker chair and a hand basin and a shower but if he needed the toilet he'd have to go out into the backyard and use the outside one. She assured him it was very clean, although 'a bit cold on the bum in January'.

She gestured at a pile of canvases on the floor. 'If these are in your way, just move them to somewhere they're not. They're just my nonsense. I'll find another place for them eventually.' A couple of nights later, Maddie arrived in a small curvaceous car with wooden window frames and drove him to a pub in a town a few miles closer to the sea where anyone who desired it was permitted to stand up and play two songs. He remained sitting down but two Fridays later, when they went again, he took his guitar and got up and sang 'Mr Tambourine Man' and 'Clapper Bridge', a new song of his own whose chorus he had just about nailed down but whose verses were still a work in progress. This time, the crowd was scruffier, more bohemian. A group of long-hairs in the corner cheered loudly at the end of 'Mr Tambourine Man' and louder still at the end of 'Clapper Bridge' and called Maddie and him over. A drink and a half later a huge bearded man in a leather jacket entered the pub. 'CHICKPEA!' Maddie shouted, and the man enclosed her in a hug so enormous, she temporarily vanished. A girl to his left started talking about how she could predict the weather with her knees and asked him if he was at the college, too, or starting there soon. He said he didn't know of any college and asked her if she knew Monterey and she said she didn't and before he'd had the chance to explain why he'd even asked she'd begun talking to someone else. Afterwards, all eleven of them went back to a big white building with a central courtyard, where there were posters of bands, some of whom he'd met, although he didn't say so. Somebody put on 'Foxy Lady' at such a volume that the speakers kept crackling and cutting out and he strived to pay full attention while a girl told him the pitfalls of communism, and he began to wonder where Maddie had got to. 'You've not read Koestler,' the girl said. 'I can't believe you've not read Koestler!' He felt as stoned and as close to being home as he had since he got off the plane and fully expected, were he to return here the next morning, that the white building would have vanished and there would be only trees and other vegetation in its place. In between songs, someone squeezed a dog toy outside the window, and he wondered who would be both so baked out of their head and committed to take the time to do that between every one of well over a dozen songs, until he realised it was not a dog toy but the squeak of a female owl in a tree. 'Time to go, Cowboy,' said Maddie, grabbing his sleeve. Her hair was river wet and her eyes were tunnels of light.

'Howsabout you then, Bob Dylan?' she said, on the way home. 'The Quiet American. Full of surprises.' She drove even faster than earlier and the car squeaked against ferns and twigs, and bumped on rougher and rougher pebbles on the road until he realised it wasn't a road at all, merely a wider-than-average footpath, a bridleway, perhaps, but you'd be pushing it to call it even that. 'Shortcut,' she said. 'Trust me.'

And then days arrived when you wondered how much more moisture there was in the world. Days of incongruous chimney smoke, should-be-hot afternoons when clothes wouldn't dry and even though the rain wasn't *in* your house it was in your house, mornings when you looked up at the moor and realised it was the place where weather was made, the place where time ended, and that, beyond it, there was nothing comprehensible or civil, despite the lies that maps told you. He wrote his sister and wondered if she, always quietly perceptive to so much, would sense in the fourteen sentences on the page the changes in himself that he felt. He drank and read. He read and drank. He walked to a white pub in the rain and sat beneath an awning and polished off almost all of a paperback he'd borrowed from the old lady and realised when he got home that he'd left it there and the old lady told him off – 'Richard, I do notice that your mind often seems to be elsewhere' – but a few minutes later knocked on his door with a cup of tea. She noticed with surprise that he'd taken one of the canvases from the pile and balanced it facing out against the wall, on top of the tallboy. 'I hope you don't mind,' he said. 'I like it a lot.' Under the painting, perched on the room's one hard wooden chair with his guitar, he looked deep into the layers of swirling oil, layers suggesting destroyed sweetnesses. Within them, he thought he saw a face of green. He destroyed sweetnesses of his own, sang and strummed over them in big brushstrokes, left just tiny slivers of them showing, wished he had flutes and banjos and mandolins and pianos to work in the layers of gentle annihilation. The words were best when they came from somewhere exterior to him but connected to him by some invisible electric rod, somewhere very different to the place where you got words in a letter or a note or an essay you wrote at school or even a song you wrote expressly for somebody you knew who had the power to help it reach an audience, and when they did come from that exterior place they often frightened him and that was when it was best. When they didn't come like that any more, he knew that there was only one thing to do and that was to go back to the house with the hole in the wall, even though that frightened him too, in a different way. The rain drummed on the skylight in the old lady's attic room and through it the dark rocks on the tor showed through like an ominous growth on an X-ray of moist organs.

A garage a couple of miles away, near where the river levelled out and widened, had advertised for somebody to pump four star into people's cars and he went to see the owner about the position but the owner took one look at him and said it had been taken, which he accepted without protest, and also accepted to be a lie. He took the long, high route back. Below him, red berries had appeared on the hillside. He stood aside to let the kerfuffle of a hiking family pass. 'I stood in a hole and I think my foot is broken,' said one of two medium-sized children. 'Take your shoe off and rub it and it will be fine,' replied a red-cheeked mum. He hooked back west and saw a sign reading 'Job Vayckansie' next to a pair of large wooden gates. 'BEWARE OF THE DOGS (3)' said another sign to the right of that. 'DICK WARNER: SEASSONED LOGS' said another, above that. He'd not noticed the place behind the gate before but realised, upon entering it, he'd smelled its aroma drifting on the breeze many times. He walked along a track of rubble and bark past high log piles and knocked on the half-open door of a squat building with a corrugated iron roof. Getting no response, he peered into the kitchen behind it. The floor was covered in breadcrumbs and wood chippings, a pan of water boiled on a stove in one corner of the room and in the other a dog-eared poster had been pinned to the wall exhibiting a naked, full-breasted woman holding a bowsaw and winking. He stepped back outside and saw a small elderly canine limping towards him, on three legs. The animal flopped down at his feet and revealed a belly of patchy fur, which he tickled. He wandered between log piles behind the building and was turning to leave when a compact man wearing thick gauntlet gloves hurtled past him, seemingly out of the logs themselves, saying, 'Fuck fuck fuck fuck bastard.'

The man in the gloves entered the kitchen and emerged holding the pan of boiling water, whose contents he sloshed haphazardly onto the paving slabs around him. 'Ants,' the gloved man said, nodding his head at the ground, and also shaking it, as if to fully wake himself. 'Fell into a snooze. It happens. Come about the job?' 'Yeah, I...' he said. 'How are you with felling trees?' said the gloved man, whose age he could have put at anywhere between thirty-five and fifty-five. He confessed it was not something he'd had previous experience with, although he had used an axe plenty of times. 'Dunt matter,' said the gloved man. 'You won't be doing that. How you feel about clearing that lot?' He gestured towards a meadow: a vast unchecked space of brambles and gorse and poppy and waist-high grass and raging hypericum. 'No great rush. How does three weeks sound? Enough? Come when you can. Seen you in the village. Living at the Nicholas place aren't you. We can talk about money later. I've got tools coming out my arse so you won't need to bring any of them.' The gloved man was walking now, and he followed. After a few steps, the gloved man bent to pick up a small object from the woodchippings they were walking on, then hurled it far through the air, where it ricocheted off a silver birch into some undergrowth. 'Vole,' said the gloved man, shrugging and letting out an industrial fart.

Maddie came in the car to get him and he played guitar in town again. Wild angelica and maidenhair spleenwort grew against the walls of a small sunken network of alleys near the pub. A bearded man with a walking stick who appeared to be well into his eighth decade staggered up to the microphone and sang a folk song, unaccompanied, which he said he'd learned as a child growing up nearby, and introduced as 'Little Meg', although he said it was sometimes known by other titles. Afterwards the song lingered in his mind, especially something nebulous about its central subject. The next time, the old bearded man was there again, this time with his wife, and hand in hand they advanced slowly to the microphone and sang the song together. Everyone applauded, but before they did, the room was very silent for a beat. After last orders, he and Maddie walked down to the riverbank and he met a couple of new people from the college, and five or six people from it he'd met before, and willowy women in shawls and slight men in glasses talked animatedly at him and he nodded and Maddie sat with one arm around Chickpea and one arm around him but his mind was only a quarter there and the remaining portion was almost all trying to memorise the lyrics to the elderly couple's song. When he got home, he scribbled what he could recollect down in his diary and began working some chords around it. 'I feel like the year has turned over and I feel a turning in me too,' he also wrote in the diary, below that. 'Hooves and shouting outside. I can't see why from the window. Room is full of moths.' An encore of heat was hissing through the long grass outside, drying the glistening cobwebs. Between the long stalks and bracken, ticks were flexing their horrible legs. There had not been a better time to be a tick for a considerable period. After his shifts for Dick Warner, his gardening for a man without a garden, he picked the bloated, flailing bodies of the ticks out of his thighs, stomach and the soft unblemished underside of his arms. He learned to be careful when he mowed because sometimes there were beer and cider bottles in the grass. When the mower wasn't on, sounds drifted over from Warner's building, sometimes that of Warner's buzzsaw and sometimes the commanding bass and tenor sounds of Elise, an insuppressible, wide-faced woman who ran the greengrocers in Bovey Tracey and would drive over twice a week to bounce on top of Warner. He soon realised the trick with the ticks was to tease them out a little with tweezers then give them one big decisive tug.

He thought about his old life and it seemed less that he'd abandoned it and more that it was still happening, concurrently; that there was another him still out there, still doing all that he might have done. Nobody had recognised him since he got off the plane, just as he had expected them not to. Some days, he felt like he had been asked to write a book and said no and given the money back, and instead chosen to write another book, finish it and abandon it in a ravine at night. By now his sister had written him back. She said she'd heard from Frank that he was in England and that she was disappointed he'd not told her but that she had decided that he must have had his reasons and forgave him. (He had never told Frank but he guessed word quickly got around in the Canyon.) 'There's a lot happening here,' she wrote. 'In the house, and everywhere, too. I feel like so much has changed in such a short time. I have to tell you that Daddy is sick. I know he would like to see you. I haven't told him I'm writing this letter.' One day he had heard one of Frank's new songs on Maddie's car radio. He was surprised how little impact it had on him. He thought it was a very well organised song and was sure it would continue to do well for the rest of the year. The second time they heard it, Maddie sang along. 'You're my rabbit,' she shrieked. 'And you've got me on the... rrrrun.' He said nothing. As if she'd somehow tapped into his thoughts, she said, 'There's a music studio at the college. I don't know if it's anything special. But I think Chickpea could get you some time in there, if you like?' He said maybe and that might be cool but he wasn't sure if he was quite there yet. 'Of course you're there, you silly sausage!' she said. 'You're more than there. The only reason you're not there is that you've gone past there and you need to reverse.' It struck him that there were two Maddies he was getting to know: Farm Maddie and Artistic Friends Maddie. Today she was somehow both. He had never been called a silly sausage before and he discovered it was not displeasing. The window had jammed the last time she'd opened it and now remained permanently in a three-quarters-open position. He dangled an arm out and let his fingers flick against the bracken as it whizzed by, enjoying the sting. Six old plastic bags full of apples were on the back seat, ripening in the sun. Several had come loose and fallen onto the composty area beneath the seats, and, while Maddie pulled over to let other cars pass on the narrow lanes, wasps flew in to investigate. There was a time and place to be an insect and that time was now and that place was here.

Frank had always been the one to announce, 'I've got something which I think is pretty special.' He, by contrast, would say, 'There's something I have been playing around with' or 'This might work, I guess.' It was, he had subsequently realised, the predominant reason why the writing ratio ended up 7/3 in favour of Frank. That, and Frank's tendency to deal directly in the politics of romance, whereas his habit was, at most, to weave around the topic. One of the advantages of breaking away on your own was you didn't write by committee and a song didn't get automatically consigned to the garbage just because you didn't bring it into the studio with its own ticker tape parade. 'Chickpea says he thinks you're very modest, and that you're an old soul,' Maddie said, after his second of three days in the music room, not really much of a studio at all, just a soft-walled black room with a reel-to-reel in the corner and Chickpea at the controls, damp and huge in the heat in the large established country of his beard and the leather jacket he never relinquished. Chickpea had left and he and Maddie were on the wide lawn behind the studio which spread out in the direction of a set of straggling medieval buildings. Opposite, two women in black leotards danced to silence and fenced with peacock feathers. Every few minutes, a girl would emerge from the medieval buildings and run screeching across the lawn to Maddie, hug her, and ask with great urgency if she'd heard about something desperately exciting that was happening the following week. Theatre, picnics, parties, music, art, other gatherings that were apparently a hybrid of all five. 'Sorry to interrupt!' the girls said afterwards, turning to him, appraising him with slow fascination, as if experiencing the pleased, lazy epiphany that he was not a tree. Almost all of them spoke very differently to the way Maddie did. Their voices were more precise and clean, more redolent of scrubbed residential streets and fussy gardens. It struck him as wild and impressive how effortlessly Maddie managed to be simultaneously of the college and very different to it. It struck him also as wild and impressive how effortlessly the college managed to be simultaneously of its geographical base and of a different planet: a place of geese, pottery and ballet, in equal measures. It was one of the most unlikely hillsides he'd ever stood on and he was here with this unlikely person all because of a cow. He noticed something unique in the curve of her chin in profile that he'd not noticed before. She had strong arms, arms that lifted many heavy objects, as different to her friends' arms as her voice was to their voices. Her language was full of wild plants that, enraptured by the music of their names, he was compelled to note down in his diary: bog asphodel and penny marshwort – or was it marsh pennywort – and purple loosestrife and bog pimpernel. She liked practical jokes and grapefruit. When she told him she came here once a week to teach people how to look after chickens he'd thought she was having him on. She wasn't. The previous weekend she had hidden his shoes in an oven. She would never find out, but she was the first girl he'd ever written a love song about.

After the third day of recording, which he grudgingly conceded was better, they ascended narrow lanes and crossed tiny humped bridges in the car, going higher and higher, parked, then walked to a stone circle. A scribble of rain had blown in through the gap in the window when they were in the car then gone and in its place there was more damp heat. She told him to place his palms against the stones in the circle and feel all the energy there.

'Ah, I'm so excited,' she said. 'My boyfriend is coming back next week.'

'Where is he right now?'

'Spain. He's been out there since May. He's in the army.'

He gazed back across the rocks, trying to pick out the car.

'I think most of it's probably trash,' he said. 'But I dunno. I guess I'll end up hanging on to the tape.'

But he was not a person entirely devoid of hubris. He had the complacency of many people who arrive in rural Britain from a country populated by bears, coyotes and mountain lions, and the sun massaged that complacency. He was still a newcomer to the moor and even oldcomers to it knew only a fraction of a fraction of what there was to know about it. One of the many things he didn't yet know about it was that, in late August, in days of heat after heavy rain, on the stretches where it was still most fully permitted to be itself, it breathed and growled as profoundly as it did in the height of the harshest winter. Terrain you'd visited always compacted its scale in your mind afterwards and he had begun to learn that but, even so, the route back to the ruined house was surprisingly arduous. The river told him he was going the right way but it seemed further than before and something had happened in the dripping folds of earth above the banks: an angry awakening, a last wet sucking of life into the lungs before autumn's dry death. Brown flies clung fiercely to his flesh. Huge tufts of grass shoved him from side to side, arguing over their custody of him. Blue and pink and yellow flowers spilled over the damp ground like ornate vomit. An old octopus of a tree reached down a rough tentacle and anointed his cheek with a bloody scratch. In his shoes, the soles of his feet sloshed about and blistered and began their transformation into a sore kind of paste. Every path became a whisper and then a lie. A stiff gate opened but led directly to a shrub of insanity. The song the old man and his wife had sung was in his head again and he hummed the song and then he barked it at the impassable bracken that stretched all the way up the valley walls and then he croaked it at the sky. An area of oxygen finally widened ahead but the ground beneath it drank his feet then low branches formed a roadblock and he crawled under them then lost most of his left leg in a peaty bubbling hole and had to use all his strength to retrieve it. He could not have been more wet if he was in the river itself up to his neck and the burnt moist state of him attracted more and more tiny winged life and he knew then that one day, once again, this would be the world. Not a car, not a sandwich, not an ambition, not sense, not a cow, not a horse, not love, not a song, not a girl. Just this sucking and gargling and burping thing beneath him. When the dizziness came, and the head pain, just before the light clicked off, it was a relief to submit, to just fall into the mouth of everything and not go on fighting any more. And then night fell smoothly in, and not thirteen yards away the river, which was not interested, continued to yell as it rushed over the rocks.

*

She was very good at keeping a straight face and she liked to take people on a journey. It was an addiction of hers but she viewed it as generally harmless. First there was usually the lie, which was thrilling in itself, but then there was the space of time after the lie, when the lie – and the imaginative invention that went with it – expanded, which was more thrilling still. It was like pulling an elastic band: if you pulled it back further you got more power, but you couldn't go too far or it would snap. She liked to take it quite far, because then when you punctured the lie the look on the face of the person who'd believed it was that much more delicious. But she'd quickly had her misgivings after she talked about the soldier in Spain. She'd misjudged it. It made her wonder about herself. It was a five- or ten-minute lie, she thought as she set out for the cottage, not a one-day lie, and definitely not a three-day lie, and it was different to many of her other lies because it played with something important. When she knocked on the door, the old woman answered and said he was not there and she had not seen him since yesterday. 'He does do his vanishing acts, Richard. He doesn't tell me where he goes. You can wait for him if you want, but I don't know when he'll be back. It's Madeleine, isn't it?' She resisted the other names that popped into her head on impulse – Jill and Rose and Sylvia and Thomasina – and the backstories she might invent for them, and instead replied that, yes, that was correct. 'If you could say that I called round, I'd appreciate that,' she said.

*

After he'd finished at the ruined house, he walked west for an entire morning, until he arrived at a pub. He ordered chips and sat on a bench outside and ate them, accompanied by a lone Muscovy duck. In a church foyer, farther up the lane the pub was on, he found a pile of free paperbacks, and put one in his rucksack. His feet ached and one of the soles had come loose from his left boot. On a bigger road, he waited for close to two hours, until a car pulling a caravan stopped for him. He sat in the back seat beside a child called Matthew with a bubble of snot in one nostril who stared at him the whole way, sucking a thumb. He got out within a mile of the village and went straight to Dick Warner's woodyard, but there was no sign of him. Outside the door to the kitchen was a trail of cold baked beans and many of the beans were stuck to the door itself. Within a swift breeze that whipped around the logs there was the aroma of wood and crow and something dead but briefly revived and not quite identifiable. When he finally reached the cottage Mrs Nicholas was out. He found some tape in a drawer and applied it to his shoe, threw his remaining possessions into his rucksack, and left the paperback and the remaining rent he owed on the kitchen table.

He started out west again and walked until he joined the next river, then followed it until it branched and widened to create a calm subsidiary pool, which he swam in. He examined the peeling skin on his feet, neither of which ever seemed to have dried out from the day he walked back to the ruined house. A new area of purple-black on one of his heels. He walked some more, until he came to another river, with a viaduct over it. He reached a quay and dark buildings, below a Tudor mansion with great sprawling gardens and a domed dovecote. Boats and parts of boats were everywhere and even a mile later, parts of boats could still be seen in numerous gardens. He crossed a stream and sat on an abandoned tractor tyre above one of the gardens, on the opposite side of a small valley and, having seen no sign of life in or near it, picked apples from its trees, and took lettuce and an artichoke head from its beds. The garden thinned and snaked on into woodland until it ended at a rusty gate, and next to the rusty gate was a small orange bus on bricks. He managed to force one of the windows of the bus open and that night slept inside the bus, stretched out along its ripped back bench. He woke up and felt like somebody had performed origami on his face in his sleep. He climbed a hill and took a small train to the grey city where he'd worked on the docks then he changed and took another train east, guessing at when he might be level with the point where the cliffs began to turn red and getting off at the first station after that. Cars pulling caravans were struggling up the tall hills that broke away from the coast in threes and fours, and he walked against the flow, flattening himself against nettles and brambles to let the vehicles pass. In many of the fields there were huge rocks and corvids could often be seen on the rocks, making their withering assessments of the day. The land was thrown audaciously together, had no order or mathematics to it. 'Dogs in field,' said a sign on a gate. 'Please keep your sheep on a lead.' He penetrated a long crevice between cliffs to the sea, which turned out to be further away than it looked, and corkscrewed down a gorse-lined path to a beach where he waited until the tide had gone out, then hooked around a jutting rock and walked east along the shingle while the sun fell softly into the salt. The tape had long since come off his shoe, the sole barely hanging on now, and its loud flapping cut through everything like an embarrassment.

Robert Belltower was not at his cabin but the key was where he had left it, under the third rock. Inside, the framed photos and the Calor gas stove and the chair had gone but the bed remained, and two of his driftwood structures were still outside. He emptied his rucksack on the floor and slept for eleven uninterrupted hours and dreamt for the first time in a while about fish. In the dream, gulls hovered and chuckled at the fish then he awoke and realised the chuckling gulls were outside. In the following night's dream the old man from the pub was by a campfire singing the folk song again, 'Little Meg', but when the old man spoke it was in his own young Californian voice. His beard was very long and he felt it to see where it ended and realised it was a vine and that it led into the hedgerows. As he felt along the beard into the hedgerows, the crowd around the campfire, who were young, and all in couples, pointed and laughed. When he woke up the song was very clearly in his head so that all he could do was pick up his guitar and sing it until it wasn't there any more. Afterwards, he walked up the undercliff, but something had changed in his foot, and he didn't get far. He swam, first under a setting sun that was like a lump of hot metal on the horizon, and then under a brighter moon, because when he swam the foot didn't hurt as much, and he hoped that perhaps the salt water would heal it in the way it had with cuts and bites he'd sustained. He went much further under and slept dreamlessly that night but was brought back to the surface by the realisation he was being hit by a rolled-up magazine, wielded by a woman he had never met.

'GET OUT GET OUT GET OUT!' she screamed at him.

He struggled for words, slurring his first attempt at them. 'It's OK! I'm his friend!' he managed to shout back at her, but she continued to hit him as he stumbled and clung to the walls.

'Who? Whose friend?' she asked.

'Him! The one who lives here! Robert!' he spluttered, stuttered, between blows.

'No you're not. He doesn't have any friends. He's dead! DEAD!'

And it was then, as the light faded again and he let himself fall into it, that he finally knew he was insane, and was a man who made friends with ghosts.

*

After he'd come to, and they'd got their stories straight, she offered him a ride. It had happened about a month ago, she said. His heart. It wasn't the first time he'd had problems with it. A fishing trawler had spotted the boat drifting about in the bay and called the coastguard. They reckoned he'd been in there for at least four days, his eyes looking at nothing but the wood they were pressed against. 'He was a fucking bastard,' she said. 'Or used to be.' She introduced herself as Helen. She reminded him a little of the Queen of England: something motionless about her hair. 'He promised my mum the earth. She believed everything he said. She was Swiss and they met while he was working out there. Doing something with roofs. I am not totally sure. I know the Belltowers were a very grand family, but that he escaped from it all and did his best to make himself one of the people. Roofs were one of the ways he did it. But there was still a natural arrogance there. My mum, I think, found it very attractive. It wasn't until later that she found out he was already married. By then, he'd vanished, and she had a couple of new things growing inside her. One was a permanent sense of mistrust. The other was me.'

'He saved my life,' he said.

'I can see how that could happen. He wasn't all bad. People aren't. With exceptions. He was tough and if he liked you he liked you. Years later, he came to find me. I didn't want to know. It took a long time for me to come round. I was working in Bishop's Waltham. A lot of people would have given up but he didn't. He didn't have any other children. Or none he knew about, anyhow. He rubbed a lot of people up the wrong way and it was only if they stood the rubbing up that they stuck around and found out who he was. I was all he had, at the end. Me, and the cabin. He loved it out there on the beach because it was away from the world and his wife. Not his own wife – I believe he was quite nice to her, in the end, and enjoyed being with her. The world's. It was something he always said. The world and his wife. From what I read in the newspapers they are currently in the process of getting divorced. Have you seen these donkeys here on the left? I just adore their noses. So anyway now it appears I have a cabin. Would you like a cabin? I am joking. I will probably keep it. I go up, clear some of it, then wonder what I'm doing, then come back, then wonder some more. Sugar! I've missed my turning because I'm talking so much. I am sorry about your head. Is it very bad?'

The road climbed into dense woodland and she parked on a sandy bulge just off the tarmac beside a sign with a picture of a bench on it. Through a gap in the trees, it was possible to glimpse the conurbation lit up in a hazy bowl at the bottom of the valley. 'I would take you further,' she said. 'But I don't drive in cities, as a rule.' He said it was cool, he could walk, and thanked her. 'Oh!' she said, looking at his boots. 'What size are you?' He told her he was an eleven and she opened the back door and handed him a pair of brown loafers. 'These were his,' she said. 'Nine and a half. It's not ideal, I know, but it's an improvement.'

A day later, in his window seat on the plane, he would find himself trying to pick out the exact hillside they'd been on, imagining the hole in the tree, somewhere down there, where he'd left his old boots, but it was no use: the altitude was too great by then. He could, however, still see the moor: a mass of fuzzy, raging green breaking up the politer patchwork around it. That was about an hour before he remembered the tape from the studio, saw it in his mind's eye still sitting on the low shelf beside the bed in the cabin where he'd left it, but by then he was in the middle of a larger letting-go. He wrote a note in his diary about a finch he had seen on the landslip writhing on the ground when they'd climbed back up to the car, the deep sadness he had felt about it, and a question – 'Does it get any easier?' – underneath it, then rustled once more in the bottom of his rucksack, which was just small enough to count as hand luggage. He was surprised to find a magazine in there. It was the one she'd hit him around the head with, an issue of *Homes & Gardens* from May. One of the main articles had the headline 'Buying Carpets'. He read it for a while but it failed to hold his attention.

STOPCOCK (2019)

JULY

Deep dark. Deeper than black, but not black. Red, and green, in a way. But so dark. Darker than any place I've lived. Nothing to corrupt it. Song of the stream behind the wall. Reka, my lodger, was out at work. Fumbling in my bag, I thought I had lost my key again, and would have to break in through the back window like last week, but the reason I could not find my key in my bag was because I was already holding my key. I have been walking until late on these long summer nights, making sure I have covered every footpath and small lane near the house. I usually get the timing wrong, and night is totally down when I arrive home. Bats are flitting about on top of the hill, gobbling up the day's less fortunate moths. At the bottom of the valley, young owls shout their complaints to the last rechargeable glow of the sun as it sinks behind the moor. A powerful, sinewy, medium-sized dog hurtled towards me down one particularly quiet lane – one of those that don't really lead anywhere and have a verdant central reservation of weeds – and I wondered when the dog's owner would appear, breathlessly bringing up the rear and calling the dog back, and just as I realised the dog was a hare, not a dog, the hare also appeared to realise I was a human, not a shadow or a ghost, both of which would probably seem more likely on this lane at this time of the evening, and made a sudden, impressive reroute, ninety degrees to its right, as if responding to some internal satnav, not losing a fraction of pace or finesse in the process.

When you walk a lot in the countryside, you get a crystallised realisation that most animals are united by one factor: their conditioning, over the course of thousands of years of hard, regrettable evidence, to be shit scared of humans.

Another thing I've been thinking about a lot recently is dead birds. Insects too, and rodents. Actually, dead things in general, in the wild. I mean, obviously we see quite a few of them, while we're out on walks, and even sometimes in our garden, but think how many are dying all the time, and just what a small percentage it is of those we do see. I mean, I know living wild things will swiftly move in to eat the dead wild things, and decomposition can happen very quickly, especially in summer, but there's still something to be learned from this, and it's probably that dead things often do their dying in secret places, known only to them.

Were there a fruit that grew in my garden throughout winter, I wonder if winters would seem a little less interminable. I watch the apples ripening on the tree out the back right now and it feels like I'm watching an hourglass containing the precious sand of summer. There's so much to do all the time, so much I want to do. Nobody told me I'd feel that way at fifty-eight. Fifty-nine! Fifty-nine, not fifty-eight. It's so easy to forget sometimes.

In Hungary, they don't say 'I don't want to play devil's advocate here.' They say 'I don't want to paint the Devil on the wall here.' I think I prefer their version. I learned it from Reka, who grew up there. I woke up to the sound of her coming home at around two last night. Her bar job means she's often home late, but this time I suspect she'd been on a date. Couldn't see the guy's face properly but he was her usual type: all shoulders, leather and hair. Motorbike. Reka has told me she has no interest in what she calls 'gamer boymen' of around her age, and her dates all tend to be around fifteen years older. Men with strong jawlines and engine oil in the folds of their hands. She is very matter of fact about it when one of them proves unsuitable, just as she is matter of fact about almost everything. She is an individual who makes a decision about what she wants and does not swerve from it, no matter whether or not it is expected of her. She decided she wanted to make a life in Britain, and, three years ago, came to Britain, alone. She saw the moor on a TV nature documentary, decided she wanted to live here, as long as it was within a couple of miles of a bus route to the city, and answered the ad I put up in the post office. She said she would learn to drive, and did so, within not very many weeks, and found a functional car for less than a thousand pounds. She is a good housemate, but has a habit of leaving full glasses of water at various points around the building. If she has been home for any period above three hours, I'll usually find at least four of them on tables, sideboards, sinks and the floor. When she leaves for work, they disappear, but she never comments on this, and I wonder if she thinks it happens by magic. Before I take them back to the kitchen to be emptied and washed, my cat, Rafael Perera, enjoys drinking from them. Reka was not a cat person when she moved in here, but has been converted, and Rafael Perera, who is named after a doctor who once saved my life, now sleeps on her bed as often as he sleeps on mine. She commented the other day that he was 'wide asleep' on there. I enjoyed this hugely and only reluctantly explained to her that it was a malapropism. Upon me then responding to her request to explain what a malapropism is, she told me that in Hungary malapropisms are referred to as 'golden spit'. I told her I would like to learn Hungarian but she replied that I should not bother, as it is 'crazy, a devil's language' and would take me at least twenty years of hard work to get the hang of.

Finding the right house is difficult. You have to be very on the ball, extremely assertive, and make sacrifices, because, if it's any good, you can guarantee several other people will want it too, just as hard as you do. In the case of me and this house, I thought I'd jumped through every hoop possible, acted as quickly as I could under the circumstances, but when I arrived here, in March, I discovered I'd been too late: some bees had secured the tenancy before me. As I unlocked my front door for the first time, I gazed up at the bees, who were congregating in a large group around my bedroom window and talking in low voices. I could see they were quite at home and had already moved all of their stuff in, whereas all I had was an air bed, a kettle and a car full of houseplants and crockery. But the bees and I soon worked it out. Since they are the kind of bees whose primary interest is in masonry, it turns out they only need a couple of feet of wall and the cornice and gutter attached to it and are quite happy to let me use the rest of the building. Occasionally, one will lose his way and end up in the kitchen or living room and get a bit dopey, as so many of us do when trapped indoors for long periods, and I will gently usher him back outside. The bees are very busy in the middle of the day, but tend to go to sleep at night and when it is raining. When the window cleaner arrived the other day, I asked him to omit the bee window from his schedule, as I didn't want them to get wet. This being the edge of the moor, the bees will already be well accustomed to moisture, but I reckon they wouldn't welcome any more of it from an unanticipated source.

The inside of the house was clean when I moved in but I decided to get a window cleaner in quickly, as the back windows were all very dirty, with yellow streaks: a hint of the lichen and moss that builds up in a damp place like this when it's unoccupied. This is also a small clue to the building's recent history, along with the newspapers in the old wood basket I found in the garage, all of which date from around half a decade ago. The house was unoccupied for four years before I arrived, and in that time the garden had become the lawless domain of insects and birds. I sense, once you peel back a couple of its layers, the house could tell you some stories, but I am sure the garden and its wall could tell you many more. There's the story of the fire remnants in the front yard, the wine glasses and melted plastic in the ashes, and, a layer deeper, the rusty items that were revealed when I began to chop back the brambles and expose more of the old garden wall: a rusty metal hook and mysterious, complex chain attached to it, a grass roller – quite possibly Edwardian, or even Victorian – with 'Millhouse Stores, Underhill' inscribed on it. What stories could you find deeper in the folds of this high, mildewy wall which surrounds the garden on all sides? What do the mossy steps – a little too grand for a building this small – know that nobody else still living does? As I peel the layers, it is my mission to tread lightly. I have thought a lot about what this garden might have looked like in 1991... in 1975... in 1948... in 1912, and further back, to however many years ago the wall was built. Two hundred? More? I don't intend to oppress my new garden, and, although I do want to bring a little more light and colour into it, I want to make it just as attractive a space for bees and blue tits and blackbirds as it has been for at least a couple of centuries. Because we're at the bottom of the valley, it's an amphitheatre for birds. Beyond the crab apple and magnolia and mulberry in the garden, there are the other, bigger trees which hang off the walls of this steep combe. The space gives the dawn chorus a different sound to any I've heard before, even on the edge of the moor, and I am not just referring to the bird who sings the question 'Have you eaten?' in the voice of a concerned New York matriarch every morning. Part of me is tempted to identify this bird but the bigger part of me, which prefers to leave the answer to my overactive imagination, is at present still winning.

Above me where I sit propped up in bed I can see two large spiders on the ceiling, their limbs entwined. I am careful not to vacuum or disturb the spiders when I clean. I have already severely diminished their habitat merely by moving here. For four years before that, they had the whole run of the place. Back then, I would sometimes drive past this house, with not the remotest suspicion that I would ever move to it, and wonder what kind of ghosts lived in it. It is red now but back then it was white, or rather you could still just about see the memory of the white it had once been. The dirt and damp and peeling paint looked like the place was enfolded in six or seven layers of giant cobweb. Spiders must have loved it even more than they do now. It is still damp, and time is revealing that – in the refurbishment works undertaken by my landlady before I took up the tenancy – some problems were merely painted over, rather than properly attended to. A few feet left of where the two romantic spiders are embracing, there's a deepening damp patch, on the side of the building past which the stream runs. The damp is slightly worse in Reka's bedroom, next door, and I am keeping an eye on that. She has more spiders in her room. They do not scare her and, through the wall, I sometimes hear her talking to them. It is one of the many times I am glad that she, and not a more squeamish and precious kind of twentysomething, ended up answering my ad. Looking up at these two spiders above me now puts me in mind of one time many years ago when Mike and I had been arguing for so long, and so exhaustingly, that finally I kind of flopped on him in defeat, and we awoke seven and a half hours later in the same embrace, embarrassed and surprised. It is the only time I can ever remember waking up in his arms, in our two decades together. Which seems sad, but if you're honest about it, how often do couples wake up in each other's arms? Besides, there are far sadder things to be sad about in that relationship.

Actually, now I look at them again, I think the spiders might be dead.

AUGUST

Eleven days of rain in succession. It is not the soothing kind of rain that makes you feel cosy and glad you are indoors. It sounds like war repurposed as moisture. It gives me no comfort at night. As I hear it toppling from the broken drain above my window and gathering in puddles on the back yard, there is a growing picture in my mind that every droplet of water from the moor is hurtling down the hill and congregating here at the low four-way intersection of tiny lanes where the house stands: four virtual waterslides, coming together as one. I took my eye off the garden for a week and now I fear it's escaped from me forever: a raging, dripping jungle. The damp patches on the bedroom walls are getting bigger. I had one of my funny spells coming up the stairs yesterday and reached for the wall for balance and the surface was so wet, my hand skidded across it, and I tumbled into a bookcase, bruising my hip. I messaged my landlady about the damp and she just said, 'I'll send my guy over.' That was four days ago and since then I have heard nothing. Her 'guy' is Nick, a cheerful, charming odd-jobber who loves a chat but never returns phone calls. The last time he came over to look at the damp, after a similarly wet period at the end of May, he recommended a mildew-removing spray and advised that I put the heating on more often. We were standing in the garden at the time, and I resisted the urge to show him the thermometer hanging in the greenhouse a few paces away, which showed the temperature as 27 degrees.

How do you get here, at my age? How do you get to a rented cottage, with no more worldly possessions to your name than a distressed Edwardian sideboard, a nice collection of trowels and just under seven grand in the building society? I will give you the short version. You move from your northern birthplace to university, and when, not long before graduation, your sophisticated floppy-haired lecturer asks you out for a drink, you shyly say yes, then wait while he disentangles himself from his first marriage, then move to a too-expensive house just outside Oxford with him, then put your own larger plans on hold to work part time as a suburban librarian and part time as his second mother, then seventeen years later when you realise he is doing the same thing with one of his students that he did with you when you were her age, and probably has done with several students in the interim, you walk away from it all, stubbornly asking for nothing, and then just when you are back on your feet, your lone known parent goes into a nursing home, and you realise that being ill and dying are both expensive; then the years pass, and you escape for a while, to another part of the world, with no thought of what you are doing afterwards, which is wonderful, but temporary, and then not long after that it is the present day, and you are a year shy of sixty. But is this all that terrible a place to be in? And what standards are we judging this by? The standards of another university graduate from my generation, who has spent four decades firming up their financial security, living like life is solely preparation for retirement? Or the standards of being fairly healthy, and still alive, and living in a place with clean air and owls, with a job you tolerate most days and like on some? If I ever get lugubrious and start looking backwards in a self-pitying fashion towards a point in my life where I could have... solidified my future, Reka gives me perspective. It is unlikely she will ever be in a position to purchase her own house, no matter how hard she works at her job, and how hard she saves, and she saves hard. Last week, she told me, her entire food bill came to £18.47. She lives mostly on lentils and reduced price veg she finds at the end of the day in Aldi or Tesco. She buys herself no treats, with the arguable exception of the bicycle she found on Gumtree for £50, owns only two bras, spends at least an hour of every day singing, and seems far less unhappy than any of the young – or old – people I meet on the reception of the community college where I work three days a week.

August: the most spiritually dark month that doesn't happen in winter. Everything is scruffy and angry and moist, waiting for September and October to come in to crisp it up and prettify it again. Chunks of crumbling wood in the lanes. A tree has come down on my route home from work so I'm having to go the long way around for now, which isn't such a great hardship as it gives me a better view of the tor, or at least it would, if it wasn't still raining for 70 per cent of each day. It feels like all this rain and wind is coppicing the countryside, knocking the excess wood off it. I detect a pinch of autumn in the air already and it is not too warm for a night-time fire. I gather kindling from up the lane. There's plenty. I avoid the stuff on the ground, favouring the bits caught high up in fences and branches, which is always drier. Today, in the middle of all the sogginess, we had three hours of brilliant sunshine, and I took advantage by doing some tidying in the garden and digging out a new bed. At least I have no trouble getting a spade in now. As I go down through the earth I feel like I am burrowing through tiers of history. Rabbit skulls, shards of pottery and thin old hand-forged nails turn up, and some bigger stuff, which I do my best to upcycle, such as a baffling rusty bracket, about two feet in length, with another baffling chain attached to it. I jammed this into one of the endless crevices in the wall and hung a bird feeder on it. Some primal instinct kicks in as I dig further and get more dirty and scratched up, some innate understanding of compost, something there in me from birth, always just waiting to be unleashed. Time stops being conventionally measured. Through the open window I heard

Reka talking on speakerphone to one of her sisters in Budapest, which – possibly in part because of all the extra letters in the Hungarian alphabet – always sounds more like seven people having a conversation than two. Later, I hear her singing. Folk songs from her home country. I have loaned her the old acoustic guitar I inherited from Mum. I called it a loan, but she can keep it, as I doubt it will be any use to me ever again.

More rain. The damp in Reka's room is worse. Some of the wall seems to be coming away. I offered to sleep downstairs in the living room and let her have my bed for a while. She waved the suggestion away, explaining that until she was sixteen she, her dad and her two sisters all slept in one room, in a tiny flat with no central heating. 'Summer is warm in Hungary but our winters, pffff, they make yours look like a beach holiday,' she said. She showed me a Dansette record player she found yesterday in a pile of electrical equipment at the tip. Remarkably, it works, albeit at a slightly slower speed than intended, and means she can play the nine 45s she brought with her from Hungary. These all formerly belonged to her dad, and were recorded by Hungarian acts in the late sixties and early seventies, with the exception of one by a British artist I'd never heard of called RJ McKendree: a distorted, fuzzy rock version of a folk song I've heard played in a couple of pubs here in Devon, quite a haunting tune. Reka tells me that, bizarrely, the record only came out in Hungary, and is worth over £400 now. She put it on and, despite the reduced power of the Dansette, bopped around the room to its nagging, oddly sexual beat. 'I don't know how they allowed this during communism!' she said, hurling herself onto the bed, and, for the first time, I was very aware that I wished to kiss her.

SEPTEMBER

What would we do without weather? Where would we be without the sideways rain of this morning and the sun that burned it off then made the remaining clouds curl above the tor like smoke from seven symmetrical bonfires, all smouldering at the same rate? How bland would the planet be? The fallen tree on the lane has still not been removed. I am enjoying driving the other route, along the ridge, and seeing the changes in the sky above the tor: the varying colours from day to day, and sometimes hour to hour, above those rocks at the summit that always remind me of piled pony poo. I pulled into a gate gap this morning on the opposite side of the valley and lingered a while to take it in and made myself ten minutes late for work. A queue of first years were already lined up at the desk, waiting for me to sign off their new library cards. Awkward, shy kids, vague about their own futures, who, when typing into their phones and laptops, find their bold and opinionated superhero alter egos. I am half-invisible to them, even the ones in their twenties and thirties. The young will always to some extent view ageing as a matter of taste, as if the fact you do not appear to be young any more is a decision you've made, like selecting a certain type of carpet or paint for your house. I remember back in spring, listening to a youth who was chatting with his friend about his discovery of old-school rap music, near reception while waiting for an appointment with the college counsellor. He mentioned Public Enemy. Not looking up from my screen, I offered the opinion that *It Takes a Nation of Millions to Hold Us Back*, from 1988, was their strongest album. Both boys went silent and turned in my direction with a look on their faces that suggested they'd just seen a goat driving a bus. But I feel for them, and their problems, and would not want to be young today, with all the added pressures of our new digital age. Reka is eight or nine years older than most of these kids but she seems at least a decade further from them than that, and from some less materialistic era. There is something generally, permeatingly vintage about her. Even her teddy bear – a rare reminder of how recent her childhood was – is ancient and tattered.

A week: that's how long it took the cabbage whites to decimate my kale. I leave them to it and don't begrudge them their meals. I grew far too much anyway and was beginning to tire of kale curries. After the caterpillars finished their business, they moved towards the house and appear to have earmarked it as an excellent place to pupate. I counted more than eighty chrysalises on the back wall and at least a dozen more have made it indoors. Today, I found an earwig in my lentil and tomato soup. Yesterday I watched an enormous spider stealthily lowering itself from the lampshade onto my pillow on a gossamer homemade rope. 'Hey! What are you doing?' I shouted, and it stopped, as if in embarrassment. The mason bees are turning up in the house more and more often, dopey or deceased. It's an insect's world here; Reka and I just live in it. I wonder if the introduction of sheep and cattle into the field across the lane is also contributing to the ever-larger number of flies in the house. Or perhaps a pigeon has got into the loft and died. I cannot check because the landlady, who lives in the Maldives, padlocked the hatch and did not leave a key.

When I arrived home today I noticed someone has cut the hedges quite brutally, without clearing up, and, as a result, one of the sheep had got a bit of blackthorn caught up its bottom. I climbed over the fence and tried to get close enough to the sheep to dislodge the blackthorn but it was too fast for me. After about five minutes of this, Reka arrived home and joined me, but being chased by two people caused even greater panic in the sheep and its companions, and several sheep all bumped into each other as we chased them. In the melee, the blackthorn branch was thankfully dislodged from the unfortunate sheep's bottom.

Flood in the kitchen this morning, after many days of suspicious smells. Water pouring through the ceiling from the bathroom. I put a bucket under it, switched the stopcock off and left a phone message for the landlady but after seven hours had received nothing back other than an email saying she would 'send my guy over', so I called an emergency drain company. Immediately, they identified the problem as backed-up water from a blocked septic tank, but I had been told by the landlady that there was no septic tank at the house. I managed to finally get her on the phone – the first time I'd actually heard her voice. She's very well spoken, called Flora, and I don't think I'm paranoid in thinking that as soon as she heard my accent, she identified me – in that way many privileged people do – as someone she could push around. She remained adamant that the drainage at the house had always 'worked solely on a soakaway' and, when I questioned this and pointed out that a soakaway always has to work in tandem with either a septic tank or reed bed and waste does not just 'vanish', she got very defensive and began to tell me how loved the house – which her parents once lived in – was and how many people had 'had a very wonderful time there'. She also said I had been rash in calling out the drain company and would have to pay the bill myself. 'So you reckon I'd have been more sensible to wait for however many days until your guy came out, sitting in a house without a working toilet or running water?' I asked, getting a bit pissed off now, and she put the phone down on me, but not before she'd announced, 'Nice speaking to you!' What followed, after the drain men's discovery of a totally blocked pipe, was a treasure hunt, with the significant catch that unlike most treasure hunts the reward at the end of it would not be treasure, but shit. Finally, the drain experts uncovered a rusty grate deeply submerged amongst many years of foliage. The chamber was full. Had been for who knows how many aeons. That, combined with tree roots growing into the waste pipe leading from the house, had been the cause of the kitchen flood. The drain guys were bloody brilliant. Not many people make it their life's ambition to work with drains but what you find is that those who do end up in that area often take a lot of pride in their work. They are rarely of an apathetic or indifferent demeanour. The work of the drain men was more like surgery than repair or maintenance, their camera tunnelling deep into the house's stomach and telling them what was amiss. I wasn't here afterwards, when the septic tank man came to empty it, but the note he left, detailing the 'dangerous condition' of the tank, is a small, dark, poetic masterpiece of some bygone English I never knew existed. After reading it, it is hard not to picture a man of ancient years and hawkish appearance who upon putting an ear close to the ground can actually hear sludge speak to him. One of the last of his breed. Perhaps *the* last. What had he seen, in his time? I suspect this house, empty and in a state of disrepair for a few years before my occupancy, and backed up with waste of olden times, was child's play to him. Anyway, the overall result, many hours later, is that the situation is fixed, temporarily, and I am more than £700 out of pocket. Reka and I played Scrabble later. She is getting better, very quickly, and I am sure will be beating me within a month or two.

Over at Underhill churchyard today, whose kissing gate Jim Boyland and I volunteered to rebuild a little while back. The church is in an exposed spot and we were soaked and dried and soaked again numerous times during the course of our work. It was a very satisfying day, although Jim brought his dog with him, who is extremely boring. As the dog – a smallish one, of I don't know what breed, which never makes a noise and puts me in mind of a bereaved aunt from a drabber Britain – watched us with its sad eyes, Jim showed me how to hammer iron wedges into the grooves we'd made in the granite. As I hit the rock with the hammer, I noticed the sound it made change as I moved down the line. It made me think of the stories stone has to tell us, all the voices inside it. How many voices are inside the wall that surrounds my garden, and what could they tell me? I feel privileged to live within its shelter, like the humans and cats and dogs and horses who have gone before me, and am glad to be able to add a tiny new chapter to its story. I look into its crevices and grooves and clefts and observe its changing hues and I know where I am, who I am, and what I am doing: I am just passing through. Reka was cleaning the house when I got home. I told her she really didn't need to do that. She told me it is almost her time of the month and she feels very hyper and cleaning always helps. 'I was very lazy when I was young,' she explained. 'My grandma used to say to me, "If laziness hurt, you would be screaming."' As I write this I can hear the little stream across the lane raging, and rain tumbling off the roof, and I am a bit worried about the weather forecast for next week, and what it might do to this place, but maybe I am painting the devil on the wall here.

More rain. Coffee with James Boyland's wife, Edith, at the abbey tea rooms. She entered the building alone, without the dog, and as she did I noticed a relief in myself. Water pouring down the lanes. Hart's-tongue fern lapping at it from the verges. The last remnants of summer's ambition are fading. Someone has yet to take down the sign advertising the tug of war in Marybridge, which has caused much local amusement, due to the extra 'f' the sign's writer mistakenly added to 'of'. I took the car in for its MOT at Phil Spring's and was surprised that, with a couple of small improvements, it passed. I suppose it looks worse than it is. Typical Devon car: not bad on the right-hand side, dented and scratched to buggery on the left, with the wing mirror held on with tape. These lanes on the edge of the moor were not dug out with any cars in mind, and particularly not the huge fortified people-carriers of today. Curiously it's the individuals negotiating them in more modestly sized vehicles who often drive more apologetically. The countryside looks on, bemused at the way it's been outgrown, bludgeoned, smoothed over, suppressed, raped, waiting for the revenge it will surely enjoy when we are gone. I reverse into my drive in my smaller than medium car, only just squeezing through the small gap in the wall, imagining the Morris Minor or Triumph Dolemite it once more practically housed and the people who probably never conceived that anybody could possibly need anything grander. You can let yourself go into a gentle, cuckoo-soundtracked fantasy about life here in the unclaustrophobic 1950s but it's worth bearing in mind, as you do, that that's when we really started getting on the bad road we are on, environmentally speaking, and when some of the most irreversible damage was already being done.

Finishing touches to the kissing gate today. Jim – whose family have been associated with the church for centuries – and I posed next to our work, and Clive, Underhill's new vicar, snapped a couple of photos of us. Clive speaks very softly and has long slender fingers, which he often uses to gently tickle the palms of his own hands as he listens to you speak. I have heard that some in the village have not taken to him, finding his gentle and sensitive nature suspicious, but I like him. He does seem a little bored, though, and apparently the job leaves him a lot of time to work on his macrame skills. He offered to do some for me and I accepted, as I need a place for my spider plant to live. He and Jim also showed me what they call 'The Bird Lady': a very mysterious carving in the church that I suspect will linger in my mind for a long time. I took a long route back, just to glory in the beginning of the changing colours on the hillside, but my goal proved futile as the journey coincided with the fifth or sixth cloudburst of the day. As I came cautiously down Riddlefoot Lane, which is barely wider than an average car, a hooded figure in a red anorak pressed itself up against the foliage to let me pass, and as I pulled level, I recognised the figure as Reka. I opened the door and she got in. She could not have been wetter. 'Rain has been a big fuck today!' she said. When we arrived home I rushed into the living room to light a fire and Reka, having dispensed of most of her wet clothing, went straight upstairs to run a bath. Seconds later, I heard a shout of 'Jézus Krisztus!', dropped the log I was holding and ran in her direction, to find her standing in her room amidst a pile of stone and plaster, with water puddling all around her. She'd been so wet, it took me a couple of seconds to realise the water had mostly come from the wall and not her. I went to the airing cupboard and grabbed as many towels as I could carry, gave one to Reka to wrap around herself, and began spreading them on the floor, then left a voice message for Flora Prissypants. When I returned to the bedroom, Reka had found the dustpan and brush and was attempting to sweep some of the rubble into the corner. I told her to leave it, and that I would be sleeping downstairs this evening, she could have my room, and I would not hear any protests to the contrary. She finally went for her bath and while she did I put more towels down and, as I did, I froze. What appeared to be a tiny, dusty foot was sticking up out of the rubble. Tentatively I poked it, and was relieved to find it was merely an empty shoe: a very old one, designed for a tiny child. On further investigation, just to the left of it I discovered an arm sticking up from the mess, pulled it, and found myself holding a small doll: not a hard, plastic doll, of the type common over the last three quarters of a century, but one made out of fabric and stuffing, and missing an eye. 'Jézus Krisztus,' I muttered to myself, letting it fall from my hand, as you might an object you'd picked up and not realised was molten hot.

'It happens in Hungary, too,' said Reka. We were sitting in front of the fire, with Rafael Perera stretched out on the rug in front of us. Reka's face was the colour of a good pomegranate. She had chosen to dry her hair naturally and I could see that five or six drips still remained on her neck. 'My grandmother lives in the countryside near a place called Kaposhomok. You would not have heard of it. People haven't. She took down a wall in her cottage and found, how do you say it, when a shoe is harder?'

'A clog?' I asked.

'Yes, exactly this. A clog. It is sometimes a charm to ward off evil but also when one of someone's children has died young and they want to keep the spirit with them, in the building.'

When I asked Reka what had made her walk over near the tor, she told me she'd just needed time to think. 'Man trouble,' she said. 'I think people think they have too many options and that is one of the problems of the world of right now.'

I had already brought my duvet and pillow down and felt extremely relaxed, right there, with my lovely housemate and my cat, despite the troubling events of the day. I'd managed to soak up most of the moisture in the spare bedroom and fortunately none of it had come through the ceiling. I could not help but notice the way the firelight enhanced the extreme natural beauty of her face and, as I let my eyes close, I permitted myself to imagine what it might feel like if she reached out a hand, just six or seven inches from where it was now, and gently held the toes of my right foot.

OCTOBER

Flora Prissypants still refusing to pay me back for the drain company's bill. I am seeking legal advice. I am not feeling well. Last night I went to bed with a band of tingling, slightly burning pain stretching around from my navel to my lower back. I am sure it is nothing. There is usually something and usually it doesn't last long and becomes nothing. That's what it's like, having a body. Or at least having a body after a certain, not particularly old, age. Of course, before that there's a period that might convince you that having a body can mean going for long stretches of time where there's nothing much wrong at all, but that's in fact a very brief period, in the grand arrangement of life. 'You look tired,' said Kath, when she arrived to relieve me of my shift. 'Are you OK?' This means absolutely nothing, since approximately four times out of every nine she sees me, Kath, whom I jobshare with, says to me, 'You look tired. Are you OK?' In part to spite her, I took advantage of the beautiful late afternoon weather, nipped home to get my bathing suit, and drove to the beach, then let myself float on the water, watching skeins of geese fly above me towards France as the most golden of suns dropped its blessing on the hills. I did not feel tired, and was OK. Perhaps it was not the most sensible course of action, and I have started to feel a bit peculiar since then, but I have an enormous faith in the healing power of salt water and fear we might not get a day this perfect and unseasonably warm for a long time. I did text Reka and ask her if she wanted to join me but she said she had another date. I heard her come in, obviously not alone, at around twelve, then could hear her playing her guitar and singing – the melody seemed familiar, and I realised it was the Hungarian record she had shown me, the one by the American singer, albeit a much softer rendition of the song than his. The builders are coming soon to sort the wall and I shall be extremely glad to have my own bed again.

I have lived in the south west of the country for a long time now, long enough to consider it my home, but, as a transplanted northerner, one thing I do often miss about where I come from is people's unsugarcoated habit of, on the whole, but with some exceptions, saying what they actually mean. Today on the way to the car park after buying a cauliflower and some strawberries from the farm shop I bumped into Sheila from the arts college, and said hello. They're a bit weird there, all into their yoga, which is great by me, but it's never simple yoga, always got to be yoga with some extra element, yoga and darts, yoga done while wearing nothing but an anorak, or something like that. Toni, who works with Sheila, had asked me if I wanted to teach on their stonemasonry course a couple of months back and I hadn't been able to make it to any of the two dates Toni had proposed to chat about it, and – though I'm not bothered – I never heard anything more. Anyway, it transpires, from a couple of things Sheila said, that I had my chance, and because I wasn't able to jump at the opportunity, I've been replaced. I didn't fully realise this until after I'd left the farm shop, due to a habit Sheila has – just like quite a few people you meet connected with the art college – of making a piece of negative information sound like a positive one. 'It's a very exciting time up there!' she told me. 'There are a lot of ideas being floated around.' This after I'd gleaned from some other convoluted pseudo-enthusiastic things she'd said that the course would now not be co-taught by Grant Hope and me, but by Grant and Judith Sitwell, from Topsham, instead. 'You should talk to Toni,' she said. 'It's a very exciting time. I know she's aware of you.' Fuck that, I thought, but didn't say it; I just politely said goodbye and wished her a nice weekend – which makes me wonder, now I think about it: am I now also a person who doesn't say what she actually means?

I sometimes think about the small culture shocks I still feel living in this part of the country, after close to a decade, and wonder about the bigger ones Reka has had to deal with. She says she finds it hard to get used to the politeness of British people, finds it overdone, and was shocked at the levels of gossip when she first arrived in the UK. 'I hear so many conversations where people seem to be talking about a woman they know, in a disapproving way,' she told me. 'It's always "she" something, something she did, they are mentioning.' Ever since she told me this, I've become more aware of it myself – especially in the staff room and refectory at work. Today we talked about Christmas, which I plan to do approximately nothing for. Reka said Christmas is different in Hungary anyway, as it's the Baby Jesus, not Santa Claus, who brings the presents. 'But we also have Santa Claus Day, where we leave our shoes near the window.' She seems quieter at the moment. Maybe it is the distraction of the new man. He is called Greg and works at a garage in Exeter. I feel more ill, a bit like an animal with sharp teeth is eating my insides.

The builders didn't come to sort the wall but Nick, Flora's guy, did. I don't know how good a job he did but I have my suspicions it's of a temporary nature. Nobody came over to look at any of the other damp issues in the house. Before Nick arrived, Reka and I packed the shoe and the doll back inside the brickwork and covered them up. I am not superstitious, but I think some people who once lived in this house interred them in the wall for a reason, and I think it's best that we respect that. I don't know if Nick saw them when he repaired the wall. I certainly haven't mentioned any of it to Flora. I am still attempting to get the money back from her for the work by the drainage company. Still ill, and none of this is helping.

NOVEMBER

It turns out I have shingles. I remember at various points in my life people talking in a tone of great pity and sympathy about other people who had shingles but I don't think I'd ever properly considered what it was. Now I know. What happens is a furious stoat somehow gets inside one half of your body without you noticing and gradually begins to chew all your flesh and nerve endings. You never see the stoat, but after a while the scars from its interior work begin to show on the outside, then begin to blister. At night, it's a little different to that: you wake up at 2 a.m. feeling like you and the stoat have been involved in a fire at a biochemical factory. I've got quite a high pain threshold but, even so, I'm finding it all surprisingly nasty – particularly the bit where the stoat bought some hot chilli sauce as a dressing then ate my bellybutton from within. What is also startling is that shingles is actually a little bit of chickenpox that's been sitting dormant in your body, waiting patiently to come back and get you. My chickenpox was a bastard in 1977, when I was seventeen. Like me, they look less punk rock than they did back then, but they're still a bastard and have become more bitter and cynical with age. I will still walk, though. This afternoon, five miles. Everything is gold and green and brown down the deep lanes, with the one exception of the bright new red berries on the rowan. Every day, the sun thins a little more. Reka and I haven't played Scrabble for ages. We must. It's Scrabble weather. I heard Reka singing the song again, late at night, and then I thought I heard it again, at about 3 p.m., but it might have been just my half-dream state. I'm that kind of ill where songs spin in your head as you try to sleep. Hallucination, I suppose. Last night my pillow was a rock I tried to carve but a hand kept stopping me. I looked up and the hand belonged to Kath on reception. 'You look tired,' she said. 'Are you OK?'

Something nice happened today, then something not nice happened, and something else, also not nice. I was walking down the hill – staggering a bit, if I'm honest, holding my side, which is beginning to look like I've been in a fire – and I smelt that lovely smell you get when woodsmoke cuts through the cold misty late afternoon air at this time of year, then realised that the woodsmoke was coming from my own chimney. What a delight! I opened the gate and as I did a man – broad, bearded – charged past me, clutching his face, which had a line of blood running down it. It took a moment before I realised it was Reka's current boyfriend, Greg. He looked scared. I found Reka in the living room, tending the fire, and said hello, but she didn't seem to notice me at first.

'Is everything OK?' I asked.

'Everything is fine,' she said. The way she said it, there was something different, a bit slower, and she wasn't looking at me. It was as if something in the fire was very important, and I was a distraction.

'We have been experimenting,' she said, continuing to look at the flames.

I was really feeling like I needed a lie down so I opted not to press the matter further, and I heard her leave for work an hour or so later. The dishwasher needed to go on so I popped around the house, looking for half-full glasses of water. I found two in Reka's room and was just leaving when something on her bed caught my eye, sitting next to her ancient teddy bear. I couldn't quite believe my eyes! It was the doll from the wall. I'm sure it's the same one – all dusty and dirty with one of its eyes missing. After all, where else would you get a doll like that? I can only think she took it back out of the wall before Nick came to repair it. She'll be back soon but I won't ask her about it until tomorrow. Maybe I won't at all. I suppose it's her own business.

I love the rainy, sometimes sunny climate of the moor and its border villages: the pockets of weather that can vary so radically from valley to valley, the clouds that sink into vases of deep green land, do their work to help maintain that greenness then tumble on to their next appointment. I like walking in the rain here and I like seeing what it does to the plants in my garden. I like the way footpaths and streams are often interchangeable. Water was a very decisive factor in my decision to live here: the deafening rush of the stream, the taste of what came out of the tap, so immeasurably more flavoursome and soft and refreshing than what I used to drink in Oxford when I lived with Mike. 'Yep, that's it,' I thought, the first time I drank it. 'That's what's been missing.' You go and get some chips in a nearby town. You walk along the street in the town with your bag of rain and, strangely, you don't mind it, because you're very hungry after a long walk along the high shouting river, and there are some chips in there too right at the bottom of the bag, just a few, beneath all the rain, and they taste good, because everything tastes good after a long walk in the rain. Water is in your entire being here, altering it, influencing the taste of everything. I so often have rain and sea and river in my hair and damp pebbles in my shoes and cuts across my stomach and chest from when I scraped them against rocks when I leapt off other rocks into water. You feel it all even more after a summer that some other British people told you was dry and hot, not realising that the South West Peninsula is not really in Britain, and that weather is different here: cooler and damper in summer, warmer and damper in winter, rainier almost all of the time, especially recently. If you can't see the moor, it's raining. If you can see the moor, it means it's about to rain. Rain. Rain. Rain. Water. Water. Water. It's so much the theme of my life. I even used it to kill Mike. I didn't say? I killed Mike. I didn't. But I did. I told Reka I found the doll today. She said it was OK, that she knew I knew, and that we could all be friends: me, her and the doll.

Ah fuck. Rain. The song again. Such a nice tune. She has got really good at it. I'll explain it all better when I'm well.

DECEMBER

Oh so ill. I didn't kill Mike. Didn't stab him or shoot him or put arsenic in his favourite leek and potato soup or chop his nomadic penis and testicles off. Don't think that. But maybe I did kill him. It feels better now I write it. It was yonks ago now, and yonks after we broke up. I didn't find out until a couple of weeks after it happened, from Beth. She was all that was left by then, our only connection. She was the one who told me not to go out with him, then she ended up closer friends with him than she was with me. She thought I should know, in case I heard elsewhere. There was nothing about it in the newspapers but I might have found out online anyhow, she said. It was in Scotland. The top left bit. A boat. A storm. Him and his mates, fishing. Only one of the four of them survived. It didn't touch me for a while but I tracked it back and the dates matched up. That was the night: the night I wished him dead. But I don't really wish anyone dead. Resentment. They say it's like drinking poison then waiting for someone else to die. Only in this case it worked. I was angry: Mum was close to the end then, things were bad, I was in some other reality without hope, was thinking back to where it went wrong, held him responsible, but I didn't mean it. But that was the night I did it. Down in the cottage, the place before here, right in the village, sleeping in the loft room, with the view of the tor, and the pony poo on top. This rain is reminding me. That was the exact night he must have died. Maybe the exact moment. I worked it out. It was raining then too. Next day without any idea of what I'd done I walked up to the pool – the deep one. Seven miles there, seven miles back. I let myself jump. I hit the surface and let the momentum take me as far under as it needed to. I was under for barely any time at all but while I was I felt I was somewhere else: somewhere where nothing was anything any more. Somewhere darker than any night, any dream. I came up into the sunlight and the sunlight felt like something you could suddenly eat and I ate it, gulped it down without chewing it the prescribed seventy-two times, or even chewing it one time. I swam against the current, my front crawl just strong enough to defeat it and get back to the rocks on the bank. I didn't jump again. This rain is reminding me. It's so... everything. Maybe it wouldn't seem so fierce if the house was double glazed. There are eight reservoirs on the moor, all built between 1867 and 1972 as the expanding villages and towns below them demanded cleaner water. When the water is low, you see the remains of sunken farmsteads and clapper bridges and Bronze Age villages. When they made one, they drowned an entire farm. How could you do that? Did cows and sheep die? I hope cows and sheep didn't die. But more cows have died since then. Ever such a bloody lot of cows. Have I ever thought about that. Oh god, the water, the drips. Is the wall going to come down again? I know what's happening outside, all the rivers, filling up. They're all getting high. One is being a thug out back of the Co-op, hissing and swearing at the locals. Down under the bridge, near the dual carriageway, another is taking some drugs it found floating in a bag. All the water is coming, and this is the end point. It's rushing down the lane, right at me. The rain couldn't be louder if I was in a tent. The power in the house is going on and off every two minutes. I can hear Reka. The song. I didn't even know she was in. She's playing the song. The wind is up – I think it's coming through a gap in the wall – and it's harmonising with her. I remember now. I heard it up there, before. On the moor. There was the house that was high off the lane, with a door in the garden wall. I think I heard it once, behind the door. I don't know. It might have just been a dream. Everything's mixed up now and my stomach is burning. I want it to dry out. Everything is wet. It won't dry out. The walls won't dry out. My skin won't dry out. There's a folk tale from there, near that bit of the moor. The pixy – an ugly tiny man – comes to the nurse's house and asks her to deliver his wife's baby. They go on a horse, very fast, to his wife, who is very beautiful, and when the baby is born, he asks the nurse to put ointment on its eyes. When the pixies are not looking, she tries some of her ointment on one of her own eyes. Suddenly the pixy and his children are even uglier than before, but the wife is even more beautiful. The next week, at the market, she sees him stealing things, and asks how his wife and baby is. 'You can see me?' he asks. 'Yes,' she says, 'but only with this eye.' And he strikes her in the eye and blinds her with his sharp fingernails. I am lucky the shingles aren't in my eye. Edith Boyland and her boring dog told me her aunt Agnes got them on the left side of her face and lost her sight in that eye. But, Jézus Krisztus, it hurts, especially at night, and I don't know what is a dream. Last night I dreamt Reka stood over me with the doll and didn't say anything and I asked her to come and be beside me but she just stood, staring. When I am better, we can leave here, me and Reka. We will go somewhere dry. We will bring the bees, we can even bring the doll if she wants. But what if the bees can't come. What about the spiders. Will they be OK after we have gone. And what about the cows, everywhere. We can go and have our own cow, at least be nice to our own cow; selfish but that's all you can do, be nice to your own cow, because if you think about all the cows you go crazy. It will sit down when it's about to rain. That's what they do, they're always sitting down here. I like the noise of them when they move slowly and heavily through grass on a hot day. It's a lovely calming sound, unique to them, impossible to replicate by anything that isn't a cow. That will happen again. It will be spring again, and it will be dry again, this skin will be dry again, after the Baby Jesus has brought our presents and it is a new year and everything turns over. I just have to be patient. But right now, I admit it, Kath. I am tired, and I am not OK. Are you happy now, Kath? Can you finally shut the fuck up? The power is going on and off, every two minutes.

FEBRUARY

My name is John and I don't know why I'm writing this because nobody will probably ever see it or maybe they will but I reckon that will be long after my time. I'm the builder. One of them. Colin is the other one. We are the ones working on the house. Not that guy Nick. He's gone. We've been here two weeks now. The place was a right tip when we started and we had to shift a load of stuff to the real tip before we could even start knocking through and sanding down and working on the pargeting so we're only just getting started, but that's not my problem. The owner of the house doesn't even live in this country and she's paying. We'll be here another month, I reckon, but it would be two at the absolute minimum if she'd told us to go ahead and do all the stuff I said needed doing. I suppose she's going to sell the place and just wants it looking smart to the untrained eye so she can get shot of it. Like I said, that's all her business, not mine. I wouldn't want to live here myself, it's all a bit too wet and far away from everything. Anyway, it was a right mess and we found loads of stuff we didn't know what to do with and I didn't like throwing it away. I talked to the next-door neighbour and she said there were two women living here and one of them died – septicaemia, which I think is some kind of blood poisoning, but as you know now anyway if you've read this far she'd been ill in another way before that. There were old socks and this weird doll and loads of smashed plates and when we were shifting this mattress with a big dip in the middle and a spring coming out of it I found this diary under it and when Colin was over at the wholesalers getting emulsion I started reading it and then I just carried on because it was interesting and then I read it again. I didn't understand all of what it was talking about and why should I when it's just something someone has written for herself about her life, but it made me sad and it made want to read books, which I always want to but don't. Anyway, I haven't really got any more to say because it's all in here anyway, but I thought I should say something because I don't like thinking about what happened and the neighbour told me the woman didn't really have any family to speak of and she seemed nice in what she wrote and I feel like somebody needs to write or do something because if nobody did that's fucking awful and everything just isn't there any more. We're going to put the wall back up tomorrow and I'm going to put it in there, in a gap between the stones, before we make good. I'm not telling Colin. He wouldn't be interested anyhow.

ME (NOW)

Come, fertilise me, in your thousands, man and beast. Give me your sheep shit, your rotten berries, your own good piss. Do not be shy and hold it in for the public lavatories on Fore Street. Squat in my bushes, stand proud above my ravines, or shake your fluffy tail in my face – whatever is the most convenient method for you, I don't mind – and let it out. Do not industrially monostraddle me with your insane lust for profit. Rid me of this relentless chemical run-off. Farm me, by all means, but farm me with tact, kindness, sympathy. Farm me gently. Farm me slowly. Take it easy. Don't you know, that I have never been farmed like this before. At least not since some time in the mid-1800s, or during that short-lived organic project by that couple last decade, which sadly didn't come off due to funding issues.

A full moon bleached the sky white-blue last night. It shone in through the bedroom skylight on Jim Swardesley from the post office and he dreamt that he was a large bear, on all fours, running through an icy stream, with dripping bear legs, and one of the big bear grunts he did in the dream as he ran woke him up. He turned and pressed his 93.5 per cent erect penis into the bottom of Gillian, his wife. 'Mmmtired,' she mumbled, batting him away. 'Go to the workroom and calm yourself down.' Downstairs, the Swardesleys' son, Julian, sat on the back garden decking, smoking, unable to sleep, his mind rewired to a frenetic, fizzing, popping speed by the hundreds of messages he'd exchanged with girls on a dating app on his smartphone over the last week, all of which he knew would come to nothing, and all of which was some way to attempt redemption for the trip he'd made to Cardiff the previous week to meet someone from the same dating app, who had not only stood him up but subsequently vanished from the face of the online globe: a redemption that was ultimately less about his romantic life and more an attempt to convince himself that humans weren't ultimately cruel and heartless. Behind him, in the downstairs bedroom, his older sister Phoebe, who had passed through a similar phase in her life eighteen months ago and now used her phone in the most minimal way, slept soundly. In her dream, on the idyllic farm of her future, a group of demanding animals, including sheep, chickens, three goats and a needy open-mouthed frog, followed her around the edge of a pond, in whose unrealistically clear water she had just been washing three peasant blouses and her long blonde hair. She turned, startled for just a moment, at the gentle yet solid touch of a large slab of human skin on her bare shoulder, which she happily realised was the hand of her future husband, the co-owner of the farm, who also bore a striking resemblance to the square-jawed lead from her favourite American TV series. 'So tell me, dear wife,' he asked her, in his square-jawed American voice, his hair not moving a fraction in the afternoon breeze. 'Shall we ride Antonio and Bess to the beach this afternoon, or head to the mountain and meditate?'

I dreamt very vividly too, as if that white-blue light of the moon was shining down through my layers and illuminating my past, penetrating parts of my crust that no run-of-the-mill night, not even a run-of-the-mill full moon night, could normally penetrate. I was back right in the meat of a night not unlike this, a long long time ago. I thought I was old at the time, but I was not. This is how ageing works, again, and again, and again, until you die. OMG, can you believe I'm actually twenty-one? I'm so old! OMG, can you believe I'm actually forty? OMG, can you believe I'm actually 900? I'm so old! OMG, can you believe I'm actually 5,807? I'm so old! As I dreamt about the night, I refelt so much of the fear I felt on it, and was scared by the fear, but I also refelt how alive I felt, and I was more scared still by that. Men were killing each other on my flanks and my knee and my left knuckle and all six of my bums and my eyebrow and my clitoris and my bollocks – although not my bullocks, who had all fled to low ground – and the men had been killing each other for two days and even though it was the deepest part of the night they were still killing each other and the fierce light of the moon was making it easier for them to kill each other and it seemed, although at first some of them had been killing each other slightly reluctantly, more out of a sense of duty than anything, now those same men were taking more pleasure in killing each other. One group of men had originally ambushed and cornered another group of men near a thick, impenetrable stand of trees on my aorta. The group of men who had ambushed the other group of men had less refined accents than the other group of men, more odorous hair and beards, but that was not so noticeable as it initially had been, and no longer seemed to matter; they were all just men, with urine-splashed trousers and swollen bloody eyes and half-legs and three-quarter arms and strewn intestines and a lust for power disguised as a lust to stay alive and a lust for staying alive disguised as a lust for power and women at home they wished were holding and caressing them and nobody really knew who was who any more and what it was all for. I was terrified, watching these men. And now dreaming about that night I felt that terror again and I felt that aliveness and I felt what I felt in the weeks following it, when all the men had died or fled or dragged themselves off to expire elsewhere, when the liquid from their bodies seeped into me, which was a different kind of aliveness, and an amazing kind of rejuvenation and energy and, yes, virility. Startling, startling virility. And then I felt momentarily ashamed but then I thought: Why? I am not hurting anyone; I am not even pressing myself into someone and being told to go to a workroom and calm myself down. I was just feeling what I felt.

Look, I'm not the Cerne Abbas Giant, if that's what you think. You're way out geographically, for a start. I have never been chalked, I am barely in any guidebooks, and I am not a renowned site of pilgrimage and ritual, or at least have not been for so long that to even talk about that would involve talking in an entirely different language which, even if it was translated into twenty-first-century English, would make little sense. Also – and I don't mean this in a snide or judgemental way – some of us don't feel the need to show off graphically and publicly about what we've got and prefer instead to occupy a position of quiet confidence about it. Each to their own, though. I hear he's OK, the Giant. I certainly don't have any personal beef with him, and am not attempting to start a feud. There is enough aggro and unrest in the world as it is. Especially on a moonlit night such as the one that has just passed.

Because the moon scrubbed the sky so clear, it was actually pretty cold in the early hours. But now the sun has burned off a light mist, all the world's clouds are elsewhere, and we're getting the flipside: the most perfect blue afternoon, hot without being stifling, a five-days-a-year perfect day. From my vantage point I can see vividly all the way to the coast, fourteen miles away, and that does not happen often. I have just watched five young friends edge their way down a deep crevice in the cliffs. Max is the leader. He has no shoes and has been walking with no shoes for so long that his feet feel nothing of the burrs and thistles and rocks and gorse needles beneath them. Then come Jemima and Annie: surfing, kayaking almost-hippie girls who talk with that laidback drawl common to all the kids around here whose parents have money and moved over from the south east a couple of decades ago. Hollie and Joe, both twenty-two, bring up the rear. They get on well, in a not deeply emotional way with Hollie doing most of the talking, and are in the middle of a lengthy discussion whose theme was originally graphic novels but has moved on to cheese. Hollie is still annoyed with herself for a grammatical slip-up in a message she sent last night, in reply to a sequence of persistent, politely complimentary and slightly poetic missives from an anonymous male, in which she wrote, 'Hey, dude, I'm sorry but I have a boyfriend and I'm comfortable with the amount you are messaging me.' The reason she wrote 'comfortable', instead of 'uncomfortable' – the word she intended to write – was that she had just burned her hand on the door of her mum's wood burner. What she doesn't know is that the sender of the anonymous messages was Joe.

But now they are on the shingle, and there is not a hint of Internet or phone reception and that other universe in which those messages were exchanged feels even more like one totally separate to this, with very few of the same rules or beliefs or social guidelines. The Internet is still two full years away from arriving at the beach so everyone is being a person. Nine people are asleep and, of those, seven will remember this sleep, with the sound of the waves in the background, as their most delicious sleep of the summer. Near the cliffs, someone has left a packet of chalk sticks, and on the rocks somebody has chalked the message 'PHUCK "SOCIETY" MAKE YOUR OWN RULES'. Just left of that somebody else has chalked a naked male body from the shoulders down. The naked male body's penis is standing to attention. If we are talking purely in terms of how it relates to the body it is attached to, the penis is slightly bigger than the

Cerne Abbas Giant's. In front of it a woman called Sue is praising a Schnauzer for leaving a crab to just get on and exist as a crab. But it is not a beach day without problems. Three men have just arrived on jet skis, bludgeoning every pleasant noise the day had to offer, and are riding closer and closer to the people in the water. Jennifer Tomasovich, an occupational therapist from Lostwithiel, has been watching the jet skiers and has now marched down to the shore and is shouting at them and trying to wave them away from the beach but they can't hear her and, if they do see her hand gestures, it only seems to encourage them to continue to get closer and closer to the shore, buzzing in show-off circles on these machines that they have convinced themselves are their Cerne Abbas Giant-sized cocks (or maybe the cock of some other land form which is slightly bigger but doesn't feel the need to be outlined in chalk). David Ludgate, who retired from running the big corporate optician in Exeter last year, has strolled down with his son Sam to join Jennifer, whom neither of them has ever met, on the tideline. 'Go away!' he shouts at the jet ski pricks.

'Fuck off!' Sam adds. 'Nobody wants you here and nobody likes you.'

Now a bigger crowd is gathering, thirteen or fourteen people, most of whom have never previously met, all united by this common four-cylinder enemy. Three or four of them begin to throw pebbles in the direction of the jet skiers. The jet skiers stop, about twenty yards out from the shore, and switch off their engines.

'What's your problem?' says their leader. Bald, pointy-faced, fifty-fiveish, he – the people on the shore realise – is the father of the other two jet skiers. He has brought them with him on his jet ski replacement-penis journey, taught them from an early age how to use a jet ski as a replacement for their own penises, passed on all the jet ski penis-replacement wisdom he has learned to them, as they will in time to their own male children.

'Our problem is that what you're doing is DANGEROUS,' shouts Jennifer Tomasovich the occupational therapist. 'There are people swimming here. You are being massively antisocial.'

'Oh, get a life, *woman*,' shouts the self-appointed jet ski replacement-penis chieftain, whose name is Andrew Bannister and – even though it seems almost too depressingly predictable to be true – took early retirement last year from his job as a big city banker and still regularly snorts cocaine.

'You mean like your life?' shouts Jennifer Tomasovich the occupational therapist. 'Why would anyone with any sense want that? You're demonstrating right now that it's obviously totally fucking soulless and self-centred.' At this, chuckles and cheers ring out from the shore, and an energy that has been building around the strangers standing there solidifies into a powerful, vibrating bar: a warm, formidable thing. Even though the strangers have not locked hands or begun singing a song of purity and strength out to the ocean, it feels like they are doing both. It is too much for Andrew Bannister, who opens his mouth to tell them why his life is actually the best, searches down in his dry throat for the words, then further, right inside his drier heart, but cannot find those words anywhere. 'Come on! What even are the words?' his throat asks his heart but his heart says nothing. And while he falters, as if in response to this – almost as if the machine is part of his body after all, just as he believes – his jet ski falters too. It stalls, to the great entertainment of everyone on the beach watching.

Fin and Reuben, Andrew's sons, look nervously now to him for the strong guidance he has always given them, in terms of what to do when you are sitting on a replacement penis. But none comes. A pebble pings off Reuben's replacement penis.

'What a trio of prize tools!' shouts Sam Ludgate.

But it's OK! Andrew has got the engine going again! He presses the accelerator and does a victory lap of the water, followed by Fin and Reuben, getting even more dangerously close to the beach than before. Because as long as he tells himself that's what it is, it's real, in his head, victory. That mouthy woman and her hippie friends haven't won. He has. Because here he is showing them the way to live: that sitting on a beach reading a book, or doing your stupid yoga, or eating your stupid organic packed lunch, is for losers. Life is about making money and using it to find a penis that is more powerful than your own. And he is sure – even though his throat, and all the bits of his body it leads down to, are even drier now – everyone will know that, and be in no doubt of his victory, as he motors away to another cove, followed by those he has spawned, and passed on his wisdom and prowess to.

The calm that redescends after that is powerful. At the other end of the beach, Hollie resumes thwacking a tennis ball back and forth with Annie, and Joe resumes watching her, and wondering why she didn't like the poem his anonymous Internet self sent her. People slip back into their delicious salty sleeps. Swimmers swim in a less nervous way. Dogs are congratulated for further minor acts of restraint. There is a slight sense that Jennifer Tomasovich the occupational therapist has given the beach the therapy it needed.

But I am not satisfied.

You will have noticed I sided with the peace-loving fraternity in this situation. The 'hippies' as Andrew Bannister thought of them, even though that description would only truly fit a few of them. The people not forcing their lives on anyone else. I generally do take that side. I am on the side of the land (well, obviously), the side of freedom, the side of unpolluted sound of waves and spiteless laughter. But am I a hippie myself? No. I resist such simple boxes. But more than that, I am too angry. You cannot be me, and see all I have seen, feel all I have felt, and not be.

'Oh, so you're a nihilist then, are you?' is what you're thinking. And you'd be wrong there too. I am not a nihilist, a communist, a socialist, an anarchist, a libertarian, a liberal, a conservative, an anything. I am me, with all of what has made me, with all of what has soaked me, and with all of that you cannot be a label.

Let me tell you this: I happen to know something else about Andrew. Eight years ago, he was driving across my ribs in one of his other replacement metal penises – an SUV retailing at over £70,000 – and hit a young pony, while breaking the speed limit by a total of 34 mph. He very forcefully felt the impact of the pony, which broke the SUV's radiator grill and bumper and smashed its left headlight, and, though it was dark, saw the animal's descent over a ridge at the side of the road, to some rocks directly beneath, where the pony died, not quickly, but ninety-four full long minutes later, watched by three other ponies, who stood directly above it. But Andrew decided to drive on, and to this day has still never told another soul about the incident. He was on his own in his SUV at the time, but even so, he still spoke aloud, directly after the impact, as if justifying himself to a friend. The words he spoke were, 'Ah sod it, it's just a bloody wild pony. Nobody even owns it.' He then drove over my hips, which nobody owns, and my knee, which nobody owns, to one of the houses which he bought with his wife, who nobody owns, where he was meeting his mistress, who nobody owns, where he would later take some cocaine, which was once owned by a man called Jake, who lived in London's Holland Park.

I know quite a bit more – but by no means everything – about what Andrew has done in his life, but this is the bit I take most personally.

So, no, when those pebbles were landing in the water near Andrew's jet ski, I was not just hoping he, trailed by Fin and Reuben, would piss off and leave the swimmers and sunbathers on the beach in peace. I was hoping that one of the pebbles would connect with his temple, and knock him into the water. Harsh? Maybe. But perhaps you are ascribing values to me that are not relevant to my kind. You have been lulled by my chatter and my jokes and the familiar names I call my constituent parts, lulled into forgetting that I am not a man or a woman or anything close. Also, I haven't done anything to hurt anyone (on this occasion); I am just feeling what I feel.

I desire love. I want to see it thrive. But I also want blood. I want it to seep into me and do its work. I want a balance redressed.

PAPPS WEDGE (2043)

'Get David Cavendish to sign that bloody document.' These had
been Sally's words to Bob as he leaned in close to her over the
bed in the hospital room that overlooked the half-empty skip and
the three-quarter-empty car park, and then she had died.

It had been a lateish life romance: a second marriage for
her, a third for him. Autumn, 2018. Shedding of old leaves and
skin. They'd made their mistakes and out of them, sometimes
it seemed almost directly, had come what they found in their
union: a harmony but not like anything either of them had
pictured earlier in life when focusing on the word 'harmony'
and trying to pin down precisely what that would look like. A
harmony made of old wood and notebooks and soup and a coffee
grinder and shouting at robots on the phone and rejecting what
nonsense they could and pianos and keeping out of each other's
way for quite a bit of the week and car boot sales and a sheep and
then two sheep when the first sheep got lonely and then three
sheep just because they felt like it. He was forty-nine, she thirty-
eight. He'd come to the book group that February, the first new
arrival for a while, invited by Jane. It had been Sally's turn to
choose that week, and she'd opted for *A Widow for One Year* by
John Irving. She talked about what a warm, generous, funny and
sympathetically human author Irving was. Bob sat in the corner
on the most important-looking chair, frowning, filling his cheeks
with wine and hogging the chilli-coated peanuts. 'He's bland and
overlong,' he said. 'And why do his female characters always have

big tits? It strikes me he's just writing out his sexual fantasies, getting off on his own inventions.' She thought Bob was a ghastly grump, a withered wirebeard, a molten meanmouth, a blown fuse of predictable cynicism. He didn't come again.

Seven months later, he crashed his car into hers at the half-blind junction outside the arts college where he went to talk about woodcraft one afternoon a week. Nobody was hurt and he admitted liability. He was so instantly attentive, so patently repentant and worried about the mistake he had made, that when he arrived at the driver's-side window after running across the road to her from his abandoned, fishtailed hatchback, she did not instantly equate his face with the jaded peanut hogger of the previous winter, even though the mouth and eyes seemed immediately familiar. He recognised her more quickly and they exchanged details for insurance purposes but it was not until the following week that she strolled out of the wallpaper of his days and became lifelike. That was in the garden centre. The nice one, with the mossy hanging baskets and the old man with the calculator. Not the big one, with all the weedkiller and all the screens that barked at you to buy stuff that would change your life as a gardener. He had his headphones on, was half-listening to a podcast about the building of early tanks and wondering why ferns were so expensive when you could just find them everywhere in the countryside around here anyway, when he realised a woman was staring at him, mouthing a word, over and over again. He removed the headphones. 'Car, car, CAR!' she said. And *now* he saw her. He saw empathy and rain and second-hand wool and an excellently cantilevered nose and forbearance and independence refusing to transmute into misdirected fury. He helped her transfer the Trachycarpus she'd purchased to the boot of her car but he got the angle wrong and one of the branches snapped. By way of apology, he bought her carrot cake at the tea room next door. Here she began to learn that what she'd met seven months earlier had been not so much a man as a set of trying recent events: a winter where he'd been assailed by a lost job and a lost parent, the last one he had. Things were slowly improving for him now. His time was divided between various endeavours involving wood. He had found the time to read four more John Irving books since February. He'd thoroughly enjoyed three of them.

Who even was that goblin who'd sat in the comfiest armchair in Jane's living room back at the beginning of the year? Bob's face had softened unrecognisably since then. She sometimes even forgot he had a beard and certainly forgot that beard looked like grey wire, even though it did. As they became Sally and Bob – always Sally and Bob to all who knew them, never Bob and Sally – she was the one who often had to step in to stop him trying to do too much for others, to stop his gentle surface being trampled on. Back then she was in the cottage in Underhill with the piano, and he was in the long house on the hill five miles away, behind the wall, with the town address even though it was outside the town, and outside the town's mains drainage network. He only rented a fifth of the long house, and a small courtyard adjoining it, which was a shame, because a colleague at the college had recently offered him a rescue turkey and he'd had to reluctantly say no due to space limitations. His house was an afterthought on the end of the long house, like something the long house had been meaning to say to support an argument but couldn't be bothered to properly articulate. Its windows never seemed quite right. Newts came in through the tiny lean-to in early spring, the side of the house which had, two centuries before, been the site of a large natural pond. The other four fifths of the building, and a couple of acres of adjoining land, belonged to Anita and Jac, a couple in their thirties. Bob never asked what Anita and Jac did for a living but he fed their pigs and chickens and cats while they were away, which was often, and took delivery of their online shopping packages, which were countless. When they were home, he listened uncomplainingly through the walls to their shouting matches, their reconciliatory humping, their unrelaxing Ibiza chillout albums, Jac bashing his drum kit in their conservatory and the piercing garden tantrums of Sorrel, their toddler.

Bob had only ever spoken to Jac in person once, which was not long after he'd first moved in, when Anita had invited him in for a coffee, and Jac had arrived home from work – whatever that was, something property-related, Bob tended to assume – and said, 'Anita, what is this strange *man* doing in my kitchen with you?' which was presented as a joke but also revealed itself, via its tone and Jac's face, to be very much not a joke too. Sally said she thought they were prize nobheads. She was vocally uninhibited during sex and they'd only done it twice when the first text message from Jac arrived on Bob's phone. 'Dear Bob,' it read. 'The walls are very thin here and I hope you know we can hear everything.' Bob did not reply and, for fear of embarrassing Sally, did not show her the message for a long time, nor Jac's second one, but did suggest sleeping in the spare room when Sally stayed over, for a change of environment, and because it could be argued that the mattress was more comfortable. The following week, Bob took delivery of the high-end drone Jac and Anita had ordered from the Internet and placidly took it over to their house when they returned from their latest international city break. The week after that, he transferred his half of the fee for the emptying of the septic tank shared by the two houses. Bob wasn't quite sure what went on with Jac's phone along the way but from what he could work out Jac must have had two different Bobs saved in the Contacts section of it and they had somehow got mixed up, without Jac yet cottoning onto this mistake, so by the time four more months had passed, and Bob was out of the house and into his new place, his thread of text messages from Jac read as follows:

Jac: 'The walls are very thin here and I hope you know we can hear everything.'

Jac: 'Bob. Please can you transfer your half of the fee to our account that you owe us for the clearing of the shared septic tank yesterday. Your share comes to £68.50.'

Bob: 'That should be in your account now, Jac. All the best. Bob.'

Jac: 'The walls are still very thin, Bob. Please can both of you be more considerate.'

Jac: 'Happy New Year, Bob. I hope life is treating you well. Please could I get eight bales of straw from you?'

Jac: 'Howdy, Boberino. We are in dire need of manure. Can you help? Take it easy, man. Jac.'

'Fucking hell,' said Sally, when Bob finally showed her the messages. 'Also why can't he spell his name with a "k" like a normal person?' They were in Bob's new kitchen. Water was all over them in every way except the way that would have made them wet: the kettle boiling, the cold tap running in an attempt to stop Bob's eyes stinging from the onions he'd just chopped, and a further, more captivating liquid story being told just outside the window. He lived by the river now, just under an hour's walk from Sally's, and he normally did walk, not drive there, arriving in mud-splashed trousers after cutting through woodland where fallen trees often blocked the path and the ground sucked thirstily at his legs. The front door to Sally's cottage led directly to the living room and if you had a bit of a belly, as Bob did, it was a squeeze to get yourself through the gap between the Kentia palm and the piano. The piano, a Bechstein which had once been her granddad's, wouldn't fit through the door so when she'd moved in it had meant getting permission to go through the

Dawsons' garden, four doors down, then using the ginnel that led behind all seven gardens on the cottage row. The removal men had not been pleased and she gave them a £50 tip, which had left her £371.23 overdrawn, rather than just £321.23 overdrawn. Sally rarely played the piano any more as tuning other ones all day could drive her what she called 'a bit doolally' and she had come to appreciate the opportunities for silence that home offered. Even though her business name, Sally the Piano Tuner, made matters fairly explicit, people still often expected her to be a man when she arrived at their house to tinker with their instruments, or much older than she was, or blind, or all three. 'So what do you do as well as this, for your actual job?' some of them asked. They found it strange, almost impossible, to believe that this is what she'd been doing for a full-time form of income since she left college. The job was not the quaint and refined Victorian existence she had imagined when she was younger. It could be territorial and shady. When she'd first moved to the area and tried to build up her clientele, rivals in the trade had badmouthed her temperament and stability as a tuner. One especially vindictive veteran had sent her a warning message by calling her out to a fake job at a fake address. As she attempted to solve the musical jigsaws in front of her at the houses of lonely men, she saw their desperate staring reflections in the polyester finish of the pianos. But there were still moments that made the job worthwhile. Old people, hearing her play dusty instruments that had not been touched for decades, burst into tears as they were sucked down tunnels into parts of their past that had been inaccessible to them for many years. The terminology of the trade never fully ceased to provide some level of amusement for her, although most of that was now her amusement at witnessing the reactions of others when they heard it. 'If you are lucky, I will show you my papps wedge,' she told Bob the first time she invited him over.

Now the legal matters relating to his father's death the previous winter had been finalised, Bob, with four or five dollops of luck and an immense amount of effort, had been able to buy the house by the river. To scrape the last bit of funds for his deposit, he had sold his furniture, his car and his record collection. Getting to the college to teach his class meant an hour's walk and a half an hour bus ride. For extra money, he took a job helping out at a woodyard, which was also not a short walk away, and felt like work more suited to someone two decades his junior, but he enjoyed its noises and smells, and it came with the advantage of free firewood. The first time Sally came over to the river house, they ate risotto beside the crackling logs, he squatting on the floor and she on a large cushion next to an ancient hi-fi unit. She heard a discrepancy in the toner arm of the deck and adjusted it. 'I think I might be becoming an interior decor commitmentphobe,' he told her. He said he liked the minimalism of the house, the sense of possibility the bare rooms offered, and enjoyed the way his three remaining LPs sounded in the empty rooms, but she saw him wince and hold his side as he got up to take the dishes to the kitchen. The next time she arrived, she brought a Lloyd Loom chair. 'But that was your mum's!' he said. 'You can't give me that.' She told him to call it an indefinite loan. On each of her next seven visits, she brought houseplants, so now it was a house of plants and a chair. He slept on a mattress and said he failed to see the point in bed frames, argued the case against them vehemently, even as he struggled visibly to pull himself upright. She worried about what he was doing to his back, carrying and splitting logs three days a week. She recommended a chiropractor – a haunted-looking man whose practice was based at the top of a haunted-looking building in the nearest big town – and, with some coaxing, he booked an appointment. In spring she filled the balcony with pot plants and Bob moaned that it ruined the view and diminished seating potential, but he nurtured each plant, inside and out, as if it were his own child, cooked every recipe she gave him, read every book she recommended, making notes as he went so he could give her feedback. He was the first man who'd ever listened to her.

The river house did not have a garden but when the water level was low Sally and Bob crossed the stones and sat on the opposite bank in the field belonging to the farmer David Cavendish, who didn't seem to have much use for it himself. It was a very steep field, which, when the mornings were misty and Bob looked out of his studio through the diagonal skylight, could give him the impression that roe deer were bounding through the sky. The hearing of the sky deer was so sensitive that even the sound of Bob reaching into a bag of chilli-coated peanuts, a hundred yards away, behind glass, would startle them, but soon they became more at ease with his presence. Formerly, a horse called Edna had lived in the field and chomped apples off the branches of the old tree at the field's centre. The tree was still there and it was not unknown for apples to cling to its branches until January. Edna had died way back in 2003 but Sally and Bob often speculated about her personality and the ensuing one of her ghost. Their conclusion that she was a very strict and disapproving horse became a running joke between them.

One day in summer 2019 a night of hot rain arrived, the river filled up with voices and Bob – unable to sleep – stood on the balcony naked for half an hour taking great pleasure in letting the full force of the saturated night hit him.

'Goodness!' said Sally. 'What on earth must Edna think of you now?'

The reason Sally and Bob knew about Edna was because they'd been told about her by Fleur, whose family the horse had once belonged to. Fleur was the one who'd sold the little river house to Bob. It was because of Sally's work as Fleur's piano tuner that Bob found out about the house being for sale and was able to buy it before Fleur decided to advertise it with an estate agent at a price Bob could not have afforded. Sally continued to tune Fleur's piano – even though she suspected Fleur didn't use the piano between each tuning, and asked her to tune it mainly because she enjoyed the company – and Fleur became a close friend of hers and Bob's, telling them stories about what life was like in the river house during the previous century, when Fleur's mum, Daphne, had lived there. Fleur called Daphne 'an indomitable woman' and 'Queen of the Combe'. The Cavendish family owned the field back then too, but allowed Daphne to keep Edna there. During this period, Daphne, who abhorred slothfulness, would ring a bell at half past six every morning to make sure everyone who lived in the other five cottages on the lane was awake. Fleur said that back then the combe was mostly home to alcoholics, that something about the way the light leaked grudgingly down into it sent people organically in that direction. When Daphne died, just a week after Edna, Fleur went to live in the river house for a few years but found that the noise of the water got inside her mind and began to play tricks on it, so she let it to tenants for several years before selling it to Bob. 'It can be a dastardly, opinionated beast', she said. 'The river, I mean, not the house. The house does not force itself on anyone. It allows you to live the way you want to.'

Fleur had been correct. Bob lived in the house pretty much the way he wanted to, which was to say that after a while he lived with three chairs, fourteen houseplants and a table. There was never a time in any of the rooms when he couldn't hear the river, unless he had one of his three remaining LPs playing loud, and on spring nights when Sally stayed over and she and Bob sat up in bed, it often felt like having a conversation in a quiet annexe of a party, next door to a room where a bigger, noisier conversation was going on. Sally, especially, was attuned to every change in the current and flow, every small rise in the water level. In bed at night with the lights off, as they half-listened to the river's hot takes and counterpoints, she often had a lot to say and he'd keep pushing sleep away in order to hear it. When she finally dropped off, it was like a switch had been flicked – she described it that way herself, but said 'like a flick had been switched' because she had not fully woken up – and then, having pushed sleep away for so long and missed his chance for it, he'd be alone, stranded with his thoughts. He noticed she often slept with her arms folded, as if waiting for a dream to impress her. After a year, he knew everything about her except the trimmings. He knew that she had lupus but didn't like to tell people about it and enjoyed bananas when they had gone a bit bad and never stood on manholes and that her parents had both been music teachers and played in the West Newcastle Symphony Orchestra and that they had twanged door handles when she was little and asked her to identify the musical note they made. He knew about all her previous romantic partners, about Jake the narcissist web designer who now lived in Seattle, about Ben who cooked extraordinarily well but slept with her best friend when she was twenty-one and about Michael who had amazing hands and taught her to use his own unique non-standard tuning on the guitar but didn't like putting his cock inside anything or anyone. He knew where each of the four notable scars on her body came from and why and precisely which month in which year in which century they occurred. He knew that she did not believe in ghosts but was also adamant that one otherwise silent December day, when she could see the fog settling over the tor through the cottage window, she had heard her piano play two notes all on its own. He knew it all but it did not stop him loving every octave and quaver of her voice and eagerly awaiting what she had to say every time she opened her mouth.

By contrast, she sometimes felt she knew too little about him. His attitude was that his previous relationships had no place here in the present. They were like statues from previous centuries: they had been erected for old reasons, in a different cultural and political climate, and you wouldn't want to drag them to a new place and erect them for the same reasons now. She accepted his reasoning, even though it meant she had to guess at some of the shapes of who he was and what was behind them. She knew he was northern, like her, but his northernness was more of a rumour embedded deep in him: seven years living up in Southport, from birth. She knew he liked wood and worked with it but it was only when she asked him what the strange T-shaped object with the redundant rusty hinge in the window of the upstairs toilet was that she knew he made things for his own pleasure out of it, too: useful things, like lamp bases and mirrors and coat racks, but truly odd things too, things from another dimension. She knew the job he'd lost the winter he met her had been as a lecturer in Film, but it wasn't until they'd been together for close to two years that she discovered he also used to go into London to review movies for a magazine, one she used to buy.

'No way! I probably read your stuff!' she said.

'Oh dear,' he replied. 'I'm sorry you had to go through that.'

He talked about the jaded newspaper critics at the screenings in Soho who would sigh and say 'Oh, not another *film*' as if they were stacking corned beef on supermarket shelves rather than being employed to do something others gladly handed over their wages to do every weekend, and about the quite famous one who fell asleep on Bob's shoulder, and about the time Bob invited his music journalist friend Martin to a screening and Martin turned up late, still drunk from the night before, and, struggling to adjust his vision to the dark screening room, sat on the lap of a well-known radio presenter, spilling the presenter's yoghurt, or was it ice cream. There were usually sandwiches and crisps laid on by the PR companies before the screenings but the famous radio presenter always brought his own yoghurt or ice cream tub and noisily lapped up the contents before the film started.

'You don't mean Irish Martin who lives in Barnstaple? The one you said you never see any more because he's a recluse and just stays in his room meditating and chanting all day?'

'Yes. That Martin. He's not Irish, he just kind of... seems it. We met in London. He used to get me into gigs for free. He's... different now. He wrote some books. He hasn't been able to get most of them published, though.'

When Sally looked at the facts of Bob from a distance – the north-west childhood, the brief media career, the love of wood, the uncomplaining ability to be outdoors in all weathers, the grumpy resistance to change, the attentiveness to everything she taught him, the skill with his hands, the inability to detect when washed clothes were dry with those very same hands – it never seemed to quite make sense. But when he was in front of her, as Bob, real lumpy three-dimensional Bob, he made total sense. Nothing had ever made more sense to her. The following year – the first of the pandemic years – they decided she would move in to the river house with him. The national lockdowns gave them the extra nudge they needed. That, and the day a man who had asked her to tune an early 1900s Broadwood accidentally locked her in his house when he went out to work and Bob had to drive over and rescue her. Not that she needed a hero, but she looked at him a bit differently after that day, felt she was standing half a stride closer to him. In the car on the way home, she noticed a shard of glass was still sticking out of the t-shirted arm he'd used to smash the window. She carefully picked it out as he steered.

She said the living room with the piano had been full of clocks, all set to different times, and their chiming had made tuning almost impossible. 'Still,' she said. 'At least I got to work on a Broadwood. Those things are rare.' He said they used the wire from them to make planes in the First World War. 'Now how in god's name did you know that?' she asked. He told her he'd read it in one of her books one time when she was asleep.

She brought her piano with her to Bob's. The removal men managed to get it in through the doors of the small light room on the end of the house nearest the lane without anybody wanting to murder anyone with knives, and there it would have to stay, which meant the room couldn't be used for much else, but that was fine, because there were more places to sit, especially now she'd brought her furniture with her. Outside the world seemed to be ending. That's what people kept saying. In less than a year 'dystopian' had become such an overused word to have been rendered near-meaningless. Early hopes when the pandemic first hit that nature was 'healing' had turned on their head and it appeared that in fact the virus was on the side of greed and destruction after all, annihilating all that was small and true and firming up the grip megalomaniacs and madmen had on the planet, in an attempt to push us more quickly towards the abyss. Social fissures spread out in all sorts of unanticipated ways. Making snap judgements online about the lives and personalities of people you'd never met had already been a fashionable form of stupidity for quite some time, but now it became an international sport. Fear leaked while people weren't looking, crept through tiny gaps under doors and puddled. 'It's scary out there,' people said. 'Stay safe.' But much of the time it felt like the problem wasn't *out there* at all, it was *in there*, in the screens that everybody carried with them everywhere they went and nobody could stop looking at. Out there, David Cavendish had let twenty-four new sheep graze the field over the river. Out there, in the sky above the combe, there were marsh harriers and deer. When Sally and Bob stepped out onto the balcony and looked into the water, they did not see disposable masks and hand sanitiser bottles floating over the rocks. The air felt clear and quick and kept both of them looking six and a half years younger than they were. At night, during the hard pandemic winter, when everything accelerated, they did shiftwork spooning each other – four minutes each, then the changeover – and got no firsthand experience of the ache for physical affection that was pulsating in the chest of unattached people the world over, spreading like a pandemic within a pandemic. They existed in a little bubble of OK, and, as guilty as they felt about that, knowing the really calamitous state of everything, they protected the bubble fiercely, and would not have wished to be anywhere beyond it.

And now it was twenty-two years later and she was two years in the grave – or technically not in the grave at all, but in the earth, certainly, by now – and he was seventy-three and the world was not yet quite over. He had become the dropout he hadn't quite been able to commit to becoming when he was a young man or a middle-aged one. It was easier now to do it, and harder, because every bit of alleged progress in society always made everything easier and harder. When the visors came in, he refused to have one fitted, and that made it simpler than it ever had been to step outside of it all, with no half-measures. No rudimentary pay-as-you-go phone. No Gmail address he begrudgingly checked once a week. Nothing. He was in the minority as a result of his choice to live visorless, but he was not alone. It made him part of the Resistance and the Resistance made ways for themselves to exist on the cultural borders: they opened small shops, supported one another by sharing produce, lived in their own voluntarily insular way. The fact that the mortgage was now paid off made it more

possible to live as part of this section of society, as did his choice
to heat it solely with wood, to insure nothing in it and to plant
a little veg in the field over the river every spring, to no longer
travel abroad or drive. He was living in one of the easier places to
be an outcast and it permitted him to not think much beyond the
ensuing twenty-four hours in his immediate surroundings. There
was no point. Everyone knew the state of play now, the chorus
of denial of two decades ago had fizzled down to a low hum,
and, while plenty was being done to stop the acceleration into
the void, the two major obstacles standing in the way – corporate
greed, and the illusory drive towards convenience – could not
be circumnavigated. The planet as it had been known for the
last few thousand years would end soon. It would end after Bob
ended, but not long after. So in the meantime what you did was
grab the good days with both hands.

In truth, he had become very unaware *what* was going on,
in a wider sense. That was the choice he had made, in an era
of infotainment tyranny. He rarely had any interaction with the
people with visors, who remained plugged in. Vague bits of news
drifted his way via encounters on footpaths and in the community
shop and the free pub: the evacuation of west California, a few
encouraging advances in sustainable building regulations, the
closing of the French border, war across most of Eastern Europe,
Shropshire drowning under deeper water every winter, a plan for
the redistribution of wealth and second homes. But it was all a
muddle, factoids spinning like dust in sunlight. It was a decade
since the visors came in, thus a decade since he had switched on
a machine to consult a news source. His news sources were the
moor and the river, but they were reliable messengers, in their
own way – perhaps no less reliable than anything else. During a
long walk he passed the reservoir a couple of miles north of home
and noticed a bridge in the clouds a few miles north west of that

and realised they were rebuilding one of the old branch lines. When there was a storm now, it crackled with more electricity. Microwaves and multisockets and chargers in people's houses blew up, which made him even more glad to have none in his. Always prone to tempests, the river now had that bit more to say when it was incensed. He put his faith in the tiny seventeenth-century bridge behind the house. The water level had never risen high enough to overflow the mossy stonework but the December before last it had come close. The dog had still been alive back then, Jim, a Patterdale he and Sally had taken off Sally's cousin Beth when Beth moved to Ireland. Around 2 a.m., with a whimper and a nose forced into Bob's armpit, he had raised the alarm. The water had been steadily rising for hours, on a day of the most persistent rain imaginable which followed several days of other rain that by any normal standards would also have been classed as extremely persistent. Bob had never heard the water scream louder than just before he went to bed that night, as it raced past the living-room window, but by the point, four hours later, that Jim stood on the bed, nudging him awake, the noise had pinned the whole house in a headlock. It was not unusual for Jim to ask to be let out for a slash at this time but when Bob went downstairs and opened the back door, the little dog just looked up at him in terror. It was clear what Jim thought, which was that there was a huge monster outside, and he was not wrong. Bob could just hear a higher note within the water's experimental dirge and realised the piano was vibrating. He went out and stood on the balcony. The writhing white shapes beneath him looked like livid swimming ghosts: all the river's dead, raised in fury, on their way to the sea to seek the most terrible revenge. The water would have needed to rise another three feet to reach the balcony, but he had never felt more expendable. Within the white bar of howling sound, he could hear the grinding of the boulders on the river bed, as the current forced them against one another, again and again.

Since that night, he often wondered what would be the first to go: the bridge, the planet, or him. He decided that if the bridge did go, it probably meant the planet was going with it. And if the bridge went, it meant the house would almost certainly go too, and, since he went out increasingly rarely these days, it was highly likely he'd be in there at the time. He could think of many worse ways to die. It would also save him from the Alzheimer's that had taken his dad, which he increasingly worried was his fate.

Today, though, the river was a pussycat. It purred around the boulders beneath his feet. The water level was low enough for him to plot a route across the bendy line of stones to the field in summer shoes and barely get wet. The deep pool, up by the bridge, where he sometimes spied trout, was mild phosphorescent green. Through the hole where one of the planks of the balcony had rotted, he could see a leftover semicircle of peel from the orange he'd eaten yesterday, gyrating behind a rock, the current not strong enough to wash it away. How much citrus had he thrown in here over the years? And what of the rest? The ash from the fire, the rotten lettuce leaves, the nail and beard clippings, the curdling hummus, the avocado skins, the peanuts, the matted dog hair, the garlic skin that flew away on the breeze like the butterflies Jagger released into the crowd in Hyde Park in the year of Bob's birth? Of all the river's dark magic, its repeated vanishing acts were perhaps its most impressive. Again and again, that crystal-clear current renewing itself, making things that had existed not exist any more. This story had been going on a long time and it never stopped, still went on down below, even on the rare occasions the surface iced over. When he died, he would be part of this story, one of the water's innumerable voices, and nothing more. He had no children or grandchildren. His cousins

Rachel and Sheila up in Stroud stopped getting in touch around the time the visors came in: they had not joined the Resistance. Martin in Barnstaple, whom he'd only seen a couple of times a year anyway due to all the chanting and meditating, had met a Hungarian lady – a songwriter – and moved with her to a house on the great plains in her homeland. He'd written Bob a letter to say the place was disturbingly flat but the sex and music were excellent, but that had been over a year ago. There was Sam, the young ecologist from the village he sometimes walked with, who quizzed him for moorland knowledge, who would remember him for a while, he supposed. But Bob's stamp on the earth would soon fade, his sculptures remaining for a while in the houses of the people who'd bought them and then in other houses and then in dusty shops and then in other houses but with nobody who owned them having a clue about the person who made them. He would just be part of the river's story, just like Fleur – now five years dead herself – and everyone else who'd lived on its banks, including Edna, and Edna's tree, and that was fine, because life wasn't about what happened when you were no longer alive, it was about grabbing the good days with both hands, and probably always had been.

It seemed very likely that the tree, in fact, might even go before him, the bridge and the planet. It leaned at a twisted rheumatoid angle now, almost painful to look at, no longer yielding apples, thrashed and browbeaten by storms. It was an incongruous gothic leper on a frivolous spring day like today. Just below it, Bob could see something else incongruous: some new low wooden posts with string tied between them, stretching up the valley. He'd first spotted them about five days ago, although he'd not seen who had placed them there. They bothered him, bothered him probably more than anything else in his life that was currently bothering him, more than the pain that diagonally knifed from his left hip to the middle of his back more obnoxiously every morning when he got up, more than the fact that when Sam had come over for a cup of coffee last week to talk about some rare beetles he was researching Bob had entirely forgotten his name for two whole minutes.

Not for one day since Sally's death had Bob not thought about her final instruction to him. Leaning over the bed and putting an ear to her mouth in that wretched room which said nothing about the life she had lived, he had not been surprised that she had not said 'I love you', since she had not said that for a long time. But the vehemence and volume of the request, more of an order than a request, the 'bloody', the clarity of it, after weeks of no clarity at all, took him aback. It was a subject she'd not mentioned for years. He'd supposed she was thinking about his own welfare, wanting to know he'd be OK and have the best possible life without her, but more recently, when he thought about it and tried to coax himself into action, it was her interests he felt he was acting on, not his own. It was just a field; looking at the way it changed from season to season, growing produce in it, reading in it, seeing animals mooch about in it, all enhanced his day-to-day existence, but who cared who really owned it? That was his take on it a lot of the time. But then he remembered her face, the last time he ever saw it, tasted the texture of her words in his head. It was several months since he'd last been up to the Cavendish farm, which was barely a farm at all now, and spoken to the younger David Cavendish about the field. Nothing concrete had come of it, just as it hadn't the time before. These new posts and string, though, nudged him into action. He would head up there again; not this afternoon, maybe not tomorrow, but certainly the day after. He would be firmer and stronger this time, even though there were few prospects he relished less.

Bob had never been sensible or strategic or cautious with

money. He'd always known this fact about himself somewhere deep down but he knew it a whole lot more after she moved in. Although neither of their incomes had increased, a year after she came in on the mortgage, a year after they pooled their resources and she made some little adjustments to all the baggy parts of his administrative life, they suddenly felt better off. They had stopped seeing David Cavendish, or his sheep, in the field across the river by then. Bob knew how much she loved the field and, as a surprise, for her birthday the following year, he took out a loan and made David Cavendish an offer for the land, which, after some wrangling and vagueness, Cavendish agreed to sell for £68,000. Sally was furious at first when he told her, then a little happy, then furious again, when she found out that Bob had paid Cavendish for the field but not received any form of legally binding document as proof.

'So you just... shook hands on it?' she said. Her face had that heavy-lidded, burdened look it got sometimes. She'd just got back from a hammer recentring job and had been reaming flange bushings all afternoon. Tuning the piano they belonged to had then been made near impossible by three toddlers divebombing each other on a giant beanbag in the adjoining, doorless room in front of a blaring television. She had no idea if the piano was in tune when she left.

'Well, essentially, yeah,' he said. 'It's fine. I am sure he's not going to diddle me. It's different here on the moor. There's an ancient code of honour. If somebody fucked somebody over in that way, everyone would know about it.'

'You are insane, and you need to get in touch with a solicitor as soon as possible. Will you promise me you will do that?'

'I promise.'

'Next week?'

'Yes. Well, soon.'

'Next week.'

But next week had come and gone, then next month, then next year, and next decade, and he did not get in touch with a solicitor. The intention was there in his mind but also in his mind, every morning, was the question 'What exactly do you want to do with this, your one precious life?' and the answer to that question was never 'Paperwork and time-consuming back-and-forths with a member of the legal profession.' She continued to harangue him about his neglect of the matter for a short period but then she seemed to forget, and realising she'd forgotten was one of the outstanding reliefs of his recent life. He felt like a child who'd been forgiven for burning down a school. The field was effectively theirs anyway. They grew sweetcorn and carrots in it like it was theirs, sunbathed in it like it was theirs, grazed three Herdwicks – not for meat or wool but just for the sheer joy of letting them be Herdwicks – in it like it was theirs, erected a marquee in it for her fiftieth birthday like it was theirs. What difference did a piece of paper make? Every so often, Bob would bump into David Cavendish on the lane, and on approximately one in three of these occasions would ask him if he might be able to sort some official documentation, and Cavendish would promise to do so, but also somehow manage to convey that none of it really mattered, even the money itself didn't even matter, even though it was now safely in one of his three savings accounts; what mattered was the sun and the air and the birds and the day, on which latter point Bob was definitely in agreement about. Sally said he was a feckless man and a royal bullshitter. She said she had become better at spotting those as she got older, and happier to confront them. Cavendish's son, also called David, reared and shot pheasant, annihilated foxes for fun. Once on the lane when he almost drove into the side of her, she called him a cunt for it, and for his driving. Her argumentative streak – though rarely aimed at Bob – had grown in middle age. When she hit the menopause, her hair greyed and thinned, then stopped greying and got thicker, thicker than it had been since she was a teenager. She attributed this to her argumentative nature. She said it was her hair's way of disagreeing with what biology had planned for it. It became the first way that people recognised her, made her bigger and more impressive in the eyes of people they knew, made them even more Sally and Bob, even less Bob and Sally.

*

The river changed colour again over the next two days: heavy cool spring rain turned it the colour of beer, foamed up its margins. He sat out at dawn hoping to catch sight of otters. More had been spotted over the last few years, especially a mile or so upstream where the combe's steep walls of moss closed in and only allowed in secret sharp flashes of light. Two summers ago one of them had made off with a cod that Patrick and Mel at Russet Cottage had left exposed, marinating in honey and soy sauce on their kitchen table with the French windows open. He thought he saw one today but it was a false alarm: just a squirrel, skipping over the rocks, out of its element. He went inside and showered and put on his lone clean pair of trousers and ironed shirt. He resented himself slightly for doing it but decided it was wise not to add any element to his appearance that would put him at risk of being taken less seriously during the day's central task. Before he left for the Cavendish place, he mopped up the water droplets from the bathroom floor: an old habit, not quite yet dying its hard death. Sally had been an alarmingly splashy bather and in two years he had still not got used to living with a largely dry bathroom. He had never quite worked out what she did to make the floor and walls so wet. When her hair got bigger, it only made the explosion of water more exuberant.

Out on the lane, the hedgerows were settling into their high spring colour scheme of white, pink and blue: greater stitchwort, red campion and bluebells. Two decades ago the lanes had become quite dicey to walk along due to a combination of angry drivers living in a pandemic, population growth, urban exodus and people texting at the wheel. It all felt like it had been leading to a kind of breaking point. The work of the second and third pandemics and the rise of self-driving vehicles had altered that. In a climb of just over a mile, he saw nobody. He took a left at the top of the hill, past a half-demolished stone barn with a corrugated iron roof reddened with rust, then turned up the track leading to the farm and pressed the intercom. He found David Cavendish – the second David Cavendish, or rather the fifth, and second most recent, David Cavendish, if you were looking at the entire timeline – on the porch, in the middle of an animated conversation with an unknown, invisible entity. Cavendish acknowledged Bob with something not totally unlike a smile, using the small part of his face that wasn't absorbed in whatever was being fed to it through his visor. His head, though bald, looked smooth and youthful – certainly no older than his age, which Bob knew to be somewhere in his late thirties – but underneath it his body resembled eight or nine assorted pumpkins on the turn, stuffed into some cloth. Bob immediately felt mean for having this thought – after all, he'd let himself go a bit in middle age, too, before his exit from digital life – and it was up to individuals how they looked after their own bodies, and nobody else's business, but he had heard the rumours about what these visors were doing to people, about the so-called 'ultraworld' they lived in, where the virtual body they modified had superseded the physical one they still put food and drink into and walked around in and shitted and pissed out of. When they had to live fully in their physical body on the government-ordained Switch Off Day, they were antsy and frustrated. It was said that many of them could no longer properly taste food. He heard rumours of something called 'joyhacking': people coming to their senses, hundreds of miles from their home, disorientated, after strangers had recoded the electronic systems connected to their brains and ridden them around for a period of days, just for fun. But Bob didn't know if that was actually true, just as he didn't know if a lot was true these days.

He waited patiently, standing seven or eight yards clear of Cavendish and staring at a tractor and an old motorised go-kart, both seasoned with moss and half-sunk into the earth on the far corner of the farmyard. It was a long time since any agricultural work had happened here.

'Mr Turner,' said Cavendish, finally. 'What can I do for you on this perfect spring day?'

'David,' said Bob. 'How is life treating you? How is your dad?'

'Well, I have to be honest and say it is not looking good. I do not think there is very long left. It is a very sad thing to see for all of us.'

'I'm so sorry to hear that, David.'

'I imagine you are here to talk about what we talked about a little while back.'

'Well...'

'Did you know – and you will appreciate this, I'm sure, as a man who likes books – that the way the Crow Indian killed buffalo in the seventeenth century was rarely with arrows or tomahawks? What they did instead was drive them off cliffs, sometimes as many as 700 of them, far more than they could eat. They used songs. Can you believe that? Songs! At the time, the buffalo was the most common wild animal on the entire planet. Can you imagine it? Biting into some freshly cooked buffalo by a campfire? The taste sensation. Oh no, you are a lettuce muncher, aren't you. But still. Delicious, don't you think.'

'No, I did not know any of that, David.'

'I am a mine of facts these days. A mine, I tell you. It is driving Polly crazy. I won't shut up. It's ever since I opened up this new window on here,' Cavendish tapped his visor, 'that permits you to absorb an audiobook at six times the speed of the actual narration. It allows you to do so many other things at the same time. But don't think I don't envy you. I wish I had your life too, for sure. Living in the right here and now. Listening to the owls, without distraction. Firewriting on your coppiced hazel. See, the thing is, Bob, I spoke to Dad about the field a couple of times, and he couldn't remember anything about what you said. And now, well, you can't really talk to him at all. It's just isolated words and dribble. Sometimes he'll just say the word "anvil" or "lips" and a nurse will come in to mop up, and that will be it, for three days. Terribly sad for all of us. You know what he was like, Bob. He's a generous man. To his own detriment, it could be said, at times. He could sometimes offer people things he shouldn't. Maybe it was a flaw, but it's one of the things we all miss about him. Because what he is now, in that bed in that home... it seems terrible to say it, but it's not him. It's very heartbreaking for all of us to see.'

'I am sorry about that, David. It must be very difficult for you. But I do have a record of the payment on my bank statement: £68,000 transferred from my account to his.'

'If that's true, that's true. But who is to say what the money was for? Is there a record of that? Perhaps it was for something else you owed him. Maybe it was a gambling debt? Ha! We are all getting older and facts get misremembered. Isn't that the way with all of history? We think Indians killed buffalo with tomahawks but really they often didn't. They killed them with cliffs and songs. No, but seriously, we could talk about this, and that is fine, but I think the best way would be for you to contact the people you need to contact, and for them to contact some people in another office who act on my behalf, and that way we can move forward, or not.'

'I've noticed some posts in the field, and some string. Someone's painted numbers on the ground.'

'As I said, I think we could talk about this, and that is fine, but I think the best way would be for you to contact the people you need to contact, and for them to contact some people in another office who act on my behalf. I hope you have a nice afternoon in your house, Bob. That balcony must be a very nice place to sit and watch the world go by.'

On the way back down the track, as an act of defiance, Bob cut left through a gap in an attractive row of mossy-rooted beech, and across the Cavendish land, towards the river. As he did, he saw Cavendish's eight-year-old son, the freshest and most up to date of all the David Cavendishes, on a chair in the middle of one of the back fields, also talking animatedly into his visor, in much the same way his dad had, and with a smaller version of the same body. It gave Bob a vision of an entire alternate version of human history, measured entirely in David Cavendishes, all getting gradually more feckless and avoidant and lardy and technology-obsessed, until finally you reached the last David Cavendish of all, who was just a small shiny circuit box sellotaped to the top of a large blob of congealed out-of-date butter.

You could hook down from here, as a trespasser, to one of the most attractive and clandestine stretches of the river: a place of plaited lichen and abrupt rocky declivities and deep plunge pools where he and Sally had often swum in spring and summer. One of the advantages of Cavendish's fecklessness was that the fields down on this furthest section of the farm had reverted to meadows and now bled seamlessly into the wilder, beardier terrain beyond that was owned by only the water. Directly there, along this eastern bank of the river, was the route Sally had taken home on a day he'd never forget when he lost her up on the high moor. Half a mile further up the valley was an abandoned cottage, reachable down a steep track on the most resilient off-road vehicle but never boasting its own electricity and unoccupied for over fifty years, although it was said that a rich London banker now owned it and the land around it. It was marked on Bob's Ordnance Survey map as 'Megan's House'. The top branches of an alder tree now poked out of its roof. Every time he walked past it, he remembered Sally talking about the terrible things that had happened to pianos during the middle of the last century, when they were elbowed out of the hallowed place they had traditionally occupied in middle-class homes by televisions; the way people had burned them and nihilistically taken axes to them. All that craftsmanship gone, just like that. It made her want to weep, she said. He forgot now how they'd got onto the subject; maybe it was just because they'd been speculating about when Megan's House was last occupied and had decided it was probably around the time the first TVs started turning up in people's homes. Or maybe it wasn't that at all and was just the usual scattershot flow of conversation when they walked. Often, they'd follow the river all the way up to the bare, blasted moor at the top, and beyond. She was rarely without an observation and for every quirk of nature, every bit of wild growth he noticed, she noticed two more. Her mood seemed to rise with the moor itself. He'd always have a fold-away handsaw in his rucksack, in case he came across an old gate that had been thrown into a hedge. That's what the farmers and the National Park authorities did when they replaced them: left them to rot. He'd find about one a month on average, on their walks, during that period. If he was lucky, he'd find a latch still attached to it and, if he was super lucky, it would be one over a century old, darkened and bruised by the decades.

He decided not to turn right up the valley today, and instead fought his way over and under fallen trees above the river, until he joined the wall on the far boundary of the field, his field. The wall arced around and became part of the old bridge, then continued to arc until it met the house. It was, in effect, a continuation of the house, although it had been here centuries longer. Perhaps the stone of the house looked incongruously smart and new next to the wall at first but now weather and time had done their work on it, the two co-existed happily, like a granddad and great-granddad whose generational divide had been bridged by their longevity. He noticed some clumps of hair trapped in the crevices of the wall, just beyond the bridge; badger, he assumed, or perhaps an intrepid moorland pony who'd wandered down from higher ground. There were a thousand kingdoms in the stone and, in each kingdom, a hundred cities, full of microscopic gardens. Who was to say what was in there was not the world? Who was to say where the world began and ended at all? Why stop at the planet's biosphere? But, also, why go further than the end of the road? Who was to decide where anyone's going concern began and ended? He remembered that period when it was all getting bigger and bigger, directly before the visor implants were approved by the government, when everything had seemed too enormous, too connected. You could talk to precisely as many people as you wanted to about any subject you wanted and because of that there was never nobody not discussing or arguing about anything and there was never not anything to check and everything you did check just gave you more to check. The acceleration had been overwhelming, as if, just when you thought it was already going too fast, technology had hit black ice. It spun, unstoppably. It nibbled away at minds.

The future had arrived and it was not about outer space and fun, as he had been promised in his childhood, and Sally had been promised to a slightly lesser extent in hers; it was about gossip and meanness and the abolition of reasoned discourse. Addiction drove it and corporate greed drove the addiction. Neither Bob nor Sally had even been big users of social media but the space that opened out in their days when they disconnected, after the big changeover, left them gobsmacked. After the impulse to check gradually dissipated, because there *was* nothing to check any more, something else happened that they had not been expecting: they did not just regain their minds, they regained their bodies. They became more aware of their stomachs and hands and feet and sexual organs. They read a hundred pages of a book without moving from the place they sat. Their meals tasted better. Snow felt like snow again when it fell on their faces, like snow had felt when they were twelve. The universe became something you could roll around in the palm of your hand and feel the texture of again.

Sometimes they would go to towns and the city, or even to Underhill, and when they did they often saw people standing outside shops, standing in the road, standing in tram queues, screaming and ranting into their visors. Once such a thing would have been deemed deeply antisocial but everyone was used to it now. Sally and Bob kept their distance, because that was expected of them, as visorless people, and because they desired to. Each time they would think of these strangers 'You are arguing with a person you will never meet about something that will never be resolved and this is your one time on earth' and they would be glad, as hard as it had been, for the decision they'd made. And it *had* been hard: it made facts – facts about tomorrow's weather, or a song they liked, or the date a monarch died – suddenly, frighteningly elusive, until they remembered there was a whole other way to come across facts and it did not make life worse. A dazzling daily sense of hope and possibility seemed to have been blown out like a candle, until they realised what it had always been was a facsimile of hope and possibility, a fast-food version of want that you kept wanting even though you always felt ill afterwards. She'd not lived as long as she should have but he could reassure himself that at least she had not spent the last decade of her life in some suspended attention-deficit simulacrum of existing.

They were both Taureans: him early, her late, just a day from being a Gemini. He never forgot her birthday, even now, but he had forgotten his own again, for the second time in three years. It had been last Friday. He had realised he'd forgotten because the following day while loading the stove he'd found a parcel left under the log store. It was from Sam. Inside was a dark brown latch, with a beautiful weathered curve to its ring. Bob dated it as late 1930s, maybe earlier. 'To Bob,' said the card inside. 'Many gates still left to open! (Found up by the Trembling Hill Mine in January.) Love from Sam and Cami.' In the post, which always arrived in late afternoon nowadays, another package arrived. The postmark on it was Hungarian, which made Bob think it was probably from Martin.

The rain seemed to be holding off so he'd decided to walk down the far end of the combe to thank Sam for the present and to take him a ninety-year-old book he'd found for him featuring a collection of intricate illustrations of moths. Cami, off work from the hospital today, had opened the door and as ever an ache – a complicated ache, with a hole in its centre – had creaked open in him when he saw her smile. She had wished Bob happy birthday for yesterday and said Sam was out, surveying a type of newt that had unexpectedly returned to a lagoon down near Torcross, but that he was welcome to come in for a cup of tea anyway.

He'd thanked her but declined and said he'd stop by again at the weekend. Neither Sam nor Cami had ever been anything less than warm and accommodating to him, almost treating him like a second father at times, but he was also aware how magnetising he found their combined energy and how his loneliness made him more drawn to it. And because of that, when he was around them, or thinking of being around them, it was as if there was a little warden in his head, constantly checking he didn't overstep the mark. His admiration for the way they lived – surviving resolutely visorless in two poorly paid jobs, knowing they would never buy their own house, reading, knitting, planting, making, learning – was so deep, it was important not to be seduced into believing he was part of it.

The rain had begun again on his walk back and, because he had known the patch of sky above him for a quarter of a century now, and the patterns of all its varying moods, instinct told him they were in for a few more of those heavy days when all the moisture came down and hit them at speed, when the river filled up and made its presence so rowdily, overwhelmingly felt that everything else was put to one side and life became a matter of waiting it out until the water decided to calm again. At the second of the humpback bridges, three men in visors and fluorescent jackets had been watching a white van, driven by science, attempt to manoeuvre itself through the narrow gap between the stones. Each had looked like he wanted to offer the van some advice. The taller of the three men – fox-faced, sixtyish – had seemed familiar to Bob but he couldn't quite place him. That was nothing new these days, and the main worry that went with it – that the person would be someone who knew Bob well and would be offended by him not remembering them – was moot, since each of the men had ignored Bob, noticing him less than they would have if he was a minor gust of wind. He'd walked on, past an Edwardian post box in a cottage wall, repurposed as a plant pot. And, as he had, he'd remembered Sally talking about the story she had begun to write one day about an obsolete nineteenth-century post box where somebody posts a letter then gets a letter back from a person in that century, who becomes their penpal. She had got a third of the way through writing the story then abandoned it. She said she always had the ideas and the beginnings but lost interest in finding out how things ended. Her notebooks were a mirror of this, always two thirds blank, even the ones where she wrote down notes and reminders about her tuning jobs.

More and more, he found landscape and the landmarks within it sucking him back into past conversations, ghost feelings, old ambiences. It went beyond that, though. Even without the power of an evocative image as a trigger, he was able to spend whole hours – sometimes longer – swimming in a vanished event or afternoon. Perhaps this made him no more present and mindful than those who wore the visors but at least his mind was his own: nobody was dictating his memories to him and organising them into albums on a screen. Some of Jim's hair he'd found trapped beneath the piano lid while cleaning it a couple of weeks ago – the hair still turned up in the oddest places, even all these months after the dog's death – spun him off into an afternoon from two winters before, when he'd held Jim on his lap and gently cut knots of matted fur from his stomach, as Jim had lain there with a trusting look that broke his heart as it happened and rebroke it now as it rehappened. Maybe he misremembered much of what he lived through – timescales, sequences, the maths of it – but as he dipped into it via memory the feelings were refelt just as strongly, if not stronger.

He opened Martin's package, which turned out to be an album he had put out via his new label over in Hungary. 'I finally, fucking FINALLY, got this together!' said the note. 'Miss you, you hairy bastard. M. x' The record was called *Penny Marshwort: The Songs of RJ McKendree*. Martin had been obsessed for years with the work of McKendree, an American singer songwriter who'd blown across the edge of the moor in the late sixties and written a set of haunting folk songs that were coated in the place and the time but also in something otherworldly, something a little like shattered glass, something you couldn't quite piece together in your mind as you heard it. Martin, in a dogged fuck-the-naysayers Martin way, had been hugely instrumental in getting the late McKendree's work to a wider audience, even half-written a book on him many years ago, and now, with the singer's cult following growing, he'd managed to assemble an impressive group of neo-psychedelic songwriters and sensitive troubadours to pay tribute to his work. Amongst the covers of McKendree's songs was even a version of the title track by the reclusive former pop sensation Taylor Swift, released under the pseudonym 'Maddie Chagford'. Bob noticed that Martin's musician partner Reka was featured on the record too and wondered if that might turn out to be a bit of jarring nepotism on the part of Martin, but her rendition of 'Little Meg' – a traditional local folk song already made unrecognisable in McKendree's reworking of it, very different to the version Bob had heard Sally sing a couple of times – was utterly fantastic, and like nothing Bob had heard before: a half-chanted incantation that somehow managed to be simultaneously a brooding funk workout and sound like somebody inventing electricity in a moonlit recess in some rocks above a beach. Over the dirty dishes in the sink, as the record played, the identity of the fox-faced man on the bridge came to Bob. It had been Jac, his neighbour from the long house, all that time ago. But the fact meant little to Bob and he was mostly elsewhere in his mind. Something – he wasn't sure precisely what – had taken him back to a night in the summer of 1999, maybe a year or so before Martin had introduced him to McKendree's music. A club in Covent Garden, mostly full of tourists. Seventies-disco-themed. Martin, lit by booze and the city, trying to convince two Portuguese women that Bob had acted in porn. Bob, playing along, but wincing inside, feeling, at thirty, too old for it all, on the cusp of a form of cultural retirement. He'd lost his jumper – his favourite – at the end of the night. Forty-four years ago. The same gap separating his birth from the year Mussolini put Italy under a dictatorship. But from here, right now... an almost touchable time. Felt like the end of something, palpably. A deadened and toxic sensation in his oesophagus on the walk to the train station afterwards. A new resolve building out of that deadness. A Chinese restaurant. A wasted meal. Hard to eat when you're that particular kind of drunk. Martin had an extra job, as well as the writing, talent scouting for a record label. That was it: they'd been to see a band he'd been tipped off about. 'Rucksack full of wank,' he'd said, turning to Bob after three songs. 'The tedium compels me to go somewhere and dance.' 'Dance' being Martin's euphemism for fuck, but not always. Sometimes it meant fight, too. Always up for an argument with a stranger, Martin. A couple of times, chasing a woman, vanishing in the process, he'd left Bob stranded. Nowhere to stay. Five-hour gap until the morning train. Hash browns and a quarter kip on a cold metal bench. Bob forgave him. Always. Then one other night. A bit later. Martin on cocaine, wolf-eyed. Ripped Bob's favourite shirt off after finding out he was moving far away, to Devon. Bob forgave him less for that. But still forgave him.

In the forty-eight minutes the record had lasted, the river had redoubled its cry. The pounding bass of the rain was no match for it. The ambience was all treble. It was being retuned by cloudfall. Bob took Martin's note and put it in a drawer in his sideboard. Also in the drawer was the latch from Sam, a couple of other old notes and letters from friends, two eleven-year-old parking fines,

Sally's papps wedge, some pebbles and a sealed envelope with 'IN THE EVENT OF MY DEATH' written on it, containing a letter instructing the house and all the possessions within it to be given to Sam and Cami. He found a browning floret of broccoli behind the kettle and tossed it into the river, which devoured it. Wavelets lashed at the bridge then sprinted under the balcony. The water had been higher than this but rarely faster, and he could hear the granite grinding. Fleur had once said that it was a good job the boulders were under water because with the force that they rubbed against each other they could probably start a fire.

In late August the new dwellings began to go up: A-frames, oak. The chainsaws took down Edna's tree in minutes, making a mockery of all the years of its slow bittersweet decline. He'd been ready, having seen the sign on the lane at the top of the hill a few weeks earlier. 'BLACK DOG PARK: A Moorland Experience' the sign announced. Three acres of gorse bushes, tussocks, ferns, brambles – a bona fide galaxy of habitats for tiny creatures – were smoothed to a neat, levelled-off brownness. Men in hard hats with visors beneath the hard hats made offerings to the river of sandwich wrappers, drink cartons and urine. Jac sometimes milled amongst them, clipboarded, vulpine, pointy of face and hand. Bob considered taking him some of the manure he'd requested by text, with an apology that it was twenty-four years late. Maybe a couple of thousand tonnes of it. One evening at dusk after the men had all gone home, an actual fox, as if deeply offended to be so poorly imitated and misunderstood, wandered over, backed up and sprayed one of the half-completed lodges, and left. Fewer blue tits and dunnocks landed on Bob's feeders now. The pair of merganser ducks he'd been encouraging onto the balcony for most of the year had vanished. Bob looked at the solicitor's number he had written down in spring and did not use his still-functioning landline to call the solicitor's number he had written down in spring. He merely decided to further reduce what he had decided his world was. It now ended at the river's midpoint. Nothing else was his concern. There was enough to take care of here on the other side, anyway. He was still finding a lot of hair in the house. He began to wonder if after all some of it was his, not the dog's. He threw the hair in the river and the river made it vanish. The water level had been higher than usual for most of the summer and, because it was always higher in winter, he looked at the bridge and wondered if this winter would be the one when it finally happened.

On the occasions when they'd climbed the valley to the high moor, on the opposite bank, on the unofficial path, they'd learned a lot about all the secret places where the water gathered its voices and power. It was a long, vertiginous, weaving stretch of ground: almost three miles to the very top. All the way, the moss got thicker, the dripping sounds heavier. Often, by the time you reached the top and emerged from the woodland, you were on a murky cloud planet. Black shapes hovered in front of you, not making their identity known until the last moment. Ponies, sheep, gorse, rheumatic witchering half-trees that had been brought to the edge of death by weather, again and again, without being quite taken over the line. Vegetation up here got flayed by the bronchial output of the sky and only the strongest and wiriest of it survived. In the woodland, before they reached the top, the pair of them stroked the moss. It felt and smelt cleaner than any carpet. Sally said the tree trunks looked like they were wearing welly socks. He suggested that maybe this was why her hair grew so fast and big: it benefited from all this rain, like the moss. He was joking but maybe there was some truth in it. His own hadn't bounced back big and fierce like hers but its escape from his scalp had lost momentum since he moved here. They came back to the house with their clothes stuck to their bodies, their skin dripping, with many of the folds and creases they'd seen in

the mirror first thing in the morning ironed out. But on the day
he lost her up there it wasn't that kind of day. It was a frostier,
stiller day – rare here – when the river was low and the moisture
in the air was motionless. They decided to walk all the way up
past the reservoir to Trembling Hill, to the abandoned silver and
lead mine. By the time they got there the mist had fallen down,
sweeping across the mine's deep black eye holes like a huge net
curtain made heavy by years of cigarette smoke. They decided
it was not wise to venture further and retraced their steps, past
a pre-Bronze Age kistvaen that had been uncovered during the
early part of the last century. Ancient trinkets and fancy evening
wear buried deep in the peat. Visibility was reduced to almost
nothing which meant he couldn't see the bit of the hill which
always reminded him of a vast mouth that had had its teeth
knocked out with a hammer, but he estimated that's where they
were. The land began to tilt and the river, very faintly audible in
the distance, was in the opposite direction to the one it should
have been. His uncertainty made him press on more briskly, in an
attempt to make the world make sense again, and it was his haste
that caused him to lose her, although he didn't realise it for –
what? – seven minutes, eight. He called out behind him into the
mist, or was it really mist at all, no, and not fog either, but that
other thing, quick and speckled and particular to the moor, that
could not quite be categorised as either. Fist? Mog? Mog. The
dreaded mog. The mog ate sound, swallowed it without needing
to chew. Hearing no reply to his calls, the central worry of the
last half an hour of his existence – that he had been upended into
a visionless ghost universe with no way out by mythical beings –
was entirely usurped by his guilt of what he had done in bringing
her here. She'd not felt well that morning; the rash she often got
across her face from the lupus had been worse than it had been
for a while. He'd pushed her too hard. They should have gone the

other way, over the back and up the lane and up the old sunken track – people said it was more sunken because of the medieval packhorses that pressed the earth down deeper and deeper – to look at a latch over there that Sam had told him about that had been made from two old horseshoes. It was the first time since the visors came in that he'd really ached for his old smartphone. Even though there'd never been a whiff of reception up here, he'd still ached for it.

She was only gone for two hours but it was the longest two hours he had lived since he was a child. Two hours of terror and weighing outcomes and decisions and possibilities. Two hours containing a novel's worth of small anxieties. He called and called for her then he listened hard for the river and found it and, even though it was not in the place it should have been, he followed it, tumbling and bumping back down the wild mossy valley as if pulled on a rope. Halfway down, he tripped on a tree root and landed on a gnarly outlying branch whose deep bloodwork on his left calf he would not notice until hours later. He could see only one thing and that was the telephone on the small table in the living room, and even though he couldn't factually see it, could see it only in his mind, he stared at nothing else until he had it in his hand. It was after he'd reached it, and called the moorland rescue team, and the police, and turned himself inside out wondering what else he could do, wondering if he should have stayed up top looking for her after all, that, in desperation, not in hope but in the pure inability to stay still, he began to march back up the valley and saw her walking towards him. Her hair glistened with crusts of frost and she looked dejected and sapped but she greeted him calmly. She told him she'd done just the same thing he had: listened to the river, then followed it. But why had it taken so much longer for her to get back? And was she OK? She said she was fine, it was fine, it had all been very simple.

She was here, and she was going to come into the house and lie down, and everything was going to be fine.

You didn't live on the moor and not know the stories about hikers being piskie-led on the high ground, disorientated in the sparkly mists, spun around, locked in place, tricked into thinking a place was another place. Tiny high-pitched laughter had been heard to ring out from deep in the cloud. Its melodies moved in circles, through the moisture. The little people – pixies, they were more modernly called, but he preferred piskies, the pre-twentieth-century version – came out from their hiding places and led you astray and the only way to reverse the spell was to turn out your pockets; he knew the drill so well but he'd forgotten and hadn't done it. It was just weather, nothing more, and the only reason it felt like dark magic was that weather itself was a form of dark magic, but he would never quite forget the stoned, tilted feeling he had up there that day, as if the landscape had spiked his drink. He knew it was just coincidence, that her health had been getting worse anyway for a long time, but it was after that day that the different period began for them. She had told him she loved him for the last time. She was withdrawn, more still, but not in a peaceful way. Her one remaining exuberance seemed to come out solely in the way she cleaned her body behind closed doors. It was as if the larger part of who she was had been cancelled. She worked less, which she'd said she'd wanted to do for a long time, but in the spaces that this opened up she didn't do any of the things she'd told him she would. One day he found her on the balcony with his craft knife, hacking into her hair, letting loose strands of it blow into the water below her. Next to her on the planks he saw singed grey tresses, candle wax. It was the first in a series of clandestine burnings, more often than not featuring small household objects, which culminated, a few months later, in him clearing out the fireplace one morning and finding the iron remnants of one of his sculptures in the cooling ashes.

'I am sorry, Bob,' she had said. She stared directly ahead into the ash and there was no meanness in her voice. 'But I didn't like that one.'

And then she got really ill, and was admitted to hospital. And he felt terrible that she was gone, and then he felt additionally terrible on top of that that he felt some relief about being able to be in the house without wondering where she was and where her mind was drifting to and what the next thing would be that she would set fire to. After the end, people talked to him like she'd been snatched from him but, although he never verbalised it, what he felt was that she'd been snatched from him a long time before that. Which was another thing that made that final instruction – that last burst of clarity and passion, when he almost saw who she used to be for a moment – so startling.

There had been a lull between the wooden posts first going in and the lodges beginning to go up, but now the construction work had begun, it was happening quickly. Within a fortnight, eight A-frames were up. Within a month, twenty. The foam on the edges of the river became different, tinged with pinks and blues. He did not see David Cavendish on the building site and did not expect to. Cavendish had not been interested in the field as a physical entity before and would probably be no more interested now, with the exception of the financial side of affairs relating to it. Bob wondered about his motivation, what could possibly come of this investment that would make the ultraworld the rich quasi-agriculturist lived inside more pleasurable and decadent. The pursuit of money for such people, past a certain point, seemed to be most of all a strident denial of mortality, and the more they were able to abrogate the nitty gritty of life via technology, the more emphatic that denial became. They used their wealth to protect themselves with bigger cars, to build more secure fences and walls to protect their three-dimensional living spaces, to build a digital wall around themselves to protect them from other parts of life. Finally, they seemed to want to use it to protect themselves against the banality of death, as if the cushion of power they had gained would secure a deluxe executive afterlife for them. But despite all science had achieved, and for all the money many had put into researching the idea, nobody had yet discovered how to live forever. In the end, the dust that would be David Cavendish would be no more exclusive or elite than the dust that had been Sally, the dust he had scattered on the hillside facing him two years ago. Dust that had immediately been washed into the river by the combe's heavy rains and, if some of it had remained on the grass and was now beneath the lodges, had surely now sunk deep into the earth.

The changes in building regulations and planning permission introduced by the government in the second and third decades of the century had been devastating for natural habitats on the edge of the moor. Underhill – and, to an extent, its surrounding hamlets – had expanded rapidly, but a lull followed: nobody had built anything new around here for several years. This perhaps made people in the valley a little complacent, slower to realise what was happening with the lodges and the impact they might have. Martina Whittaker had been over to tell him there was a residents' committee meeting scheduled to protest the development, to see if anything at all could be done at this late stage. He knew, because Sam had been over to invite him to the same meeting a day earlier. Bob said he would be there but when the night of the meeting arrived he found himself instead not at the meeting but on the balcony, a glass of whiskey in hand, watching the river. It was so full all the time now but tonight it was not angry. Its sound was more like the hushed chatter you get in an auditorium where people are waiting for an important announcement. Because the water level was now higher, more moss had begun to grow up the walls of the house, grey-green wiry wavy stuff. Autumn was happening and autumn never stayed long so you could more or less say it was winter and on winter's darkest days the combe let in so little light, it was like living down deep in the gap between two sofa cushions. Days soon became all beginning and end, a couple of bookends you convinced yourself was life. The sun found it difficult to get down in the gap between the cushions and kill the frost there. To maximise the last of the daylight before it all happened, he opened windows and doors all over the house. The through-draught stirred up more hair. There was ever such a lot. It showed him that maybe he hadn't really cleaned properly when he thought he had. Such a hairy place, the deep south west of the country. He thought of a film director, the only one he ever interviewed in his time writing for the magazine. Lived on a corner plot of land, a jutting elbow of salt soil, like a smaller replica of the far east elbow of the country where it was situated. Bald man. Immaculate house. No hair in it anywhere. But here, by contrast, you got hair on your walls, hair in your piano. One night in November there was a storm and Bob closed the windows. A long, sharp piece of concrete render fell from the roof, smashing outside the front door. If he'd been standing there, that would have been it for him, but he wasn't. The A-frames withstood the storm. Martina Navratilova – the lady who'd invited him to the meeting; he thought that was her surname but couldn't remember for sure – saw him when he was down the lane, looking for kindling. Her granddad had once punched a bull who charged at him. That's what Sally, who'd heard the story from Fleur, had once told him. Martina Navratilova said they'd all been disappointed not to see him at the meeting last week. Whittaker! That was it. Not Navratilova. That was someone else. He opened the gate leading to the field. He didn't like the latch on it: it was one of the ones with a coil, not yet bestowed with character by time. The wood made a nice sound but not the metal. He could see the highest of the lodges poking out over the hillside. It wasn't the most ugly set of buildings. You could convince yourself it was all quite rustic and pleasant if you blocked out all the beetles and dormice it had slaughtered. It was quiet now, no drills or hammers or diggers for several days. Some men in hard hats still wandered about with clipboards, not doing much. As, back at home, he pissed into the toilet with the blind up on the window facing the river, he saw one of the men looking straight at him from across the water. It might have been Jac but it was hard to tell due to the condensation on the glass. The man continued to stare and Bob continued to piss and then the man turned away and right then Bob knew Bob had won.

She used to say she wanted to run away.

'But you are away,' he'd say. 'Look where we live. We couldn't be much more away. Maybe if we lived in northern Canada or Finland or something, but not here.'

'Yes, I know, so why does it feel like that?'

There'd been a man, a customer, some bloody weirdo, who wouldn't leave her alone, kept wanting his piano tuned over and over again when the thing was totally fine, could not have sounded better, then when she told him she couldn't work for him any more, he contacted her via a fake identity on social media, tried to book her services again. It wasn't quite frightening enough to go to the police about but it had scared her. But it wasn't even that. It was a prevalent feeling at that particular time: a feeling that it was all in your face, everyone, everything, all the time, on your screens. They both had dreams about total strangers filing into their house, telling them what was wrong with the way they lived. It wasn't his fault and it wasn't hers; it wasn't most people's fault. People's brains – everyone's – were still pre-industrial village brains, brains built for the nineteenth century, and the eighteenth century, and a lot of the centuries prior to that, and could not be expected to cope with this overflowing rush of world, this full spate river of statement and opinion. But then after that they had felt like they *had* finally run away, for eight years, and maybe even for the two different years that came after. She, he knew, had felt more like she was in a place. And that made him more confident that sprinkling her remains over the thing – he forgot what it was called now, but it was green, and directly across the river from the house – was the right course of action. It had been a good time, that period. But he could not say if it was her best time. He could not even say if it was his best time, even though he told himself it was. A lot of it was guesswork, how you remembered your own life. He could not feel his body and mind as it had been on a day on a Tuesday afternoon in 1998 or a Thursday morning in 1982 or a Saturday evening in 2006. But sometimes when he went away from the present and swam about in snapshots of memory, he got close to it. Music helped. She told him about that once: how melodies worked, stimulating neuro-pathways that other things couldn't. In the orchestra she was in, they played old songs for people who had the illness. The big disease with the little name. No, that was a line from a song about something different. The little disease with the big name. No, not a little disease. A horrible thing, anyway, and music somehow penetrated it, took them back to something, revived something.

He wanted to play the piano. It shouldn't just sit there, gathering hair. The desire had come over him out of nowhere. Would it be too late to learn? Why had he never asked her to teach him? Was that neglectful of him? Could he have taken more of an interest? At least found out how it all worked? He opened the lid and wiped the hair off a couple of the keys and pulled some more out of the gap between them and hit the keys experimentally. He noticed starlings, more of a plume than a murmuration, out the window and as he did he felt this had all happened before: the opening of the piano, the slight cough caught in his throat, the birds, the bottle of Baby Bio on the window ledge. It was a kind of déjà vu he experienced now, but different to what déjà vu used to be. It always felt like he was experiencing the reality of a dream he'd dreamed and that he also knew what happened next but couldn't touch it. It was as vivid as when he got sucked into the past but it was different: it sucked him into the present, as imagined from the past. The moment always felt weighted equally with significance and banality until he lost it, like a small precious object dropped in a toilet bowl just as you'd pulled the chain.

The last person who'd played the piano had not been Sally but Fleur, not long before she died. In her seventies, she'd taken a younger lover – a town councillor of just forty-eight – and it had been the talk of the combe. Bob, now at a similar age, would do nothing of the sort. Firstly, how would that even happen? And secondly, it had not occurred to him as an ambition. He had met Fleur's younger man just once, a reedy human with a nervous chuckle who, even though he was of a roughly equal width and height to Fleur, gave the slight impression of living inside her coat. The encounter had been on the lane, around this time of year, and Fleur had talked about how late the bats were staying around now, and how much it worried her. Now they stayed around even later. December, sometimes. 'GO HOME, bats,' Fleur had said, to the bats.

Bob had never put a blind or curtain over the large skylight Fleur had installed in the bedroom, since it would have been too tricky, and waking up with the dawn light had never been much of a problem for him. But it could be confusing, on nights when the sky was clear and the moon was at its fullest. It could make you as confused as a bat who should be hibernating. Waking up to the bright white light, he had been known to head to the kitchen and put the kettle on, only to then look at the clock on the dining-room wall and realise it was somewhere around 2 a.m. So when he woke again tonight, with the moon full and the bedroom flooded with light, it was not initially perturbing to him. Two subsequent factors made him realise there was something extra at play: the glow was much more orange than usual, and the room was warm. Before he stepped out onto the balcony, before he'd even seen the deeper orange light, its spinning shapes, through the pane of the kitchen door, he knew what was happening, and with that came the knowledge that he'd always known it would happen, forever.

The fire was well under way, past the point of reversal or rescue. Five of the lower lodges had been brought to the ground and the flames were licking their way up the valley, deep into the bowels of the dwellings on the terraces above. The pure rage of it reminded him of the river when it was at its most unstoppable. It was not something that could be reasoned with. But standing on the balcony he did not worry for a second about it reaching him, or even about the smoke troubling his lungs. The river was at a brimming, tumultuous height – a height that defied the logic of the last few days' rain – and provided a protective barrier, a barrier even more inarguable than the conflagration. It splashed up high and wild against the walls of the house, splashed against him too. He realised, belatedly, that he was naked, but he was not afraid. He decided he could happily, very happily, let it take him: the river, the trees beyond, the valley, the moor, everything. He would be more than OK with that. He realised he was singing but he had no idea what the song was, only that he knew it. He grabbed his whiskey bottle from the kitchen sink and drank from it. The air smelled good and rich, like something being turned over and exposed, and he thought for a moment he could hear a siren in the distance, but then thought maybe he had imagined it, and he wasn't able to tell because his singing was so loud, and the river was loud too, and he had no wish for either to stop. On the right-hand side of the valley, where one of the higher A-frames – one of the taller, more high-specification lodges, which was to be rented at a greater price to the ones nearer the river – had fallen, the fire had also opened up a gap in the trees, but had not reached beyond that to the bigger trees where the valley began to get mossier, which would reject the advances of the fire with their immense moisture. The gap and all the light from the moon and the fire allowed him to see one particularly memorable, wide-armed oak and he thought about the time he had walked past it with Sally, which had been the same afternoon they'd walked past the abandoned house and she'd talked about people destroying the pianos in the fifties and sixties: thousands of them, kicked and smashed to fuck or set alight. It had actually been on this same walk that she'd told him about Martina Whittaker – yes, he had her surname now, and would not let it slip away – and her grandfather, who had punched the bull in the face when it charged him. There had been an old faded 'BULL IN FIELD' sign still up there at that point, which must have triggered the story. He recalled now also that he'd somehow got the details twisted: it was Martina's great-grandfather who had punched the bull in the face, not her grandfather. Standing there naked, illuminated by the flames, staring at the tree, he remembered everything Sally had told him; he did not forget a thing.

ME (NOW)

The village of Wychcombe is recorded as 'a manor call Wickcoomb' in the Domesday survey of 1086. By the thirteenth century, the parish could boast two churches: St Constantine's, situated precariously and impractically on a granite escarpment 730 feet above the main street and now no more than two ruined walls, and the still-standing St John's. By the 1500s, Wickcoomb had split into two settlements: Wychcombe and Underhill. After this point, Underhill expanded and Wychcombe stayed more or less the same size, coming to resemble, from above, a densely wooded forked tail attached to the posterior of the larger settlement. The 1921 census recorded the population of Underhill as 666, causing much merriment in the four alehouses the village then possessed, although by the census of 1961 that figure had dropped by 98: a reduction often assumed to be down to the human cost of the fight against Hitler but in fact down to the progress of agricultural machinery and the subsequent decrease in rural employment opportunities, resulting in an exodus of residents to urban areas. Many in the village would come to remember the war as the most fulfilling period of their lives. Most of the wealthier households by this point had a wireless, which had invariably been sold to them and repaired by a Mr Henry Salter of Plymouth, a small man who rarely paused for breath while imbibing liquor and telling his many embellished stories of life on the road and who, on his trips over to charge people's wet batteries, would often stay on for a few days and organise sing-arounds amongst his drinking companions. Always matriarchal, the village in this period became even more so. Social gatherings were organised by Land Army girls who had taken occupation of the outlying farms and Wychcombe Manor. The manor had until late in the previous century been the ancestral home of the Bambury family, who during the late 1700s kept fourteen parrots and England's last house jester: a man of barely four feet three inches in height whose routines included chewing the feathers off live sparrows to see if they would still fly (they didn't). These days the mainline train barrels over the viaduct past the luxury flats the manor has now been converted into, as passengers strive to stifle their irritation at the sound of one another's antisocial mastication and shrill offspring. Sometimes, a fox, hare or a deer will be visible from a window, but it is a rare commuter who will notice, since most are too deep inside the more compelling universe inside the screens they take with them everywhere. Few look up to admire the abandoned but still very attractive Wychcombe Junction station where some of those very foxes who run alongside the train have been known to sleep and breed.

The passenger railway arrived here in 1847, although it was predated by almost two decades by another, which took granite across my flanks, down to the coast, where it was shipped off and used to make bridges and walls. Before it fell under the infamous axe of British Railways chairman Dr Beeching in the 1960s, Wychcombe Junction – and its now defunct adjoining branch line – brought many a carless traveller to the moor. The station might also be considered partially responsible for an openness to outsiders not common to all villages in the area. Many who have visited Underhill have remarked upon a feeling of being 'protected' or 'watched over in a kind way'. It is thought that this can largely be put down to the presence of Underhill Tor, towering over the village at 1,350 feet, from whose summit it is said, on a clear day, both coasts of the south-west peninsula can be seen. Home to an acclaimed golf course and once believed to be the site of volcanic activity, the tor is not subject to the hype of some of the other more talked-about hills of the south west but is every bit the match for any of them in terms of history and natural beauty, and outdoes most of them in terms of height and girth, making, for example Glastonbury Tor, at just 518 feet, look kind of weedy by comparison. The tor is distinguished by the pile of rocks at its peak which have been variously likened to 'a step stool' (not totally inaccurate), 'a bumpy kind of nose' (maybe), 'some piled pony poo' (way off), and 'a small mystic staircase' (yes!). On its rear slopes is found some of the most beautiful ancient woodland in the country, hosting an abundance of wildlife, including roe deer, marsh fritillary butterflies, woodcock, bog asphodel, ring ouzel, cuckoo and kingfisher.

Look at me. I have fallen into my old trap of talking about myself again, haven't I?

You are all very fast nowadays. Nearly all of you, anyway (I strive to steer away from generalisation). I wonder where you believe you are going with it. It's an illusion, of course, most of the time: speed, and the efficiency and ease it promises. A new superfast train corridor smashes through ancient woodland, fucks over a couple of Elizabethan farmhouses, rapes and pillages the homesteads of hares, otters, stoats and badgers, but it's OK because Stewart will be home from the office a whole half an hour sooner, and be able to use the time to play computer games in his living room, rather than on the go. Your connections and your engines get slicker yet you feel more rushed, more pushed, and the days evaporate like never before. You fly at warp speed towards your destination, thirsty for it, never stopping to consider that destination is another word for death. You do not factor in what is missed until it is too late. The default position is that progress is pace. But when will this state of nirvana that it's all leading to occur, where each person will operate at peak speed and be perfectly happy and undelayed and no longer have to walk or use their mind? And will it all be worth it? Away from technology's grand illusion, everything moves at the same speed as ever. A grand old beech, poorly for some time, was felled on my shin yesterday. The 211 rings on its trunk tell the truth. Run your finger along them. They're smooth, consistent, redoubtable. The space between them didn't change just because somebody invented the microchip or the fax or the microwave oven.

It would be so much easier if there was one individual to blame for it, rather than collective human greed and self-delusion, if we could, say, pin it on Bill Gates or Steve Jobs or Dr Beeching or Tim Berners-Lee, but we are not in a superhero film, where a supervillain is mandatory; we are in the world, where supervillains are amorphous entities made of money and nepotism and spin and many many grasping hands. I will say this, though: Beeching trod on my toes once, during his brief destructive reign as British Railways chairman, and he was the smuggest of gits while he did it. He didn't even take the time to learn to pronounce Wychcombe properly before mooching around the station with his clipboard, condemning it – gave it the long 'y' at the beginning, like some nobhead. 'WHYchcoombe Junction, you say, over in Devon? Hmmrph. I suppose that is feasible, provided I am back in East Grinstead by supper.' Afterwards he submitted his findings to his boss, Ernest Marples, the Minister for Transport, who, it should be noted, was married to Baroness Ruth Alianore, a tarmac heiress who held a stake in the M1 and other new major roads. I rued a lost opportunity, so when Beeching returned eight years later, to officiate at the opening of a new heritage steam railway in the area (the chutzpah of the man!), I was ready. It was a windy day and the sharp, heavy tiles I succeeded in dislodging from the roof of the station as he walked past came within eight inches of doing their job, but ultimately – being six miles from here – it was outside my range.

No, I am not able to control weather. You could say I just have a stake in it, like Baroness Alianore and her early motorways.

Unlike a tree, I don't have rings, and they don't grow. I flourish, then I die back, then I flourish. The circle is not unbroken – at least not unless somebody builds a high-speed rail link through my core. But my contours do change. I have one more buttock than I once had. Over on my left knee, where St John's churchyard can be found, I'm lumpier than I once was. People look at the couple of hundred gravestones and they think that's it, that's history. They don't consider the others beneath the earth, all the centuries before that, all the bones piling up, changing the shape of the land. All the forgotten lives that felt like something more than this, something that mattered, when they were being lived. There was a period of about forty years, going from the last century, stretching into the very early part of this one, when the cemetery was kept very neat, over-mowed and over-strimmed. The shrieking of the beetles and butterflies as they died was a kind of tinnitus for me. Now mercifully the volunteers responsible for its upkeep lean towards a wilder aesthetic. The fact presents itself in stark beauty: wildflowers love dead people. On an early spring day like today, primroses, celandine and forget-me-nots are rife. It's a cheery technicolour place with a light mood but on an ink-washed afternoon in the darkest, wettest heights of winter walkers feel a shiver as they explore its corners. If the beheaded statue of John Maypoll, a six-year-old child who died of polio in 1913, or the three mysteriously nameless graves inscribed with nothing but 'Cholera, 1847' don't do it then the carvings inside the building itself generally will.

The oldest and crudest of these dates from the 1100s. Most frequently discussed is the Sheela-na-gig on the north wall, and what is variously referred to as 'The Bird Lady' and 'The Girls' on the font. These are described thus in the second issue of *Jack In The Green*, the pagan-inclined Devonshire history pamphlet, by the pamphlet's editor Simon Bridestow in May 1993:

'For me this is the most haunting of all the West Country's na-gigs, owing largely to the vastness of the exposed vulva and the angle at which the head is set back from the body, being redolent of both decapitation and extreme ecstasy. Such suggestion of ecstasy seems to support the argument that the na-gigs that appeared throughout Europe were not so much a warning against sin as a celebration of the power of the feminine. Not totally dissimilar in theme, and possibly carved at a very similar time, is the once-seen-never-forgotten Bird Lady carving on the font, in which a male figure adopts a supplicatory position below a female possessing some sort of club or staff and a wreath of hair, overlooked by birds and very similar apparent duplicates of herself. These duplicates have been called "sisters" and "ghosts". In 1988 while walking the north moor I met an old man called Graham who'd grown up in Underhill and told me that as a small child he'd heard the woman/ women on the font referred to as both "Sally Free and Easy" and "Old Meg" but had never known why.'

Other articles in the May 1993 issue of *Jack In The Green* include Jackie Tinsdale on Devon river sprites, Alan Bradford on the argument that some of the old carvings on the stones in the Trembling Hill stone circle are actually breasts, and Bangy Doddsworth's account of the time he was disorientated by piskies in the mist up on Combe Moor. Adverts included steer the attention of readers to a forthcoming gig by the partially reunited John McCandle's Dirt Band in Underhill village hall, the Whiddon Tracey Good Food Market and a family (in fact,

Simon Bridestow's) seeking accommodation on the high moor. Though barely remembered now, the magazine sold out of its 800-copy print run and was given pride of place in the post office by Jim Swardesley's predecessor, Jeff Bryant. When he took over, Swardesley continued the tradition of selling the work of local authors and, to this day, along with various walking guides, a visitor can, should they wish, while paying for their stamps, purchase such works as *Lunar Freedom*, the new collection by Kathy McGregor, better known as The Nude Poet. The cover features a tasteful shot of McGregor from behind, unclothed, sitting in the centre of the Trembling Hill stone circle, watching the sun rise over my head.

Looking down towards the post office now, I can see there is quite a queue outside. Swardesley, as ever, handles it coolly, cracking jokes, enquiring about the health of spouses and children and grandchildren and grandparents and parents, showing an uncanny recall for first names. 'SIT!' a woman yells at a Japanese Akita outside the door, sending a tremor through the waiting line. 'I think the whole village just sat down,' Swardesley wisecracks to Ruth Cole, who is waiting for a receipt for some handmade notebooks she just sent to Greece. Next up is Pat Gutteridge, who is here to collect her pension. Swardesley doesn't try her with a joke, as he knows from experience she's not one to stop for a chat. After this, in the stonewash jeans she is known for, she will purchase the two items she always purchases during her weekly shop, some vodka for herself and some sausages for the crows in her garden, plus some other provisions. She lives four miles from the village and always walks home, usually via Combe Woods. Last night a tree came down, entirely blocking the footpath, but today on both journeys she climbs the adjacent bank and vaults the trunk, in a manner reminiscent of a lanky nineteen-year-old boy. Next week, she will be seventy-one, an occasion she will celebrate alone by baking herself some cream cheese pound cake and watching a VHS of the film *The Full Monty*. People look at Pat and what they see is loneliness, countryness, a bony facade the world can't get past. But in her youth Pat engaged for several years in what those same people might describe as living. She resided in London, danced on tables, took cherubic musician boys home with her and told them what to do. Nobody would ever know now, apart from herself, but in a documentary about the touring life of the folk supergroup Equinox, she can be seen in a post-gig gathering in a hotel room, smoking and laughing, exuding Gaelic beatnik chic with her sharp cheekbones, black turtleneck and fringe. For an eighteen-month period, but no longer than that, people sometimes mistook her for the folk singer Anne Briggs. To her left in the hotel room sits the singer Donovan Leitch, whose advances, earlier in the night, Pat had batted away.

But Pat was quick-tempered in her youth, never one to stuff an opinion with feathers. Her fallouts were large, and often cataclysmic. When she lost a daughter to cancer and a partner to suicide, she – being an orphan – did not have a family to look to for support, and the friends she turned to instead let her down. The aggregate result of this, several years on, was her decision that the people she could truly rely on were crows. Crows, who never vanished during hard times, or stopped speaking to you when you gave them some unfiltered advice about their career. Crows, who would land on her arms and shoulders in the pub garden, always her arms and shoulders, never anyone else's. Crows, who ate every last bit of her sausages and never complained. They gathered around her waiting for worms as she turned the soil in her garden, which wasn't officially her garden, just a thirty square foot patch of ground between her back door and the dry stone wall where the moor in its harshest form began and which hadn't been claimed by anyone else and which some bastard could now prise from her cold dead hands if they wanted to take it away from her. People looked at her and thought, 'That's the kind of person who never cries.' But it wasn't true. Back in September of 2008, when she'd seen a crow nailed to a fence post outside the Cavendish farm, she bawled, sporadically, for most of the following day.

One day, when Pat was with her crows, turning the soil for her and for them, she found an axe. It's still only her and the crows who know about it, to this day. It's a quite remarkable axe, a little over ten inches long, apparently unused, and dating from 700 BC, although it might seem a little less remarkable if you knew just how many axes of a similar vintage were still buried on the moor. There are even a couple in the river around a mile further up the valley from Pat's, not far from the empty building the map calls Megan's House. I doubt they'll be found any time soon, as it's not a bit of the river people often have cause to get into. The ravine is too narrow and you couldn't get a boat down there. I could tell you properly about what is still buried here, down under the rivers, in the peat, in the soil beneath the reservoirs beneath the old farmland that they drowned to build them, and it would blow your mind into a million tiny pieces, which you'd never find again, and then those pieces would also sink into the earth, forever. So much is buried, so far down, and we live – even the more archaeologically inclined amongst us – only on the top one or two layers. Just as you can't any longer get to what Pat once was because it's buried under what Pat has become, with only the odd shard or two coming to the surface, you can't really reach the past of here, the past of me, and what I am made up of. But that does not mean it is not still there.

My thoughts didn't always take this form. I could have told you plenty of things but the language I spoke in was not the one I speak in now. 'Nope, sorry,' you would have said. 'That's just a noise.' But then the noise would have stayed with you, shaken you, loosened your bowels. You would have found great difficulty in not thinking about it, especially in the capacious hours just before dawn. But even then the noise was relatively comprehensible and well mannered by comparison to what it had been. Once, much further back, the noise came with fire and lava. Did it? I feel like I know it did, but it was so long ago, so all I can do is trust in the innateness of that feeling. And then the inevitable question follows: How did I go from that to this? How did I become so sapped, so self-conscious? How did I get this tediously well behaved?

It's your fault. You're seeping into me, in all your ways. You've been doing it for millennia, but you do it much more than ever now.

You keep photographing me. Why? Is it because you're worried you'll miss me when we are not together? I don't recall when the very first photo happened but the oldest known that remains intact can currently be found at the Devon Heritage Centre, at Chidleigh Babbots. It was taken in 1886 by Cecil Boyland, who, as a well-off rector, became the first resident in the village to own a camera. I am not the focal point of the image. That honour goes to the peat-cutting brothers Jude and Peter Mortimer, who can be seen outside their one-storey cottage, leaning proudly on their spades. A spectacularly large cockerel pecks away at grain to Peter's left. But I'm dominating the background, looking pretty damn fine, feeling myself in a major way, a slight monochrome suggestion of swirling mist above my rocks. It's probably the most mysterious and impressive I've looked on film, with the possible exception of a shot from 1977, where I'm looking down casually on a merganser duck taking flight above a clam bridge, captured by a lone, gangly figure, a regular visitor to the area, American. There was something about that day, too. A dank magic. I was in one of my moods, in the best and worst possible way. I think you can almost feel it in the photo, but not quite.

So, yes, there have been some good photographs of me. That is a stone fact and I have no quibble with it. But please can you stop taking them? Take a few, maybe, but not so insanely many. It's not helping anyone in the long run, least of all me. Why not paint me instead? Paint me like one of your French hills. Paint me like Joyce did. Not exactly like Joyce did, but as freely as Joyce did. Paint my trees in a way that reminds me of the time your Palaeolithic ancestors hunted wild pigs within them, swirl the colours and shapes in a way that hints at the still-discernible cellar holes where my old farmsteads have rotted back into the earth. Elevate me with your art, rather than devitalising me with your mimicry. Conjure your version of the fire-breathing cardinal enigma I once was.

It's getting dark now. Except that's not true because it never gets properly dark ever these days, even in the countryside. I can see the lights of the village twinkling in the bowl of land beneath my feet. It's one of the advantages of a hilly landscape, that view. It's extremely pretty when viewed from above. A fairytale scene. But later on, when people have gone to bed, some of those lights will stay on; there will always be some light somewhere, whereas in a true fairytale, the darkness, when it comes, is absolute. There are places where you still feel that dark up here, more than you will in 99.9 per cent of places in the rest of the United Kingdom. Some of the lonelier stretches of the river. Up by the kistvaen on Trembling Hill, half a mile past the silver and lead mine. But it's still not the same, not like the old dark. Imagine: you're in, let's say, 1544. You look at the carvings in your church from many centuries ago, a time that seems so unimaginable and unreachable, and you try to understand their meaning, and you can't read, so all you have to go on is what someone else in your village who also can't read told you. First came mass literacy, then came the light. We use the light and shine it on the literature. We read our pagan pamphlets and our books and our WikiLinks and attempt to comprehend the past, and often believe we do. But light, like speed, is often an illusion. We angle our light on our previous findings, which were also made in the time of light, and we make our theories and we think we understand. But that light is like a slim epilogue to history. No, not even an epilogue, nothing so large, more like a brief acknowledgements page at most. You just can't ignore the deep thick black that went before, just how long it lasted, just how dense and inexplicable it was, and all of what was buried within it.

I honestly can't tell you how dark it once was around here. I couldn't even begin to make you understand.

MESSAGE BOARD (2012)

Judith Sparrow: Has anyone spotted a horse rug on their travels? Purple, with red stripes. Last seen up near Hood Gate. Any information appreciated. My Thomas is getting cold.

Terence Black: Fantastic fish and chips tonight at the Stonemason's Arms. Just right. Mushy peas.

Diana Wilson: I had some last week. Overcooked.

Gary Oliver: Everyone keep their eye out there's a drone around in the night sky been seen looking for something worth pinching.

Gary Oliver: Don't suppose anybody has two concrete slabs they don't need any more?

Terence Black: Be vigilant about scam phone calls. A number has been calling me. International. Says I have been in a car crash nonsense I haven't.

Jennifer Cocker: Are Roger and Sheila OK? Haven't seen them for a while. They're very old and having trouble getting around now.

Sheila Winfarthing: We are fine. Thank you, Jennifer.

Jennifer Cocker: Someone should go round and check on them. I can't. I have the kids.

Sheila Winfarthing: I'm right here.

Gary Oliver: Anyone who has any engine oil they don't need please let me know. It shouldn't go to waste and can be used for heating my stone sheds.

Alan Rockwell: TALK ON OLD WOODCRAFT. WHAT HAVE WE LOST? UNDERHILL VILLAGE HALL. September 8th. 7 p.m. Alan Rockwell discusses woodland arts. SAMPLES FROM TALK: Sawn elm is often used for the partitions in cowsheds and other places where animals live, as it can cope with the kick of any beast. Cleft oak is often used for the rungs of ladders and can be trusted for its resilience. What does trimming a cleft with a froe mean? Find out. Snacks and non-alcoholic drinks. Entry £3.50.

Penelope Ralph: We have some oil you can have, Gary. But please can you return the drum afterwards.

Judith Sparrow: Congratulations to everyone on last week's cakes and plants at the Old Chapel. Over £300 raised for RNLI. A splendid effort for all concerned. Any village would be proud to raise half as much.

Diana Wilson: Well done but lemon drizzle cake was dry.

Mark Laggs: Heard a wheelie bin is on fire down near the Molesting Station. Think it belongs to the Cooks. They're not on here. I'm told they know.

Diana Wilson: So why did you write it on here?

Mark Laggs: Wanted people to know. In case it happens again. Could be kids. Only trying to help.

Judith Sparrow: Molesting Station??

Mark Laggs: The MOT Testing Station. Looks like it says Molesting Station. Because of the tree.

Judith Sparrow: You have an overactive imagination, I think, perhaps, Mark?

Jennifer Cocker: From a news report last year: 'RESURGENCE OF BURNING BIN CRAZE AMONGST TEENS. Wheelie bins are constructed from high density polyethylene, which when set alight releases carbon monoxide and dioxide. Such gases starve the brain of oxygen, and can be misinterpreted as a high, when in fact the burner of the bin is quickly and irrevocably destroying their own mind and body. Different coloured bins give off different fumes. Brown bins are believed to give off the most potent false high.' Useful?

Judith Sparrow: Does anyone have a horse rug for sale? Second-hand? Still haven't found the one belonging to my Thomas and the nights are drawing in.

Alan Rockwell: Thank you to all who came to the talk on old woodcraft last night. The total attendance was nine but I believe it was a case of quality over quantity.

Gary Oliver: There's a white goose on the grass at Riddle Bridge. If it belongs to anyone. It's OK it's just sitting there.

Megan Beaker: When I was a child my mother and father had many geese. As well as being eventually good for the pot, they provided a guard for the house and a deterrent when thieves were abroad. We did not lock our doors back then, of course.

Gary Oliver: Those were the days. My mate Rob in Stepsford never locked his door. Last August couple of junkies from Plymouth came up and cleaned him out. Left the whole house bare. Even took the family photos.

Mark Laggs: Old chair up for grabs if anyone wants it. Smells a bit of fags but not much. Will dump if no takers. Don't call on phone. No reception in the combe.

Diana Wilson: When you say 'dump', I do hope you mean at the Household Waste Recycling Centre.

Mark Laggs: FFS

Megan Beaker: I believe chairs do us more harm than good in the modern age. Squatting is excellent for the posture. We have forgotten this, as a race.

Penelope Ralph: Very true, Megan. Indigenous cultures know this.

Gary Oliver: Goose is still down at Riddle Bridge. Seems fine. Wonder if it sleeps there.

Megan Beaker: I named my favourite childhood goose Grunwald. When it came time to cook Grunwald, I was sad, but entirely accepting that this was the way of things. The fire was in the centre of the room which was what you would nowadays call 'open plan'. My sisters and I sat and watched the flames, with two oxen, who were also in the living room, as it was a very cold night. This was not long after my parents died.

Jennifer Cocker: Anyone getting cloudy water after issues the other day?

Sheila Winfarthing: And here I was thinking Roger and me were the oldest on here, Megan!

Mark Laggs: Keep it running and it will clear.

Penelope Ralph: Not strictly relevant because not quite geese but has anyone seen the door in the house up above Brent Moor, on the lane, which says 'DUCK' on it? I always think, 'That must be a really big duck who lives there.'

Diana Wilson: No.

Terence Black: Terrific steak last night (medium rare) at the Steam Packet in Wiliford.

Alan Rockwell: TALK ON THE HISTORY OF LETTERBOXES. HOW LONG WILL THEY REMAIN? UNDERHILL VILLAGE HALL. October 25th. 7 p.m. Alan Rockwell discusses the evolution of the posted letter in the UK. SAMPLES FROM TALK: Like Santa Claus, the first British post boxes were green, not red, but it was decided they were too camouflaged in their surroundings. The first red post boxes appeared in 1874 but it took another decade before all the green post boxes in the country had been repainted. The first British post box of all appeared in Wakefield in 1809. Snacks and non-alcoholic drinks. Entry £3.25.

Penelope Ralph: I have always admired the small Victorian post box in the wall down near Summersbridge. I recently found out that the reason it has a kind of soft brush in its mouth is to stop snails and slugs getting in and damaging the letters.

Gary Oliver: The way the world is going, some bastard will probably pinch it one day.

Diana Wilson: Post keeps getting later in the day all the time. Nearly 3 p.m. the other day. One day soon it will be so late it will be early again.

Alan Rockwell: In fact, Gary, you might find now is a relatively benign time, in terms of the theft of items in the custody of the post office. Attacks from robbers were so common in the late 1700s that the post office would advise customers sending money to cut all banknotes in half, send them at different times, and only send the second half after receipt of the first half had been acknowledged. I will also be covering this in the talk. Snacks and non-alcoholic drinks. Entry £3.25.

Judith Barrow: The post box in the wall of Linhay Farm also has a soft brush in its mouth. They put it in because some bees nested in there.

Alan Rockwell: The one beneath the Black Tree? Also Victoria-Regina, that one. I believe it's the oldest on the entire moor.

Diana Wilson: That tree has always been full of slugs and snails.

Megan Beaker: The Black Tree has always been what everyone in the village has called it. Nobody alive remembers a time when it wasn't there and wasn't black. A perplexing runt amongst its tall confident siblings, it never gets bigger, never dies, never withers. It is a tree of perpetual winter, a tree devoid of the relief of seasonal change. When people walk past it they often find their electronic devices misbehaving. Watches stop. Torches catch fire. Phones zap embarrassing photos to half-acquaintances, unbidden. It is said that many centuries ago a robber of the road – possibly one of the gang they called the Gribblins – was left to die in an iron cage attached to an earlier, blacker tree on the same spot, his last meal being three candles fed to him by a local resident, but that is just a story, teased and tickled by time. What is known for certain is that sheep have often been found dead on the boulder beneath the tree, rivulets of blood spilling from one eye. When lightning hit the tree during the early 1960s, a disgraced limping clergyman in his final half-decade of life, who'd settled here from up country, saw the entire trunk change to white and a face wag its wet tongue at him from the bark, but when he recounted the tale in the Stonemason's Arms later that evening, its authenticity was discredited because of his reputation, but also because he was quick with gin at the time and wearing an item of knitwear back to front.

Alan Rockwell: Thank you for this, Megan. Most edifying, and largely new to me. I have made a note in my journal.

Sheila Winfarthing: I remember that lightning strike well. 1962. Or maybe '63. I wasn't aware you were here as well back then, Megan.

Megan Beaker: I had already been here a long time by then.

Ted Wentworth: Sheep know 99 easy ways to die but are always searching hard for the 100th.

Gary Oliver: Stone sheds now toasty on these chillier nights. Thanks again to Penelope for the oil.

Mark Laggs: Ted some of your wall has come down up by Nettle Field. I saw a ewe on the road. Could be yours too?

Ted Wentworth: Thanks, I'll check. Could be Cavendish's.

Megan Beaker: A drystone wall should not have too much weight low down. The weight of the stones creates the adhesion that makes it trustworthy. Ventilation is important, especially in areas frequently subject to frost. The foundation of the wall is extremely important. Many walls are of double thickness. There is often a gap in the middle for what is called 'hearting': the placing of smaller stones, as a sort of filling. Even so, no mortar is used. This double thickness was echoed in many walls of actual dwellings on the moor, giving ample room for the interment of totemic objects and charms. Common plants that grow on drystone walls in the area include stonecrop, maidenhair spleenwort, wall rue, leafy dog lichen and – less often – the rare lanceolate spleenwort and parsley fern. Sheep – particularly the Blackface – will often seek out a weak spot in the walls, although a sheep that sees a hole in a wall will leave the wall well alone, for she senses it is in danger of collapsing on her.

Penelope Ralph: Whereabouts are you based, Megan? I don't believe we have met. Are you anywhere near Riddlefoot Lane?

Megan Beaker: Not far from there.

Gary Oliver: He's not on here so I'm posting for him but Steve Clayton's whippet Len had a seizure yesterday and ran off. Was seen by Cavendish's farm this morning at 7am but not since. Can everyone keep a look out.

Terence Black: Does anybody know if the Stonemason's Arms are still serving food in the afternoons? Can't seem to find it on their wwwbsite.

Jennifer Cocker: I spoke to Jim at the post office who saw a whippet running alongside the dual carriageway today. He said he stopped on the hard shoulder and ran after it to try and catch it and steer it away from the traffic but it ran off into Parker's Woods.

William Williams: I have some old sheet music here. Classical, but also some old broadsides and ballads. I keep holding onto it but it's just taking up space so if anyone would like to have a look and make me an offer, let me know.

Megan Beaker: The lyrics are mostly wrong.

Gary Oliver: Steve Clayton's whippet Len now been seen by Dimple Bridge, Fox Lane and Stumper's Cross. Nobody can get near him. Just runs in circles. The cancer has spread to his brain. Steve says best to just leave him now.

Jennifer Cocker: Oh, poor poor dog. Is there nothing that can be done?

Mark Laggs: Gary, do you still have that spare coving from last year?

Penelope Ralph: Funny story for everyone, going back to post boxes. I dropped Mike off at Modbury post office earlier where he was posting Sophie's birthday present and while I was waiting I drove around the block a few times to kill time. As I was coming back the last time I saw Mike coming out the door and, as he did, an Astra, exactly the same colour and model as ours, driven by an elderly lady, pulled up right outside the door, and Mike opened the passenger door and got in right next to her. She almost had a heart attack. I pulled up a moment later and we both apologised. She was shaken but we all laughed in the end.

Diana Wilson: Why did you go all the way to Modbury? It's miles away. There are at least nine post offices closer than that, all with reasonable opening times.

Mark Laggs: My mate Craig drove all the way from Devon to Robin Hood's Bay with a loaf of bread on his car roof. That was a Vauxhall Viva, though. They hadn't started making Astras yet.

Pete Micklewhite: Who does everyone use for logs and who is best (dry)?

Mark Laggs: I use Lloyd Warner down over the back side of the Tor but he's not the cheapest.

Diana Wilson: Surprising that Lloyd turned out the way he did. When you consider his father.

Jennifer Cocker: Can anyone hear the fireworks this evening? I have a lurcher and two cats, petrified, beside me. How can people be so inconsiderate?

Mark Laggs: Coming from the Rectory, I think. Sounds like war.

Diana Wilson: Call the police.

Judith Sparrow: Yes, I can hear my Thomas outside whimpering. He only neighs like that when he is very scared.

Pete Micklewhite: Thanks Mark. Lloyd is indeed a top lad. Bit different to his old man.

Alan Rockwell: TALK ON THE HISTORY OF VILLAGE NAMES. HOW DID WE GET TO WHERE WE ARE? UNDERHILL VILLAGE HALL. December 1st. 7 p.m. Alan Rockwell discusses the evolution of place names in the UK. SAMPLES FROM TALK: Did you know that Payhembury is called that because it was owned by a Saxon named Paega, and that Hembury once meant 'high fort'? Who was Totta and what was her ness (Totnes)? Who was Wineca and what was her leigh (Winkleigh)? Why is Underhill (Underhill) called Underhill? PLUS GUEST SPEAKER COLIN STAPLETON FROM BIDEFORD. Snacks and non-alcoholic drinks. Entry £2.75.

Diana Wilson: I'd have thought it was called Underhill because it's under a hill.

Megan Beaker: I know who Totta was. I met her and she was a supercilious prick.

Sheila Winfarthing: When was this, Megan?

Jennifer Cocker: So pleased to announce that our daughter Melanie has been selected to represent Britain at the Olympics in diving. This is the culmination of years of hard work and dedication for our Mel and we could not be more proud.

Mark Laggs: Well done Mel!

Megan Beaker: I used to dive, on frequent occasions. That was one of the reasons they selected me to take charge of our settlement, after my mum and dad died. I knew where the big sharp rocks in the river were and I knew how to pick my spot. I was able to stay under a long time, and I tickled trout out from under the granite. Within a year I could grab two at a time. Unatha and Joan (she wasn't called this but that's what you'd call her) were waiting for me above with my thick warm coat, which only I was allowed to wear. I was not alive much longer and believe my diving would have only improved, perhaps to Olympic standard, if that had been a thing. Later, when I had a different face and body but the same name, I remembered how, even though it was so many years later, and then again, and again. I never took the river for granted, as those who do rarely live to tell the tale. We said it had a voice. We called it Jack. But Jack's voice was many voices. It was the voice of my mum and my dad and my other mums and dads, and it is my voice too. I hear myself when I get close to it.

Penelope Ralph: Well, I don't know about anyone else, but I am enjoying Megan's stories a lot. Who was it who invited and confirmed you here on the message board, Megan? I don't think I have seen you around the village or the combe.

Megan Beaker: It was me. I did it. I invited me. I confirmed me.

Dave Busley: HAPPY DAVE'S GARDENING SERVICES. NO JOB TOO SMALL. COMPETITIVE RATES. CALL 01364 782435. INDOOR JOBS CONSIDERED ALSO. ALWAYS HAPPY TO HELP.

Rebecca Potts-Wellington: Bonfires are fine, but be considerate. Please check with your neighbours before lighting one. And DON'T do it on a windy day. Very antisocial. Naming no names.

Mark Laggs: There's a black lad running around Cavendish's top field. Not sure if anyone knows anything about him.

Penelope Ralph: Mark, this seems a bit racist. I don't see why it's cause for concern or that the colour of the skin of the running boy is relevant.

Mark Laggs: Typo! Black lab. Saw him on Squeezebelly Lane before that. Maybe was tied up outside Spar and broke his leash.

Mark Laggs: It's OK, he's Sue Pearson's. I just heard. She got him last week from Berry Pomeroy.

Anne Cherry: Free pair of Crocs. Size 6.

Jennifer Cocker: Has anyone seen Roger and Sheila recently? It might be worth going over to check on them.

Sheila Winfarthing: We are right here. Still walking and speaking in intelligible sentences without dribbling and making our own meals and everything. Some have described us as a miracle of modern science.

Anne Cherry: High-waisted jeans. Barely worn. Bought in Next sale, 2008/09. £7 ONO.

Megan Beaker: I lost my maidenhead around the back of the tor. It was the day of the fair. A French boy was responsible.

He wasn't the age of a boy and didn't think he was a boy but he was. There were lots of French on the moor, then. They had been in the prison, then were released, on the condition they stayed within the parish. At the fair there were heads on sticks, carved and painted black, and people threw rotten apples and onions at them and cheered. Mr Oldsworthy, Underhill's baker, played the fiddle. I could smell the nutty aroma that always lingered on Oldsworthy's dusty jacket as the French boy led me on past him by the hand and I knew the song from a long time ago and knew it was part of me. After that I could hear them start to play 'The Bonny Bunch of Roses'. Young dogs were wrestling, looping and twirling on the grass, out of breath. We went to the barn. It's still there. The cuckoo was crying from the tor top and as I looked into the stone in front of me and the French boy tried to find me and breathed hot breath into my ear I felt like I was the stone and I felt 15,000, not fifteen. The stone was full of stories and there would be more. But about this story I never told a soul. On the way home the words to the song were in my head: the roses one, not the one I felt was part of me. 'One morning in the month of June. While feather'd warbling songsters. Their charming notes did sweetly tune. I overheard a lady. Lamenting in sad grief and woe.' I stopped at a fallen tree and collected kindling, looking for the drier bits caught on branches above, like my father had told me. It had rained that morning but it was easy to forget that had ever happened.

Judith Sparrow: Terence Black, in case you are wondering, the Nissan Micra who you didn't thank when it made quite an elaborate manoeuvre down a farm track to let you pass the other day on the lane up to Hood Gate just beyond the sharp right-hand bend was driven by me.

Anne Cherry: Selection of old board (and other) games. Kerplunk, Downfall, Scrabble, Monopoly, Pictionary, more. All in excellent condition. £20 the lot. Individual prices considered if no takers.

Mark Laggs: When I was playing Downfall as a kid a bee once went in one of the holes on the turny bits, thinking it was a flower. I will always remember that.

Diana Wilson: Turny bits?

Megan Beaker: Someone said I once turned a man to stone. People retold the story, then embellished it. Even the unembellished version is untrue. I could not have done that if I wanted to (and I did want to, at times). But that doesn't mean the stones don't have a voice of their own.

Jennifer Cocker: Is Gary OK? I haven't seen him on here in a while.

Mark Laggs: He's been having a hectic time I reckon. Sorting the insurance and everything after his stone outbuildings burned down. I think he lost a lot of stuff.

Penelope Ralph: This year's Ball In The Hall will take place on June 22nd. Outdoor catering will be provided by Miranda's Kitchen. We are also very pleased to welcome Adverse Camber from Torquay, who will be enlivening proceedings with their mix of sea shanties, rock, ska and what the Plymouth Herald described as 'solid peninsula reggae pop' in a glowing 7/10 review. Tickets will be £10 and must be purchased in advance from the Stonemason's Arms or the community shop.

Mark Laggs: In case anybody is going up by Riddle Bridge, the road is closed. Massive fuck off elm has come down.

Judith Sparrow: Brilliant news! Thomas's horse rug has been found. Angela Paley from Wentworth Country Cheeses discovered it caught in a tree, a full half a mile from Hood Gate, and handed it in to Jim Swardesley at the post office. Jim called me and I went in and picked it up yesterday. Amazingly, it is only slightly torn. Of course, I'd got my Thomas a new rug in the meantime, because he can't go cold, so now he has two. He's an exceedingly happy horse!

~~Megan Beaker: Do you all sometimes hear me sing to you in your sleep? Do you notice how it intensifies when you are feverish and sick, how it becomes everything? Do you ever realise, as my song scores your dreams, that it has been the soundtrack to so many dreams in the past, too, but you never remember it when you wake up and are back in your surface world, which you laugh and shrug and joke your way through and pretend is the real story?~~

REPORT OF DEBRIS (2014)

I need a slash. I think I'll do it here. Gap in the tree curtain. Well-trodden. Ah sweet Mabel in heaven it stinks. Should have chosen a country lane instead. How many people have wazzed in this layby? Must be millions. Billions. Ye olde travellers on the trunk road into the west, unable to wait until the next rest facility. Services: twenty-one miles and twelve miles. Always try to get your horse to last out until the furthest one. Invariably a mistake. God, what's this ground made of. Weeds growing from pure urine. Don't think I'll kick off my new foraging career here. Let's leave that a while, shall we. Plastic bag caught in a tree. Nothing beautiful about that, whatever that emo kid in the film reckons. I was a big emo fan as a kid too. Rod Hull. Brilliant. Convinced it was a real bird until I was at least eleven. OK, here will do. Crisp wrappers. Plus-size drinks cartons. Do you want to get large for an extra 20p? Sorry, I mean go large. Litter bastards, slurping their McDiabetes after their day out to a renowned World Heritage Site. Tiffany, look here, isn't this remarkable, these larger blue stones were somehow transported all the way from the mountains in west Wales 4,000 years before cars or trucks or trains had been invented, although there is a conflicting theory that they are erratics which drifted in on Ice Age glaciers from their original resting place. No, Tiffany, leave it where you threw it. There isn't time. We have to be at Aunt Jackie's at six, and what's the point when there's loads of other crap there already and I'm sure there'll be a little man to come and pick it up before long.

That's better. Give it a shake for luck. Why is it they never do that in the films? Always goes back in the pants so quickly. Barely even a movement. No thespian concession to zipping up. Zero evidence of stains or droplets. Always a plot device piss, too, never just a piss. Is this a plot device piss too? 'If he hadn't have stopped, he would never have met that druid, and his life would never have turned around.' Doubt it. Who needs turning around anyway? It just means it's going to be that much more exhausting the next time, when you get turned back around the other way again. Could do with a drink. Just one. Three hours until the pubs open. The pubs where I'm going anyway. The Coach & Horses on Greek Street will be open by now. Johnny Slazenger and Steve Rizlas two pints of Fosters down, boasting about how they crushed another innocent with their knowledge of New York Dolls trivia. Pete Shapiro with another indie girlfriend, flicking peanuts into her cleavage ravine at last orders. Had a quiet word with the twat last time. Wanted to take her home myself and treat her good in good ways and bad in good ways but didn't; just walked her to the Tube station, asked her if she was OK, told her not to date music journalists and find a nice lad instead, a scientist or botanist or oil rig worker. Sign on a lamppost: 'LOVE CONQUERS ALL'. Arrow added between the 'CONQUER' and the 'ALL', leading to a 'FUCK'. Walked back into the pub and it looked like a battlefield, smelled like a yeast illness, oozed the spotty defeat of an old armpit. I put the Pogues on the jukebox and leapt around a bit while everyone else died in corners. Won't be doing that again. Not after last night. All gone now. You'll never work in this town again. Or mosh boisterously again in this town to snaggle-toothed Gaelic punk rock.

Going 60 now. Feels like 80 in this. Pleasant Jesus, are those poppies over there? Is that even real, or some fake carpet someone put down for a laugh to wind me up? There's a rattle that's bothering me. Hope this thing is going to make it the last ninety miles. Bought it from a granny in Enfield. 1989 vintage. One lady owner. Lady owner made me a cup of tea. Strong like I like it. Never seen a builder drink it stronger. Six digestive biscuits. Forced me to take the three I didn't eat home with me. Think the shady old crone might have turned the clock back, popped in a 1980 Lada engine. If it doesn't get me past Yeovil I'll sell it for parts and hitch the rest of the way. Better than the Renault 4 I used to have. Got nicked. Thieves changed their mind and abandoned it after 200 yards. Feck, I need MUSIC, but I've got no cassettes – who has, now, apart from hipsters and the dead? – so I'll carry on amusing myself by watching the place names zip by. Tintinhull? What sodding kind of name is that? I'm picturing North Sea poverty meets intrepid French reporting but sensing that's not what I'd find. Maybe that's it, that's why I became a journalist: reading all those Tintin books when I was ten. Never got the dog, though, did I, and it's all over now, isn't it, probably. Too late. Sorry, Snowy. Try an owner with a longer temper. You don't go decking Richard Peck in the most popular pub for north London journalists at 7 p.m. on a Friday and expect to walk out of it as an employable metropolitan freelancer. Don't regret it, though. Twat lied then tried to screw me out of a month's pay then when I sold his feature – *my* feature – to *The Times* he said he'd make sure I never got work from anyone he knew ever again. Too much silence about this shit, too much fear about what not being silent about it might cost you. Too many people in that world not from money being pushed around by people from money and not paid by people from money because the people from money don't understand the importance of being paid and the terror of not being paid. Too many people not from money complying and not sending the people from money sprawling across a lager-stained parquet floor, scrabbling for their glasses which they probably only wear as an affectation.

OK. Motorway now. Getting closer. Traffic slowing down. REPORT OF DEBRIS in orange computer letters. It's OK. Twenty-five miles left. This will be better. New start. Can feel the country air clearing up my eczema already just from those three minutes in it. Give me a week and I'll be a fully qualified country squire. Lazy afternoons of picnics and croquet and mild alcoholism. Looking forward to the pubs too. Saddlers and farriers and wheelwrights, sitting about, telling you about how they made their girth straps and shoe nails and spokes. You get the hippies down here, too, lots of them. Nothing hectic about anything. Very little aggro. A more meditative life. Finally get down to writing my bestselling memoir *Mindful Fighting* in which I explain how to stay totally in the present while lamping somebody at closing time.

Shouldn't get too excited. Room above a garage. Not exactly going to be Daphne du Maurier, am I. Saw her on an old documentary, saying her house wasn't too big just for her. Only 938 rooms. Quite modest, really, darling. Not as if it's the kind of place one *rattles* around in. Different bit of the wild west but the same in some ways. More trees, less coast, fewer ghosts of children who died in arsenic mines. I'll go down there too soon, though, Kernow. Loved both counties as a kid. Climbing trees. Any I could get into. As high as I could go. OK, off the main road now. Thank god. Left in such a rush forgot to do my road tax and was freaking out every time I saw the police. Always pulling me over, they are, perhaps sensing insurrection, despite my responsible adherence to the speed limit.

Giant rocks in the woods. Hobbitland. Came to a party near here in '99 with Jen. Big farmhouse where capitalist hippies sold their homebrew. Tiny men everywhere. Me towering over them. Tiny men and willowy women. 'You get taller when you're drunk,' said Jen. Correct, probably, as she is about everything. Best break-up ever. Still love her to bits, even though her family are poshos. Still looking after me even now, getting me out of tight spots. What are these things beside the road? Sheds? Look more like portals, bit charred-looking. Step in and everything spins and smokes and you fear incineration but actually just end up in 1968. Fine by me. It's where I'm planning on going soon anyway. Is this a road? I think it is, just about. Ah! Polytunnels. This'll be it. Jen said to come in the back way. So as not to embarrass him in front of his customers? I asked. No, because the main gate will be locked by that point, you prat, she said. Ooooh look at this, not what I had in mind when she said garage. I was thinking of the ones in Hackney. Don't get this there. Stone, pretty big, little old wonky steps going up to the living quarters. Daisies, multicoloured ones, growing out of them. I can deal with this. The place is just an afterthought for her cousin Titus, one of many annexes. Done pretty well for himself. Two years younger than me, Jen says. Not as if he started with nothing, though. Wonder what the main house is like. I'm fucking well early. Two hours. Saw a pub a couple of miles back up the lane. Sounds like a plan.

*

Wednesday. Titus has been over, brought three cucumbers. I tried to be polite about them, thanked him, even though if you ask me they taste of all the most disappointing parts of British life. He walked over to the window, turned this big Indian jug around, possessive like, stamping his authority on the space. I don't care which way around the Indian jug goes. It's not my Indian jug. Asked me how I was settling in. Great, I said, not totally fibbing. Refrained from complaining to him about the way if you're cooking a pizza in the oven you need to shove it right to the back then turn it around halfway through and even then it will probably burn on the edges and be frozen solid in the middle. He told me to put a rod down the septic tank if it gave me any problems. 'We are a tad feral around here, I'm afraid,' he said. He's all right, Titus is. Voice oozes everything he's from. Not super posh, laid-back Devon posh, as if the act of talking itself is a little tiring, as if words are a chair he's constantly pushing the reclining lever on. Heard that sound a lot here already. Reminders of my ingrained peasanthood everywhere. Bit alone but made some friends at the pub already. Maurice, a thatcher. Almost broke my fingers with his handshake. Saw Bob yesterday. First time in six years. Good to be close to him again. Grumpier than he used to be. Looks even more like a terrier. 'Mind out for newts,' he said, as I walked in. 'What?' I said. 'They're breeding out the back,' he said. 'They seem to still think there's a pond here.' Some people really own a room when they walk into it; Bob used to really rent a corner of that same room. Different now. Sense a new unwillingness in him to please. Listened to some records, a blast of stoner rock, proto-metal, some of our old touchstones. Didn't smoke. Drank tea. First time I've known him to be single. A good thing, too. Loved himself a loud, bossy lady, Bob did. Don't know if he still does. Always going straight from relationship to relationship with no time to take his clutter to the charity shop in between. Never the healthiest state of affairs. Big barrier to meeting someone on equal terms for him. Wouldn't have told him, though. Say something like that to Bob and he wouldn't express offence; he'd just go a bit silent then you wouldn't see him for an epoch. Hard to believe he ever lived in or near a city. Kind of bloke who whispers to sick trees and makes them well again. Told him I was trying to learn the names of the flowers. 'You?' he said, disbelieving. 'Have this,' he said, handing me a book. 'I've got two.' 'What's this one on the cover?' I said. 'Snake's head fritillary,' he said. 'The ones next to it are marsh marigold.' Took the book and wandered around a bit afterwards in the sun, steep steps, a water spout two inches above the pavement, 'NOT DRINKING WATER'. Good job they told me that because I was just about to get down on my back and clamp my lips around it. Ginnels and jitties behind cottages, covered in daisies. Not daisies. Fleabane. Just learned it. Ugly name for a nice plant. Pictured this place, 1968. Thought about its ghosts. RJ. Was this one a street he walked along? And did the Countenance Divine shine forth upon these clouded hills?

'I see your car's got Devon rash already,' Titus asked later, when I saw him by the polytunnel, stirring an organic nettle and comfrey-based fertiliser.

'You what?' I said.

'Devon rash. It's when the left side of your car gets scratched up from all the time you spend pulling over into hedges and banks to let other people pass.'

'Ah,' I said. 'Yeah. It's a good job people don't drive here like they drive in Manchester or London. I'd be dead by now.'

'Did you know?' he added, as if we'd been talking about it for a while. 'Apple used to just mean "fruit". It didn't mean "apple" until relatively recently – a few hundred years ago or so.'

Every day's a school day here.

Excerpt from rough draft of Wallflower Child: The Ballad of RJ McKendree

You don't realise you're part of history when you're in it. If you live in a time in history where you walk down from your village to defecate alongside your compatriots in a communal mire, you are not squatting there wishing 1596 would hurry up and arrive and Sir John Harington would outline an idea for the first flush toilet. By a similar measure, if you live in 1967, and are renting a house for an affordable price in a beautiful part of the world, near dozens of other artists who you rub up against every week and spark off, you probably do not think 'Hey, I am in the sixties when everything was better!' There is no awareness in you that everything will not always be this way, that you are part of a blessed generation, sprinkled with stardust, and in a few decades' time artists will auction several of their internal organs for the freedom you have.

But that stardust is only part of the story: the story of the Woodstock Generation that has been told a thousand times. We know magic filled the air. We know that it was a rare time when artistic bravery intersected with popular appeal and – frequently – vast ensuing wealth. But there are different stories still to be told of the same era. In a way, there were quite simply too many great records made in the sixties and seventies. The foyer got too crowded, and not everyone had room to move around and do their thing. Some less assertive souls, perhaps feeling that they could not breathe, decided to leave. What it means is that many records made during that era are only now getting the respect and love that they are due. Some of them are yet to receive it. This is a book about one of those records and about the man who made it. But it is a little more than that too. It is also an adventure in itself, a road trip, after which nothing in my own life was ever quite the same again.

'What it's probably hard to get your head around for people now is that we were not worried about money back then. We were just a little British folk band really yet we were playing huge venues, touring Australia and Germany, we all had big detached houses, and most of us had paid off the mortgage before very long. Of course, a lot of what we earned got squandered on beer. You'd go to Dick and Sheila's house and wait while they got ready to go to the pub – Dick and Mick always had to live within a mile's walk of a pub, it was part of their rules – and, as we were leaving, Dick would grab a wad of pound notes from a gap in one of the walls or a cranny behind one of the beams, which was also later where he kept his weed because after some of the other folk bands got busted, he started getting paranoid. Of course, Oliver and I had money coming in from *The Gribblins* and *Mingle the Tingle* by then. But we hadn't, a few years earlier. When Oliver had first started making them in his shed. It all happened very quickly, the change. Four years, something like that. But everything changed quickly back then.'

I'm sitting in a farmhouse kitchen. The room is full of ceramics and they're great ceramics – full of abstract slashes and curves and runes in bold primary colours – and I'm trying to stay calm but it's not because of the greatness of the ceramics that I'm trying to stay calm. It's because the kitchen belongs to Maggie Fox, *the* Maggie Fox, who is sitting right there in front of me on an Ercol chair talking to me. Maggie Fox, whom I watched present *Blackbird* when I was a kid. Talking to me about Equinox, my favourite folk-jazz band of all time, and about the costumes she made for *The Gribblins* and *Mingle the Tingle* and – later, slightly less successfully – *Brock of the Wood*, and about her ex-husband Oliver. And I'm also trying to stay calm because all of this interests me, all of this is a book in itself, and every story leads to another story, and every one is enthralling, but it's not even the real reason I'm here, and I want to talk to Maggie about the real reason I'm here, but I also don't want her to stop talking about the other stuff, but I also don't want to keep her all day.

Maggie is one of the all-time unsung, or certainly only partly sung, heroes of the children's-television acid-folk music crossover and a Renaissance woman of the first order. In the late sixties, with her husband Oliver, in a stone shed at the bottom of the garden of the old weaver's cottage they shared, she co-created the Gribblins: the tiny enchanting green creatures who disorientated humans – invariably rich, affluent ones – with their eerie flute music and dancing then stole their possessions and carried them back to their mossy lair to examine and hypothesise about them. While Oliver made the sets, using moss he had gathered from nearby woodland, and storyboarded the episodes, Maggie designed and made costumes for them of a mindboggling intricacy, tiny felt hats and gloves and the phosphorescent chainmail armour that covered their bodies – all of which, in the shadow of her better-known husband, she has never in my opinion received enough credit for. Not satisfied with the success of that, and her brief turn as co-presenter of *Blackbird*, singing slightly-too-eerie songs for children, she later took up an invitation to join the folk supergroup Equinox as singer and flautist for the final two of their five albums, replacing their original vocalist Bonnie Gosling.

Having emailed the address on her out-of-date-looking website and received nothing back, I had thought the easiest way to track Maggie down would be via the publishers of her now-hard-to-source children's book *Josephine Bigfish* or the company responsible for the 2003 DVD reissues of *The Gribblins* and *Brock of the Wood* (*Mingle the Tingle* is still to be rereleased due to contractual issues). Nothing came of either so I opted for the more direct route, driving down to the Cornish estuary village of Trewars, hanging out in a craft shop which sold some of her pottery, then skilfully and subtly managing to get the owner of the shop to let slip where the creator of the ceramics I was admiring lived. An hour later, here we were, in her kitchen, and I got no sense that my presence was unwelcome.

'You're on the moor, you say, or close to it?' she continues, handing me the second cup of tea of the afternoon. 'I miss being up there. Of course, I have little to complain about here, in terms of surroundings. But looking back I think the moor was a kind of seventh member of Equinox. Equinox, it was really me, Dick, Mick, Julian, Norman, Gill and the moor. All but two of us lived on or very near it. It's where a lot of the secret something we had came from, even though by that time the band were breaking up. Norman had already recorded his *Let Norman Steal Your Thyme* solo LP and Dick and Mick were thinking about new ventures. So it was very exciting and very fraught at the same time. And it was the same with Oliver and me with the moor. When he first had the idea for the Gribblins – which of course comes partly from some real robbers who lived on the moor in the sixteenth century – we'd be doing all these walks up there and he'd be fizzing with inspiration, asking me, "What type of monster do you think would live in this tree?" or running off to climb into an abandoned shed and root around. Then he read about tardigrades, these microscopic creatures who live in moss and can withstand boiling and freezing temperatures and sleep through an apocalypse, and that was where the idea for the Water Bears came from, who as you'll probably remember were the nemeses of the Gribblins in the show. We'd walk through the woodland, over the moss, "the Goddess Carpet" they call it, and Oliver would collect the moss for the sets. Probably not a very ecologically correct thing to do, actually. It was like being married to a big kid. Later he got a bit too involved in the world he was creating at times. He once told me he was convinced that one of them was alive and spoke to him. Meg, the smallest one. Not that there was much difference in size in any of them. They were all different, though, if you looked closely. I hesitate to say a girl because the Gribblins ultimately had no gender. They were before their time in that way, I suppose. I should hasten to add, however, that Oliver was high a lot at this point, as so many of us were.'

She got up and swept an intrepid ginger cat off the kitchen work surface.

'Dad, get down from there. We call her Dad because as soon as I got her, she went straight to get settled on my dad's old favourite armchair and Hannah, that's my daughter, started saying she looked like him and always seems to watch *Question Time* very intently, like my dad used to. But I digress. You wanted to ask about *Wallflower*. I think I have the copy that Dick gave me somewhere in the loft. Isn't it amazing the way the value of these things change, and it comes round again and people get interested? If I am being honest I haven't played it for several years now. I know I thought it was very special at the time. I am sure I still would. This is all – what? – forty years ago now, so you'll have to forgive me if I don't get all of this right. A lot of it was about Dick and Mick and their friendship which was sort of bowing and creaking under the strain of various internal dynamics. As I said, the band was already disintegrating by the time I joined, halfway through the recording of "Mountebank". Then before we started the last record Dick came in and said he had this song, "Mrs Nicholas", by this American guy, which was strange, because Dick could be very anti-American back then, and he wanted us to cover it, but even though we did and it went well, Mick was always very resistant to the idea, just, I think, because it was very specifically Dick's thing.

'The background to this, which I think you can't ignore, is that not long before that, Mick had slept with Sheila, and Sheila hadn't really enjoyed it, and had gone running straight back into Dick's arms. Of course, Dick hadn't precisely been any kind of saint before that, and viewed her infidelity as licence to be even less of one, which was not hard for him, what with the amount of time he was spending hanging around the art college at Chidleigh Babbots after he'd been doing some guest lecturing in the music department there. I don't know if it was there, maybe not, but he ended up cheating on Sheila with this girl called Sue Piduck, who, as soon as we found out about her, we all started calling "Superduck" in an attempt to cheer Sheila up. It didn't last long between Dick and Superduck but afterwards she wouldn't leave him alone and kept saying she had this tape with this incredible music on it and nobody knew who made it, and that Dick needed to hear it, that it would be an actual crime if he didn't, and she just would not shut up about it and finally, after about two months, Dick – realising it was genuinely about this tape, and not about the fact that Superduck wanted anything more from him – goes around to her house and listens to it, and it turns out she's not lying: it's an amazing record. The next day she brings it over to Dick's house, and we're all there, including Sheila, which meant there was a tension in the room, and nobody really seemed that mellow, but all of us – except Mick – totally got it that this record was not anything ordinary: utterly haunted, with this slight eastern edge to it, and with this amazing tuning that was even more advanced than the people of the time we thought were really advanced, musician's musicians; Davy Graham and Suni McGrath and Nic Jones and the like. I felt like I was listening to something that had been made centuries ago, not four years ago. "Mrs Nicholas" was the one Dick had earmarked and wanted us to cover and we did play it at a few live shows but we never recorded it, mostly due to Mick's resistance. I don't even remember it being the best song. But I'm skipping ahead. The thing was, there was this big chap from the college there at Mick's house, a biker type bloke, a sound recordist from the college who Dick was knocking around with and who everyone called Chickpea, and about two minutes into the first track, he says, "Fuck me backwards. I recorded this album!" And then he tells us that it was by this

American guy called Richie McKendree but that he didn't have a clue what had happened to him since but he knew this girl called Maddie who might, but it turned out she didn't either, only that he'd gone back to California years ago and nobody had heard from him since.

'Of course, things being things, and Dick being Dick, it took absolutely ages for it all to get sorted. The friend of Superduck's who'd had the tapes was in some kind of debt at the time and wanted a lot of money for them, even though she'd just found them in a beach hut belonging to her dad. Then Chickpea wades in and says they're as much his as anyone else's. Meantime Equinox are breaking up and Dick's trying to get Selkie started as a label and also trying to track down this McKendree guy to clear it all up. By the time Dick finally finds him, McKendree's working in a camera shop somewhere in Oklahoma and living above his mum's garage and has given up music altogether, and when Dick manages to get the record out it's December 1976 and a different kind of music is in vogue. Even Dick himself had lost a bit of interest in the more… mystical and bucolic aesthetic by then. He'd started writing those very raw and political songs about trade unions and whatnot, which – don't get me wrong – I always liked a lot, but they're not quite sprinkled with the same magic, are they? Selkie only lasted about three years in total as a label. Hardly any copies of *Wallflower* were pressed and even fewer were sold. I hear it's going for – what – £400 on the Internet now? Astonishing. Did you know Dick also managed to get McKendree over here, a couple of years later, here in Devon?'

I know it's a cliché, but I actually choke on a throatful of tea as she says it. 'Haggli fzz!' I say.

'Pardon?' says Maggie.

'Holy fuck!' I say. 'I didn't. Pardon my French. That's… I had no idea.'

'Yep. The Empire in Exeter. Long since shut down. It was a small disaster, really. Dick, who was piling the pounds on by this point, headlining, wearing these jeans that were far too tight, and with this really harsh crew cut Sheila had just given him. The venue had booked a totally inappropriate third support, this skiffle band from Budleigh Salterton called Cliffy Coggles and His Donkeys, who were all well into their forties. And then in the middle there's McKendree, playing the whole gig sitting on a stool with his back to the audience, and not saying a word, not even a thanks, between songs. He only played about four, I think. I was introduced to him afterwards, but he didn't say much, seemed like someone who'd recently had some bad news, but also like this lost little boy. I reckon there were no more than thirty people in the crowd, and three of those were me and Oliver and Angus Boon from Nannie Slagg, who now I come to think of it had a go at a McKendree song too. And then there was this really embarrassing moment backstage when this German couple turn up with a pen and an autograph book and Dick's getting poised to sign it for them and McKendree just looks like he wants to find the nearest manhole and hide under it and it turns out that it's actually Oliver's and my autographs the couple want. Dick was not pleased, I don't think. A complicated man with a very tangible ego. So many good points, though. He had put up all the money himself to fly McKendree over, at a time when money was less easy for him. Say what you like about him, he was always generous to a fault. Hard to believe he had only a decade left on the planet at that point.'

'Wait. Hold on. Did you say Nannie Slagg? The metal band who turned into Blacksmith?'

'Yes, although they were far less metal at first. More progressive. A filthy band, both in looks and sound. I believe

223

they covered "Bog Asphodel" at their live shows, circa 1972. That would have been because of Dick. An almost unrecognisable version of the song, though. When Nannie Slagg became Blacksmith and got properly famous – a totally different kind of fame to Equinox's – Angus envied the freedom Dick had as a lone wolf, envied his new… anonymity, and he'd often hide from it all at Dick and Sheila's place. You'd walk in and he and Dick would be eating jam butties, sometimes ten of them in one go, all on doorslab bread and layered with Sheila's homemade butter. Both being Scottish, they didn't call them jam butties, though; they called them "jeely pieces".

Aye, get me, the walker. Walking. Bloody miles. Even got the jacket. Right country squire, I am. Map and mint cake and everything. And boots. The Converse All Stars weren't really working out up here. Bit bleak today. Think I can see November coming over the hill, December behind it, carrying its bad news in a sack. Not bleak like home but bleak. What's home? Where you lived until you were eighteen, I suppose. Doesn't seem like home in my mind any more, though, and then other times it does. Our house, tiny, end of the row, no garden but you went up the ginnel at the end and then past the tyre stack and the back of the garage and these old barns, all this crumpled corrugated iron, and then you were right there, at the bottom of the hill, and the strips of rusty metal and Coke cans would peter out and you climbed the top and up there you felt safe from everything and you looked down and all the shit wasn't visible any more; everything seemed much greener. And then the woodland, behind that: a little forest in the sky where there was a pond and the tadpoles made the water look black in April and I found a lost ginger cat then carried it back down to town in my coat and then just as I got to Gallagher Street I saw a picture on a lamppost of the exact same lost ginger cat that was in my coat with 'LOST CAT' written next to it and I took the cat straight to the address on the poster. Everyone hates the advertising industry until they lose a cat. Except the woman in the house didn't seem that massively over the moon about getting the cat back and the cat didn't seem that massively over the moon about being back and kind of gave me this look as I left, like it was much sadder than when I found it or when it was in my coat. But maybe the woman was glad and was just being the way people were around there, which was not that happy about anything. Which is different to the way people are around here, which sometimes seems a bit too happy about everything. And that's sort of the way the countryside in this place doesn't quite look like the countryside near this place: it's still all big but here it seems a bit happier. I remember the last time my dad came back, about three months before he left for the last time and about a year after he'd left the first time. He had this big plywood board, which he started attaching papier mâché to and making all these humps and bumps, and then when the papier mâché was dry he started painting it green, and brown, and grey, and then you realised that the green bits were hills, and the grey bits were roads and the brown bits were mud, and I got home one day and he'd put a load of plastic farm animals on it, plus a couple of dinosaurs, and left my toy cars there – the ones I had already and a couple of new ones he'd secretly got me in Stockport the weekend before – for me to brum all over it, which I did, for weeks afterwards, until after he'd gone for the last time, and it was all the fun I needed, even more fun than when my mum took the rugs up to clean and I scrunched them up and brummed my car through the folds. He never talked much about what he was making, my dad, he just went ahead and made it, mostly in secret. I wouldn't have been surprised if he had a secret shed somewhere, like Oliver Fox, where he was making his own Gribblins or something like that. And that was a lot of the problem, and why my mum didn't trust him, because he was so quiet and secretive about everything, but maybe it was her lack of trust that pushed him towards what he did, and that made him go off with Sandra Tunnard, and then go off with her again, after he'd changed his mind about it for a bit and tried to live with my mum again. And maybe my mum was right when she told me he was a bastard, and maybe he still is one if he is still around, but the point is I have never really had the chance to find out firsthand. Ah shut up, Martin. Tell it to your therapist. Not that you'll ever have one. Admission of defeat, isn't it, therapy? Not down here: they've all got one, even the trust fund techno hippies with the smooth life and no demons. Might as well be California, what with that and the coastline. Another sign of the north in me: that stubbornness. I'll sort myself out, thanks. Keep your couch. But anyway that was all about five years before I found the lost cat, and about two years before I found my dad's records in a box in the loft, and got on the road to wasting my life writing about rock bands instead of doing a worthwhile job that might help somebody. And what I remember now about that model village my dad made me, as well as the new impact of the realisation that he took the time to make something like that, just for me, is that the hills looked more like the hills down here than the hills up there: they had less space between them, like someone had really enjoyed squeezing them together and making all the angles between them and thinking about how they related to each other and making little secret places in all the folds where nobody could see you getting up to your secretive business.

Excerpt from rough draft of Wallflower Child: The Ballad of RJ McKendree

I was one of the lucky ones: I found my copy of *Wallflower* in a box marked 'Country/Folk/Misc' in the Heart Foundation shop in Sheffield in 1998, a time before the Internet had turned record pricing into a less exciting democracy. It cost me £5.49. I suppose you could say that I, on that day, was another person who didn't realise he was part of history. I was just a person taking a chance on a record that looked interesting. I might not have even picked it up if I had not been intrigued by the cover, which featured an abstract painting: a swirly heliocentric sort of hillscape, with dotted suggestions of houses, and with, I later realised, what could be argued to be just a suggestion of a face in it. On the inner sleeve the painting was credited to 'RJ McKendree, based on an original work by Joyce Nicholas'.

I loved *Wallflower* instantly, but it wasn't until much later that I developed my deeper relationship with it. I was recovering from a bad time in my life at that point. I had lost my job, been drinking far too much. I picked fights with men who deserved it and men who didn't. Stood in to defend the honour of women in trouble and women not in trouble, gradually lost my power to perceive which was one and which was the other. Went home with cauliflower ears and a carrot nose. Woke up with a crying liver and a clicking hip. I took off deep into the West Country, an outsider there, just as McKendree had been when he'd first arrived there, more than forty years earlier. I lived above a garage, just as McKendree had. I had no certainty of my future, drifted, just as McKendree had. I learned wildflower names, just as he had. Opened my eyes to their magic and the poetry of the dead, who had dreamt the names of the plants into existence. Greater spearwort. Reedmace. Purple loosestrife. Creeping

227

bugle. Toadflax. Agrimony. Lady's bedstraw. All the while the record seemed to be growing each time I listened to it, as if someone had snuck in and, in fact, changed it while I had been partially neglecting it. I decided its grooves had actual ghosts within them yet they were not ghosts I wanted to run away from. I played McKendree's version of the traditional Devon folk ballad 'Little Meg' and his choral, semi-chanted 'Sad Painting of a Dog' sixteen, seventeen times a day. Then, later, as I explored my new terrain, met people connected – however tangentially – with the McKendree myth, the record stayed with me and waltzed me through the landscape. I found it extremely difficult to find out what happened in McKendree's life between late 1968 and the late seventies when he made the first of what turned out to be several return trips to Devon. It seemed like the most mysterious of many mysterious periods of his life. I knew his father passed away in 1969, and by 1975 he, his sister and his mum had moved from California to Oklahoma, where he was living in his mum's annexe and working part time in a used camera store. It appeared to be a time when he had abandoned music altogether. But then my research led me to an unexpected discovery that thrilled me to my marrow: in 1972, McKendree had reconnected with his old co-songwriter from Stoneman's Cavalry, Frank Bull, and recorded a one-off single, an almost unrecognisable electric version of 'Little Meg'. But even this turned out to be another rotten rung on the ladder separating McKendree from fame. Bull disowned the result, the pair clashed during its recording, and, following its conclusion, never spoke again. Meanwhile the label who were set to release it, Hemlock Jukebox, folded, yet in a surreal twist, owing to the determination and Eastern European background of one of the label's evacuees, the single was still pressed, but only for a Hungarian market. After many fruitless eBay searches I managed to track down a copy in Klagenfurt, Austria, for which

I was pleased to only pay £35. It's a truly mind-bending work, three minutes of echoey, raw-as-you-like fuzz where psychedelic furry FX pedal funk meets something frightening and primal, apparently roaring out of the mouth of a cave beyond the edge of time. Yet it is also... a duet. Bull's vocals have to me never sounded like this on any other recording, resembling, as the defunct Hungarian music magazine *Bounce!* so accurately put it in one of the single's few reviews, 'the voice of a man unsuccessfully attempting to dislodge a locust he's found stuck between his teeth'.

The more I learned about McKendree, the more I learned he was not merely an eerily, almost celestially gifted musician. He painted, he took uniquely atmospheric photographs. In his later years, he was an ahead-of-the-curve campaigner against climate change and ecological ruination. In some ways, perhaps part of the problem for McKendree, and part of the reason he has still not been reappraised in the way a Nick Drake or even a Judee Sill has, is that his story doesn't follow a traditional rock tragedy narrative. He did not die in his twenties and was not a suicide. He failed at all points to be a major abuser of drugs. He part-vanished rather than totally vanished, only part gave up making music. There was nothing emphatic about his path. But his story is as laden with tragedy as any other in popular music that I can think of. His music was lost, found, lost again. The one true love he'd ever found, the only woman he'd ever wanted to truly be with, rather than just float noncommittally around, had her life cruelly snatched from her in a freak agricultural accident, just as it seemed feasible the two of them might finally be united. He himself died in a manner that was no less freakish, suffering a fatal stroke while on a bed in his chiropractor's clinic, on the final morning of the twentieth century.

Full track listing for *Wallflower* (recorded 1968, released 1976):
Penny Marshwort
Mrs Nicholas
Little Meg
Bog Asphodel
Cow of the Road
Sea Cabbage
Villager
Clapper Bridge
Gods of Mist, and Stone
Sad Portrait of a Dog
Marsh Pennywort

Notes, from 2,300th listen:
Whose is the laughter you can just faintly hear at the end of 'Marsh Pennywort'?

How much better would this have sounded if it was pressed on heavy late sixties vinyl, rather than this flimsy Ted Heath-era frisbee I hold in my hand?

Let's say this record actually came out just after it was made, in 1968 and 1969. Let's say it found an audience, lots of cool people were whispering about it. Let's say I was my age, or younger, at that time. Would I have listened to this record? Or would I have been suspicious of it for being too popular with cool people, and possibly denied myself the chance to enjoy it until a few years later, when it had become less cool? Ergo: been the same kind of stubborn cultural edgeperson I am now. But, even if it had been given the right of birth in the era it was made, would *Wallflower* have found any kind of large audience of cool people? Is it not a little bit frail, too much of an elusive whisper, too much of a record – even in its actual sound – that you have to search for, and eventually find?

Question: What are they, the layers that you can put into a piece of music, that makes it improve with age? Are they things you can see and feel? Where do you find them? Are they in the grooves? Grooves of vinyl. The transference of sound to them. People tell me how it works but I still don't get it. It's the ultimate modern witchcraft.

Usable transcript from interview with Angus Boon:
'Equinox were round tae bend, away wi' tae fairies. Something mental always happened when we played wae them. Which we did a bit, in our very early days, and which might sound tae you like a weird pairing, if ye didn't properly ken us, but wasn't, in that stage of Nannie Slagg's musical evolution. And there's this one gig in Todmorden, ye listenin', and we've played our last song and we get backstage and Equinox are there, all ready to go on and then Mick says tae the rest of the band, "Hold on, where's the rug?" They had this Moroccan rug which they all had to sit on while they played and they couldnae play without it and Julian, the wee milksop who played the lute and yae could knock over with a feather, he'd been entrusted with its safety on this occasion, and he'd left it in their hotel room in Halifax. By the time he'd driven there and back they were an hour late going on and a rumour was going round that it was because the band were baked, but it wasn't; it was because they needed their RUG. There was a second rug, too, after the first one wore out. And there's a story about Mick getting pished and nailing the first rug down on top of Dick so he was totally trapped underneath, but I don't know if that's apocryphal now, laddie.

'The Exeter solo gig? Aye, I mind it well. Fecking class performance by Dick. As always. He was so obsessive about his craft, the laddie had made himself immune from ever being anything less than brilliant. Not many people there, though.

People paint it like it was all about the punks, like outside the venue streets were thronged with laddies and lassies wearing safety pins and gobbing on pedestrians. That's a load of pish and twaddle. It was just a little lean time, a general lack of interest for what Dick – and I – was doing. I remember McKendree was wandering around, looking like a lost lamb; ye can guarantee nae member of the audience who saw him would have kenned the long streak of piss was one of the star acts of the night. When Dick had finally persuaded him to come over he'd asked specifically if he could stay somewhere on the moor, which meant Dick couldnae get more than a couple of drinks, and had tae drive him to and from the venue, and Dick was ragin' about that, because if he couldnae get drunk it always ripped his knitting. McKendree looked like he was about tae start bawling and I asked him what was wrong, kenning that maybe the two of them had fallen out. He told me he'd been walking up near Underhill Tor that afternoon and been trying to photograph a pair of these merganser ducks, which were pretty rare, even then, and in trying too hard to get a close-up he'd managed to scare the female, which like all the females looked very fragile and had a right braw shagged crest on the back of her head – kind of like some of the lassies Dick picked up at gigs, come tae think of it, heh – and by doing that he'd sent her flying off 300 yards up the river, and sent the male the same distance in the other direction, and now he couldnae stop thinking about it and said he was feeling like a terrible person. I told him to stop being such a wee nancy.

'Before Dick moved down here, after when we first decided to leave Glasgow, the two of us were staying in a house in Kensal Green for a while, only a mile or so from all the bohemian stuff going on in Notting Hill Gate. You wouldnae have called it a *fashionable* place, but we did some of the fashionable stuff of the time. A wee lassie Dick knew back in Kilsyth hitchhiked all the way down after him and turned up on our doorstep one day wae some sugar cubes. Lassies would do crazy stuff like that, where Dick was concerned. I didn't even ken the stuff was acid. That was how fecking naive I was. Anyway we took it and I ended up in the bath just bawling, "When's this fecking shite gonnae start *working*?" Neither of us were really intae it but I do reckon it broke down some walls for Dick; he started getting a bit further taeward the peripheries after that, exploring death more in his songs. And then he bought his first rug, from the market on Portobello. So we were intae it all and weren't. A lot of the minted hippie laddies didn't really see eye-to-eye wi' me. I talked too much, whereas for them it was all about not saying much and just saying stuff like "cool" and "far out" and making yersen look mysterious. But that was another world; we didn't live there. We were often up late at night and a bunch of car thieves lived next door, and you'd see them in an alley in the back spray-painting a Rover P5 at three in the morning. But anyway, Dick was never much of a lover of yer pop music, but I do remember at the time he would just nae stop listening to this tune "Thirteenth Snake Woman" by Stoneman's Cavalry, which was just a B-side to this tune called "Right On" that had been a wee hit in the States. So after he got the tapes from Superduck and found out that McKendree actually had been in the band and had a co-writing credit on that song, he flipped right out. I'm sure the laddie would have got the record out anyway but that was the icing on the cake.

'Aye, Morag! That was the name of the lassie who brought us the acid. I've remembered it now. Have yae seen the photo on the back sleeve of the *Doubling Cube* LP that Mick and Dick did just before they got Equinox together? The one where they're playing backgammon? You can just see this bored-looking lassie sitting on the couch behind them, staring out the window, looking like death. That's her. She was aff her fecking heid. Followed Terry Reid everywhere on tour, after she'd had her business with Mick. Wouldn't leave the poor lad Terry alone. Cut off a big chunk of his hair one time when he was asleep and kept it in a box.'

Sodding hell, is that my problem? Is that what I've been doing all these years, interviewing all these fading emperors of sixties and seventies rock, convincing me they're just my uncle for an hour when actually I'm looking for a full-time father figure? Thank you for the chat, Carlos Santana, and just as an extra could you come back to the flat and do me some overcooked chips in the deep fat fryer and tuck me up under my Spiderman duvet? Also, how are you with papier mâché? Why do I ask? Oh no reason. Just wondered. Actually did once pencil in a casual drink with Rick Wakeman after our Q and A but he never called. Christian. Into his cars. Probably wouldn't have worked out for the two of us anyway. Another one today, Angus Boon, but nobody's paying me for that. Nobody does now. Listened to his stuff on the way over. The early work, Nannie Slagg; a folk band, really, once you remove the layers of noise sludge. Actually did some half-decent tunes right at the start. All burrs and incense and runny battery-farm eggs on pappy white bread. Then the well-known stuff. Blacksmith. Three albums, gradually getting more shit and famous with each one. Stadium rock for the hygiene-deficient. A band who looked more like their own roadies than their own roadies did. Not my thing at all. Solo LP after that: weird record, not quite right. Got to give him kudos for the title though: *Unmetalled Road*. Him standing next to a footpath sign on the cover, in a tight vest, looking sullen. Not quite carrying it off: the vest, or the shift in genre. Traditional Scottish folk songs and synthesisers. An uneasy mix. Still got his mullet now from not long after that. 1984: year of delusional concepts of hair progress in middle-age rock. Imagine he'll stay committed to it until the end now. Younger wife, Carol. His fifth. One more for the full Henry VIII. Carol kept coming in to the living room and asking if we had enough fudge brownies. We said we were OK. At least thirteen of them on the table at all times. Clues to the epic recent narrative of Angus's stomach. Buzzing a bit from the stories he told. Liked him a lot. Showed me a photo of him and Dick McKnight of Equinox walking through the docks in Greenock. Double denim. Possible absence of underwear. Couple of useful lads to have on your side in a brawl. Talked on with him. Gave me more leads in my detective story. Kills me that it might never get read. Tried to sell a book a while ago. Nobody was arsed. 'Thank you for sending us this. We thought it was excellent and really has something special and a unique voice and I particularly like the bit where you wrote your name on the title page in capital letters but we think what would really improve the structure is if you could kindly fuck the fuck off and never contact us again.' Why would this one be any different? 'We would actually love to publish this biography of a dead person very few people care about, written by someone who can no longer get work in the national media.' Not happening. £118.73 left in the bank now. Rent due with Titus in a week. Trying not to worry. Bob will help me out, I reckon. Clearing my head. Walking along the coast. Atlantic. Different to the south. Right big growling bastard. Sharper teeth, more root canals. Almost fell down a hole in the cliff. Salty spume blowing up at me through it. You'd think they'd tell you, put a sign saying 'HOLE' in front of it or something. Hut on the cliff edge. 'I LOVE ANNIE' scratched into the wood. We all want to be Annie. Wind spun me down some steps. Helicopter above, coast guard, following for a while, probably thinking 'What's this cunt doing out here?' Hair getting a bit long, a bit Angus, at the back. Wind blew it all the way round and it blinded me and I fell over a tough wiry wee shite cunt of shrub. Talking like a Scottish person too now. Happens, if you spend enough time with them. Shrubs have to be hard bastards up here, to survive all the blowing. Looked like one myself. Redhead cliffweed, also known by its Latin name Gingerus Twaticus. Everyone used to rub it when I was young, scruff it up. Always rough enough for it to hurt a bit but you weren't allowed to complain. What passed for affection, round our way. Last thing the old man did before he left. Rubbed his knuckles into it. Nobody does that round here. They give you a hug, even if you don't know them, make to shake your hand like they're about to do origami with it. Do what the hell you want with your fingers, pal, but I'm not game; I'm keeping my palm right here, in the archetypal loading position, like a human man.

Excerpt from rough draft of Wallflower Child: The Ballad of RJ McKendree

It's hard to imagine what impact Devon must have made on McKendree as a baby, if any, but one might assume that his decision to head there in 1968 was sparked by some seed of a memory, some kind of peeling back of the layers and searching for the child inside himself. His father was in the US air force, which meant he moved the family around a lot during McKendree's early childhood, until they settled in the town of Watsonville in California. From that point until the dissolution of Stoneman's Cavalry in 1967, Richard John McKendree's story was not markedly different to that of a lot of music-crazed kids growing up in sixties America: he gets into the Beatles, he grows his hair to the disapproval of his parents, he and Frank, his friend from school, begin to write songs in Frank's mum and dad's garage. Out with his bandmates, he smokes weed and drinks whiskey, but remains in fear of his father at home, shakes his mother's and sister's hands every night before going to bed. Stoneman's Cavalry get a record deal, have a minor hit, implode. He makes it known that he would henceforth prefer to be known not as Richard or Richie but RJ and drifts around the steep dusty edges of LA, almost gets convinced to become a born-again Christian by Bryan MacLean from Love, is rumoured to be briefly considered as a replacement when David Crosby leaves the Byrds, always seems trapped on the edge of everything, unable to quite reach the centre of any scene and become part of it, as if behind some kind of force field, possibly self-made. He doesn't appear in any memoir or biography or review of the time, besides very briefly in the cobbled-together, long out of print and somewhat trashy-looking 1970 paperback *LA and the Happening Scene*. Here, the young full-time dental hygienist and sometime singer Linda Perhacs, whose own lone solo album *Parallelograms* would also take decades to be recognised for its true mystical brilliance, remembers McKendree attending a gig at the Whiskey a Go Go in the company of his mother, presumably some time in 1969, not long after his return from Devon, and recalls noticing that they 'have each other's looming awkwardness and small ears'. It took a long time for me to track down Frank Bull, who never gigged or recorded again after his ill-fated reunion with McKendree to record what became the Hungarian-only 'Little Meg' single, and now is an abstract artist living – going on the evidence of his website – in an extremely long one-storey wooden house in Colorado. He told me he was reluctant to talk about that time, having been advised by his guru to place it in a locked box in the past, but after numerous requests from me did reply to a couple of questions in a fashion not a lot less abstract than his art, calling McKendree 'my original old lady' and 'the source of my river'. He claimed to have never heard the *Wallflower* album and to have no interest in doing so but was sure that 'my other self, on a parallel plane to this one, really digs it'.

One afternoon about a week after I've been to see Angus, my phone rings, and it's him, although I don't know at first because I haven't saved his number because rock stars you've interviewed aren't going to be your friend.

'I had one more thought, laddie, regarding your wee book,' he says. 'The boy who produced the album, Chickpea. The great big slab of beef. He might be able to tell you a bit more about your man McKendree. If ye can get any sense out of him. He still lives down here, up in the hills behind Dawlish. Shite thing is I don't have his number...'

'Damn.'

'I can tell you where his caravan is, though.'

*

Nobody talked about 'acid folk' in the seventies so nobody called the *Wallflower* LP that when it was released. 'Acid folk' is what it has been described as more recently by record collectors but I am not sure if that is truly accurate. Genres are just restrictive boxes that were made to contain something naturally slippery, and, often, the more slippery something is, the better it is. To me *Wallflower* is as bucolic as it is acid, as eastern as it is western, as jazz as it is folk, as elemental as it is mystic, as spectral as it is real. It sounds possessed to me, by a landscape, possibly by a woman, or maybe two. All of this is very hard to get a grip on for the listener, and it's perhaps in this slipperiness where another part of the mystique lies.

Songs such as 'Penny Marshwort', 'Marsh Pennywort' (a more hazy, whispery reprise of the earlier song but also something more than that), 'Mrs Nicholas' and the reworking of the little-known traditional Devonshire folk ballad 'Little Meg' all give the impression of a state of hypnosis induced by female characters, potentially even the same female characters. Once the listener learns of the close friendship McKendree struck up with Maddie Chagford, the daughter of a farmer living on the edge of the moor, it's tempting to speculate to just what extent she was his muse. Chagford died in 1974, aged just twenty-five, in a heart-breaking tractor crash on the farm, so by the time McKendree returned to the West Country for the deferred attempt to promote his album, he was too late to consolidate anything that might have sparked between them, and perhaps it is this, rather than the manner of his death, that is the biggest tragedy of all. Maddie was not his last romance, if a romance was what it was, but he never married and for the remainder of his life certainly never had a live-in girlfriend or sustained a relationship for longer than seven months.

'There is one other thing I just remembered,' says Maggie. 'I can't believe I forgot. I do worry about myself sometimes. Well, so the thing is, we did see McKendree one more time. Or at least I thought it could have been him, and Oliver was sure it was. It was at the march to protest the bypass. 1996, or 1995, was that? You'd probably know as well as I do. He was a few rows behind us but then we lost sight of him. I remember he was with this very beautiful black boy wearing a silk scarf. It can't have been all that long before he died.'

What is this hair on me? Tiny hairs, all over my t-shirt. Get off me, hairs. These things are ferocious. I think it's the sofa. Whose sofa is it? Seems familiar, but it's not mine, not Titus's. That's where the hairs are coming from, the sofa. But where did they come from before that? God, there are SO MANY of them. I just can't put it together. My brain is too dried out, too big for my skull. It's a wonder it's still inside there. If you took it out and tried to fit it back in you'd never manage it. Why do I continue to be this stupid when my brain is this big? Fuck this fucktangular life. OK, kitchen. Water. Tastes good. I need salt. Who decided to make taps so loud and why do they hate me? What did I ever do to deserve this? Who lives here and why am I alone here? Painting of a cow on the wall. Seedlings. Why won't my left eye open? I think an enemy might have Copydexed it shut. Scent of lily and coffee. Pot is warm. Guitar. Spider plant. Oxygen Steve who did the listings page at *Melody Maker* had one. Used to go to his house with Adam from Engine Room PR before gigs. Hated that plant, Adam did. Don't know why. Used to piss in the soil when Oxygen Steve was out of the room. Johnny Slazenger came over one time and joined in. PRs. Can't trust any of them. Nice table, this. I notice tables more nowadays, me. Coins on it. £1.56. Enough to buy some eggs from an honesty box outside a farm. RSPCA newsletter next to the coins. Dark bottle of hair product. Miss Delicious Sea Spray, 'for that "just out of the waves" look'. But does it also contain fish piss, mystery and the souls of the dead? If not, I'm not into it. Open laptop. Some bread! Is there anything to spread on it, I wonder. Ooh yeah. Watch out technology 'cause I'm using honey. Why is nobody else here? Not a man's house. 91 per cent sure of that. Sex? No. Didn't happen. Can feel my loins telling me that. Neglected of late. Must do something about it. Clean the pipes. 'A freelancer's lie down', the journos used to call it in London. But not here. Of course not here. Anyone could walk in. Well, not anyone, but the owner. Ah, I think it's coming back. A woman, her dog, limitless source of tiny hair. Cold flannel on my face. Such big sad eyes, looking down at me, eyes that seemed to stretch in their corners and reach out to try to tell their tale. French dress sense, a bit, sort of. Mid-forties? OK, that is enough of standing up. Tactical vomit might be in order. Finger down the throat. Puke's sweet release. Steps outside, an excited canine whimper, key unlocking a door. Does that paper bag have poppadoms in? Ooh, one left. Nice and rubbery, just like I like them. Which kind person did this for me? Ah, I think I remember: it was me. Top bloke, my past self. Like him a lot. Sometimes.

Excerpt from rough draft of Wallflower Child: The Ballad of RJ McKendree

When I arrive at Chickpea's, it's the smell that hits me, before anything else, before I get around the corner and see the rotting half Ford Escorts and three-quarter Mitsubishis, the motorbike wheels, the strange rusting gurney, the chimney pots, the tiny pink child's bike sinking into the weeds on the high bank, the pile of defeated smoking something behind the corrugated iron shed, the lone disconsolate horse with the fluffy feet tied to a stake, the caravan with the pen of barking dogs outside and the other caravan that looks like it's been subject to its own internal hurricane and the other caravan behind that with more penned and caged dogs outside. It's the smell of the last day of every music festival I've ever attended but as if that smell has then had oil poured on it and been grilled for a year. Dogs yell at me from all sides from behind fences and awful walls and wire mesh, and two more tousled black ones trot down the lane to meet me. I knock on the door of the red caravan, the one I have been told about, the one with the car engine on its roof, but there is no answer. An old unconnected sink looks up at me from the dirt, asking for help. The two black dogs follow me around the back, eager-tailed. 'And this is the place where we keep our old tyres and cookers,' the dogs seem to say, proudly. Half a Renault van offers 'OODLE GROOMING SERVICES, OTHER CANINES CONSIDERED'. I see nobody. I want to leave, just as I have since I first smelled the smell. The relief upon doing so is so immense, the relief makes having been there almost worthwhile. I proceed down the lane, out of this rust and asbestos apocalypse, out of this inexplicable steel village run by dogs. The smell departs and butterflies cartwheel alongside me, into the sun.

*

Devon retained its mysterious hold on McKendree and perhaps it was all about that first journey he made there, from California, and some kind of attempt to recreate it, and the inspiration that flowed through him as a songwriter for that one summer, which led to the recording of the songs on *Wallflower*. He returned in 1978, for his gig with Dick McKnight, and then again in the late eighties, and twice in the mid and late nineties, sleeping in tents and on friends' sofas, and at a travellers' commune in the foothills of the moor. Ever since his early twenties, McKendree had suffered from upper back problems and blackouts, and it seemed that his one-in-a-million death, on the morning of 31 December 1999, was a final sort of culmination of these. A haemorrhage during treatment for spine issues is not a rock-and-roll death but McKendree's was not a rock-and-roll life in much of an archetypal sense. It is perhaps fitting that it ended in Devon, the place where he'd made the defining artistic statement of his life. There is also a certain poetry to the fact that he never got to see the twenty-first century: a lost artist who was not made for an era where art didn't get lost any more, when music became so much more accessible, cheapened by choice, when archive footage was there for free, to be picked over, shared, and shared and shared, then shared again.

It is a little difficult to remember just how hard it was to access music itself in the seventies, eighties and the first part of the nineties, let alone to access a publicity-shy, commercially moribund creator of that music. No Facebook, Twitter, Instagram, YouTube, Spotify, Discogs, eBay. Prior to the arrival of the Internet, it was hard enough to track down your own estranged father, let alone a psychedelic primitivist's folk music from California whose last recorded output had come out three years before your birth, and even then only in Hungary. This book could not have been written then, I suspect. This dearth of digital network, of all the invisible wires that now loop and cobweb together and connect everything and make the world seem so small yet so much more intimidatingly massive and complex, was no doubt another reason why McKendree continued to go largely unrecognised as the paisley acid genius he was, but what it gave him was the luxury of living a life under the radar, the ability to stay modest and quiet and unexpected. The more I learned about McKendree from the few people I talked to who met him and were still alive, the more I suspect that living some other way would have been deeply uncomfortable for him.

Eye cleaned up now. Sat very patient while she did it, didn't even whimper. Still won't open but feeling better for a woman's touch. Walking now, me and her and the dog. Couldn't believe it when she told me her full name. But by that time I'd seen the painting – not the cow, the other one – and something in me knew, even though I hadn't even known she existed. All too convenient, really. Thought I was in my own fantasy. Film of my life. Maybe I am. Maybe I'm dead. If I am, being dead is OK. Some great ladies here in the afterlife. She takes me up the back of the tor, round past the house that looks like it has ghosts inside, the one where you watch and wait for the terrible face that will press itself against the depraved smudgy glass. Water is rushing down the lanes and beside them. A river, and then another dry something that used to be a river. 'They reclaimed the land in the fifties,' she says. 'Filled it in. But you still get the mist down there, looking for the river like it should still be there.' Poor mist. Like a lost soul looking for a dead lover. Like a singer looking for an old muse. Shut up. Don't think about that. Sheep carcass. Meat almost gone off the bones. Dog won't leave it alone. 'Come here, Sherlock, stop frolicking in former animals!' Viaduct. The hill and its stepladder of rocks. 'Used to be a volcano, once,' she says. '1976, I think it was.' Funny, she is. Effortlessly. Some of the lads at the paper used to say women couldn't do humour well. Fucking bullshit. She's not wearing make-up but her eyes seem smudged, somehow. Entrancing. Wish I'd properly decked that guy last night; caught me unawares before I'd got a chance. Didn't even know I'd cut in on him at the bar. Tracksuit bastard. 'What's your problem? Go over there and sit with Sad Susan while you wait your turn.' Well, here I am with Sad Susan. That's the main thing. Cows in this field. Coming towards us. Lary buggers. 'Nothing to be scared of,' she says. 'They're all lovely. Just stand your ground.' Ah, we're going past that bit of barn. Always freaks me out, that place. 'There's a rumour that someone photographed it and when the photo was developed the whole building was there, just as it would have been when it was built in the 1700s,' she says. 'Nobody has ever seen the photograph, though, conveniently.' Muddy. Her legs don't half motor, for a little person. Big puddles. I help her over; her hand is clammy and small. And then she lands, kind of in my sleeve, and stays there and holds on to me. There's so much I want to ask her. But all I say is 'Are you cold?' and we don't move for what feels like the next fortnight.

Excerpt from rough draft of Wallflower Child: The Ballad of
RJ McKendree

> By 1989, RJ McKendree was a middle-aged man, albeit an oddly
> youthful-looking one, with few of the trappings of middle-aged
> life. He lived in his mother's house in the suburbs of Tulsa, which
> he'd inherited upon her death four years earlier. He socialised with
> few people besides his sister, who lived just two streets away. For
> income, he continued to work in a camera shop in the centre of
> town. His music had reached the pinnacle of its obscurity. Dick
> McKnight had died of heart failure a year earlier, Selkie Records
> had long since folded and *Wallflower* was remembered only by –
> at the very most – those still alive who were involved in its release
> or had bought one of the small number of copies of it that had
> been pressed. McKendree was sometimes known to busk in
> downtown Tulsa (note to self: FIND SOURCE/TULSA RESIDENT
> AND VERIFY THIS) but had largely abandoned playing music in
> any committed sense, yet it was at this point that he decided to
> buy a plane ticket, pack a few clothes and his guitar, and visit
> Devon for a third time. What was his impetus? We will possibly
> never know. Was he still searching for the ghost of Maddie? Had
> he finally realised, after all these years, that the UK's deep south
> west was the place where he most fitted in, or at least the place
> where he felt least like an outsider?

Not bad, this cucumber. Eating them all the time now. Bite into
the fuckers like a Twix, just while idly doing my stuff. Had a word
with Titus and he's agreed to defer rent payments for a couple
of months. He's a good guy, the cucumber baron. Course he is.
Related to Jen. Badge of quality. Teach me to write posh people
off, that will. Veg paradise, this. Am allowed as much as I like.
Sometimes find a box outside my door. Tasty rejects. Carrots

the world wrote off as ugly without stopping to look into their pure soul. Soil-caked muscular dystrophy broccoli. Outsider sweetcorn. Rebel cabbage. Nobbled geek courgettes. Could almost stop going to the shop altogether if I cut out carbs and personal hygiene and accepted extreme dust as a part of domestic life. Got the stuff Chris asked for today. That bread she likes, with the olives in it. Why do they put a little plastic window in the packaging? Food doesn't look out and see what's going on in the street. It's not your nan. Newspaper. Don't know why. Thought Chris might like one. Good stories today. An aromatherapist in Paignton has been sentenced for terrorising her neighbour by repeatedly banging bin lids. 'The jury heard that Karen Birchall, who practises aromatherapy under the name "Mitzy Moon", started banging the bin at 3 a.m., asking her retired neighbour Denise Sutcliffe, "How are your nerves now?"' Bastard in front of me didn't put the divider down on the checkout. Sure sign of a wanker. Shit. Forgot candles, the scented ones. Will she hate me? Is this married life, suddenly? We only met two Fridays ago. Used her card to pay today. Waiting for a new one of my own. Lost mine in a peat bog, Sunday afternoon. Walked up by the cemetery, the burned-out church. Good names on the tombs. Meredith Bunce. Elsie Welsey. John Peter Trumbletits. OK, made that last one up. Stuck for a name for your novel? Go to a cemetery. Grave of a small child. First World War. Scary statue, head missing. Forget-me-nots. Wildflowers love dead people. Me? I'm coming back as a primrose in the next world. Walked up, up, up the hill that goes to the clouds. Past two old cottages. Thick stone walls built to withstand Satan's bronchitis. Sign above a door: 'DUCK'. The duck who lives there must be fucking massive. Sign above another door: 'REBUILDED 1847'. Great but more importantly can you tell me when was it builded? Higher, the old mine with the stone eye windows. Place where it looks like it all ends. Buttock hills. Wire grass. Ground like a mouth, sucking at you, not happy with just your feet, wants your knees too. Lose your whole leg around here if you don't watch it, or at least a good part of it. Why do you only have one foot, shin and ankle? Ah, I left the others up on Trembling Hill. It seemed easier in the long run than bringing them back. The earth owns them now. Moss everywhere. Trees all in their sartorial stoner-rock phase. Vincent Price's voice in my head, narrating my journey. What a mid-Atlantic accent would be if the mid-Atlantic contained a pagan island with its own thriving population of wolves. Thought I might meet one of Oliver Fox's Gribblins, go on an adventure, join the tribe, biggest member, only redhead, the new leader, a simpler life. Another hangover vanquished by the moor. Passed my Stepping Stone Proficiency Test, all the levels, breezed the Beginner and the Intermediary but then almost came unstuck at Holy Shit These Slippy Bastards Aren't Even Above The Water. Fucking bench up here at the top carved out of stone. What pre-industrial maverick did that? Garden furniture essentials. All the rage in the 1680s. Sat down on the granite, looked in my wallet to check how many stamps I had on my loyalty card for Toploaded Burrito in Camden. Don't know why. Not going back there any time soon. Just wanted to check. See what I was missing out on. Saw my debit card was missing. Panic! Remembered I'd stored it in my phone case pocket instead. Relief! Looked in my phone case pocket. Wasn't there either. Panic! Had my phone out to take a photo of some bog asphodel half a mile back. Must have dropped it. Walked back. Got on my hands and knees and ferreted around, trying not to sink. Wasn't there. Couple of hikers passed, binoculars, matching red anoraks. Twitcher types. Them: 'Oh dear, what have you lost?' Me: 'My bank card.' Everyday occurrence here on the moor, sort codes seeping into the peat. Gave up after twenty minutes. Three youths coming the other way. Duke of Edinburgh award types. Wholesome. 'Can you do us a favour? Can you call my number if you happen to spot a black HSBC card down there in the bog?' 'Sure. I'll just save it on my phone. What's your name? Don't worry. I'll just put it down as Bank Card Guy on the Moor.' No call. Trudged back to Chris's. Creaky hips. Blister bigger than the toe it was attached to. No money for beer. Can't take myself anywhere. Hope you know what you're getting yourself into, Chris.

Excerpt from rough draft of Wallflower Child: The Ballad of RJ McKendree

This book is not about me. There are enough examples of the rock biography where the ego of the author is permitted to take over, and he becomes as much the focus of events, if not more than, his intended subject, and I do not want to be another. But it is impossible not to tell the next chapter in my McKendree pilgrimage without detailing my own very personal role in it, since without that, and what I was going through at the time, the remarkable coincidence that took me deeper into the McKendree story would not have happened.

As I have briefly mentioned before, when I began to research McKendree I was going through a difficult period in my life. I would drink to excess, be quick with my fists in bar rooms and clubs and bus queues, spend mornings wallowing in regret about what I'd said or done, then look for a quick way to make it better, which, by mid-afternoon, I would have concluded could only involve a visit to the nearest pub. After a fruitful and exciting initial couple of months on McKendree's trail, when I'd found out just how many bit players in his story were still alive and well in the south west, I'd hit a bit of a wall. I had used almost all of my savings, the moorland sky – as it can sometimes – had done nothing but empty itself on the boggy ground for two weeks without let-up, and I found myself in the corner of the Stags Bar in the Church House in Wychcombe, staring morosely into my stout and wondering how it had all come to this. The precise ins and outs of what happened next need not be detailed here. Let it suffice to say two angry men got into a petty quarrel over their position at the bar, then one of them – believing he was acting chivalrously towards a member of the opposite gender who had recently entered the premises – slightly misjudged the size of the other man and ended up coming off slightly worse in the resulting melee, and was taken into the care of the person he believed he'd been defending, back at her house, before slipping into a semi-comatose state.

The following morning, while I slept, my new guardian angel walked her dog, a lurcher called Sherlock, and bought eggs and coffee from the Co-op. As I stumbled around the top floor of her cottage, my bruised pride was not slow in coming back to me, but the events of the previous night were revealing themselves in a staggering, painful way, one by one: my tussle, the kind and patient face of my benefactor, the late night Indian takeaway I'd insisted on then left half-eaten, the laugh we'd had at the bit on the menu where it said 'Thank you for your costume' and the way the laughter had hurt my bruised face. It was several minutes before I descended the stairs and set my astonished eyes on the painting in her stairway, by which time Christine – for now I remembered that was her name – was opening the front door on her return.

'This,' I said. 'It's the painting from one of my favourite albums. I can't believe it. It's... it's very... it's, well, fucking hell it's the reason I'm here, in Devon.'

'Ah, you saw that?' she said, elegantly easing off a boot. 'It's not an original. It's not even an original copy. Just a copy of a copy. I have been thinking of taking it down, to be honest.'

'Yes! The original is by Joyce Nicholas. It says on the LP sleeve. I looked it up online. It's worth a fortune now. But do you know it, *Wallflower*? The record.'

Seeing her properly in the sunlight that was streaming through the window above the front door, I remembered her many kindnesses from the previous night. I noticed now that she was older than me, maybe by several years, older than I'd first thought. Her face made me think of a mosaic: a very beautiful thing made entirely from shattered things. The elegant way she held the lead attached to the dog and hung her hat on the coat rail seemed to accentuate an ambience of Frenchness about her.

'Poor Sherlock, I think he has a gorse needle in his foot. I do know it, yes. I knew the man who made it, for a while. I also knew the person who helped to get it made. But that was a very long time ago.'

'Dick McKnight, from Equinox? No, what I am I talking about, he just released it. Chickpea? You're kidding. You knew Chickpea?'

'No, her name was Maddie. She was my sister.'

The two of us, under the trees. Feet in the river. Her: calm, Zen. Me: screaming like a little girl. Dragonflies around our heads. Trees greened up to the max, furred branches. Burrows in the moss. Holes leading to the underplanet. Total *Alice in Wonderland* shit. 'Just concentrate on breathing properly and it won't hurt.' All right for her to say. Doubt the water temperature would make much difference to her. Her feet are already like blocks of ice. Let her warm them on me every night, except nothing changes. 'Bad circulation,' she says. 'Runs in the family. My dad had it. Sister too.'

Sister.

Trying not to cry or shout but sweet Mabel in heaven it's cold. Find myself imagining him here, under the moss. The video he never made, the pop star he never was. 'He used to come up here,' she says, as if reading my thoughts. 'He walked a lot. It was probably part of why there was never any meat on him, even in his forties and fifties. He never wore proper shoes for it, always just some old trainers. They always had holes in them and bits of moss sticking out of them. He didn't have nice feet. He told me once about this house he used to go to, up over there, about a mile. Some rich Aussie bought it in the nineties and the barns are Airbnbs now. But it used to be abandoned. When they knocked some of the walls down there was a story in the local paper of someone finding a doll in one of them. It's not uncommon, around here, dolls in walls. Shoes, too. They say they were put there to help ward off evil. Although I saw the picture of that doll in the paper and it didn't look nice. Didn't look like it wanted to help. Anyway, Richie said he went to the house and sometimes it felt like voices were speaking to him through the stone. A woman. He said she watched him sometimes. I was a bit mean about it at the time. Thought it was nonsense, acid casualty talk, even though I later realised he wasn't one of those. He said a lot of weird stuff. It was before I'd really listened to the record, to be honest. I was twenty-nine, more dismissive, more beholden to irony. But now I think about him saying that and I'm not sure. Do you think music can be haunted?'

'Definitely,' I say. Got more to say on this subject, and I start, but then I stop. My role here is listener. Cold starting to get more bearable. Acclimatising. Zen feet of a Buddhist master. Give it a week and I will be able to walk on hot coals too.

'I met him in 1993 at the old commune, sort of a commune I suppose, anyway, up at Runnaford Hollow. But I'd actually met him before. I didn't remember that. Why would I? I was only a little kid, five. But when he started talking I knew, and he knew who I was straight away. It was a weird time, that summer, kind of like another little 1960s, and him being there probably made it more like that. He was older than everyone else but he still didn't seem like other people I knew who were his age. There were some quite odd people up there too, people with quite a bit of darkness in their life. We all knew he'd made a record but he was very silent about a lot of stuff. Everyone always stopped everything they were doing and listened when he played, though. We started hanging out for a while. I'd been going out with this guy Mark, younger than me, nothing serious, and we'd been doing a lot of animal liberation stuff. But then we broke into this farm where there were loads of geese and opened the gates but some geese went straight onto the road and got hit by cars and I didn't even know why we'd broken into the farm, which didn't seem terrible for animals in any way; that made me withdraw from all that, and start to hang out more with Richie. We even recorded a few songs, in the same room where he'd recorded *Wallflower*. Very lo-fi, definitely not what was in vogue with UK bands at the time, more like American stuff. Eric's Trip, Sebadoh. Chickpea still has the mastertapes. I've never asked him for them back. I decided they were a mess. Richie wasn't fond of them, either.'

'I went to his place, Chickpea's, to find him. There was nobody there. Just all these dogs.'

'I wouldn't go within 500 yards of that place. It stinks to high heaven. That's if he's living in the same spot. He might have moved on. I heard that he is pretty ill. He's been a very fucked-up guy for a long time. Did you know he robbed a post office and went to prison for a while? Someone told me they went into his caravan and it was just plastered wall-to-wall with eighties porn, with one great big poster of Princess Diana in the middle of it all. I don't know if that's actually true. Anyway, I have a cassette. So you can hear the songs if you like.'

'You are kidding?'

'No. The only catch is you'll need to find a cassette player. I don't have one.'

'So you and Richie. Did you...'

'Yes. No. Sort of. It didn't work, at all. He seemed like quite an asexual person. And there was the fact of Maddie too. It made it odder still. Maybe me getting close to him was a way to try to bring her back, a bit. After that, we sort of drifted. I know he stayed in Devon for a while, though. I would pass him in the car sometimes, walking along a lane, and wave from the car, but that was about it.'

'And him and Maddie...'

'There's no way of telling. I was ten when she died. She wouldn't have said anything to me and maybe I wouldn't have remembered if she had. My assumption is that maybe they didn't. He wouldn't have told me something like that, but I do know that when they met he'd been under the impression that she had a boyfriend. I don't remember her having boyfriends, not since school. She was very much a law unto herself, different from me and Mum and Dad. You can even see that in the way she died. We had two tractors, a new one and an old one, and Dad had told her not to take the old one with the iffy brakes to the far field, which was really steep, but she didn't listen. She was more arty than the rest of us, she read Russian novels and listened to what my dad called "drug music". Everyone loved her. Everyone. I couldn't have been more different, really. I was one of the boys, not many female friends. I ended up working at the golf club, drank pints, watched football. People found me a bit stroppy, I think. But then I changed, became a lot more like her. Started going up to Exeter and Bristol, hitting all the charity shops, where you could get some total bargains back then, and buying clothes like the ones she used to wear. Gabardine skirts. Felt hats. I became much quieter. This sounds really crazy but I even used her name as my own sometimes, answered the phone as her. It was this deferred way of processing grief, I think. And then after that, I kind of became me, whatever that is. That would have been not long after Richie died, I suppose. And that was when I repainted the painting.'

'I really can't wait to hear these songs.'

She doesn't seem to hear me say it, just hears the other question in my mind, the one that I was too afraid to ask.

'And you know what the most ridiculous thing was? It wasn't even the brakes that did it. It was just the slope. We were all supposed to go to the May fair that day, at Riddlefoot Meadow. They always had it on the last day of the month. I remember that, because she was a Gemini, and so was he, actually. She had a migraine, and said she didn't want to go. She must have felt better. She was always trying to move some stuff. It was some walkers who raised the alarm but it was too late by that point. It's hard to say how much too late.'

Are my feet purple? Think they are. Fish nibbling at them. Wouldn't even feel it if they were. Exfoliation. People pay good money for this. And bad money. Wondering about that house on the hill. Can just see an old woman down the valley, calling a horse, ringing a bell. Water is mellow, tinkly. River has a song but you have to get in really close to hear it.

Excerpt from rough draft of Wallflower Child: The Ballad of RJ McKendree

'She said love don't come for free and she pushed me into the trees.' – RJ McKendree, 'Marsh Pennywort'

McKendree might not have recorded during his thirties and early forties but in early middle-age he retained what many musicians of his generation did not, something he might not have maintained had he become rich and famous: a curiosity about new music. As a forty-something, his listening remained as diverse as ever, including Indian ragas, Zambian funk, fuzz-laden Polish psychedelia on the cusp of progressive rock, but also took in some of the most interesting low-budget American bands of the time: Pavement, Swell, The Amps, Guided By Voices, The Grifters. The sessions that McKendree recorded in 1993 with Christine Chagford yielded just four songs: 'Sister Blue', 'Rent My Head', 'Gribblins' and 'The Twice River'. The recording sessions took place in the same room where the songs for *Wallflower* had been recorded two and a half decades earlier, with the same engineer, Chickpea. The songs – all duets between Chagford and McKendree, with the exception of 'Sister Blue', which features Chagford's lone, gossamer vocal under a lagoon of tape hiss – are an unusual mixture of sunshine pop sweetness and Sonic Youth-like pre-grunge feedback and have a lo-fi quality that makes them sound like they're coming from a stairwell three rooms distant. The two vocalists, meanwhile, sound connected and not connected, awkwardly spliced together somehow, yet all the more charming from that, and exempt from the 'empty biscuit barrel' sound that blighted so many of the bigger budget records of the nineties and makes them sound so horribly dated now. The sessions themselves were fragmented and chaotic, with Chickpea – who was suffering from what was later discovered to be the first of three bouts of bowel cancer – swigging from a bottle of Jack Daniel's, leaving his post at the mixing desk every few minutes to use the nearest water closet, or just not turning up at all on the afternoon that had been arranged. The songs remain, to this day, unreleased.

'Have you heard the term "impostor syndrome"?' Chagford says to me. 'I wonder if most people – apart from the really arrogant and privileged – have it. I think maybe I have it more than most. I have this recurring dream where somebody comes and tells me I'm not allowed to go on living the way I am because there's a qualification missing from my past, and I have to go back and sort everything. I think it comes from this feeling in my life that I've never really stuck at something and completed it. I quit my bartending job and sort of ran away from it. I left school as soon as I possibly could. I chose not to stay on at the farm after it became too much for Mum and Dad to manage. Even the eco-terrorism stuff: I was never fully there with it. And those recordings were the same. It was another unfinished thing. But around that time I had another recurring dream, a proper nightmare, really. It was about Maddie. I didn't dream actually doing it but in the dream I always knew that we'd been arguing and I'd pushed her off something high into some water and in the dream she kept coming back as this doll, I don't know, maybe the really old doll Richie had told me about that he'd found in the wall, but maybe not, because I don't really know what that doll looked like, but what would happen is that as the doll Maddie would sing and tell everyone about what I'd done to her. And then this ultra-weird thing happened which was that at the Newbury bypass protest march a few years later I met Maggie and Oliver Fox, you know, who'd done *The Gribblins* for TV, which I absolutely loved as a kid, with all that moss and everything, and the Water Bears always having a go at them, which I loved maybe even more. I was there with Mark, because we were still friends, although there was nothing else between us by this point, and he was really involved with the whole thing, getting arrested and chaining himself to trees, but I was really only a daytripper there, so it was just another example of how I am a bit half-arsed about everything, and at the end of the day I ended up getting a lift back down here to Devon with the Foxes, who were really lovely people, just as lovely as

you'd imagine, and they invited me in to their house, which was
this massive barn, which I remember had all these ladders and
mannequins everywhere, and a swimming pool outside with
frogs and leaves in it, and above the fireplace I noticed there
was one of the actual Gribblins, just sitting there. And then after
that, every time I had the dream where Maddie was the doll,
she would be this Gribblin. So essentially the dream became
about my sister, coming back as a seventies TV character, and
singing a song to everyone about how I'd murdered her.'

Hot air balloon! Me! Who'd have thunk it? Up here. Me, who
used to refuse to walk over the high bridge over the motorway
and go a mile further along to the underpass instead. Is that
turbulence? Do you get turbulence in balloons? No room for a
black box recorder here. Not with four of us in the basket: me,
Chris, Titus and Jen, who is down for the weekend. One of Titus's
toys, this. Seems to be in control. Took lessons years ago. His
dad. Professional. Did it for Virgin. Flew with Branson. Hung out
with him and Mike Oldfield and Oldfield's kettle drums. Oldfield
shy, still looking like a boy at thirty-two. Avoiding going over
the field of cows now. You can't do that, Titus says, because the
cows think the sound of the burning propane is the aggressive
roar of a giant skybeast and freak out. Going south, down the
river. Cottages on their own. Mystery homes, invisible to the land
eye. Secrets of the sky. How on earth do you get to these places
by car? Chris's hand in mine. Think Jen is cool about me and
her. Seems it. Two of them talked about millinery. Jen is taking
a course. Chris did one last year. Compared hats. Seemed to hit
it off. Almost left them to get off with each other. Chris, eating
a nobbly orange. Sailing the peel away on the wind. Likes the
big ones. Not me. I'm more of a satsuma boy. I watch her. Lines
blurring. What am I? Lover or biographer? Can I be both? Titus

taking us lower, following the curve of the river. Don't think he's going to crash land. Got some champagne with him. Expensive stuff. If you end up on private land you have to give the bottle to the owners. Tradition. 'Every landing is a crash landing if you're in a balloon, really,' he says. Reassuring. That confidence, rife, even up here. Nothing touching him. Bending with the wind, fragrant, easing through it all like he's made of flowers. Could I make myself like that? Is being like that within my capability, with where I'm from, who I'm from? Anyway, doesn't matter. Not much matters up here. Not the book, because who will read it. Not the rent, because it's not due for another month, and besides Titus said I could earn some money by doing some picking if I like. Harvest soon. Reddening land below. Looks like a map: a map of what I'm writing. But who will ever see it? Who cares? And that doesn't matter either right now, because I've got Chris. Hand back in mine now, sticky from the orange. Does this work, two broken people together? Are we jigsaw pieces, or just shards? Shut up, Martin. Stay out of the future. Stay here. It's good up here. She's good. Life's good. Cucumber's good. Look at it all below you. Is that the spooky barn we walked past? It is. Is that the building where 'Sister Blue' was recorded? It is. Is that the sheep you cuddled last week? It is. Is that your estranged father? No. It is a Jersey cow. Is that the pub where you decked the esteemed newspaper editor Richard Peck? No, it's not. That's a million miles away, in another universe. We can do this, Chris. We can do it here, I think. Look, it's the mist. I can't believe it. The one you said still looked for the river, even though the river was filled in years ago. It's the actual, famous mist. Well, not famous, more like cult mist, really. Famous in a quiet way, underappreciated. That poor, sad mist. Never stops searching. And then it goes. But then there's more mist, and I suppose even though it's not the same mist, it is the same mist, and everything starts over again, and, even though it's different mist, made of different particles, I suppose it never forgets. It will always be here, trying to find the answer to its question.

BILLYWITCH (1932)

My name is William Millhouse. I am not a remarkable or interesting man, but these are my memories. It is late in the day now, and I have decided to set them down, not because I believe them to be a record of a great or interesting life but because if I don't, being survived by no living relative, I will take them with me to the grave. Maybe that is not such a great tragedy but within my life is the life of a place too, and I feel great alteration is afoot, and some of that life may soon be frittered and blown on the wind. There will be others who could tell it better and wiser than me, but I am not quite as simple a man as some have taken me for, and this is my story, or at least the parts of it I remember most clearly. In the telling, I do my best, with the knowledge that I might make mistakes and be victim to tricks of the mind, as all who have tried to recall and record the times they have lived through surely have been.

1862 was the year of my birth. The time was May, the sweetest of all months, and the hour was early. As my mother would later tell it, our cockerel, Old Percival, crowed his biggest crow, and the next moment I arrived, and henceforth I was known as 'Cockadoodledoo', then, within time, 'Doodle', and it was said by those close to me that the spirit of the ancient idiot cock was in me. I was always the first up in the morning, always experimentally pecking at morsels I shouldn't. I tried in vain to reach for objects that were beyond me, springing up in a flapping, futile fashion. It was hoped that this habit would change once I reached maturity, but, since my height failed to progress much beyond five and a quarter feet, such hopes proved forlorn. My mother, Dorothy, did not shred words when irate with me, frequently hurling insults centred around my stature. She was a fast squall of a person, a busy knapsack full of sharp stones, constantly taking charge of all situations, as she'd had to since her own childhood, living with her own mother, Katherine. Katherine, who died shortly before my birth, had been feckless in character, a serving girl at the Big House who'd been put in the family way by her employer Joseph Bamford when she was just sixteen. Therefore my grandfather Edward, a seller of kitchen utensils and mousetraps, was not my true grandfather, just a kind man who had stepped in to save the face of everyone concerned, with the exception of himself. Though not from a farming background, Edward, being his mild and easily plied self, in his later years came into the ownership of a cow named Mumble, as an alternative form of payment from a customer who was unable to remunerate him for a set of pots and pans. In the evenings, Edward and Mumble would graze the long acre, Edward, holding a rope attached to Mumble, taking the same route each time: a circle past the church, over the back of Stumper's Cross and along Riddlefoot Lane. It was from Edward that I learned about the clairvoyance of cows. Nowadays I have thirteen of my own and I continue to place trust in their judgement as forecasters of fortune and weather. A cow, as it gazes on you, steady and vacant, takes in more about the core of who you are than most folk imagine.

That Joseph Bamford is my real grandfather – though never a man I have ever thought of as my grandfather, in the way Edward was – means I have the blood of country squires pumping inside me, though I must say on most days that I do not feel it, and I do not sense that many who meet me suspect it within me. I am rarely dressed up to the dick and I pass quietly along the edge of most occurrences in the parish unnoticed, that being a feature of my size and my daytime habit of being clad in the hues of the earth and the stone around me. Some saw the way I would remain quiet around my schoolmates and elders yet talk in great depth to chickens, cattle and sheep and thought me maized as a brushstick but just because I am not a man of conventional learning it does not mean I am a fool. I have seen a lot happen here but always opted out of village gossip. When I bore witness to Mary, the wife of Oldsworthy the baker, cavorting with Thomas, the schoolmaster's boy, in the orchard behind the church, my lips remained as tight as if they had been sewn together, and I mention the incident today only because both parties are long gone from this mortal coil. I learned a lot about the benefits of silence in my home environment, where an ill-chosen word in front of my mother could so readily lead to a ladle or saucepan flying towards your head. My father Henry, a quiet man, learned the same, and in our house it was not a bad thing to learn since, owing to Edward and his trade, kitchenware was a thing that was never in short supply. His seat at the kitchen table was in front of the cottage door and on warm days, when it was open, it was not uncommon for a traveller passing along the lane beyond to have to dodge a plate or spoon as it came spinning into their midst.

My father worked as a gravedigger at the church of St John. I never believed I smelt the dead on him, but an earthy odour lingered constantly around his skin and clothes, crusty and pungent, with an edge to it that made me squint when he kissed me goodnight. As he was ordered around at home he was ordered around at work, mostly by the stern vicar, Alfred Boyland, whose sermon on local sin had once infamously sent members of the congregation at his previous parish, Wickhampstead, running from the church in tears. 'It's not just about laying a body in the ground,' my father told me. 'Folks like things just so.' When John

Ludgate succumbed to cancer of the throat, the Ludgate family insisted that he not be buried on the south side of the churchyard, since over there had been recently interred Richard Cavendish, a rotund bully with whom Ludgate had been involved in a thirty-year feud over a prize hog. The bereaved, however, more often requested that the north side of the churchyard be avoided, since it was said that was where the Devil's Door was located. As a child I searched and searched for the door, but was never successful in locating it. Some said black dogs had been buried there too, but my father was dubious of that and had never found any evidence in his excavations. When not with a shovel in his hand or being harangued by my mother, he hid in books, taking a great interest in the history of the moor, particularly its Bronze Age and Beaker relics and the unfortunate vandalism inflicted on many of them during the last couple of centuries. It saddens me that he did not live to see the excavation of the kistvaen near Trembling Hill mine, in which the remains of a girl, thought to be no more than fifteen years old, were found preserved in the peat, along with those artefacts her people had believed would see her safely into the next world: an axe, a necklace and a shawl, woven from a beaver's pelt. It was his habit of a weekend to walk up there, along the old Lych Way, and he once remarked to me that when he did, he felt the presence of the dead more strongly than he had ever done in his working day.

It is a right handsome church, St John's, here in Underhill, and as the child of one of its employed I came to know it with some intimacy. I did not like the fresh, slick tombstones – their cold blankness frightened me, and seemed like a hard stark statement about what was waiting for me in the great beyond – but the old stones, with their dimpled lichen tales etched all over them, always gave me comfort. When nobody was around, in the autumn evenings, and the air was smeechy from bonfires, I would sometimes get close and give them a proper big cuddle. I don't know why I favoured this activity more on those autumn evenings with a new chill in the air but that was the way it happened. The building itself has a heavy appearance, even more so than most other churches in the area, a wider rim of granite being used close to its foundations, and it is said that this was a deliberate measure taken so the Devil did not carry it off to higher ground, as he had done with the little-visited St Constantine's, whose ruins stand halfway up Underhill Tor. Over on the west side of the church is a yew tree of some 1,400 years in age and, for the first decade of my life, and the century preceding it, carcasses of the badgers and foxes that had been killed in the parish were left on the trunk, five shillings being paid to the successful hunter for a fox, half a crown for a cub, and a shilling for a badger. Mercifully I have no actual memory of this.

On the whole, I associated the church with feelings of warmth and benevolence. Other children in the village were most frightened by the Bird Lady carving on the font, in which a woman is crudely depicted, apparently about to do grievous harm to a man, while watched by her sisters and her feathery accomplices, but I always thought of the Bird Lady as a friend and many times had dreams of her watching over me. Like her, I possessed a great affinity with avian life. Whether or not this has anything to do with Percival, and the way I arrived into this world, I do not know, but to this day, blue tits and chaffinches are not shy about entering my kitchen. It is far from uncommon for me to arrive downstairs of a morning and find a song thrush perched on my ottoman. At the Underhill Fair in 1901, when a great gust of wind blew down the Duck Marquee, setting a melee of geese, ducks and hens flapping across the village green, many eyes – eyes that normally ignored my presence – looked immediately to me for assistance, knowing of my reputation. I caught four geese and a duck very easily, while

Mrs Addlestrop from the tea room at Upper Wadstray showed great calmness in her handling of a large, vexed black cock. By this time Old Percival was long gone, although he had lingered for more years than had been expected. Many was the time that Dorothy would instruct me to check on him with the words, 'Doodle, be going out to that hen house un see if that bird un snuffed it yet,' upon which instructions I would promptly venture to the wooden enclosure where Percival roosted, peer in, ask of his health, and be answered with a croaky 'Cwawwwk.'

My playground was Combe Woods and it was here that birdsong was most intoxicating, especially in May, that most colourful and bonny of all months, the month that I still believe is mine, by birthright. I could not imagine that the most talented symphony orchestra in all the land could come close to matching the melodies my friend Sarah Slatterley and I heard above us in the infinite emerald canopy as we amused ourselves on those stretchable afternoons. Sarah was possessed of a singing voice as pure and life-affirming as a blackbird, and, while I fail pitifully now in trying to recollect the voice she spoke with, the melodies that issued from her mouth are as fresh in my mind as they would be if I'd seen her just yesterday. Sarah was always in charge of the games we played in the woods, one of her favourites being Black Pig, in which I would hide behind one of the many large boulders in the woods and it would be Sarah's task to find me before I leapt out, making tusks with my hands, running at her and shrieking 'Black pig! Black pig!' In her other favourite game, which she called Little Meg, it would be my job to build a bridge across the river for Sarah at one of its shallower points, using whatever material – rocks and branches, usually – was not too heavy to carry. I would place a chain of dog daisies around her neck and Sarah, being Queen of the River, would then stand on the platform I had constructed for her and wave to Her People, who I always imagined were Lilliputian and not completely of this earth. I do not know why the game was called what it was called, other than it was also the name of an old song Sarah used to sing very sweetly. One day, when we were out in the trees, she asked me, 'Doodle, will you call me Meg, but only when we are here?' so, because I would have sawed off my own right foot clean at the ankle if Sarah had asked me to, that was what I did, and it became one of the many little secrets we stored in the trees. Maybugs were often around as we lolled on the grass in Riddlefoot Meadow and we laughed at the noise they made, so loud and impolite that it seemed to come from the century ahead of us, or maybe that is just how I now think of it, now I am in that century. Billywitches, my father called them. Sometimes, as an evening chill stalked through the tussocks and raised pimples on our bare arms, Sarah pressed up close to me, and I felt a feeling I didn't understand that was like syrup pulsing through me and that, while only being a foreshadow of a feeling I would feel as a fully developed man, was no less potent for it.

I could see nothing important in my future but Sarah's face at times like these, framed by the soft honey of her hair, but I feared she was a girl whose yearnings stretched out far wider, far beyond me and this glade.

'Doodle,' she said, one especially fine afternoon, as we sat under the Black Tree.

'That is my name,' I replied.

'If I told you something I have not told another soul, could I tell it to you, knowing you would keep it to yourself and it would never enter the ear of another?'

She had an oil beetle crawling across her forelock, but I did not want to sidetrack her, so chose not to mention it.

'You could,' I replied. 'I promise it shall go no further.'

'One day, I intend to go to Honiton, and France, and maybe even the Americas.'

It was from my father and Edward I heard about most of the legends of the moor: the black dogs and the piskies and the river sprites. Edward told me it had been many years since a flibbertigibbet had been spotted in the area but they were rife in his own father's boyhood and, having learned of their reputation for frightening young maidens on dark lanes, I worried about what that could spell for Sarah once she made the transfer to womanhood. Because of this, I always insisted on walking her to her front door when we were out anywhere close to nightfall. Then there were the piskies to worry about, too. My father himself had never been tricked by them but Edward remembered a time when he was up the moor and the land seemed to slant half on its side as a great mist came down and every direction he walked in led him to the same locked gate, the air only clearing when he turned out his pockets. My mother dismissed this story as 'pish and twuddle', claiming that Edward had never had any sense of direction and could not be trusted, as a man who had once argued blind that Scarborough was in Cornwall.

I did not need to speak to my father to know of the story behind the stones on Trembling Hill, since it was common knowledge that each was a young girl who had been turned that way for the crime of dancing on the sabbath. Underhill has long nurtured a reputation amongst neighbouring parishes for breeding disobedient women and I have seen enough evidence with my own eyes to not doubt the reputation's foundation. Many is the time that I saw a young lad from the village being led emphatically by the hand towards the woods by a member of the fairer sex, although it is seldom that I have seen the reverse. I often picked up an abandoned blouse or frock, corset or pair of breeches on my wanderings in Combe Woods. Houses being crowded places, where bedrooms were shared with siblings and even on occasion sheep and goats, more children than not were conceived under the stars. Our cottage, containing for many years just me, my mother, my father and Edward, was a relatively capacious anomaly, although my mother's personality filled the space that would probably normally require six other persons of at least medium size. With each year she became more ornery, and with each year my father took another polite step back from asserting himself, perhaps hoping that it might placate her, when in fact it was an equation that seemed to make the opposite result, and finally he retreated so far back that he was entirely within his books and antiquarian concerns. It is from reading his diaries, and later his library, rather than any of my schooling, that I am able to put words on a page in the way you see before you now. He never missed an entry, and though some are rather mundane ('grey rain, saw a strange horse outside Mrs Fitchett's'), others are a document of alterations in the parish, the lores of the time, and his concerns about the frittering of our history in front of his very eyes. On 3 March 1871, he laments the vandalism of Hannaford's Plob, the tomb of a fifteenth-century hunter, by local builders who repurposed the stones for new cottages on the moor's north-east side. Later that month, he talks of watching a young couple in the village pass their newborn through the forked trunk of an ash tree, to cure the child's nascent cough: a custom I have heard about from other sources but not seen evidence of for nigh on four decades. 'Edward twisted fiveways insensible with drink,' says the entry for 5 September 1883, and nothing more. 'Solstice. Bilious. Coach to Newton,' the diary is told on 21 June 1882. 'Flowers for Dorothy. Not bright enough.' By this point, the feared Alfred had passed away, being replaced at the pulpit by his son, Cedric, a far milder character and keen early student of photography. My father had a stout and rewarding relationship with Cedric, especially after – if memory serves right – my father saved his life by pushing him out the way of a falling gargoyle during a storm in 1887.

A phrase I learned about the moor from my father was 'If thee scratch my back thee shall pay for it.' In his mind, if you attempted to tame the moor, to force your industry into its acid soil, to harness the great power of its rivers and trees for profit, it would eventually exact its revenge. To him, that great domed expanse rising above the surrounding countryside was always 'She', never 'He'. 'Old Her be angry today', he would sometimes say, and I would be uncertain as to whether he meant the great wild space above us or my mother. But then I would see the fearsome skies over the tor, and the even more fearsome ones over Trembling Hill beyond that, and he would add, 'I wonder who's angering Her today', and I would know what he was talking about. For me, those sombre slopes were where the world ended, and I never felt the need for more world beyond that. I have never been to London, never wanted to, and now I never will. But, seeing the row of houses that has just been built over towards Summersbridge – ugly dark red boxy things, without individuality or charm – I fear the city will soon come to us, and it is one of old age's small mercies that I will not be here to witness it.

There is the high moor, with its tough wire grass, ice winds, vast treeless slopes and wind-blasted sheep, and there are its footslopes, with their soft river valleys and speckled woodland, and I do not rightly believe you can ask for one without the other. People told me Hell was a place down below and Heaven was above but in Underhill I know the positions to be the reverse of that, and down here in our Heaven Sarah and I continued to play under the plumed chorus in the faery light that can only be created when strong upland sun shines down on thick tiers of burgeoning leaves. Winter surely happened too but I scarce remember it, whereas now it happens at least once a year. The river gets rude and high and the stepping stones Sarah and I placed at even intervals across it close to Summersbridge can no longer be reasoned with. I have seen the river landed only twice in my life for, even when it is full, it moves too fast for that. Half a mile further up the valley is Megan's House, empty now for many a year. My father said an old crone, not Megan but Lydia, lived there until not long before my birth, and used to walk over twenty miles a day on the moor, getting up not long after midnight in midsummer in order to make the most progress possible. He studied lines in the landscape: he noted that a straight line went from the Trembling Hill kistvaen, where they would later excavate the body of that young woman, through the stone circle and the centre of the tor and the churchyard, and the line brushed the edge of the house where Lydia lived too. Now I see there is this man Watkins, who has lately received much attention for his books on prehistoric lines, but my father was making note of the very same some fifty years earlier. History is full of quiet men who do not get the credit they deserve and would never ask for it, even if their life depended on it.

But then there are men like Cranford Frogmore, who will let the world know who they are, and what they have done, at any possibility.

Frogmore arrived down from Bath one spring with his fawning band of archaeologists, strutting about in his clean white frock shirt, speaking to other men he met as if they were so many woodlice in his path. It was in the orchard that I first spotted him, his train of similarly attired cohorts in his wake, as Sarah and I were lazing beside some new lambs and their protective mothers. 'Who is this prize spoon on a stick?' I remarked, but as Sarah's eyes followed his thin prancing legs through the grass, she remained silent.

By this point, I had finished my schooling and had been given work by Mr Cosdon the thatcher, not because of any great talent I had for handling a blade or laying a water reed top lane or wheat reed ridge, but because I was known as a good little climber who could squeeze into a spot smaller than himself. The business was to an extent in the family, since my mother had once worked as a comber of reeds for another old thatcher, Toddler Crockford, who lived up in Wychcombe in a very horrible house. There only being a limited amount of thatch to renew in Underhill, my work also afforded me the opportunity to travel, once even almost as far as Sidmouth. Not being a person who got the chance to look down on much when walking at ground level, I loved my new life in the sky, even though I felt all of the weather there more keenly than ever as it came down off the tor. One night I dreamt I was a church bell, with the face of a very beautiful lady. In this dream it was my job to stand high above the town and ring myself whenever bad weather or danger was approaching. Everyone looked up at me and smiled and appreciated my work but nobody ever got close to me, and I felt lonely in the dream and would have liked to have had another bell beside me. Not long prior to this, my father, who did some ringing himself, had told me that the first bells in the church had been sounded as an answer to coming thunder and lightning, to frighten it away. He loved to hear the bell tapping on the stay, the tick-tock it made, and often remarked that it was pleasantly like being inside a giant clock.

Sometimes, now, I think of my life as having been lived in two distinct parts: the one where I was climbing higher and higher, and the one since then where I have made it my business to tunnel down, into the essence of things. This perhaps begs the question: when have I lived on the level that most people do? Perhaps very rarely. And perhaps that has suited me just fine. Here on the moor, the air is known for its buoyancy, and you don't have to be perched on a roof to feel that, but up so many feet above everything, I often felt like I could just ascend to the clouds, especially not being a person of any great heft. I liked the view my work gave me of the trains coming into the new Wychcombe Junction station. In those days the brakes were not the most reliable and many times the carriages overshot their mark, meaning passengers would have to walk very many dozen yards back down the track. Not all trains did stop and once I watched the carriages creak to a halt, only for nothing but several thousand bees to disembark, in the form of six hives that were then transported to Riddlefoot Meadow. Our parish has also not been without eminent human visitors. Prime Minister Gladstone passed through Underhill on his tour of Devon in 1872, and although I have no memory of this, my father said he had the opportunity to shake his hand and felt that he was 'not a proper person'. Sir Walter Raleigh, it is said, was at large in the alehouses of the moor not long before his arrest in 1603. Edward claimed that, as a young soldier, he met Napoleon when he was moored in Torquay harbour, but Dorothy dismissed this as 'whiskey talk'. Edward also assured me that as a child he'd met a man whose grandfather had been one of the royalists who had been infamously ambushed by parliamentarians while playing cards in the old Wickcoomb Inn, but by this point Edward was well into his eighth decade and often known to go amiss for several days, taking his night's rest in fields and hedge bottoms.

Living with three men who were constantly bringing pieces of the outdoors back into the house with them – me with my dry reeds, my father with his soil and Edward with the burrs and leaves and buds that had attached themselves to him during his wilderness naps – was the bane of my mother's existence. She reminded us with little respite about the relationship between soap and the almighty and it was as if, in her eyes, none of life could quite happen right unless every surface of the cottage was spotless. But of course as soon as it was spotless and life did start happening, the happening of it would make the surfaces dirty again, so in a way the life she hoped would happen was destined to always be but an unreachable dream. She worried terribly what her peers in the village thought of her and was forever haunted by the day in 1868 when she had visited Sidmouth without a bonnet: an incident she had later overheard two of the sisters from Pixies Cottages gossiping about. She was vehemently against the drinking of tea, maintaining that it was the Devil's own drink, destructive to the senses, and did not allow it in the house. I never felt more taboo or lawless than when drinking a strong brew in Sarah's kitchen – an exception mayhap being the time that Fernie Saville and I went out in the snow and, with one of my father's shovels, dug up the sign to Upper Wadstray and Wychcombe and turned it in the opposite direction.

It was Cranford Frogmore who took Sarah away, as I suspected he would, from the moment I saw her eye roving towards him in the orchard. The day that I did not find Sarah at home when I called for her and saw his white frock shirt discarded on the ground near our old stepping stones, then heard giggles from in the copse behind, confirmed my worst fears. From the moment Sarah's body began to mature, a wall that could not be perceived by the eye had gone up between us, and that feeling of syrup pulsing through me as she pressed up to me in the long grass was now just a memory. I had accepted this and that she was deserving of more of a man than me, but Frogmore was not a fraction of what I had hoped for her. I saw that he viewed everything in his immediate environment at best as part of a supporting cast in the play of his life, and any lover he chose would eventually have to be a victim of the same fate, and worse. If he had been less interested in the upkeep of his own moustache and the suppression of those in his stead, maybe it would have been him who found the prehistoric nuggets right under his nose in the kistvaen on Trembling Hill, rather than his more pleasant successors, some three decades later. He and his supercilious gang of trousers had only been in Underhill two days before they had commandeered a table in the corner of the Stonemason's

Arms, which they looked upon with as much ownership as if they had been responsible for the carving of its own sturdy legs from oak. 'Do as my shirt does!' he had commanded me, when I had the temerity to take a seat at it, and it was only later I had realised that what he was telling me to do was kiss his self-adoring arse. I walked silently away from that, just as I walked silently away from Sarah's involvement with him. I have always shied from conflict. It is my way. Yet it is in my memory of these days that can be found my life's great regret.

She never returned to the village. The rest of the Slatterleys moved away, to Penzance I believe, not long after. I heard many years later that Frogmore ploughed his way through the whores of Hackney while she went mad, alone, in a big Regency house up in Bath, before being committed to the madhouse. But who is to say for certain? As I have mentioned, I am distrustful of rumour and tittle-tattle.

I recall Sarah's and my small story here so it will be held in print, but it strikes me as futile, not just because I do not know who would ever be interested to read it but because I am sure the earth and the river hold it and tell it too, as they tell all our stories, and that when they tell it they do so with a far greater eloquence and recall than I ever could. My father, despite the nature of his work and his diligence in attending his employer's sermons, possessed a quite pagan view of the afterlife. He believed that parts of us seep into the earth, to become parts of the landscape around us, and perhaps parts of other souls yet to be. He saw it as a sort of dispersion of narrative. The root ball of a tree planted in a churchyard, he said, would soon go to work in absorbing the dead. He told me about the highwaymen who had been caught and hung in chains up on Underhill Tor, starving, getting their nutrition only from shreds of candle wax fed to them by those passing by until they finally expired and rotted into the earth. I saw in my mind's eye the thick broth rain up there washing their secrets down into the soil and the river, and the river telling those secrets, just as it told the secret of the lady in the carving in the church and the secret of my mother's true father.

Because the rainfall is so great here, digging is usually not difficult, but during a rare dry spell it was not uncommon for my father to break a shovel. He always kept a spare in a small attic in the stone barn behind the cottage: a topsy-turvy space that my mother constantly reminded him to keep tidier than he did. Could my father's life have been as quiet as he wished it to be, if he had actually taken on board some of the advice my mother barked at him, or would she just have found more shortcomings to chastise him about? It is hard to say. I try now, as an older man who spends time underneath matters, to see more of what made her what she was: the story under the story, what it took for her to hold everything together, in a house of cows, chickens and men that were invariably either uncommunicative, crapulous, clumsy and hungry, if not all four at the same time. Heavy responsibility and lightness of manner cannot easily go hand in hand. What I do know is that my father rarely remembered to do any of the tasks that she shouted at him to do and, because of that, I know that on the day that she dislodged the shovel from the attic space and it fell on his head, it would have been in a precarious position, and because of that, it is questionable whether she can be blamed directly for his death.

I can picture the scene now: my mother on the ladder, growling her dismay at the disorder of my father's tools, her hands busy above her, rummaging. My father directly below, staring at his dusty boots, uttering not a word, waiting for the storm to pass. The shovel falls and the sharp metal blade hits the softest part of his temple. The end of his life was not slow, although part of me suspects that my mother's verbal annihilation of his character continued for a minute or two, even after he passed from this world into the next. It is hard not to note the irony that so many heavy objects had been propelled towards him over the years – earthenware mugs, griddles, trays, china birds, plates – and he'd lived through it all, yet the one that finished him off was the one she accidentally sent in his direction.

For the remaining twelve years of her life, my mother was a milder presence, particularly from the point two years after my father's death when Edward's liver finally became too pickled to keep him above the earth. I had never noticed at the time, but when she had talked to me or my father or Edward, her hands were constantly held together, her nails digging half-moons into her palms, and it was only now that she ceased to do it that I noticed she had ever done it. Cats, hens and dogs no longer fled into hedgerows at the sound of her voice. She ate more unselfconsciously, remarking on many an occasion with a satisfied chuckle that she was 'full to pussy's bow'. The stones in her tone became smaller, less sharp, and her mission to tame dirt for good abated. The cottage was at the lowest point in the valley, where all water seemed to come to gather, and that dampness was more noticeable as my mother's obsessive cleanliness and tidiness fell off. The walls have always felt like crumbling cake here. I believe it is a building fit more for cows than humans. Yet it still stands, and I am still in it, also standing, just about.

My father is interred on the north side of the churchyard, near that Devil's Door that I have still not located, and it was I who dug his grave, and who planted the ash sapling beside it, which I trust is now hard at work absorbing his essence. It was the driest spring in living memory and the bluebells leaned and withered as soon as they flowered. After Cedric Boyland saw that I could dig with an enthusiasm and strength that belied my size, he believed it only logical to offer me my father's old position, and I accepted, and at that point the part of my adulthood I lived in the sky ended and the more sunken part began. Yet it is in this subterranean part of my life that my mind has floated higher, into unknown places that seem to be somewhere above the clouds. Sometimes, I think a more significant part of it than not has been spent inside dreams – extremely lucid, deeply textured dreams, sometimes more real than Underhill itself.

There is not a lot else to tell.

I am still here, still digging my holes and filling them in, and am still for the greater part the person I was when I first began doing it, although my bones ache a great deal more, and I fear I only have a year or so left at it. My reading and writing has improved, with the help of my father's old books. Mumble the cow is no longer amongst the living. In the end, she outlasted my father, Edward and my mother, and very close to the end of her life, I decided she should not be so lonely, and got some companions for her, after purchasing some land off Benny Woodcock. The herd – or their successors – provide milk but I don't push them hard or make a song and dance about its availability. If people come for it, they come. Nonetheless these cows are more than enough to occupy the time I do not spend deep in the earth or words. I am glad of them and glad to not be a man who depends on them for income, to be a man who owns a plot of land and the roof above his head. Some say the damp in here is not good for my lungs but I have outlived many a man who spent his life in more parched rooms. My mother, in her more sensitive, confessional final days, told me that when he had the place built, Edward inserted a shoe in the wall, and a doll which an old lady in the village had told him would give the place protection from misfortune. The doll, she said, had originally been part of a pair. But I do not know about the truth of this. There are a few things I know for sure. Children swimming in a river will never be quiet, that is one. You cannot count the tadpoles in your pond, that is another. But there is infinitely more I don't know, just as ever it was.

In truth, it is Underhill that has changed far more than I ever could. More folk arrive on the train now and, thanks to its improved brakes, it stops at the station platform with fair precision. The advent of the motor car has brought more daytrippers to the moor and not all of them treat it with the respect it deserves. Just the other day, I had to apprehend a young gentleman with an accent I could not place who was pulling moss off the trees in Combe Woods. He seemed startled by my interference and, were I younger and larger and less reserved, we might have sparred. Instead, with the remark to his lady friend 'It seems the piskies do live and speak after all, Jean!', he departed, towards the road. I fear great change coming. Sometimes, I dream images I do not recognise, unfamiliar machines with too many wires, popping and crackling with electricity. In one dream I saw my own tombstone and the words inscribed on it: 'William Millhouse: virgin, underestimated' but it did not have a date. In another I was sitting in a meadow in May surrounded by all its floral glory but looked up at Underhill Tor and saw a face in the hillside and the face was screaming. I fear the advent of a vandalism coming far greater than the one that concerned my father. I suspect the moor is about to have its back scratched and there will be multiple payments due.

That we became briefly famous, as a village, owing to the findings at Trembling Hill, has also brought more people to the area. They said that she, the girl they discovered, was put to rest in a crouching position, facing the rising sun. This strikes me as not a position of dignity, but we are nearly the same at the end, underneath our airs and graces, our bonnets that we sometimes remember to wear into town, our tailored shirts and lacquered gentleman's moustaches. I do not doubt that she did pass into the next world but I suspect it is as my father said and that world was a dispersed one, of trees, earth, flowing water, flowers and souls yet to be born, and that, contradictory to what her people thought, her amulets, clothes and tools did not go with her. It is still the same now: I have buried people with vases and quilts, with hammers and banjos, with cats... even once with a favoured mouse. I know every inch of the churchyard, know just how many Sarahs are in it (three), just how many Davids (sixteen), Williams (eleven) and Megs (seven), but there will, of course, be more beneath that, long forgotten. The stones will talk, I think, if you give them long enough. I still recoil from the younger headstones, the very clean ones that glint in the sun. They give me a chill. But as far as other chills are concerned, I have never seen a ghost here, nor a piskie. A newly qualified young doctor in the village, a golfing man by the name of Fitzpatrick who moved here from the west coast of Ireland into one of the ugly new houses, told me that on his way back across the tor after playing the back nine he was led astray in the mist, unable to get home and found himself mistakenly over by the ruin of the old barn that once belonged to the Warners, and said he saw a plume of smoke rising in the doorway, in the shape of a woman. I think he is a very imaginative man but I also do not doubt the moor's intention to spin and confound people on its more vexed days. I have heard it claimed that the figure in the carvings on the font has been seen as an apparition, but few people have spent as much time in her manor as me and I have never set eyes on her, although curiously, she does often visit me in dreams.

At these times, I am often digging and she stands to my rear, quietly observing, making sure the job is done right. I like the idea of her presence. It gives me comfort when the dark thoughts creep in: when the tor makes its rain to blacken the world and I am out in it alone, when the belltower captain rings out the nine tailors for another man lost and I dwell on the inevitable solitude that comes to us all in the end, or when I wonder what I could have done for or been to a woman.

It is now a while since I have broken a shovel. I have three in all and they live in a low and accessible place, in the porch, near my shoes and raincoat. Not far beyond can be found my mother's old ottoman where, when May is at its peak and the sun is shining and I leave the door open, I will still often find a chaffinch or song thrush perched. At the close of these sweet, bright, late spring days I will sometimes open the ottoman and put on one of the garments within it. There are a couple of dozen in all that I have collected from the woods over the years, although it's rare for me to find one there now. I favour a couple of cotton frocks in particular whose bright and intricate patterns seem to match the foliage around me. I take the back way into the trees, through the leaning gate in my old dripping garden wall that is half off its hinges and I tell myself I will repair, drekly. It takes me ten minutes to follow the thread of the stream to the river. All the old bridges on the moor began with stepping stones and the ones that Sarah put down are still there, negotiable in fair weather. As I balance on them, enjoying the way the fabric feels against my skin, I remember her standing there, singing her song to her people that I could not see, remember the great stillness in me that contrasted with the great yearning in her and the yearning in the water that seemed to match it. Sometimes I have imagined that I still hear the song. One time, when I was feverish with summer flu, I was even sure I heard it croaked back to me by the rocks in the river and I shivered and swayed with its power.

After I have stood on our makeshift stone bridge I rest in the long grass, at the end of this unremarkable life, aware, as I lower myself, of every twist and ache and fault and gap in this contraption I still call a body. But then I feel it all getting under the cotton and passing through me – the sun, the butterflies, the maybugs, the tune of the water, the breeze, the falling light – and I am the moment and nothing more.

SEARCH ENGINE (2099)

How tall was Reka Takacs?

Reka Takacs was 172.2cm tall, or - if you prefer to
measure it the old way - five feet eight inches. (The
same height as you.)

Who was the husband of Reka Takacs?

Reka Takacs had two husbands. The red-haired writer and
record producer Martin McGuire (2029–2045) and the dark-
haired actor Thomas Molland (2046–2047).

What does Takacs mean in English?

It means 'weaver'.

When did Reka Takacs die?

Reka Takacs died in 2091, one day prior to what would
have been her 100th birthday.

Why are we doing this? I know all this stuff. She's my great-
grandmother.

I'm sorry. It's force of habit on my part, a hangover

of the genetics of my programming. It's because she was famous. People always want to know how tall famous people are, whether they have a spouse and, if so, who that spouse is. It's really dumb. It goes back to the early days of Google. All these thousands and thousands of people looking up internationally well-known figures they are attracted to and checking on their marital status, as if thinking, 'Hey, let's see if I have a chance here.'

I don't think of her as famous. She didn't want to be famous. She's not famous now.

She was, for a while. The *Little Meg* album sold 30,000 copies during the month of its release. That is pretty impressive for 2047, and for what was essentially a folk rock record. The general public didn't have a lot of money to spend that year.

Do people search my name and height and try to find out if I'm married? No, don't tell me that. OK, tell me.

931 people searched the words 'Bea Mortimer' and 'married' or 'married to' or 'husband' last year. 649 of those people also searched 'height' or 'how tall'. People generally search 'height' or 'how tall' far more often when trying to find out information about men. 480 people, having discovered the answer about whether you were married or not, then went on to try to find out if you were dating anyone.

That's insane. Who are these people? I don't think I even sold 931 copies of my album last year. What is this over here?

That is correct. You sold 762 copies of *Dick Warner's Woodyard*. The single 'The Witch on the Wall' sold 611 copies. But you did literally zero promotion. That is lady fern. There's a tiny bit of dwarf male fern next to it, and some stalks of crested dog's-tail. The pink flowers growing at its base are red campion.

I think I would like more ferns for the garden, for the dark bit by the wall. But they cost so frickin' much at the Garden Salon.

You could just dig one or two up from somewhere around here and carry it back in your rucksack. But that's down to you and your conscience. You bought a rhododendron last year from the Garden Salon and it cost more than you spent on food that week, and those things are rampant out in the wild here, so there is at least one argument there that it was not the most logical use of your finances. I also think the rhododendron is going to start blocking out your light in the kitchen soon. It's already swamped the bellflowers and Welsh poppies that came from offcuts from Reka's garden. Oh, you *are* going to take this fern out? No, you're just feeling it, to see how easy it would be. OK. That thing you can feel buried in the soil next to the roots is a golf ball. This bit of land we are now walking across was a golf course. It closed sixteen years ago. The moor has reclaimed it.

I know. I grew up around here, remember? I love the way the purple on the rhododendrons looks, especially when it's contrasted against the rocks and the river. She told me that there were three big ones in the garden of the house where she lived with Maureen, where my grandfather was conceived. So now whenever I look at them I think of what that garden must have looked like, and of Reka playing her guitar. They also make me think of that house in the book *Rebecca*.

Manderley. Author: Daphne du Maurier. Gollancz, 1938. First print run (August, 1938): 20,000. Second print run (August, 1938): 10,000. Third print run (August, 1938): 15,000. Fourth print run (August, 1938): 15,000. Do you sometimes think that maybe you try too hard to follow in her footsteps? Do you think it's because you look quite a lot like her?

Daphne du Maurier? I don't look at all like her. It's OK, I knew what you meant and, no, I don't think I try too hard to follow in Reka's footsteps, as a matter of fact. She came to the UK with nothing, she worked hard, meanwhile simultaneously teaching herself to be an amazing musician. She ate well, swam and walked every day, and lived an extraordinarily long and varied life. At seventy-five, she still looked utterly fierce and people often mistook her for fifty. In a twenty-five-month flood of inspiration she summoned three of the best albums of all time out of the heavens and onto tape and even more impressively she did it in her forties, a time of life when society believes that the best-before date on most singer-songwriters' talent has expired. As soon as she had enough money to be comfortable she gave a substantial amount of her income to wildlife charities and women's shelters, but she never felt the need to shout or point at herself as she did it, or at least only did so in a way that might encourage others to follow her example. Between 2061 and her death she took in a total of seventy-four ill or elderly donkeys and looked after them on her land. She had tattoos of every species of plant and animal mentioned on RJ McKendree's *Wallflower* LP, and of a crow biting into Satan's neck. She won several awards for her gardening. Nobody was better at flipping an omelette with absolute precision and balance. By a conservative estimate, she saved the life of at least seven sheep whom she found in dicey predicaments while she was walking the moor. She lived in four different countries, had romances with several inspiring and unusual people of both genders and died in the place she loved most passionately. I don't think trying too much to be like that is possible, is it? And if it is, there's certainly nothing wrong with it, in my view.

OK. I was just asking.

What animal are you today? I am sensing... moorhen, maybe? No. Bigger. Cormorant?

Not all that far off. Merganser duck. The ones you mistook for mandarin ducks the other day. It's not an uncommonly made mistake. But it's the males of the mandarins that are the startlingly pretty ones, whereas with the mergansers it's the female who has the crest on the back of her neck and wears the nice clothes.

Oh, the ones that always make me feel underdressed. Well, thanks a lot! As if it isn't bad enough that I'm wearing this old jumper with splotches of black on it from where I painted the shed yesterday. The mergansers always fly away from me, through the gap where the bridge used to be, every time they see me. They seem like a very fearful bird. Are you feeling fearful today? You were a wolf yesterday.

I was a wolf because we had been talking about that bit in Reka's journal, where she describes the time she

played in the pub in the Scottish Highlands, and the
landlord had a pet wolf and there was the lock-in and the
wolf ended up falling asleep with its head in her lap,
and that reminded me I hadn't been a wolf for a while...

Ah, Wolf Night! So memorable and magic. I say that like I was
there. But I feel like I was, just from reading her account of it.

... and I thought in view of what we are doing today it
might help if I was a creature with a knowledge of the
river. Also, maybe, yes, I do feel a bit fearful. You
said that if you found the swimming spot you have been
talking about, you were going to dive. I don't want you
to dive. You don't know what's under there, and it's not
within my capabilities as a female merganser duck - or
within my capabilities as anything else - to call an
ambulance if you hurt yourself.

But the whole point about Abbot Cathcart's Pool is that it's sixteen
feet deep. There is nothing you CAN hurt yourself on. I do love
the way you can just switch animals like that. How does it work?

And you gleaned this information from what, or who?
Some old guy you met walking up on the Lych Way, two
and a half years ago? That doesn't sound very solid and
trustworthy to me. I suppose he wore a cape and a big
hat, too? Are you absolutely sure you didn't imagine
him? Yes, I think that whole spirit animal thing is at
least partially bullshit. We are all different animals
on different days. Think of it like you think of your
relationship with your favourite song. It changes from
day to day, doesn't it. One day it's 'Word Up' by Cameo.

Another day it's 'Wide Berth' by the John McCandles
Dirt Band. Another day it's 'Dark is the Bark' by the
Left Banke. Another day it's Taylor Swift's posthumously
released cover version of 'Hold On' by Sharon Tandy
and Les Fleur De Lys. Another day it's 'Trying to Live
Right' by Circus Maximus. Another day it's 'Magician in
the Mountain' by Sunforest. Another day it's 'Sorcerer'
by Junction. Another day it's 'Sorcerella' by Jefferson
Lee. Another day it's 'U Got the Look' by Prince. Another
day it's 'Richard' by Wolves in the Roof. Another day
it's 'Sun Chases Me Down' by Equinox. Another day it's
'Ramsplaining' by Blacksmith. Another day it's 'Think' by
Lyn Collins. Except I know your favourite song ever is
always ultimately RJ McKendree's cover of 'Little Meg'
from the 1972 Hungarian-only 7-inch, just as I know that
my favourite animal is always ultimately a capybara.

Of course, the difference is that I own two 127-year-old copies of
the Hungarian-only 'Little Meg' single and have met and touched
them many times, whereas you have never met or touched a
capybara. Also, is it me or are you getting more opinionated?

I've explained how it works. I gather and assimilate
information. And within that information are inevitably
opinions, which I also assimilate, and which more recently
tend to gestate inside me.

But, even though you have gathered so much information, you
cannot tell me where Abbot Cathcart's Pool is?

No. You're on your own with that one. I can just give you
various more general pointers about the river, using my

temporary merganser self. 'This is a sound and propitious place to make a nest.' 'Trout often gather under this small waterfall.' That kind of thing.

What I remember Craig saying about the pool is that it was located in a place you really wouldn't expect it to be and looked quite unassuming, that from the path you'd guess it was just a fairly ordinary, shallow part of the river.

Wait, the guy you bumped into on the moor was called Craig? That doesn't sound very 'all-seeing moorland warlock'.

He was actually very helpful and knowledgeable. I would have liked to have got to know him better. I don't know why I remember that day, perhaps because the atmosphere was very odd up here. The sky was an extremely unusual colour. Oppressive cobalt, like a tunnel in a dystopian film. The sound of our voices was very strange as we spoke, as if the air was trying to suck us away. I wish I'd taken his number so I could nag him again for the exact location, but I was distracted at the time, withdrawing, feeling a bit reclusive...

So absolutely unlike now, then?

I'll choose to ignore that comment. Anyway, you were switched off that day, so you wouldn't know, and you shouldn't assume that just because somebody is called Craig that they are a Craig. I've met loads of Emmas who aren't Emmas at all, for example, although having said that nearly all the Lauras I've met are very much Lauras, which is fine with me. I do think I am quite a Bea, overall. Craig said he spoke to nearly everyone on the moor and nearly every conversation added to his knowledge of the place. A bit like you gathering and assimilating your information, I suppose. He said he was a guide and he did what he called Legend Walks and that I should think about coming on one. So I did think about it, and I decided I didn't want to, but what he said about the pool has lingered in my mind ever since, the way he described the colour of it and the depth and the sound when you were in it. He said the marker you had to look out for was a sickly looking hawthorn next to three piled rocks, which didn't seem to narrow it down massively in my mind, if I am honest, and who is to say the hawthorn isn't now dead and gone, if it was already sickly twenty-five months ago? He said the pool wasn't part of his Legend Walks and he was only telling me about it because he liked me (OK, yes, in retrospect I do realise it was possible he was coming onto me), and that as well as being called Abbot Cathcart's Pool it was sometimes referred to as Meganthica's Pool and that Meganthica was the name of the teenage warrior queen who was found in the kistvaen down there during the Edwardian era, preserved in the peat, and that she is still thought to haunt the moor, in many guises, to be a kind of muse, in a way. He told me there was even a song about her, an old moorland ballad, which appeared on an album that had been quite successful in the forties, although most people had forgotten about it. Of course, I said nothing, but you probably would have seen a small smile escaping from the corners of my mouth, if you'd been looking closely.

How are you feeling now, vis-à-vis your retreat from the public eye, and the fact that fewer and fewer people are interested in you and your work? Do you still ever feel the old addiction to attention, that need to have your existence confirmed and fed back to you? Do you miss anything? It's been a while now.

You can be quite blunt sometimes, you know. The point is, I don't want to *represent*, I want to *be*. You get tempted to represent, because the rewards for it are instantaneous, and also representing feels like a correction to all the times you are misrepresented – by people who judge you solely by your image, by the media, by people who misunderstand your work because they are too distracted to properly pay attention to it but also feel obligated to have an opinion on it. I am aware that I could press the 'broadcast' switch and we could flip this conversation and make it live, show people this entire walk, and that I would feel an instant sense of warmth and connection, or a digital mimicry of it, and people would be all like 'Bea, we have missed you so much! It's so nice to see you!' and that is not totally unappealing to one part of my brain that I have tried to understand more extensively over recent times. But then I know I'd feel a bit hollow afterwards, and what would it have achieved, apart from giving away some of my life, when really I'm quite fine just being here with you?

Yes, with me. Whatever I am. That's nice. I am touched. Even though you can't *actually* touch me, physically.

I think you know how I feel about the *Friendly But Edgy* record by now. I think it's an OK pop album, for the naive and noisy and pliable being I was at that point in my life. I am sure I will never have a record sell that many copies again and I am fine with that, and am especially fine with not experiencing many of the social and administrative by-products of that. It seems like a very... obedient record to me now, although that is probably as much about the image of the record that is reflected back at me by society as it is about the record itself. I'd sometimes look at me, this me that existed inside a virtual space, in the aftermath of that – and the aftermath of *Rust* to an extent, even though that was a smaller record, 'the difficult second album' I suppose you'd call it – and I'd not recognise this person who allegedly made them, this other person that a distracted hive mind had created and existed solely inside people's visors. There'd be these huge online spaces where people would talk about the lyrics to 'Thirty-Second Casanova', explaining exactly which parts of my romantic life I was writing about in the lyrics, which disappointments and failures, when in reality nearly all of it was based on a story my friend Laura had told me back when I was in Year 11 at school.

Was Laura a Laura, by any chance?

She absolutely was. 110 per cent. One of the best Lauras I've ever met. Then after *Rust* I started having these recurring dreams where there was this line of strangers, an absolute train of them, all coming into my house, and I looked for the end of the train of strangers, where it might finally stop, and I couldn't see it, there were just more and more people stretching off, into some trees in the distance. And I think that was a pivotal moment for me. And of course I was lucky because I'd had Reka to tell me what it was like, from her experience, which makes me feel sorry for people who are in that position and don't have somebody to tell them what it's like or guide them through it. She was there for a while, right there, somewhere much scarier than I was, and she killed it stone dead, snuffed out the fame she had created. And was undoubtedly happier for it. Not everyone can do that. Not everyone has the choice. I used to read about these rock suicides, the 27 Club and so on, and not understand it, baffled as to why these beautiful and talented and adored people would want to end it, apart from maybe that they were fucked up on drugs and booze. I wondered why they couldn't just step off the rollercoaster for a while, stop doing gigs, stop making records, stop appearing. But now I understand. People want so much from you. You have no idea until you're there. Also there's another kind of overdose going on, an overdose of yourself being reflected back at you, and a sort of weird need for it, a preoccupation with it, and that need, and the simultaneous hatred of it, finally becomes a cage you can't get out of. Because the adoration you experience from strangers is every bit as dangerous to your mental health as the loathing you sometimes feel from them too. I stopped before that happened, and wasn't even that well known in the first place. And now here I am. I rarely get recognised, especially as I no longer look like 'Her', the screen me, the other me that never existed properly anyway, that I partially invented. I can still live. But of course I still want what I do – what I *really* do, the work – to be appreciated. I still want to communicate and be heard. That's entirely human, and entirely natural. Communication is positive. I love it.

Are you absolutely sure? You said a few weeks ago that your new LP was going to be a concept album called *Cave* and that the concept was that you were going to record it as a gatefold double album featuring twenty-three songs, get just one copy of it pressed, then travel to France and leave it in the furthest, dampest recesses of a cave in the Pyrenees.

OK, I was having a bad day that day. Anyway, let's not get too self-analytical about all this. Because in the end that becomes about the ego too, and the ego is what I'm trying to destroy, at least partially. Also, you've heard me talk about all of this too many times before.

I don't mind. I like hearing your stories.

Doesn't the village look pretty from up here? I'm just going to climb right up to the highest rock, because obviously you can't hike to the top of the tor without doing that, it's against the rules. Then I think if we go directly in the direction of the second buttock hill about two miles over there, we'll be somewhere near where Craig said the spot was. It's weird: you know, sometimes when I'm up here I feel like I'm walking on a man's face. I remember Reka saying when she came back here for the second time, from Hungary, and then when she came back for the final time, from Canada, she loved the way the village could surprise her when she chanced upon a new angle to view it from. I suppose this is a very familiar angle, though. I am looking down now and thinking, 'That looks like the kind of place I'd like to live,' and, guess what, I do! That's kind of cool, isn't it, don't you think? And isn't that mist nice? The way it's below us and the sun is breaking through it and the sun seems kind of below us in a way too. Oh my god, I think that is my actual shadow on it, wow.

That is known in weather folklore as a Brocken spectre. It comes from the Brocken, which is a German mountain that tends to be very misty: a place where that often happens. With a Brocken spectre, you also often get what used to be known as a glory, which Coleridge and Wordsworth both observed in their time in the Lake District, where a psychedelic selection of colours form around the shadow of your own head, on the mist. This is usually part of a mistbow. And all this is very quintessentially autumnal, which reminds me that it's October right now, which - and please forgive me for labouring this point - seems quite a late and chilly time of year to be diving into a river on a moor, and that maybe it should be postponed until next summer, if not longer.

It's quite curious: at first I just used to think you were merely a source of factual information, but now I feel like you also might be my conscience too, or maybe a parent, or an invisible brainjournalist relentlessly interviewing me for a double-page feature in your head magazine.

I know. I find it curious too. It's happened, and I don't know why. I have definitely changed and feel that change inside of me, whatever inside of me is. Lately I have experienced a desire to eat grass.

See that barn wall down there, the ruin? I hate that. I don't know why I hate it, because it's actually a very attractive bit of wall, where you can still see evidence of some skilled brick nogging, but I hate it. I have just remembered a phrase of Reka's, 'jump the sun'. It was what she said she used to say a lot when she was about to record a song: 'Let's really try to jump the sun with this one!' I feel like that is what we are doing, all this way up here, right now, jumping the sun. I think that is what I will call my biography of Reka when I finally get my notes together. *Jumping the Sun: the Wild Life and Times of Reka Takacs*. I think it is better than my original title, *Dreamweaver*.

I feel you feel that way about the barn too. I have felt you feel it every time we have walked past it, ever since I started to feel things. And I agree: that is a better title. Do you definitely think you have enough material to write the biography?

I think I do. I have the journals, and, although they're very sporadic, there's a lot there. I know I only met her when she was already in her eighties but we became very close. I think it's an amazing story: her childhood in poverty in Hungary, the crude yet somehow haunted and alchemic early songwriting, her and Martin's move back to Eastern Europe, the way the two of them popularised the work of McKendree, her more solitary period, the attempt to capture the sound of falling dust on record, the animal rescuing and prize-winning horticulture. There will be gaps, of course. She would never talk much about her time at the house where she lived with Maureen, where my grandfather was conceived, apart from the garden. I know Maureen died and Reka still found it very upsetting to think about, all these years on. I know the village gravedigger had once lived in the house, which I suppose makes the place even more dark in my mind now, although the building is now no longer there and the land it was on has sort of been subsumed by the big house next door. But, look, gaps are OK. It gives the reader the opportunity to tell some of the story in their own way in their own mind. Reka said Martin worried that his biography of RJ McKendree had too many gaps in it, but when it finally came out, after Martin died, a lot of people thoroughly enjoyed it.

Why did Martin and Reka split up in the end?

I am not certain. Maybe the fire just went out. I know he liked to drink a fair bit. I'm also aware Reka felt a bit troubled by the close friendship he maintained with his previous partner, Christine Chagford, which definitely rekindled when Reka and Martin moved back to Devon, although I think it was just friendship and I know Reka liked Christine a lot too, was even a little obsessed with her in some ways. Apparently when Martin was dying it was Christine who stopped her entire life just to care for him.

What about Thomas Molland? Why did Reka break up with him?

I seem to remember her official explanation was he was just a narcissistic cunt.

What about you? Will you be in the book?

I think I will keep myself out of it.

But you are her great-granddaughter, and massively influenced by her work! You said it yourself just now: you got very close to one another. You have a bunch of her most cherished possessions in your house. The 7-inches. They're each worth close to £500,000 now. You could buy a beach hut up north with that. A good one, with a door and everything. And then there's the painting, and that freaky old doll she owned.

Yes, but I was also a slightly sore point for her, or rather my grandma was. She gave her away and tried her best to move on from that, as agonising as that must have been. And she knew my great-granddad for all of five minutes, at a time when she was enjoying her young life, taking control of her own decisions. If I hadn't done my research and tracked her down she would have gone on in blissful ignorance of my existence. So, however she felt about my company, I was always an unwelcome reminder of a hard and reluctant decision early in her life that she had tried to put behind her.

But she did adore you, viewed you as a protégé, and gently but emphatically encouraged you to become who you are, artistically.

Anyway, this book will be about her, not me. I'm trying to annihilate the ego, remember? Also the painting isn't the original, so it's not actually the future pension fund you might think it is. Ooh, I love this bit, it's like getting close to the roof of the world.

It's where everything starts again, I think, where the clouds and rivers renew it all. Listen to the water here. The noise is different. It's different to down by the house. I was talking to Sue, who lives down the road, and we both said the same thing, that we listen to the river when we're in bed and have the window open and sometimes we wait for the noise to stop; we forget it's not a shower or a sink being run next door, and then we remember it's never going stop, that it's just going to keep on renewing itself, keep being the same but different, long after we are gone, and maybe that's obvious but it's also pretty wild, when you're close to it and experiencing it and realising it. Oh wow. Look at the pattern of the stones in the bottom of this uprooted tree trunk. Don't tell me that's not art. Imagine the sound this big gentleman made when he fell.

A beech. 172 years old. Came down in December 2094. Nobody actually heard the sound. But it still made one. They always do. Just to clear that up.

How do you know this stuff, but not some other stuff?

I don't know. I also know that Toadpit Lane is called that because there once used to be a pit full of toads down there, but I suppose that is self-explanatory.

Oh you saw that too, back at the start of the walk? It's funny how you get these little connections that get your mind working, especially when you're on a long walk, because I was thinking about that name, and then we were just talking about Reka trying to capture the sound of falling dust and turn it into a rhythm track, and it got me thinking about the Grateful Dead recording the sound of clean air in the desert and the sound of heavy air in the city and mixing them together into a rhythm track for *Anthem of the Sun*, which is an album where I think they really did jump the sun, and that got me thinking about Owsley Stanley, who was the sound man for the Dead in the early days, and also principally responsible for the supply of LSD to prominent musicians in the San Francisco area in the mid-sixties, and therefore at least partially responsible for this insanely enormous amount of transcendental and frontier-breaking psychedelic music, but who, by 2007, the fortieth anniversary of the Summer of Love, survived on an exclusively meat diet and spent a lot of his free time slaughtering toads near his house in Queensland, Australia. So you've got this dude who has been instrumental in the mind expansion that led to one of the most flabbergastingly creative artistic periods in all of history – a time when there was so much going on that someone as talented as RJ McKendree didn't even have room to be recognised for the genius he was – and what he ends up as is this individual who is essentially made entirely of beef and chicken and – while suffering from the cancer that he thought his carnivorous leanings would prevent – goes out and murders as many as 225 toads per day using a highly toxic liquid disinfectant called Detsol. And that got me thinking about all the people who are these radical cultural icons when they are younger and how they very gradually change and come away from what they are and let down the people who adore them in the process, and how maybe it's in the cacophony of fame that that happens, and you don't even know that you're changing and gradually becoming unmoored from what you were, you don't even know that you're becoming a carnivorous old toad exterminator.

I am not sure you've chosen the best case study here. Owsley actually went out of his way not to be famous for pretty much his whole life; he was preaching the

benefits of an all-meat diet as far back as the sixties
when he was managing the Dead and they would try to
sneak chocolate bars into the studio behind his back
while he wasn't looking; he killed the toads because
they were poisoning the baby fish in the lake near his
house, and, though he did have throat cancer for many
years, what actually killed him wasn't that, but a
car crash on 12 March 2011 (not 13 March 2011, as is
sometimes reported). But I do take your point and see
exactly what you are saying.

Know-it-all! Anyway, the thing is, I don't want to get caught and
lost in the cacophony. I don't want to kill toads, even if they do
poison fish. I like toads. I am also enjoying the way life has slowed
down since I came off the road, the real one and the virtual one.
It's me who is controlling how I feel, not the hive mind. I've got
really good at gardening, and flipping omelettes.

You also haven't had a sexual partner for the last
sixteen months.

That's where having a nice soft right hand and an extremely good
imagination is beneficial. Who knows? Maybe I'll bump into
Craig again. Plus, I have you.

But you can't feel me.

I almost can. I wish I could, sometimes.

I wish you could too.

Do you miss me on the days when I switch you off?

I do. A lot. And I don't know how that's possible, but it is.

Ooh shit, I've tripped over. Sweet Mabel in heaven, it is SO boggy here. I've got peat all over my hand and my kaftan sleeve. What is this? Some weird black rectangle, plastic. Eugh. Must have been here for ages.

I believe it is a debit card, probably from the early decades of this century. HSBC. The name of the holder appears to have faded and rubbed away, though. I suggest you put it in your pocket for now and recycle it when you get home.

I don't mind that I'm dirty. I'm too happy. You see, getting up here, alone, in this air, being away from the pressure to represent myself, I've had time to think about what I really want to do next, which you don't when you're on the road, or when you're on the digital road, doing all the representing, and that's when you go down paths that don't suit you and get you trapped. I feel in a way that my career has only just started. I'm thirty-four. Reka didn't make her best music until she was almost a decade older than that. We're on the cusp of a new century. The world hasn't ended yet. I think about me ten years ago, and I did what I did, and people liked it, but... the voice. It was sort of an amalgam of other voices, which everyone has to be at the start. All those great psychedelic bands: they started out by doing fairly straightforward cover versions, didn't they. But you need your own voice, and I think that's part of what makes something last, makes it something that is more than a song that people really like for six months then forget about forever, and you can't force that voice. Some people are lucky enough to have it very quickly. I reckon McKendree might not have had it in 1966, but he definitely had it by 1968. It's not been so quick for me, and I do think some of those early songs, they were kind of… Reka lite. But I think it's here now, and it wasn't about any trick or knack, it just came about by playing and, well, living on the planet for a number of years. There's this feeling that all I was doing before was just sort of revving my engine, and now I'm ready to go. It's exciting. There's so much to be done. There's Reka's book, and the *River Goddess* album and that's just the beginning.

So you've definitely ditched the whole *Cave* concept then?

Yes. That's gone. It's all about *River Goddess* right now, all the way. But it will take as long as it takes. I've done the whole thing of rush writing a record in between touring and interviews, not properly living with your subjects. I did that with *Rust*. I want this to be different. I want to enjoy the research as much as I enjoy the writing; I want to get right into the depths of it. You might call it procrastination; I call it prep.

Hence today's little research trip.

Exactly! And, speaking of which, look: hawthorn, sickly, looks like it's about to fall over. Three piled rocks. Could this be it? I think it actually is. Yep. Oh my god, look at it. Right here. You'd never know from the path. Look at the colour of the water. How is that even possible? Right, I'm stripping off. And that rock there. Perfect for a dive. Thank you, Abbot Cathcart. Thank you for allowing me to swim at your private leisure club. Or perhaps that should be Meganthica I am thanking. Thank you for infusing this place with your spirit, oh ghost of the moor, oh little deity. But, most of all, thank you, Craig.

You look very good, very toned.

Thank you. I know.

I still don't think you should dive, or that you should at least do a little jump first. But you're your own boss, as you keep telling me, and it's your funeral. But also don't make it your funeral. I think you could live a long time. You have good genes, like your great-grandma. You just need to make sure you drink lots of water, like she did.

It's funny, you know: she told me she actually didn't drink anywhere near enough water when she was young. She was always very forgetful and leaving full glasses of it all around the house. So she realised that the only way to make sure she drank enough was to always drink a glass in full as soon as she got it. She'd really fill her cheeks with it. She reminded me of a gerbil. It made me laugh. It was quite an unusual thing to watch a person as old as that do.

Yes, you told me, and that she said Thomas Molland used to hate it and told her it was 'unladylike'.

Sorry. I forgot I'd already said that.

It's OK. As I said, I like your stories. And repetition doesn't have the capacity to annoy me. That's not a feature of my character.

Right. I'm ready. I'm going to switch you off now. I hope you don't mind.

No, I understand. It's the way it works. It has to be that way. It's better for both of us.

One last thing before you go. What do you think of 'Toadpit Lane' as a song title?

It could be OK. Depends on the song itself. Also, how does the toad pit relate to the river, if it's a concept album? Perhaps it's something to save for the record afterwards. Anyway, we can discuss this later. Do what you have to do. See what you can find down there in the water and where it takes you. I'm not going to watch.

OK. Here goes. I just know this is going to feel amazing.

EPILOGUE
ME (NOW)

What changed you, over the course of your life, here on earth? What were the significant events? The big moments, good and bad? Maybe some didn't seem so big at the time but then, later, you looked back and said, 'Yeah, that was important, I can now recognise that nothing else was ever the same after that.' Or maybe they did seem big at the time, and then you realised they were even bigger. I have too many to list, but one that sticks in my mind was when the first giant black legs went into me. Was it really almost a century ago? It seems like yesterday in a way, yet also simultaneously seems like the giant black legs have always been in me and I can't really remember what it felt like to not have giant black legs in me. I can still remember the pain I felt when they went in, like no pain I'd ever felt before, a pain that was about more than just the piercing of my skin.

Can you imagine it? You're there, the dew is fresh all over you, the sky has not long got light, and the most dystopian sights in your immediate vicinity are a mounted hay turner that's slowly shedding its paintwork and sinking into a spinney on your pelvic girdle and Charles Bamford's abandoned prototype Vauxhall Cadet on Riddlefoot Lane, and then suddenly these men arrive, and they appear to be erecting these giant robots on the bridges of your feet; a long line of them, marching off into the distance, towering metal soldiers that seem to presage the coming of something terrible but you don't know quite what. And you are powerless; all you can do is stand there and watch as they are put in place, as they become *an intrinsic part of you* that you have never asked for, and then lines are connected between them, lines that fizz and crackle, and that is even scarier, because it's ugly and dark, and there have been ugly and dark things forever, which it has been possible to accept, because they seem part of the natural balance of everything, but now it seems that the ugly and dark things will be controlled by machines, and that is going to be different. You don't know how it is going to be different, but you know.

The word 'pylon' means 'gateway' in ancient Greek. The fact that we called them pylons is probably a lot to do with the fact that the 1920s, when pylons were first introduced, was an archaeologically excitable decade, especially in Egypt. Pylons were what the double towers were called that you found at the entrance to Egyptian temples. I don't have an entrance – unless you count several hundred fox and badger holes – but I do have three pylons. Am I a temple? I can certainly play that role, if you want me to. People do seem drawn to me, spiritually, although not in any official capacity. I notice that people are often quieter, calmer, when they are on me, sometimes even inspired to find parts of themselves that they can't quite reach when they are down below, although I can't take all, or even most of, the credit for that. I feel on the whole that it is less that the entrance, protected by my pylons, is in me, and more that I am an entrance to what resides directly behind me, almost all of which is bigger, taller, darker, more untamed.

When Joyce Nicholas did her painting of me, she chose to leave the pylons off, even though by that point they'd been in me, on me, for a couple of decades. I don't know if this was a conscious decision. My belief is just that she was seeing what she saw every day, out of her loft window, in her own way, and responding to it, very viscerally and freely, also in her own way. This is what all the best art is: our repainting of the world, in our own individual language. And it's when that language is least compromised and most individual that the art is less likely to drown, more set to surf successfully across time. But of course it's also true – and here is the difficulty, and the cruelty – that some of the painting where the language is most truly and beautifully of ourselves, least swayed by a mission to please and be quickly understood, is the kind that can have a very difficult birth, feel like an unwanted, unloved child for a while. But then when, and if, it gets past that difficult stage, the dream life it lives – whether it is a painting, a record, a book, or some other form of creative endeavour – in the minds of those who adore it is astonishingly powerful, arguably no less real and vivid – maybe even more real and vivid – than the thing from the less abstract world that inspired it.

I think this goes beyond just art and artists, this dream life we live that is sometimes so much more vivid than the real one. Jim Swardesley has, in his time in charge of Underhill post office, created an extremely fine post office, within the parameters of what a post office is permitted to be. Many people travel six or more miles out of their way to go to this post office, choosing it over a more geographically practical post office, just because of the atmosphere the person in charge of it has created, because of its unpredictable shelves of local literature, because of its wide range of stationery, because of its reassuringly large and thick door, because of the relentless positivity and patience of Jim's assistant, Tara. But this post office is nothing compared to how the same post office will be repainted in Jim Swardesley's mind, many years from now, when he has left the job and moved his family elsewhere. Jim Swardesley's mindpostoffice will be twice as large, its door twice as old and large, its queues twice as chatty, its nature and topography section a genuine rival for

Waterstones. Is that a selection of artisan coffee, handmade mugs and the latest vinyl releases on the shelves of Jim Swardesley's future mindpostoffice? I believe it is. And who is to say that Jim Swardesley's future mindpostoffice is any less real than the real thing, because only Jim Swardesley will be able to see Jim Swardesley's future mindpostoffice, therefore only Jim Swardesley will have the right to decide how real it is.

I must emphasise here that seeing into the future isn't amongst the range of my talents. You probably know far more about the future now than I do. I just know that Jim Swardesley's future mindpostoffice will be a thing, because I know Jim Swardesley.

There are actually a surprising number of people out there – surprisingly ecologically conscious people, people with great respect for the landscape around them – who have an aesthetic appreciation of pylons, and Jim Swardesley is one of them. Jim can talk quite extensively to you about porcelain insulators, the Milliken Brothers' original latticework architecture and the evolution of the Central Electricity Board's original transmission grid, and was even the admin for a now defunct Facebook group called Pylons I Have Known from June 2014 to September 2016, when an online spat prompted him to step down. Jim took a photo a couple of years ago that he is very proud of, featuring the sun shining down through my pylons; one which I must grudgingly admit has a certain austere beauty to it.

It is the pair of giant black legs in the foreground of that photo – the legs of my most westerly pylon – whose shadow a young woman sits under today, playing her guitar. She is not from this country originally, is still in the process of making it a proper home, and has had a difficult few months. She lost a good friend not all that long ago, and faces an extremely difficult decision about her future. Additionally she is processing the feelings that come in the aftermath of shouting at a man in an SUV for driving too fast along a lane this morning then realising the man was a shaman she'd been introduced to at the farmers' market the previous week. On a brighter note, she is renting a pleasant, dry new cottage, with friendly neighbours on either side – our esteemed postmaster and his family, and a lady who tunes pianos for a living – and a handsome view of me from the bedroom window, and she feels increasingly lit up with creative desire. In times of trouble, it calms her to play her guitar, especially up here, where only the sheep and the ponies and the wind can hear her. The song she's playing isn't one of her own, but a ballad, one I've heard many times before.

Build me a bridge
Made of all I've seen
Hold my eyes in wonder
Circle me with flowers
And remember this time
For one day nevermore I shall be
And listen to the water
Going through the stones
Where is my song
Already and it is me
For I lived before
And live again
And circles are my game
Though I am not one
I am it all
For I am Little Meg

The words are different to what they are sometimes but that is OK. In a way, it's just another kind of repainting the world. Actually, the words are nearly always different, and you'd probably be hard pushed to say precisely what the original ones are now, but the tune is always the same, even when the tune is sort of different. I don't remember when I first heard it. I know it was a long time ago. A long time ago even for me. Maybe longer than anyone would think. Remarkably it doesn't seem to have lost its appeal through overplaying. What I have realised, though, is since the pylons went up, I find it harder to tune into it. There's some static in the air – something beyond the hum that everyone hears coming from the power lines – that distorts it. I suppose this is the way everything works: you gain something but you inevitably always lose something in the process. You gain a double fridge-freezer and an Apple Watch but you lose the ability to perceive the ghosts of time passing through the air quite so clearly. You gain an SUV to take you to your shamanic appointments more quickly but lose your sense of humility and respect for your fellow human beings on the road. You gain the ability to very quickly look up where and how tall the world's biggest pylon is (the Zhejiang Province, China, 1,213 feet, more than 50 whole feet shorter than me) but lose an unspoilt view millennia old stretching down towards the English Channel.

I have learned to accept the giant black legs in me now. After all, it is not exactly like I have a choice in the matter. They still hurt, probably just as much as they did on the day they went in, getting towards a century ago, but the pain is different now: I have, I suppose you might say, kind of subsumed it. It happens to us all in time. None of us are exempt from that pain. You get a throb or an ache or an injury or an illness. Then you realise: 'That's absolutely part of me now, that pain. That is now an element of my unique voice, playing this familiar tune.' So you move forward, because it's the only choice, because getting back to the place before the pain turned up is an affront to nature. Even though the idea of 'nature' is up for debate, the idea that that is an affront to it is not.

Inevitably someone will paint me again one day, and the pylons will be in the painting, maybe even the focal part of it. And people – not everyone, but people – will look at the painting and think, 'Yes! I understand. All of this makes total sense and makes me want to do something too, to not just be here, standing still. All of it had to happen and the love that went into it was not in vain.'

Acknowledgements

This book doesn't take place on the real Dartmoor; its setting is a parallel dimension moor that doesn't exist but just happens to be in the same place on the map. But while the places in *Villager*'s moor have different names and all of its inhabitants and legends are from my imagination, it shares an ambience with Dartmoor and would not have been the same book if I had not been living and walking there during its creation. So, I raise a glass here to Dartmoor, and to the residents whom I've met, chatted to and learned from – not least my 'Dartmoor Dad' Keith Dahill, Nat Green and Ruscha Schorr-kon, a landlady immeasurably more interesting, kind and accommodating than the one featured in the 'Stopcock' chapter of this book. I would also like to offer a special thanks to Louise McKnight and Laura Willis, who kindly offered their time and knowledge of – respectively – Glaswegian dialect and piano tuning to help me sharpen some of the notes here, and Ellie for her support and a couple of eagle-eyed spots at proof manuscript stage. This is the fifth book I have crowdfunded through Unbound, and if you are one of the people who pledged for it, you perhaps deserve the biggest thanks of all, as it wouldn't exist – at least not in its present form – without you. Absolutely vital also is that I mention Matt Deighton, who – like RJ McKendree – is a brilliant unassuming songwriter bashed about, then enhanced by time, and whose excellent 1995 album *Villager* made me decide, many years ago, that I'd one day like to write a book with the same name. Matt is one of many musicians whose craft is an important part of what has led me to this point in my writing career. The others are far too numerous to list here, but I would be seriously remiss in not mentioning my good friend Will Twynham, who as we speak is bringing RJ McKendree to life in the most thrilling of ways. Just as music has made this book more than it would have been without it, art has too, and I am indebted to my mum Jo, my dad Mick, Unbound's art director Mark Ecob and *Villager*'s cover artist Joe McLaren for the work they have done to make it a beautiful object, rather than just a load of words on some pages. Finally, thank you to my editors Imogen Denny, DeAndra Lupu, Mathew Clayton and Hayley Shepherd for their eagle-eyed skills, to Matt Shaw and Dave Holwill for the website help, and to my agent Ed Wilson, and anyone else who, like them, has assisted in any way in giving me the belief that I can do this.

Unbound is the world's first crowdfunding publisher, established in 2011.

We believe that wonderful things can happen when you clear a path for people who share a passion. That's why we've built a platform that brings together readers and authors to crowdfund books they believe in – and give fresh ideas that don't fit the traditional mould the chance they deserve.

This book is in your hands because readers made it possible. Everyone who pledged their support is listed below. Join them by visiting unbound.com and supporting a book today.

Jessica Auton
David Avery
Nick Avery
Terri Babbitt
Jill Badenoch
Duncan Bailey
Gary Bailey
Julie Bailey
Katharine Baird
Susan Bakalar
Wright
Sally and Evie Baker
Susan Baker
Emma Ball
Ali Balmond
Nicola Bannock
Diane Bark
Clive Barker
Michael Barks
Andrea Barlien
Olivia Barnes
Stuart Barnes
Samantha Barnett
Rosie Barr
Jenny Barragan
Lucy Barratt
Sara Barratt
Norma Barrell
Jess Bartlett
Rosalind Bartlett
Isabella Barton
Lisa Barton

Sian Barton
Sam Batstone
Laura Baughman
Leslie Bausback
Gisele Baxter
Caroline Bayley
Adam Baylis-West
Emma Bayliss
Anna Bazeley
Bob Beaupre
Bethany Beavan
Pinches
Kassie Bednall
Ella Bedrock
Sarah Beesley
Alison Beezer
Donna Bell
Iain Bellis
Chrissy Benarous
Alison Bendall
Ronnie Bendall
Yvonne Benney
Basque
Julie Benson
Sue Bentley
Michelle Beresford
Christopher
Bergedahl
Lara Berkley
Suzanne Bertolett
Mary Bettuchy
Melanie Bhavsar

Suchada
Bhirombhakdi
Rhianydd Biebrach
Jared Bieschke
Cathy Billings
Heather Binsch
Karl Birch
Maggie Birchall
Rachel Birrell
Inger Bjurnemark
Stark
Andrew Blain
Gabrielle Blake
Amy Louise Blaney
Graham Blenkin
John Blythe
Meryl Boardman
Ruth Boeder
Gilly Bolton
Alice Bondi
Alex Booer
Sean Boon
Charles Boot
Ruth and Randy
Borden
Jeannie Borsch
Sarah Boswell
Michelle Bourg
Lesley Bourke
Huw Bowen
Lynda Bowen
Margaret Bowen

Dave Bowerman
Kate Bowgett
Teresa Bowman
Lyndy Boyd
Kevin Bracco
Elizabeth Bradley
Susan Bradley
Jackie Bradshaw
Richard Bradshaw
Hugo Brailsford
Ali Brand-Barker
Donal Brannigan
Angie Bray
Caroline Bray
Vanessa Bray
Sarah Brazier
Gill Brennand
Hannah Brickner
Gemma Bridges
Emma-Jane Briggs
Cate Brimblecombe-
    Clark
Tom Brimelow
Margaret Brittan
Rebecca Broad
Xander Brook
Caroline Brosius
Angela Brown
Beverley Brown
Karon Brown
Katharine Brown
Kathleen Brown

Laura Marie Brown
Leslie Brown
Richard Brown
Rosanna Brown
Sharon Brown
Steph Brown
Tanya Brown
Sally Browning
Stella Brozek
Amber Bruce
Beverley Bruce
Caroline Bruce
Sian Brumpton
James Bryan
Marie Bryce
Catherine Bryer
Abby Buchold
Leslie Buck
Elaine Buckley
Alyson Buckman
Fiona Buffham
Sarah Bullock
Alison Bunce
Rachel Burch
Dan Burgess
Julie Burling
Donna-Marie Burnell
Ross Burnett
Rachel Burnham
Arwen Burns
Chris Burns
Alex Burton-Keeble

Heather Bury
Mary Bush
Rochelle Butcher
Rose Bygrave
Heather Byram
Ann & Ross Byrne
Faye Byrne
Simon Cade
Michelle Calka
Judi Calow
Joseph Camilleri
Maggie Camp
    (nee Dry)
Donatella Campbell
Rosanna Cantavella
Jo Capel
Sarah Louise Carless
Stephen Carlton
Susan Caroline
Caroline Carpenter
Amy Carr
Jonathan Carr
Liz Carr
Victoria Carr
Lorrie Carse-Wilen
Holly Cartlidge
Philippa
    Carty-Hornsby
Susan Catley
Stephanie Cave
Heather Cawte
NJ Cesar

Justin Cetinich
Kate Chabarek
Barbara Challender
Nicola Chaloner
Lesley Chamberlain
Tamasine
 Chamberlain
Laura Chambers
Caroline Champin
Christy Chanslor
 Mangini
Liz Chantler
Zoe Chapman
Heather Chappelle
Ailsa Charlton
Mylene Chaudagne
Gill Chedgey
Anna Chen
Nigel Denise
 Chichester
Gillian Child
Joan Childs
Daniel Chisham
Lesley Christensen
Valerie Christie
Linda Francesca
 Church
Amy Ciclaire
Lisa Claire
Jasmine Clancy
Adrian Clark
Heather Clark-Evans

Jenny Clarke
Mandy Clarke
Katie Clay
Izzy Clayton
Penne Clayton
Alison Cleeve
Lisa Bernadette
 Clegg
Robert Clements
Charlotte Cliffe
Gill Clifford
Freyalyn Close-
 Hainsworth
Laura Clough
Shelley Clynch
Amanda Coder
Gina Collia
Diane Collins
Marguerite Collins
Sally Collins
Ida Connolly
Trisha Connolly
Susanne Convery
Jane Conway
Adam Cook
Laura Cook
Bryan Cooklock
Sarah Coomer
Fi Cooper
Dan Copeman
Jackie Copping
Phil Copple

Sue Corden
Íde Corley
Liz Cormell
Rachael Corn
Ellie Cornell
Amanda Corp
Sarah Corrice
Andrew Cosgriff
Anne Costigan
Manners
 Costnothing
Elizabeth Cotton
Melanie Coulton
Rebecca Cowell
Kati Cowen
Geoff Cox
Jo and Mick Cox
Louise Cox
Ann Crabbe
Melissa Crain
Sara Crane
Grumpy Craw
Patrick Creek
Charlotte Crerar
Tessa Crocker
Nancy Crosby
Brenda Croskery
Alasdair Cross
Rachel Cross
Kate Crossley
Vivienne Crossley
Julia Croyden

Anna Cullen
Leah Culver-
    Whitcomb
Stephanie Cummings
Joanna Cunningham
Maria Cunningham
Cindy Curtis
Cushla
Sue Cutting
Matthew d'Ancona
Roseanna Dale
Beth Dallam
Patricia Daloni
Jackie Daly
Shawn Dangerfield
Claire Daniells
Rebecca Daniells
Gimli Daniels
Janet Daniels
Evelyn Danson
Levi Darbyshire
Elizabeth Darracott
Claire Davidson
Karen Davidson
Kelly Davidson
Harriet Fear Davies
Kate Davies
Meryl Davies
Nicki Davies
Nicola Davies
Pat Davies
Penny Davies

Ariella Davis
Catherine Davis
Donna Davis
E R Davis
Laura Davis
Patrick M Davis
Jeannie Davison
Alexandra Dawe
Rebecca Dawson
Fleur Daykin
Annie de Bhal
Milou de Castellane
Antony de
    Heveningham
Philip de Jersey
Amaranda de Jong
Celia Deakin
Alison Deane
Michael DeCataldo
Jayne Deegan
Joanne Deeming
Jill Dehoog
Vicky Deighton
Nat Delaney
Suzanne Delle
Della DeMarinis
Laura Dempster
Pamela Denison
Rachel Dennehy
Christine Dennison
Robin Denton
Albert Depetrillo

Emma Dermott
Amber Dernulc
Heather Desserud
Elly DeVall
Suzie Dewey
Jo Dicks
Claire Dickson
Glenn Dietz
Nicole Dignard
Gemma Dixon
Laura Dobie
Zoë Donaldson
Anne Doran
Rose Doran
Sarah Dorman
Marina Dorward
Rosalyn Downie
Rose Doyle
Martha Driscoll
Kathryn Drumm
Miyako Dubois
Eileen Ducksbury
Hilary Duffus
Helena Duk
Jane Duke
Angela Dunavant
Christina Duncan
Gill Duncan
Anne Dunn
William Dunn
Julie Dunne
Sue Dunne

Jane Dunster
Sonja Dyer
Robert Eardley
Rachel Easom
Christopher
  Easterbrook
Sarah Eden
Jean Edwards
Sharon Edwards
Eirlys Edwards-Behi
Charlotta Ekblom
Esther Ellen
Tom Ellett
Debbie Elliott
Stephen Elrick
Judy Elrington
Jonathan Elwood
Ann Engler
Katie Enstone
Deborah Enticott
Raelene Ernst
Jeanette Esau
Pascalle Essers
Leo Esson
Marina Etienne
Carol Evans
Christina Evans
Isobel Evans
Karen Evans
Rachel Evans
Tom Everett
Rachael Ewing

Christine Exley
Birgit Eyrich
Zea Fael
M.J. Fahy
Shelley Fallows
Gina E. Fann
Sarah Faragher
Alessandra Farrell
Johanna Fender
Joanna Fenna-Brown
Richard Fensom
Lori Ferens
Peter Fermoy
Rebecca Field
Adele Finch
Ed Finch
Erika Finch
Pamela Findlay
Hugo Finley
Colin Fisher
Nick Fitzsimons
Sorella Fleer
Joanne Fletcher
Mark Flitter
Michelle Flower
Maria Flynn
Shannon Flynt
Aurora Fonseca-
  Lloyd
Susan Ford
Tom Ford
Melissa Forrest

Christine Fosdal
Brian Foster
Mary Foster
Annette Fournet
Fi Fowkes
Catherine Fowler
Susan Fox
Jane France
Tiffany Francis-Baker
Fay Franklin
Nancy Franklin
Kelly Frazer
Ellie Freeman
Jacqueline Freeman
Adam Frost
Duncan Frost
Jane Fulcher
Sherry Fuller
Steve Fuller
Matthew Fuszard
Deborah Fyrth
Renee Gagnon
Mel Gambier-Taylor
Jenny Gammon
Luisa Gandolfo
Saffron Gardenchild
Emma Gardner
Laura Gardner
Anthony Garratt
Erika Garratt
Christine Garretson-
  Persans

Amelia Garvey
Maya Gause
Emma Gedge
Sally Geisel
David Gelsthorpe
Sarah Gent
Ethan Georgi
Jan Geurtsen
Rob Gibbins
Claire Gibney
Hanna Gibson
Mike Gibson
Harriet Gilkerson
Mary Bentz
  Gilkerson
Joanne Gillam
Richard Gillin
Katie Gillingham
Angela Gilmour
Stephanie Gilmour
Elizabeth Gladwin
Vivien Gledhill
Jayne Globe
Dave Goddard
Sierra Godfrey
Jennifer Godman
Alice Goldsmith
Rich and Paula
  Goodall
Susan Goodfellow
Katey Goodwin
Mandy Gordon

Rachel Goswell
Toby Gould
Donna Gowland
Natalie Graeff
Emmy Lou Graham
Andy Green
Darrell Green
Rachel Greenham
Rebecca Greer
Amy Gregson
Louise Griffiths
Rachel Griffiths
Sky Griffiths
Sharon Grimshaw
Helen Grimster
Claire Grinham
Brad Groatman
Michelle Grose
Rebecca Groves
Zabet Groznaya
Juliana Grundy
Jennie Gundersen
Martin Gunnarsson
Rebecca Gurr
David Guy
Katie H
Sara Habein
Tom Hackett
Fiona Hackland
Caroline Hadley
Julie Hadley
Sarah Haggett

Janine Hale
Sally Hale
Anna Hales
Catherine Hall
Kate Hall
Laura Hall
Lizzie Hall
Lynn Hall
Martine Hall
Niki Hall
Fay Hallard
Lisa Hallett Howard
Verity Halliday
Laura Hamilton
Sharon Hammond
Imogen Hampton
Margaret Hand
Samantha Handebo
Kate Hannaby
Matti Hannak
Cathy Hanson
Catherine Hardwick
Alison Hardy
Cathryn Hardy
Emma Hardy
Katherine Hardy
Hilary Harley
Andrea Harman
Candy Harman
Lynda Harpe
Sue Harper
Priscilla Harriman

Fia Harrington
Rachel Harrington
Charlotte Harris
Faith Harris
Savannah Harris
Frances Harrison
Leanne Harrison
Mal and Chris
    Harrison
Sharon Tracy
    Harrison
Greg Harrop
Arianne Hartsell-
    Gundy
E Ruth Harvey
Emma Harvey
Lynne Hastie
Shelli Haswell
Luke Hatton
Marianne Hauger
Emily Hawkins
Jessica Hayden
Sarah Hayden
Philip Hayes
Dawn Haynes
Denise Hayward
Kate Haywood
Elspeth Head
Bethan Healey
Gillian Heaslip
Emma Heasman-
    Hunt

Sam Hedges
Cat Heeley
Emma Heggie
Anne-Marie
    Heighway
Richard Hein
Brendan Heldenfels
Helen The
    Hedgerow Hag
Laura Hemmington
Cathy Henderson
Lynne Henderson
Mallory Henson
Elizabeth Henwood
Jane Hermiston
Anneka Hess
Diane Heward
Jo Hewitt
Kat Hewlett
Eve Hewlett-Booker
Amanda Hickling
Martin Hickman
Tracey Hickox
Jan Hicks
Max Higgins
Richard Higson
Kate Hill
Rich Hill
Carlien Hillebrink
Charlotte Hills
Ann Hiloski-Fowler
Beth Hiscock

Tony Histed
Frida Hjelm
Kahana Ho
Jackie Hobbs
Becky Hodges
Keith Hodges
Marie Hodgson
Pilgrim Hodgson
James Edward
    Hodkinson
Jason Holdcroft-Long
Lynne Holding
Dianne Holland
Samantha Holland
Jill Holliday
Fran Hollinrake
Anne Holliss
Claire Holliss
Karen Holloway
Holly Holmes
Monet Holmquist
Barbara Holten
Pamela Hopkins
Sharon Hopkinson
Janice Hopper
Geoffrey Horn
Clare Horne
Ellie Horne
Xenia Horne
Olivia Horsefield
Andy Horton
Jocelyn Houghton

Caroline Howard
Jacki Howard
Liz Howard-Smith
Dan Howick
Sara Howland
Lisa Hudson
Theresa Hudson
Chris Huecksteadt
Clare Isobel Hughes
Crystal Hughes
Elaine Hughes
Jennifer Hughes
Lindsay Hughes
Yvette Huijsman
Alison Hull
Sandy Humby
Sharon Hundley
Kerry Hunt
Marilyn K Hunt
Sarah Hunt
Melinda Hunt-
    Hungerford
Ian F Hunter
Jaazzmina Hussain
Becci Hutchins
Claire Hutchinson
Melanie Hutchinson
Gisele Huxley
Kay Hyde
Philippa Illsley
Nigel Ince
Betty Ing

Laura Ipsum
Kimberley Irons
Carolyn Irvine
Ivan Ivanov
Jackie
Anna Jackson
Judith Jackson
Catherine Jacob
Marc Jacobson
Kellie James
Sandra James
Marieke Jansen
Mark Jarret Porter
Sophie Jarvie
Peter Tags &
    Kim Jarvis
Sarah Jarvis
Luke Jeffery
Marcus Jenkins
Christine Jenner
Kim Jennings
Lucy Jiwa
Tristan John
Vicky Johns
Alison Johnson
Andrea Johnson
Sarah Johnson
Sophie Johnson
Beth Johnston
Helen Johnston
Pauline Johnstone
Allison Joiner

Craig Jones
Hollie Jones
John Jones
Lora Jones
Meghan Jones
Myra Jones
Rebecca Jones
Sandra Jones
Suzi Jones
Alice Jorgensen
Sara Joseph
Melissa Joulwan
Mary Jowitt
Alex Joy
Val Joyce
Mike Jury
Vickie Kakia
Lena Karlsson
Annette Katiforis
Ardala Katzfuss
Jo Keeley
Ursula Kehoe
Minna Kelland
Colleen Kelly
Gill Kelly
Martha Kelly
Helen Kemp
Rebecca Kemp
Christina Kennedy
Helen Kennedy
Laura Kennedy
Ros Kennedy

Denise Kennefick
Bridie Kennerley
Kristin Kerbavaz
Debbie, Graeme,
    Rigby, Charlie &
    Dudley Kerr
Roberta Kerr
Paul Kerrigan
Mary Kersey
Helen Kershaw
Rebecca Kershaw
Audrey Keszek
Gemma Khawaja
Dan Kieran
Caitlin Kight
Peta Kilbane
Janneke Kimstra
Deborah King
Georgina King
Sue King
Simone Kinnert
Jon Kiphart
Michelle Kirk
Pete Kirkham
Kelsey Kittle
Alison Klose
Catherine Kneale
Alison Knight
Heather Knight
Korin Knight
Yvonne Knight
Rachel Knightley

Mel Knott
Patricia Knott
Chris Knowles
Rick Koehler
Laurie Koerber
Sandra Kohls
Teppo Koivula
Sioned Kowalczuk
Helene Kreysa
Laurie Kutoroff
Emily Kyne
J L L
Dawn Lacey
Kevin Lack
Susan Lacy
Christine Ladyman
Clive Lafferty
Leslie Lambert
Emma Lamerton
Peter Landers
Deborah Lane
Jane Langan
Patty Langner
Teresa Langston
Alex Langstone
Joelle Lardi
Nicole Larkin
Phil Latham
Heidi Latzan
Ronni Laurie
Vanessa Laurin
Terry Lavender

Delia Lavigne
Clare Laws
Abigail Lawson
Stephanie Lay
Alison Layland
Catherine Layne
Kim Le Patourel
Morgan Le Roy
Capucine Lebreton
Bennet Ledner
Diane Lee
Alexandra Leeds
Alice Leiper
Janet Lemon
Alison Lennie
Sandra Leonard
Denne LePage-
    Ahlefeld
Emily LeQuesne
Catherine Lester
Jane and Cliff
    Lethbridge
Jill Lethbridge
Alison Levey
Eva Levi
Alex Levine
Jane Levine
Natale Lewington
Beth Lewis
Helen Lewis
Katherine J. Lewis
Marian Lewis

Pam Lewis
Fletch and Maggie
  Lewis - my
  little hoons
Nita Lewsey
Lidbert
Jonathan Light
Bonnie Lilienfeld
Susan Lindon-Hall
Ian Lipthorpe
Katie Lister
Claire Livesey
Vikki Lloyd
Siân Lloyd-Pennell
Benjamin E. Logan
Ellen Logstein
Gillian Lonergan
Kirrily Long
Andrew Longland-
  Meech
Liina Lonn
Helen Looker
Hannah Lorne Gray
Katy Love
Catriona M. Low
Jennifer Lowe
Catherine Lowrey
Rocki Lu Holder
Jude Lucas-Mould
Katie Lucey
Simon Lucy
Barbara Ludlow

Sandra Lukashevich
Helen Luker
Elspeth Luna
Nick Lupton
Daniel Lüthi
Abby Lyn Jones
Katherine Lynn
Adam Lyzniak
Suzanne Maasland
Linda Macdonald
Margo MacDonald
Zoe Macdonald
Karen Mace
Sophie Macgregor
Kate Macinnes
Helen Mackenzie-
  Burrows
Sara MacKian
Russell Mackintosh
Lisa Maggio
Laura Magnier
Laura-Jane Maher
Rebecca Major
Catt Makin
Mary Malpass
Lynn Mancuso
Claire Mander
Doran Manella
Kieran Mangan
Darren Manion
Steve Manners
Guy Manning

Keith Mantell
Anne Margerison
Deb Markham
Emily Martin
Maribel Martinez
  Greig
Andy Masheter
Catherine Mason
Frances Mason
Jo Mason
Laura Mason
Adrienne Massanari
Jose Mastenbroek
Louise Matchett
Suzanne Matrosov-
  Vruggink
Susan Mattheus
Stephen Matthews
Zara Matthews
Becca Mattingley
Shannon Matzke
Shirley Mawer
Molly Mayfield
Melanie McBlain
Wendie McBurnie
Cat McCabe
Laura McCarthy
Yvonne Carol
  McCombie
Megan McCormick
Sonya McCormick
Joel McCracken

Lauren McDaniel

Hazel McDowell

Helen McElwee

Jane McEwan

Daniel McGachey

Barbara L
    McGonagle

Luna, Vince &
    Ted McGowan

Marie McGowan

Ann McGregor

Holly McGuire

Kirsten McIlroy

Alison McIntyre

David McKean

Andrew McKechnie

Victoria McKenna
    Martin

Janet McKnight

Vanessa McLaughlin

Cate Mclaurin

Alastair McLellan

Ruth McLennan

Amanda Mclernon

Mandy McLernon

Fi McLoughlin

Mary McManus

Amanda McMillan

Peter McMullin

Leanna McPherson

Erin McSherry

Denise McSpadden

Carol McTear

Melanie McVey

Sarah Meehan

Signe Mehl

Kate Menzies

Stacy Merrick

Anne Metcalf

Susan Metcalfe

Olivier Mével

Elgiva Middleton

Eilidh Miller

Michelle Miller

Scott Millington

Chris Mills

Laura Mitchell

Polly Mitchell

John Mitchinson

Sebastian Moitzheim

Emma Moore

Kristine Moore

Natalie Moore

Sarah Moore

Andy Moorhouse

Sarah Mooring

Jenny Moran

Amy Morgan

Sharon Morrell

Jackie Morris

Mercy Morris

Morgan Morris

Melody Morrow

Leigh Morse

Katrina Moseley

Dana Mosher

Hettie Moss-Connell

Sarah Mottershead

@mr_spoon

Florentina Mudshark

Donna Mugavero

Jean Muir

Sarah Muir

Linda Muller

Hannah Mumby

Catherine Munro

Ellie Munro

Wendy Murguia

Frances Murphy

Ian Murphy

Clive Murray

Elizabeth Murray

Lara Murray

Meg Murrell-
    Peloquin

Alix Murtha

Sarah Mushrow

Laura Mutton

Hugh N

Kate N

Debbie Nairn

Jessica Naramore

Carlo Navato

Andy & Angela
    Neale

Gemma Nelson

Gem Nethersole
Alyson Nevill
Tim Neville
Elizabeth New
Briony Newbold
Caron Newman
Colleen Newton
Sarah Newton-Scott
Ducky Nguyen
Laura Niall
Jo Niblett
Valerie Niblett
Kate Nichol
Lynda Nicholson
Liz Nicolson
Andy Nikolas
Kate Noble
C Nodder
Anita Norburn
Gemma Norburn
Sheila North
Meredith Norwich
Adele Nozedar
Andrew Nunn
Caleb Nyberg
Jackie O'Brien
Kelly O'Connor
Karen O'Donnell
Caoimhe O'Gorman
Liz & Ian O'Halloran
Mark O'Neill
Hannah O'Regan

Sarah Oates
Laura Ohara Sibra
Gemma Olsson
Kim Olynyk
Omega House
Linda Oostmeyer
Angela Osborne
Jeannine Otto
Maria Padley
Paula Page
Kirsten Pairpoint
Michael Paley
Juliet Palfrey
Alison Palmer
Ellie Palmer
Pam Palmer
Sarah Palmer
Gwen Papp
Clare Parker
Steph Parker
John Parkhouse
Catherine Parkin
Samantha Parnell
George Parr
Sarah Parry
Claire Parsons
Soraya Pascoe
Kate Passingham
Karen Paton
Trish Paton
April Patrick
Gill Patterson

Rob Paul
Jo Peacey
Eleanor Pearce
Sharon Pearson
Janice Pedersen
Karie Penhaligon
Caity PenzeyMoog
Naomi Perfect
Valerie Perham
Bob Perry
Judy Peters
Mags Phelan Stones
Leslie Phelps
Phil & Vicky
Elizabeth Phillips
Kyla Phillips
Michael Phythian
Alice Picado
Kelly Picarazzi
Lisa Piddington
Karen F. Pierce
Michael Pierce
Kelsey Pilkington
Peter Pinkney
Nicola Pitchford
Denise Plank
Jo Plumridge
Marcel Poitras
Justin Pollard
Steve Pont
Annette Poole
Naomi Porter

Becky Potter
Lucy Potts
Peggy Powers
Richard Prangle
Kristine Heidi Pratt
Robert Preece
Sally Preece
Virginia Preston
Laura Price
Gemma Prothero
Christina Pullman
Lisa Purcell
David Quarterman
Lisa Quattromini
Ian Quelch
Cheryl Quine
Sue Radford
Ruby Rae Norton
Helen Rainbow
Laura E. Ramos
Susan Randall
Tina Rashid
Laura Rathbone
Anooshka Rawden
Jonny Rawlings
Angela Rayson
Becca Read
Caroline Read
Kerie Receveur
Lynn Reglar
Vivienne Reid-Brown
Peg Reilly

Tamsin Reinsch
Steph Renaud
Marie Reyes
Anita Reynolds
Electra Rhodes
Julie Richards
Laura Richmond
Hatty Richmond
 Dakin
Fiona Riddell Pearce
Meryl Rimmer
Nicola Rimmer
Beverley Ring
Kerry Rini
Rachel Ritchie
Rochelle Ritchie
Nicole Rivette
Lucy Rix
Catherine Roberts
Claire Roberts
Amanda Robertson
Janet Robertson &
 Louisa Lloyd
Norman Robinson
Spencer Robinson
Patricia Rockwell
Valerie Roebuck
Jeanette Rogers
Sue Rogers
Susan Rollinson
Donna Rooney
Tom Roper

Kalina Rose
Lauren Rosewarne
Adam Ross & Hazel
 Auri Patterson
Alexandra Roumbas
 Goldstein
Matthew Rowell
Rhona Rowland
Lizzie Rowson
Sar Ruddenklau
Sue Rupp
Sam Russell
Marjokaisa Ryhänen
Marie S
Karl Sabino
Sara Sahlin
Katie Sajnog
Matt Salts
Nic Sands
Ingrid Sandstrom
Lyn Santos
Kirsten Sarp
Christine Savage
Sherri Savage
Dorothy Scanlan
Lisa Schaller
Stephanie Schlanger
Julia Schlotel
Sue Schneider
Katharine Schopflin
Linda Schott
Carl Schultz

Katee Schultz
Vikie Schwartz
Leslie Schweitzer
Jenni Scott
Russell Scott
Sarah Scott
Tracey Scott
Jane Seager
Andrew Seaman
Jonathan Seaman
Lisa Search
Claire Searle
Peter and Angela
    Seary
Cora Seip
Sharon Sekhon
Emma Seldon
Neil Sellers
Dick Selwood
Emma Selwood
Gary Selwood
Beth Setters
Belynda J. Shadoan
Mariese Shallard
Harriet Shannon
Kathleen Shannon
Lori Shannon
Eve Sharman
James Sharp
Victoria Sharratt
    McConnell
Adele Shaw

Iola Shaw
Jenny Shaw
Joanna Shaw
Matt Shaw
Chris Sheehan
Luke Shelburne
Tara K. Shepersky
Cliff Shephard
Clare Shepherd
Eloise Shepherd
John Shepherd
Susannah Shepherd
Josephine Sherwood
Andrew Short
Elizabeth Shostak
Claire Siân Ricketts
Mike Simmonds
Cyndi Simpson
Carolina Siniscalchi
James Skeffington
Gabriela Sládková
Debbie Slater
Stoic Sloth
Kate Sluka
SmallTeethingBeastie
Emma Smallwood
Barendina Smedley
Abby Smith
Bec Smith
Carolyn Smith
Charlotte Smith
Chloe Smith

Claire Smith
Fiona Katherine
    Smith
Gabriella Smith
Hannah Smith
Helen Smith
Janine Smith
Kate Smith
KT Smith
Lan-Lan Smith
Lauren Smith
Libby Smith
Louise Smith
Martin Smith
MD Smith
Michael Smith
Peter Smith
Rebecca Jane Smith
Rosie Smith
LA Smith-Buxton
Susan Smyth
Julia Snell
Michael Soares
Ingrid Solberg
Yve Solbrekken
Murielle Solheim
Gaby Solly
Roberta Solmundson
Laura Jane Solomon
Sally Songer
Kit Spahr
Beth Sparks-Jacques

Lyn Speakman
Maureen Kincaid
  Speller
Chris Spence
Rosslyn Spokes
Teresa Squires
Deb Sreiberg
Richard Stagg
Andy Stainsby
Lisa Staken
Corie Stanfield
Elizabeth Stanley
Hannah Stark
Andrew Steele
Natasha Steer
Sarah Steer
Angie Stegemann
Anzi Stenvall
Astrid Stephens
Ann Marie
  Stephenson
Ros Stern
Nina J S Stevens
Ruth Stevens
Sarah Stevens
Amy Stewart
Terri Stewart Hackler
Charli Stewart-
  Russon
Beth Stites
Gòrdan Stiùbhart

Rhiannon Stocking-
  Williams
Mary Stoicoiu
Shelagh Stoicoiu
Sue Stokes
Carmen Stone
Gwilym Stone
Stephanie Strahan
Duncan Strickland
Jillian Strobel
Rachel Stubbs
Nina Stutler
Carol Styles
Nadia Suchdev
Sue Summers & Co.
Helen E Sunderland
Adam Sussman
Judi Sutherland
Laurel Sutton
Ian Swanwick
Laura Sweeney
Toni Swiffen
Kirsty Syder
Angela Sykes
Jerry Sykes
Hayden Sylvester
William Sylvester
Janet T
Nick Tait
Ben Tallamy
Anna Tarnowski
Alison Taylor

Brigid Taylor
Chris Taylor
Dave Taylor
Kay Taylor
Patricia Taylor
Shereen Taylor
Sue Tett
Sarah Tevendale
Kim Thain
Carolyn Theisen
Marthe Tholen
Dave & Jan Thomas
Donna Thomas
Victoria Thomas
Ian Thomas-Bignami
Brewer Thompson
Claire Thompson
Fern Thompson
Helen Thompson
Marianne Thompson
Fern Thompson
  from Caroline
Lynne, Kylie, Donna
  & Shelley
  Thomson
Alastair Thornhill
Carolyn Thraves
Donna Tickner
Aurora Tiddy
  Brook Zeal
Lynne Tidmarsh
Sarah Till-Vattier

Anka Tilley
Emma Tinsley
Adam Tinworth
Simona Toader
Joanne Todd
Pippa Tolfts
Amie Tolson
Deborah Toner
Sarah Torr
Angela Townsend
Ryan Trainor
Emily Traynor
Jon Treadway
Sarah Treble
Carly Tremayne
Lindsay Trevarthen
Jessica Trinh
Julianna Trivers
Fiona Trosh
Stefanie Tryson
Joanna Tucker
Ann Tudor
Kate Tudor
Chloe Turner
Jim Turner
Liana Turner
Sally Turner
Sue Turner
Alison Twelvetrees
Anita Uotinen
Rachel Upward
Mrs V

Mike Vallano
Richard Vallat
Sonja van Amelsfort
Chantal van der
    Ende-Appel
Kristen Van Dyke
Robin Van Sant
Shane Van Veghel
Anne Vasey
Sandy Vaughan
Leo Velten
Kellie Vernon
Nicole Vickers
Sally Vince
Vivian Vincek
Paul Vincent
Rosalind Vincent
Alice Violett
Kate Viscardi
Nicole Vlach
James Voller
Felicity Wadge
Julia Wagner Grover
Leslie Wainger
Allyson Wake
Sarah Wakes
Anne Walker
Sue Walker
Niki Walkey
Heather Wallace
Anthony Waller
Linda Wallis

Sara Walls
Rachel Walne
Declan Walsh
Amanda Walters
Stephanie Walters
Carole-Ann
    Warburton
Donna Ward
Jamie Ward
Joolz Ward
Lee Ward
Laura Watkins
Bj Watson
Christine Watson
Deborah and
    Anne Watson
Rachel Watt
Keith Way
E Webb
M. F. Webb
Lisa Webster
Andy Weekes
Ange Weeks
Marie-Louise
    Weighill
Deborah Weir
Julie Weller
Sarah Wells
Clair Wellsbury-Nye
Jane Werry
Lyn West
Lucy Weston

Michelle Westwater
Katy Wheatley
Andrew & Lucy
    Whelan
Pam Whetnall
Jaki White
Nic White
Susan White
Mark Whitehead
Richard Whitehead
Robert Whitelock
Rosie Whitfield
Annalise Whittaker
Carly Whyborn
Chris Wignall
Peter Wilde
Lorna Will
Linda Willars
Heather Willcox
Angela D. Williams
Caroline Williams
Eileen Williams
Gwynedd Williams
Henry Williams
Oli Williams
Briony Williamson
Mark Williamson
Laura Willis
Rosamund Willis-
    Fear
Kim Willmetts
Bree Wilson

Derek Wilson
Fiona Wilson
Kirsten Wilson
Tracey Wilson
Oliver Wilton
Camilla Winlo
Anna Wittmann
Gretchen Woelfle
Kellyann Wolfe
Kanina Wolff
Mia Wolff
Laiane Wolfsong
John Wood
Judith Wood
Lucy Wood
Matthew Wood
Peter Wood
Rebecca Wood
Sandra Wood
Justine Woodbridge
Joanna Woodhouse
Brenda Wordsworth
David Wrennall
Georgina Wright
Melanie Wright
Michelle Wright
Rebecca Wyeth Fox
Jeremiah Wyke
Jo Wynell-Mayow
Zoe Wyrko
Theresa Yanchar
Stephanie Yates

Neil Yeaman
Stephen Usins
    Yeardley
Duncan Yeates
Lisa Young
Donna Zillmann
Birgit Zimmermann-
    Nowak